ALSO BY EVONNE WAREHAM
FROM CLIPPER LARGE PRINT

Never Coming Home

Out of Sight
Out of Mind

Evonne Wareham

W F HOWES LTD

This large print edition published in 2013 by
W F Howes Ltd
Unit 4, Rearsby Business Park, Gaddesby Lane,
Rearsby, Leicester LE7 4YH

1 3 5 7 9 10 8 6 4 2

First published in the United Kingdom in 2013
by Choc Lit Limited

A CIP catalogue record for this book is available
from the British Library

ISBN 978 1 47123 624 2

Typeset by Palimpsest Book Production Limited,
Falkirk, Stirlingshire
Printed and bound in Great Britain
by MPG Books Ltd, Bodmin, Cornwall

MIX
Paper from
responsible sources
FSC
www.fsc.org   FSC® C018575

For my father, who would have been astonished.

CHAPTER 1

It was a dark and dirty alley and a very expensive dress.

Madison Albi hesitated. She *really* didn't want to go in there. Not in a shimmery little cocktail number and a pair of strappy sandals. *Hell, not even in boots and a protective suit.*

Without her permission her foot took a step forward.

She peered into the shadows, wrinkling her nose at the smell. Stuff was rotting, down in the darkness. She didn't want to know what. She shivered. *If you plan to go wandering around in the dark, you really should bring a coat. But who planned* this? A puddle of something that looked like oil gleamed in the lights of a passing car. It had to be oil. It hadn't rained for days. Unless it was . . . blood?

Huffing out a breath, she pulled herself together. This was *so* stupid. She was spooking herself into nightmares here. All because she'd thought, just for a moment, that she'd felt something.

A burst of power, like static, in her head.

Huh! She'd had one glass of tepid white wine at the reception – which had been one glass too many, given the way it tasted – and now her imagination was working overtime.

Disgusted with herself, she turned away, trying to ignore the treacherous pull of disappointment.

She'd been so sure, just for that moment . . .

She took one step away, then another. Then stopped.

'This is crazy.' She swung round and marched back to the entrance of the alley. 'What are you – a scientist or a wimp?'

She didn't have to go in. She could stand right here, where there were street lights and traffic. She glanced around. *Hmmm.* This wasn't exactly the centre of London. It wasn't that light and there weren't that many cars.

She cast a longing glance up the street, at her apartment block. Lights, people. *Warmth.* So near and yet so far.

In the other direction the section of the new development still under construction was a desolate wilderness of scaffolding and creaking tarpaulins. Was that the source of that burst of . . . whatever it had been? Was the sense she was picking up, of a presence – a presence that could connect to her mind – one of the security guards at the building site? She breathed deep. No – that was wishful thinking. There was no guard on the site. The security patrol came by every hour in a nice, *warm* van, to check the place out.

Which left her with something else. Something lurking in the alley between the two abandoned shops, boarded up, marooned and derelict, destined for demolition the moment a legal quirk over ownership was finally settled.

A sudden gust of wind set something flapping on the construction site. The sign proclaiming the second phase of the development to be nearing completion, and ninety per cent sold, was rippling as if it were alive. Madison shivered. *If you've got any sense you'll go home, now. In ten minutes you could be sipping hot chocolate in your dressing gown.*

But then you would always wonder . . .

Resigned, she took another step towards the alley. It really wouldn't take long. A simple matter of collecting the power of her thoughts and projecting them into the darkness. The likelihood of there being any response was minimal. Less than minimal. *You've been looking for long enough, and you haven't found anything yet.* Dropping her shoulders, which had unaccountably hunched themselves up around her ears, she breathed deep, focusing.

This she could do.

The probe went in smoothly, her mind expanding into the gloom in a controlled sweep, searching for connection. Sorting, sifting, sensing.

A thrill of excitement flared. There *was* something.

She leaned forward eagerly. *No, dammit!* The impulse that was jittering out of the alley was coming from the small, fuzzy mind of an animal. Probably a rat. She shuddered, snapping off the contact. There was nothing there. No ghoulies or ghosties. Nothing human.

She brushed her hands up her arms, feeling gooseflesh. *What are you doing? Standing in the cold, communing with a scavenging rodent!*

Time to get real.

Go. Now.

As she moved, her heel twisted under her. Cursing softly, she stumbled sideways before regaining her balance.

And then, without warning, it came again.

An incredible surge of power, roaring out of the darkness, sweeping blindingly over her.

Even as a hand went to her throat in alarm, she felt the click in the back of her brain. Like coming home.

Then, in a rush, he was on her. Towering over her.

Light glittered on the metal bar, clutched in an upraised hand.

'No!' It came out as an ear-piercing scream.

The bar dropped.

In the sudden silence she heard it hit the ground and roll away.

'Oh God.' The voice was dredged up from somewhere very deep. Rusty. Older than dirt. 'Didn't know . . . woman . . . shouldn't be here . . . not safe.'

He was swaying towards her, invading her space.

With no room in her head to think, she put up her hand to shove him back. As the flat of her palm connected with his shoulder she felt him flinch violently. The gasp he gave echoed in her own lungs.

Like a lightning bolt, even as she was withdrawing her hand in panic, skull-splitting pain arced out of him, and into her. Splintering into her mind. Threatening to engulf her.

She opened her mouth to scream again, for both of them. The sound died in her throat as the pain broke off, as swiftly as it had come. There was an abrupt, sickening blackness.

Then her assailant dropped like a stone, out cold at her feet.

CHAPTER 2

Madison crouched by the inert body, teeth chattering. Her heart was hopping about in her chest like a demented frog, making it difficult to breathe. She steadied herself, reaching out a tentative hand to his neck, feeling for a pulse. His skin was colder than hers, but the beat there was strong.

He wasn't dead.

Relief flooded her, followed by irritation.

'Come on, Madison, get a grip. You don't kill someone by poking them in the shoulder.'

She leaned in, looking him over.

She couldn't see much in the dim light, except that he was big. Dark cap, dark beard, dark over-coat. The clothes didn't tell her anything she hadn't expected. A touch confirmed it. She withdrew her hand quickly from the greasy collar of the coat.

The man was a derelict, one of the homeless who lived on the street and slept in doorways or wherever else they could find. She blew out a breath. She'd worked at the lab with most of the rough sleepers from this part of outer London. He wasn't one of them.

She felt around in the dark for the slim, gold evening purse that held her mobile phone. *Find the bag, get the phone, get help, get the hell out.*

The bag had to be close; it had been in her hand when all hell broke loose.

Triumphantly she located the fine chain of the handle and pulled. When the chain gave way, she almost lost her balance. Totally confused, she found the broken end and traced it back, groaning as realisation dawned.

Her bag was under the body.

She was going to have to kneel down, to push him out of the way. With a sigh, she hitched up the hem of her dress.

After three unsuccessful attempts to roll him over she gave up. She couldn't even slide her hand under him, to drag it out.

'Sod it, sod it, sod it.'

They were completely alone; off the road, at the mouth of the alley that opened into the narrow area in front of the shops, that had been used for parking. Residents were still parking there, and would be until the building site was finished. Madison scanned the scattering of cars. No other human being in sight. The foyer of her apartment block glowed invitingly, just yards away. It might have been on the far side of the moon. She could be along the road in less than a minute, but if a car reversed in here while she was gone, trying to park—

She sat back on her heels. She had to get him

somewhere safe. Safer than this, anyway. Which meant he had to be awake. Offering up a brief, silent prayer, she leaned over to tap his cheek. Tapped a little harder when she felt the flicker of movement.

Her heart lifted in relief when he coughed and muttered something she mercifully couldn't make out. Breath hissed in her throat as his head flopped sideways, into a small patch of light, and she saw the green and yellow of old bruises on the side of his face and neck.

Someone had beaten him. Viciously.

No wonder he'd come at her with an iron bar. Blood was welling from a fresh cut over one eye.

She took her hand away sharply as a long shudder went through him.

He was waking up.

Thank God. Her knees were killing her.

She just managed to get out of the way as he rolled over, wincing.

'Holy hell, it's an angel. Two angels.' The voice was husky but sounded more normal. Deep. No accent. He was squinting at her, fingers feeling up into his hairline. 'Bloody heck! What did you hit me with?'

Madison was too busy helping with his efforts to sit up to argue the point. *Boy* he was big. Solid. *And still uncoordinated.* She dodged a flailing hand. Up close and personal he didn't smell too bad, considering. Not like she expected a date to smell, but bearable.

With a brief pang for her dress, she knelt forward, bracing her arm to let him pull himself up. A surge of vertigo swept out of him and over her, then was gathered up and gone. Somehow he managed to get his feet under him and they made it over to a low wall. He collapsed on to it with a groan, dropping his head into his hands.

'I must be losing it. Did you punch me, or what?' He shook his head gingerly. 'You must have a right hook like a battering ram.'

'I think I just got lucky.' He was staring up at her, owlishly. 'I just finished off what someone else started,' she explained.

'Oh. Yeah, right.' He scrubbed a grubby hand over his forehead, looking puzzled when it came away wet. Madison found a handkerchief and handed it over. He mopped at the cut, looking around vaguely. 'There were some kids. Uh – couple of weeks ago. I was sleeping . . . Three weeks? Yeah – three weeks.'

'They attacked you?'

'Mmm.' He shifted position on the wall, uneasy. 'I think maybe . . . Did I mistake you for them? That they'd come back?'

'Doesn't matter.' She was feeling around on the tarmac, where he'd been lying.

He coughed, hunching over, peering at her. 'What are you doing?'

'Looking for – ah!' She pounced on the bag. Opened it. And found her sleek, black phone was now in about six pieces.

'Where is he, then?'

'What?' She was only half-listening, intent on the wrecked phone. She prodded it. It was clearly beyond hope. 'Where's who?'

'Boyfriend, date, whatever,' he prompted.

'Oh.' She shook her head. 'No date. No boyfriend.' She followed his eyes down her dress, which now had a spreading stain on the hem. 'It was a work thing. Reception. The mayor, people like that.'

What are you doing standing here, discussing your social life with a bleeding man? Need to take control here. The phone is gone, but he's awake and talking, so it's probably okay to move him.

'You know you shouldn't be out alone.' He was frowning, words slurring. 'Woman on her own. S'not safe.'

'I can take care of myself.' *This from the man who came at me with a metal bar?* 'Look, if I help you, do you think you can get up the road, to that building?'

He sat up, focused. 'Yeah. I can make it. But why would I want to?'

'Why?' She turned to face him, confused. 'So we can get you medical attention. A doctor—'

'Nah.' He was shaking his head from side to side, for emphasis or to clear it. He didn't look too happy with the movement. 'Don't need a doctor.' He waved a hand. 'You've done the good Samaritan thing, getting me up off the floor. I'm not planning to sue you for putting me there, so you don't have to hang around. Go.' He made a shooing gesture that almost had him off the wall.

Madison stared at him. 'You think I'm just going to leave you here? Five minutes ago you were out cold. When you came round you were seeing double,' she accused.

'Yeah.' Somewhere in the matted beard there might have been the skeleton of a smile. 'Two angels.' He mimed looking round. 'Now, where did they go?'

For a second, fury sparked brightly in Madison's chest. He was laughing at her. *Right, if he doesn't want help, that's fine.* She didn't have to stand here in the cold, arguing. Her teeth were chattering. Her dress, her bag and her phone were probably beyond repair. She'd done her bit all right. Anyone with an ounce of common sense would have walked away already.

She swung on her heel, hesitated, swung back.

To hell with that. Common sense could take a hike.

His chin was slumped, the wide shoulders drooped and his arms were buried in the folds of his disgusting coat, holding himself precariously together. Whoever or whatever he was, and whatever he said, she couldn't leave him alone and hurt, here in the dark.

But that's not all, is it?

She could feel the need, clawing inside her like cramp. She was never going to walk away. Not from something like this. A reckless exhilaration was fizzing in her blood. She hadn't imagined that surge of power. Her ears were still ringing with it. She'd felt his pain, mental and physical. This . . . he . . . was the most exciting thing she'd encountered since . . . since . . .

There had never been anything this exciting.

She couldn't let him go. She had to get him somewhere safe, where she could assess him properly. Which meant she was going to help him, whether he wanted it or not.

When she went, he was going with her.

Without pausing for thought, she grabbed his good arm and yanked.

Taken unawares, and still unsteady, he came up with a rush.

Before he could protest, or evade, she shoved her shoulder under his and began to pilot him up the street.

He hauled in air as if she'd sucker-punched him. Her hand on his wrist stopped him slipping out of her hold.

'I said I wasn't going with you, lady. What part of no don't you understand?'

'All of it.' She gritted her teeth and kept going. 'Just walk, will you.'

The way he was leaning on her told her he'd be flat out again if she let go. She was pretty sure he knew it too, which was why he stopped trying to shake her off.

Until they reached the front of her block.

'No! No way!' He swore violently and dug in his

heels when he saw where she was heading. 'You can't take me in there!'

'I can and I will.' She tightened her grip and ploughed on. 'This is where I live.'

'Lady, you're crazy.' He flapped his hand. 'You got a porter, concierge or something?'

'Of course. Mind the step.' He stumbled, then got his feet co-ordinated. They were both breathing heavily. 'What's the problem?'

'What do you think? One look and the guy will be calling the cops.'

'Not when you're with me.'

'Not even if I was with the Queen! I'll be back here in the road before you can turn around. S'no point.'

'We'll see – but as you didn't want to come with me in the first place, why are you arguing?' she asked sweetly. When he didn't answer she put her hand behind his back to shove, getting a muffled curse of pain in response. It tweaked her conscience, but not much. Her shoulders were aching and they were almost at the door. 'Stop making a fuss and get a move on, before we both die of hypothermia.'

The lights in the foyer skewered his eyeballs like lasers. With one thing on his mind – getting off his feet before he fell down – he changed tack, towing his captor towards the nearest sofa and flopping out of her grasp into the soft depths. Absently he stroked the red leather. Expensive.

13

Nice place his angel lived in. Angel. Pity he had to pick a bossy one. But with his luck – except – what did he know?

'How do you feel? Better?'

He hadn't realised he'd closed his eyes. He opened one. *Better* didn't describe the river of pain coursing across his left shoulder, nor the aching nausea of the too-empty belly, not to mention his head, which he was trying to ignore, but in her terms he probably was *better.*

And she'd sounded so full of hope.

Now there was a word that hadn't been in his mind for a while.

He grunted, which seemed to satisfy her. Maybe he *didn't* feel so bad. He was getting warm, for the first time in a week, and the sofa was doing good things to his weary bones. Left alone, he might stretch out for a while. But that wasn't going to happen.

The little guy from the reception desk had trailed them to the seating area, open-mouthed. Now he was shifting from one foot to the other, looking unhappy. No surprise there, seeing that he had a vagrant in his hallway, messing up his designer décor. Plus he was going to offend one of his tenants. Probably a good tipper, too. She looked like a good tipper.

He transferred his open eye to the angel. Actually she looked plain good, except she wasn't plain. *Losing the thread here.* Tall, slim, brunette. Long hair. Straight. Shiny. The gold dress clung in some interesting places. Pity about the oil stain. He sat up a fraction straighter, so he could see the rest. Excellent legs. Fuck-me shoes. Now there was a thought. A very old, lost-in-the-past thought.

His mind hazed. Something about her—

There was a reason he was here, but he couldn't recall it.

She needed someone to take care of her. Maybe that was it. Alone on the street at night, wearing all that gold round her neck.

He focused on the heavy gold chain. It glittered in the strong light and he looked away. Maybe he *should* stick around. She wanted him for something. Stick around, he'd find out what.

Fat chance.

The little guy had started his pitch. Wouldn't be long now and he'd be out on his ass. *May as well make the most of the sofa while it's available. Catch a few Zs.*

'Miss Albi. Um . . . I really don't think I can allow this.' Madison looked up from studying her captive. He seemed to have passed out again. Straightening her shoulders, she fixed Scott with her coolest stare. The concierge swallowed bravely. 'My job is to keep people like him out. And he's dripping *blood!*' Scott's voice dropped to a horrified whisper.

'Only on to his coat. It's not going on the furniture.' Madison frowned, wondering what had become of her handkerchief, then brushed it aside to focus on the concierge. *Do not give in. Smile nicely, act gracious. Lie. And slip him a tenner.* Good thought. She conjured the smile.

'I know this is difficult, Scott, but we only need a minute. As soon as I get him back on his feet and into the lift, we'll be out of here.'

Behind them the street doors opened, with a blast of cold air. Madison nodded towards the pizza delivery man who'd come in with the air. The scent of garlic and tomatoes wafted round the lobby.

'Why don't you go and see to that, and when you come back, we'll be ready to go.'

Scott looked unconvinced, but went.

'Told you so.'

The captive was awake and watching her. Smug.

'Shut up, you, I'm thinking.'

She saw him take a breath to respond, then decide against it and let it out again, collapsing further into the leather sofa.

While she was thinking she went back to her inspection. The dark cap was pulled down over matted hair. Stubble – no, make that beard – obscured most of his face. The heavy overcoat, buttoned at the throat, had been good once. When it was new. Some time back in the last century. Way back. The fabric was shiny with wear in some places, stained in others, but there were signs that someone, presumably its inhabitant, had tried to clean and brush them away.

The hair under the cap was dishevelled but not lank. It was midnight dark, except for a splatter of silver at the sideburns. What she could see of the beard was black and silver, too. His head was down, sunk into his chest, so she couldn't check out his features.

The fresh cut over the eye was oozing now, not dripping. In a proper light she could see that it had been half healed but had re-opened when he fell. With his head down, the bruises were less obvious. He'd been heavy enough when she'd manhandled him in here, but the ancient overcoat hung loose on him. She suspected he was gaunt for a man of his build. The ragged edges of a pair of grey trousers showed under the coat. The trainers were the most disgusting pair she'd seen in a while.

They would be going straight in the bin.

One of his hands, grazed at the knuckle and ingrained with dirt, was splayed out, limp, on the seat beside him. He was scrubbing awkwardly at the cut with the other.

'Here.' She found a lipstick-stained tissue in the bottom of her battered evening bag, tore off the stained part and handed it over.

'Thanks.' It was no more than a mumble, but it did get his head up.

The eyes were dark, possibly blue. Clouded and unfocused.

His head drooped again, but he still held the tissue, so he hadn't drifted off.

Almost absently she scanned him; a fast, non-invasive once over. What was coming out of him

17

now was the standard soupy muddle of thoughts she could pick up from any passer-by, on any street corner in London. The sort of stuff she'd learned to tune out, aeons ago . . . Nothing special.

Shit! Had she made a mistake, dragging him in here?

She hesitated. She didn't normally do this. It was against all her principles. But this wasn't exactly normal. She gathered her thoughts and probed into him.

'Fuck! Don't do that!' He jumped, wincing away from her. As if she had slapped him.

'You can feel it?' Shock spiked through her.

'How can I fail to,' he flapped his hand as if he was warding off a troublesome insect, 'when you're coming at me like a boot to the head?'

She pulled out of him sharply, heart rate accelerating and decision made.

'Right, here's the deal.' She leaned over him, talking fast and close to his ear. Scott was walking back towards them. 'You go along with everything I'm about to say and you get food, a bed for the night and fifty quid. In exchange you help me with a couple of experiments.'

'Mind experiments?'

She caught her breath. Exhausted and in pain, he was still as sharp as a razor. 'Yes. Mind experiments. Nothing painful, I promise.'

'Huh!' He hunched away from her, chin down. She was getting used to the look of the top of his head. 'Hundred.'

'What?'

'Hundred pounds.'

'In your dreams. Seventy.'

'Hundred.' He was looking sideways, over her shoulder. 'Make your mind up quickly, lady. Your little pal is almost here. Got a pretty determined expression on his face. I reckon I'm gonna be out on my ass in about ten seconds.'

'All right!' She capitulated, exasperated. 'A hundred. You'd better be worth it!'

'Always do my best to satisfy a lady.' He leaned back on the leather cushion. There was a distinct gleam in the dark eyes.

'You've certainly recovered.' She put all the ice she had into her stare before turning away. *What have I done?*

She squared her shoulders. He was big and undoubtedly smart, but so was she, so that was no problem. He was hurt, which gave her the edge. She pushed down a qualm. He was better off with her than out there on the street, in pain. She could handle him. She had to. He had something she wanted. Really wanted.

'Scott.' She moved forward, smiling. 'Please don't give me grief on this.' The folded note in her hand disappeared smoothly into Scott's top pocket. 'It's just—' she shrugged, looking guilty. It wasn't that hard. She didn't like lies, and there were far too many in her life already. But she had to get Scott onside. If he made a fuss – hell, she was *not* going to lose this guy. She had the speech planned. It wouldn't be a lie. Not exactly. She revved up the smile. 'Like you said, he's bleeding. He was on the ground behind my car. I could have clipped him when I backed in.' *Maybe – if he'd been anywhere near at the time.* 'I don't want any trouble. If I can get him upstairs and cleaned up, he'll be out of here by morning. We'll use the service entrance.' She put all the reassurance she could into her voice, then held her breath.

Scott was wavering visibly. 'Well – I suppose he's your guest, like, isn't he?' He made up his mind. 'All right.' He rolled up the sleeves of his uniform and leaned over to grab one of the captive's arms. 'Come on, sunshine, on your feet. And mind you behave yourself with the lady.'

'Yes, guv. Obliged to you, guv.' Over Scott's head Madison met eyes with the wickedest gleam she'd ever seen. Then he winked. She swallowed a breath. The next few days were going to be . . . eventful.

Scott had got him up, but he was floundering, favouring the left side of his body. The one she'd thumped in the alley. She swallowed down a twinge of guilt, and moved to take his arm gently, letting him settle his weight against her in his own time.

'Thanks.' The word was a whisper against her ear. She looked sideways. As he stooped they were on the same level, and she met his eyes again. Navy blue. Softer now, but still knowing.

She was about to take this stranger into her

home. A place she didn't even take her friends. She shivered, hoping he didn't feel it.

Scott was getting impatient.

An unlikely threesome, they shambled towards the elevator.

Scott was back on the ground floor, soaping his hands in the cloakroom, when the door banged open behind him. His sister, Sandra, stood in the doorway, holding a mop and bucket.

'Wondered where you'd got to.'

'Had to wash my hands, didn't I?' Scott shook water off his fingers. 'Been up to the penthouse. Helped Miss Albi take a man up there.' He smirked when his sister's eyebrows shot up. 'Some old vagrant she nearly ran over. Filthy, he was.' Scott fastidiously adjusted the cuffs of his uniform. 'Too soft-hearted, she is. Wanted to make sure he was all right. I'd have left the bugger there.'

'Yeah, well, you would.' Sandra advanced towards the sink. 'You know Miss Albi, she's dead kind to everyone, treats everyone proper. She's a really nice lady. For a spook.'

Scott's head jerked. 'You don't want to go saying that. That's just stupid gossip.'

'Might not be gossip.' Sandra flounced as she put her mop in the sink. 'That place Miss Albi works. Research laboratory – *mind* research. Got to be top secret, innit? Spooks and stuff.'

'You want to keep your mouth shut,' Scott

warned. 'If Miss Albi hears you talking like that she won't want you cleaning her place.'

Sandra sniffed. 'Know when to be discreet, don't I?' She turned off the tap. 'Bit risky though, innit, taking in some bloke off the street? You reckon she's all right up there?' Sandra frowned, concerned. 'She's got some nice stuff, and she's all on her own since that chap of hers went. Pity about that.' Sandra gave a sentimental sigh. 'Right before the wedding and all.'

'Better before than after,' Scott said sharply. 'You don't want to go talking about *that,* either.' He adjusted his tie. 'She'll ring down, if she wants anything. You get on and do the lobby, while it's quiet.'

Madison shoved her key in the lock, one eye on the captive. *Really must get a name.* He was propped against the wall, head down. Scott had scarcely handed them out of the lift before he'd pressed the button to descend. The lift foyer to the penthouse was tiny, but it had still taken them an age to cross it. She looked him over, mouth twisting. Exhaustion was closing in on him. *Him.*

'Do you have a name?' She pushed the door open.

'Mmm.' He was swaying. She grabbed him before he fell. If he went down, she'd have to call Scott to get him up again.

'Not far now.' She hauled on the front of his overcoat, holding him upright with teeth gritted.

22

She felt him pull in a deep breath. Some of the weight eased. 'Okay?' she checked, cautiously.

'Yeah.' For a moment they stood, looking at each other.

His eyes were surprisingly alert, long lashed. Madison felt colour coming up into her face. His body leaned against hers. Close. Hard. Warm. Warm was good, except—

She swallowed. Behind her was the open door of her home. Her refuge. What was she doing?

'S'all right.' His voice was husky. 'We have a deal.'

'I don't know what you mean.' She tried to sound brisk.

'You're worried about taking me in there.' He nodded behind them. 'And if you're not, then you ought to be.' She couldn't really tell, under the mat of beard, but there might have been a twisted grin in there somewhere. 'I'm assuming there isn't a husband/lover/boyfriend lurking?'

He's going to find out, so why hide? 'No.'

'No one to object if you bring your work home with you.' There was definitely amusement in the voice now.

Madison felt a familiar stir of resentment. Women had to be so careful about things a man wouldn't think twice about. It got under her skin, but now wasn't the time. Even so— 'I wouldn't be with a man who wanted to dictate what I do. And I'm not afraid of you,' she added, for good measure.

He was staring at her. 'That so?'

'Yes.' She pursed her lips, trying to ignore the squirm in her belly. This was getting to be quite a night for half-truths.

His eyes were still on her face. 'You sure? Only you did such a good job, fibbing to Scotty-boy—'

'If you were listening, you know I didn't – fib.' The childish word suddenly made her want to giggle. She resisted, sucking in her cheeks.

'Sophistry.'

Madison blinked. 'What?'

'You heard. Didn't think someone homeless would know a big word like that?' He was baiting her again. Temper stirred.

'I make it a rule never to prejudge anyone I meet.' *But you may have underestimated this one.* She ground her teeth. 'I misled Scott. I admit it – so sue me. It got you up here.' She met his stare. 'I repeat, I am not afraid of you.' *Make something of that, mister.*

'Good, because you don't have to be.' Abruptly he gave up the contest. She saw a shadow of pain cross his face. Anger faded as her heart twisted in sympathy. 'I can be civilised,' he added. 'Your person and your furniture are quite safe.'

Bitterness, under the flat tone?

'Good to know.' It was disconcerting to hear the quiver of relief in her voice. She took his arm again.

They made it into the hall. Madison took a second to breathe, wondering how the place appeared to a stranger. She'd chosen the coral paint to be warm, welcoming. Not that she ever welcomed anyone. Not since Neil. She stepped past that thought.

'Right.' She straightened up. 'I'll fix us some food, while you take a shower.' She frowned. 'Will you be able to manage that?'

'I'll manage – I'll find something to hold on to – unless you're offering to prop me up?'

She wasn't going to dignify *that* with a response. 'There are clothes—' She gestured to the hall cupboard. 'They should fit.'

She opened the door and rummaged. She knew Neil wasn't coming back, but she hadn't been able to get herself together to dispose of his things. They'd made it as far as a couple of plastic sacks in the closet by the door and no further. Now she was glad she'd lacked the courage for that final step. Neil and this guy were much of a size.

She unearthed the black bags and pulled out jeans and socks, a soft plaid shirt, which gave her a pang under the heart, and a nearly new sweater, which didn't. Digging deeper she found an unopened pack of boxer shorts, and turned with the pile in her arms.

'These were on their way to the charity shop, so you can keep them. Afterwards.'

'After you've had your wicked way with me, you mean?'

She ignored him, looking at his feet. Shoes would be a problem. Neil had small feet for a six footer, smaller than this one. Those trainers were *too* disgusting. He'd have to go without until the stores opened tomorrow. She caught herself up. *Making plans to take him shopping?*

He hadn't moved to take the bundle, so she put it down on the hall table.

'Not coming back?' He nodded towards the pile. 'The previous owner?'

'No.' She hoped her body language was telling him not to go there. Giving him Neil's clothes was one thing, explaining— 'I assume you don't have issues with pre-owned?'

He shrugged and winced. 'Not if he doesn't.'

'He won't.' *Can't.*

He was leaning against the front door, as if he still hadn't quite decided whether to bolt. 'And they're part of my fee – after you've sucked out all I have to give and spat me back out.'

'You have a wonderful turn of phrase. It's your mind I'm interested in, *that's all*!'

'Didn't imagine anything else. No, wrong. Imagined, maybe. Expected? No.'

It took a second for her to realise he was laughing, not wheezing.

He looked dreadful, haggard and drawn and bruised, but he was laughing, head tilted, inviting her to laugh with him.

She almost wanted to.

'Actually.' He put his hand to his face, rubbing the cut as if it hurt him. 'Despite my boasting downstairs, I'm not sure I'm in a fit state to accommodate a lady. Even one who only wants

26

my mind. I think you may have wasted your money.'

'I haven't paid you yet.' She pulled his hand away from his face. 'You'll make it bleed again.'

'Sorry,' he muttered, closing his eyes and leaning more heavily against the door. She stared at him. He hadn't struck her so far as the kind of guy who apologised much, so he had to be feeling pretty bad.

Very cautiously, she flicked a probe into his mind. In and out, before he could sense her too deeply.

Even the half-second of contact was enough. Three different sorts of physical pain, confusion, gnawing hunger – and something that felt very close to total exhaustion. His system was just too overloaded to cope. It was swamping him. He was hanging on more or less by willpower alone.

Touched by something she couldn't identify, she put a finger to his bruised cheek.

'What the hell happened to you? Who hit you?'

'Before you, you mean?'

'I thought we'd settled that. I apologise.'

'Me, too.' He shrugged himself up, wearily. 'I scared you.'

'We scared each other. You were expecting them back, weren't you? Who was it?'

'Dunno. Couple of kids with boots and sticks. They'd had a few beers and were looking for some fun. It wasn't anything personal. I was just there . . . wrong place, wrong time.'

She felt anger rising inside her. She knew it

27

happened. It didn't make it easier to hear. 'That's evil.'

'Fact of life on the street.'

'How can you choose to live like that? You don't seem to have an abuse problem, you're educated, articulate—'

'Hey now, lady, don't go using those big words on a dumb slob like me.'

'Don't play the fool.'

'And don't you pass judgement.' There was ice in his eyes. 'You don't know anything about me. All I am to you is a piece of meat – raw material for your experiments.'

'No!' She reacted indignantly. 'A subject, yes, but never less than a human being. A person, doing a job, for a fee.'

She let her eyes challenge him.

He was the one who looked away.

'What d'you want me to do then, to earn my money?'

'Shower and food first, then we'll talk. Bathroom is that way.' She scooped up the clothes and shoved them at him. He fumbled with his left hand and wedged them against his chest with the right. She reached out to stop them falling.

'Look, how badly are you hurt?' She remembered the pain she'd felt in him. 'Do you need a doctor?'

'Nah. It's bruises, mostly, and I think my collar-bone is busted. That's why the problem with the arm. Everything will heal, but—' He stopped.

Madison waited.

'I think you'll have to give me a hand with the coat.' Clearly he hated asking for help. Alpha male, cornered. 'I don't think I can get it off by myself.'

The material felt slippery under her fingers. She tried not to think about where he'd been sleeping lately and concentrated on getting him out of it, with a minimum of pain. There was one of Neil's top coats at the back of the cupboard. He could have that, too. Then she could burn this one.

They were both panting by the time they had stripped the coat off him.

'Can you manage the rest?'

'Yeah.' He nodded – convincing her, or himself? 'Just give me a minute.' He sucked in air. 'Where was the bathroom again?'

'That door. There's soap and shampoo. Towels on the shelf.'

'Thanks.' He peeled himself off the wall. 'You . . . you've been great. Shame about the dress, by the way.'

Madison looked down at herself, regretfully. Even her favourite dry cleaners – specialist and expensive – weren't going to be able to rescue this.

'Great shoes, though.' He stumbled into the bathroom.

Madison stared at the closed door. Neil had been a shoe man. She had a whole closet full. Seduction slippers.

'Oh *shit*.' She wiped a tear off her face with the back of a grimy hand. She didn't have time for this. She had things to do.

Out of the ravaged dress and bundled into jeans and a sweatshirt, with her hair tied back, she nudged the thermostat on the heating up a notch. She could hear the shower running.

Satisfied, she padded into the kitchen. If she could get in a short session tonight, tomorrow she would take him to the lab and throw everything she had at him. She chewed her lip. Physically, he was a mess, which might be why he was so susceptible to her. She'd be as ruthless as she could stomach, but it was going to take a while. He hadn't specified a time limit for earning his hundred pounds. *Not so smart there, buster.*

She filled the kettle and flicked the switch. She needed coffee. It would probably work for him, too. Plus some sandwiches. Maybe soup?

She had the fridge door open, looking for cheese, when the phone rang.

'Madison? Where did you get to? I've been ringing your mobile all night.'

'Hi, Jonathan.' One handed, she poured hot water on instant coffee. 'Mobile is ever so slightly FUBAR.' She glanced over at the dismembered mobile phone sitting on the counter, well beyond any of her engineering skills, and sighed. 'Long story.'

'Hmm.' Jonathan didn't sound impressed. 'Don't you know it's not polite to run out on your escort before the end of the evening? You go with him, you leave with him. I thought all nice girls knew that?'

If I was one of those *I wouldn't be planning to do what I'm going to do to the man currently in my shower.*

'I'm a scientist. It sort of cancels out.' She sipped coffee. 'Anyway, I thought you'd pulled with that gorgeous waiter. I was trying to be tactful.'

'Dalliance, mere dalliance.' Jonathan waved away the idea of the waiter. 'You know Ashley and I have an exclusivity agreement – but I don't blame you, cutting out. Boredom doesn't describe it. I wish I'd thought of it. I'm not cross really.' His voice dropped and softened. 'Just making sure you got home safe, sweet pea.'

'I did.'

'Good to know. I'll see you in the morning, then.'

She hesitated. 'Yes.'

Jonathan took about five seconds. 'You don't sound too sure – ah – Heaven be praised. You've got a *man* there.'

'No!' She heard the hiss. 'All right! Yes.'

'And you're wasting time talking to *me*?'

'He's in the shower.'

'All wet and waiting? God, you little minx. Who knew you could move so fast? You didn't find him amongst the soggy canapés, so it had to be on the way home . . . oh no!' Jonathan's voice rose half an octave. 'Please don't tell me you've been trawling the back alleys, *after dark*! Mad, it's not safe. And to take him home! You get that pretty boy from the reception desk right now, to help you throw him out. I'm going to stay on the phone

31

until you do. I don't care if he's naked. Give him a fiver and tell him to come to the lab in the morning for the rest.'

Madison bit her lip to stop herself laughing, hearing the concern in her colleague's voice. 'That's very sweet of you, Jon, and I do appreciate it, but it really is perfectly okay. He's too beat up to do me any damage. In fact it was the other way round. I thumped him—'

'You thumped him? Why? What did he do?'

'Misunderstanding,' Madison cut in quickly. 'We straightened it out. It's fine, honestly. He's fine. Well, actually he's not, and he won't let me get him a doctor—'

'Mad,' Jonathan broke in ominously. 'Tell me this man is not going to die on you? Go into a coma? Something permanent *and difficult to cover up.*'

'We're spooks, we can cover up *anything.*'

'You watch too much television. Or maybe not enough. Look, sweet pea, I love you, but Mad is not just a fond nickname. Get rid of him. You do not need this in your home. He'll come to the lab for money. They all do.'

'Cynic.'

'Realist. Turn him loose, please.'

'If I do that, I'm afraid I'll never see him again. He's . . . resistant.'

And yet she'd felt, somehow, as if he was searching.

Wishful thinking.

32

'He's something special, Jonny. Power like I've never experienced. And he can feel me. He knows when I'm inside his head.'

'Oh God. How many glasses of paint stripper did you have at that bloody do?'

This time she did laugh. 'One, and that was one too many. Look, it's okay, Jon, I know what I'm doing. I'll bring him to work in the morning and you can see for yourself.'

She heard Jonathan exhale. 'Well – if you're dead set on keeping him, do you want me and Ash to come over? Act as bodyguards?'

'It's a lovely offer, but no. It really isn't necessary. I *will* call you if I need you.'

'Promise?' Jonathan was weakening. 'Uh – I still think you're crazy, and I won't sleep a wink with worry, but if you're sure . . .'

'I am. I'm a big, bad scientist. I can do this. Goodnight, Jonny. And don't fret. I'm quite safe.'

She replaced the receiver, smiling. She did feel safe. It was the captive who needed to watch out for himself. *You really have to find out what his name is.*

She looked at the clock, frowning. He'd been in the shower over half an hour, which ought to be long enough to wash off the grime, even the ingrained stuff. Thorough was good, but enough was enough.

The bathroom door was still shut.

'Hello?' She knocked. 'I made coffee.'

No response. No sound of running water. No sound at all.

33

She turned the handle. The door wasn't locked.

He was lying on the floor, naked except for the shorts.

'Blast!' For the second time in less than two hours she crouched beside him, heart thumping, Jonathan's scare scenarios lurid in her head.

When he moved – a small nestling gesture that tugged at her overworked heart – she could have broken into song. She leaned closer and was rewarded by a faint but audible snore. She leaned back, not knowing whether to laugh or cry. He'd neatly sidestepped her plan to begin experiments tonight.

He wasn't unconscious.

He was fast asleep.

Balked of her objective, Madison sat on the floor beside him. She was going to have to get him up sometime soon, and into the guest bedroom, but she might as well take the chance of a quick physical appraisal. Not as if she had anything else to do, and she was pretty sure he wasn't going to volunteer her a look at his injuries. She brushed off a flicker of conscience. She really did need to get an idea of what sort of mess he was in.

The face, shrouded in beard, eyes closed, was still an unknown quantity. His hair, newly washed, was dark and springy. She caught her fingers in the act of stretching out to touch, and pulled back sharply. His body, and she could see virtually all of it, was a complete surprise. Hard, toned, muscled. Way too lean for his height, but otherwise

34

breathtakingly perfect. She'd expected signs of privation, but there was nothing. He was strong and fit. Ripped, even. Who knew?

And much younger than she'd thought. The silver in the hair had thrown her off. Early thirties, at a guess. Lying on his uninjured side, his left shoulder was swollen, the flesh discoloured by bruises, confirming his diagnosis of something broken. Somehow she had to get him medical attention. There were healing cuts and more old bruises in other places, souvenirs from the kids with boots and sticks. Nausea grumbled in her stomach. All that hurt, for a sick thrill.

And aren't you planning to do the same thing to his mind? Work him over, for your own pleasure?

Not pleasure! This is my job. This is science.

And you don't enjoy your work?

'I won't leave him damaged and in pain, and he'll be paid.'

And that makes it all right, does it? But of course, he's only a down-and-out. Something you found in the gutter.

'That's not true, but if he chooses to degrade himself—'

Sometimes it's not a choice. You know that.

Madison let out an exasperated snort. She was talking, *out loud*, to a voice in her head!

She leaned against the bath and focused on a spot where the wall tiles joined, clearing her mind.

Why guilt? Why now? The lab had to have subjects. She worked with residents from a number of homeless shelters. No one was harassed. They were all volunteers and they were treated with respect. Hell, she even had a few who were regulars. They were good material and they didn't talk afterwards. *Or if they do, no one much listens.* She shook her head. Why was this one different?

Because you more or less dragged him in here, and you're not planning on letting him go in a hurry. And he has power. Of his own. You want to teach him to use it.

She snapped back, feeling dizzy. Apprehension tugged at her stomach. Did she really—

She shook her head again, gritting her teeth. Enough with the self-examination. She was tired and hungry and off balance. Right now she had to get six-foot plus of inert, naked male off the floor and into a bed.

She scrambled up, considering the problem. A wet towel? Ice? Both? *Each!* Should she just get a blanket? He looked very peaceful, but the floor was chilly and hard. Probably no worse than where he'd been sleeping, but even so—

She put her hand on his arm. His skin was smooth. Besides the bruises there were scars. A jagged, newly healed slash along his side that had probably come from a knife. And then something older. And more puzzling. A slight puckering of the skin in the crook of his elbow. Plastic surgery?

Curious, she traced it with a finger. There was definitely something. A skin graft, to cover a birthmark or a tattoo?

Shrugging, she shifted position, watching his ribs rise and fall.

Clean, warm and in a secure place, his system had simply sandbagged him, taking what he'd been fighting not to give. No wonder he'd fallen asleep, even on so inhospitable a location as the bathroom floor. Her hand drifted over his chest. His stomach was flat, with an intriguing line of soft hair disappearing into the top of the boxers.

With a gasp she pulled her hand away, horrified at herself. Checking out his injuries was one thing, ogling and pawing him, when he wasn't awake to know about it—

Face flaming, she got to her feet. Filling a glass of water, she splashed a few drops on his face.

He came awake quicker than she expected, propping himself on his good arm and blinking at her. After a second of blankness, his eyes focused. Recognition.

'Mmm.' He yawned hugely. 'Did I go under again?'

'You were asleep. Come on.' She'd become quite adept at sliding an arm under his, to get him on his feet. She tried not to think about smooth, exposed skin. He pulled against her, half-heartedly. 'There's a perfectly good bed, on the other side of the hall. Just a few steps.'

A mix of coaxing, bullying and threats got him into the bedroom and sitting on the edge of the bed.

'Feet up.'

He resisted at first. He was strong, even two-thirds asleep. She'd almost given up when he lost interest and let her scoop him on to the bed and roll him away from the injured shoulder. She wrapped the duvet around him. On an impulse she couldn't identify, she bent and dropped a soft, fleeting kiss on his forehead. His eyes flickered open, muzzy.

'Here you are, practically naked in my bed – one of my beds. And I still haven't found out your name.'

For a second the eyes cleared, as if he understood her. He muttered something. She leaned forward to hear. It was barely a breath and then his eyes closed, shutting her out.

She frowned. He wasn't making sense, or she hadn't heard properly.

What she *thought* she'd heard him murmur was 'Don't know.'

CHAPTER 3

Madison opened her eyes slowly. Light was filtering through the narrow gap she always left between the curtains. The enticing scent of brewing coffee drifted over her. She stretched luxuriously. It must be Sunday, or Neil would have woken her.

Her head jerked up. Neil was gone. There was no dent in the pillow next to hers. No pillow there at all. If she could smell coffee then there was only one person who could be making it.

She slid out of bed quickly, reaching for her robe.

He was sitting at the kitchen table, with his back to her, hands wrapped around a large mug. Her eyes travelled to the machine on the counter, staring. He'd figured out how to make it work. Wouldn't you know? It had to be a guy thing. Sandra cleaned the monster every week, but it hadn't been used since Neil—

She swallowed hard, eyes abruptly filling with tears.

'The brew's fresh. Want some?' He was getting

up to pour it for her, but she waved him back to his seat, keeping her head averted. Finding a mug and filling it gave her a moment.

'Uh – good morning.' She leaned against the counter behind him, sipping. That sweater had never suited Neil. She'd pulled it out last night because it had a fastening at the neck that would be easier on the injured shoulder. It looked better on him than it ever had on Neil.

The disloyalty of the thought rocked her.

Then he turned, and she got a look at him that wasn't clogged with tears.

The beard was gone.

The face was all planes and angles, the mouth sensuous and firm. There were hollows where there shouldn't be and dark circles under the eyes, but they hardly mattered.

Something in her belly clenched, then relaxed. Warm.

He was studying her, warily.

'There was a razor, in the bathroom.' He looked uncertain, misreading her silence. At least she hoped he was misreading it. With an effort she pulled herself together.

'No problem . . . er . . . did you sleep all right? With the shoulder?' She dragged out a chair and subsided into it. With luck he'd just think she wasn't a morning person.

'Yeah.' The puzzled look was still in his eyes. 'Thanks for putting me to bed.'

'It seemed better than your choice. The

'bathroom floor,' she reminded him, when he looked even more confused.

'Oh – yes.' He frowned. 'I must have been pretty hard work last night.'

'Some,' she agreed. 'Look, won't you change your mind about seeing a doctor? I can run you down to A&E.'

'No.' He moved too quickly and winced.

'You're still in pain.'

'No hospital. No doctor. I'll take analgesics, if you have them, otherwise, I'll manage.' There was an edge of something in his voice that she didn't understand. It sounded like desperation.

She got up and found some tablets, grimacing at the eagerness with which he accepted them. 'It would be better if it was strapped up. You'd be more comfortable.'

She could see he wanted to shrug in response, but had more sense. His head was down, studying the mug.

'Hospitals ask questions. They want to know things I can't tell them.'

She hesitated, then decided to let it go.

'Hungry?'

'Starving.' He looked up and grinned. It did something very peculiar to the base of her throat.

'Breakfast, then.' It came out husky.

Covering her confusion, she went to the fridge. Every week Sandra unpacked the shopping ordered online and delivered to the apartment. Every week Madison reminded herself to alter the automatic

41

order that replaced all the things she and Neil had cooked and eaten together. Every week she forgot and Sandra took away or threw out the unused food. Now Madison was glad she'd had the lapse of memory.

She unshipped bacon, eggs, sausages and mushrooms.

'Full English breakfast?'

'Please.' He got up. 'More coffee?' He refilled both mugs. 'I didn't want to disturb you, so I just put the machine on.'

Neil's coffee maker, Neil's razor, Neil's clothes. 'No problem.'

It felt strange to be cooking breakfast with a man sitting at the table again. Strange, but not wrong.

She dished up and put it in front of him. 'Heart attack on a plate.'

'Right now I don't care if you've laced it with arsenic. It looks wonderful.' She sat and watched him tackle the food with a concentration that gave her a totally unexpected sense of pleasure. Halfway through he looked up.

'You're not eating?'

'Toast, in a minute.'

'You should have some of this. You cooked it.'

He held out a forkful of bacon. After a second's hesitation, she took it, then let him pass her a mushroom.

'No more. You finish it.' She licked sauce off her fingers. 'We're sharing breakfast and I don't even know your name.' She watched closely, knowing she wasn't imagining his sudden stillness. 'I'm Madison Albi.'

'And I can call you Miss Albi, or is it Ms Albi?' His eyes slid away from her.

'Dr Albi, actually, but Madison will do.'

He'd pushed his plate away and was fiddling with his mug, which was empty.

Madison leaned back. 'And you are?' she prompted.

'I can't tell you.' His eyes were everywhere but on her.

'Can't or won't?' She held her breath.

'Can't.' Cornered, he had to look at her. The bleakness in his eyes flared in her heart. She could feel it spilling out of him, and the well of despair behind it. 'I can't tell you because I don't know.'

He put up his hand to cover his eyes and she knew he was trying to block her out, but the emotion was too strong. It was seeping over the table to her, choking in her throat. She put out her hand, to touch him.

'Take it easy.'

She sat quietly, trying to give him what strength she had, without invading him. It seemed to be working. There was colour coming back to his face. He dropped his hands.

'Better?' she asked softly.

'Yes.' The word was slow, considering. The dark glance was wary. 'You get this a lot, do you? Strangers you've picked off the street eating breakfast and then telling you they don't know who the fuck they are?'

43

'I think I can safely say that this is a first.' She paused. 'If you're trying to ask why I'm not more surprised, then I have to tell you that you did give me a strong clue.'

'I did?'

Madison nodded. 'Last night, when you were half-asleep, you said you didn't know your name. I assumed I'd misheard, but when I thought about it some more, it made a certain kind of sense.' *But I wanted you to tell me.*

'I wish it did to me.' He balanced his hands on the edge of the table, palm down. 'I have no idea who I am. I have no memory of anything beyond the last three months.'

'You just woke up one day, in an alley somewhere?'

'Close to the railway line, near Paddington Station. Apparently I'd been sleeping in a nest of cardboard boxes. It looked like I'd been there for some time. I was cold, dirty and hungry. I was dressed in the clothes I had on last night – ragged and filthy – and I didn't have any fucking idea who I was, or how I got there. It sounds impossible, but it's the truth.'

When he looked up from studying his hands and she saw the desolation in his face, she knew it couldn't be a lie.

'There has to be a reason. A head injury?'

'That's what I thought, but there's no evidence.' He bit his lip. 'I did go to the hospital. They couldn't find anything. Eventually they turned me out for

44

wasting their time.' He held her eyes, steady. 'I don't blame them, but I've not been near one since.' He shifted awkwardly and his eyes dropped away, but not before she saw the memory of anguish in them.

'No.' She tried to imagine how it would feel. Isolation. Panic. She couldn't even come close. 'You can't remember anything at all?'

'When I try, there's just this . . . it's like a wall. And . . . my head aches.' His eyes skittered away for a moment. 'Once I got as far as the letter J. I don't know if it means anything. I have dreams sometimes, when I almost know—'

'And then you wake up.'

The smile was heart-tuggingly rueful. 'Yep.'

'You think J is your name? Part of it?'

'It's all I have. What I've been using. J-A-Y,' he spelled it out.

'Jay.'

Madison got up, made toast and put it on plates, giving herself thinking time.

She put one plate in front of him and sat down again. 'This isn't my field, but I don't see how you can suddenly become amnesiac without trauma. If there's no physical injury—'

'It has to be emotional trauma. My mind is running away from something.' His voice grated.

'Maybe,' she admitted cautiously. 'From your description, it seems as if you were already home-less when you woke, in some sort of trouble, anyway – so that wasn't necessarily the result of the memory loss,' she mused. 'Substance abuse?'

45

'Not as far as I know.'

'Nothing fits.'

'Tell me about it.'

'No, you tell me. You say it's like a wall?'

'That I can't get around. Do you want to come in and find out?'

Madison drew in her breath sharply. 'You mean that?'

'Why not? It's what I'm here for, isn't it? So you can mess with my mind?' His eyes were narrowed, sizing her up. 'This is what you do for a living, right? You're a scientist, doing mind experiments?'

Madison chewed her lip. The lab wasn't a secret, just . . . discreet. Her other subjects knew exactly what went on, so why not him? There would be forms, waivers – and payment. She had arrangements in place. She could get him into a hostel – regular meals, health checks, the chance of a fresh start . . .

But if he is what you think he is, what he might be . . .

She sat forward, folding her hands. 'What do you know about mind reading?' She forced her voice to be crisp and businesslike, waiting for the laughter and the jokes.

'What's to know?' He wasn't laughing. 'Officially it doesn't exist – except in fiction or on the stage . . .'

Madison took a shallow breath. 'But?'

He shrugged his good shoulder. 'Military authorities are supposed to have been trying to make it work for years – if you believe the conspiracy theorists.'

'Do you?'

'Don't know if I care either way.' Something flickered across his eyes. He frowned. 'I suppose . . . Maybe there are more things on earth, Horatio, and all that – a lot of people believe in that thought-reading stuff.' The frown deepened. 'I don't know . . . I suppose . . . it's sort of like science . . . *Science* is interesting.' He focused on her face. 'You're the real deal though. ESP, telepathy, whatever. You can actually *do* it.'

'Mind reading isn't exactly ESP, or telepathy. Not the way that I do it.'

'No?' There was interest in his eyes. Genuine interest, not the look she so often encountered. *The one that said 'humour her'*. 'What *is* it like?' His eyes were sharp and alert, fixed on her face.

'It's more a matter of focus.' How to explain the unexplainable? 'I don't channel into someone's mind and straight into their thoughts, word for word. I pick up . . . brainwaves, I suppose you'd call them, which is a kind of telepathy – but to actually read, that requires a degree of concentration. It's like a probe, a direction of energy—' *Why are you sharing this? You never share this.*

He hadn't noticed her sudden hesitation. 'It's not a random thing.' He nodded, clearly pondering. 'You have to be able to process and handle raw data. What sort of results are you getting?' His

47

attention sharpened on her again. Her face warmed under the intensity of his stare.

'I . . .' she hesitated, confused. *But what's the point of stopping now, if he's going to be part of it?* Her shoulders relaxed a fraction. 'Nothing is clear cut.' She couldn't help the tiny sigh. 'I get results, but they're tangled, impressionistic. When people imagine mind reading they think of a verbatim record – monitoring exactly what's taking place in someone's brain. For me it's more about emotion than logic. I sense what people are feeling.'

Abruptly the wash of pain that had flooded out of him last night came back to her, leaving an acrid taste in her mouth. She picked up her mug and drank the dregs of her coffee, bitterness chasing acrid. 'The facility I work for is a charitable foundation, researching the heightened use of the senses in a therapeutic context.' She stopped, checking on his expression. The official-speak that she always found mildly embarrassing didn't seem to bother him. 'I've done some work on memory, but my particular area of research at present is connection. Basically, I'm trying to find ways of making mind-links that might eventually be used for therapeutic purposes. But that's a long way off.' This time she held in the inevitable sigh. 'So far, simply making coherent links is proving difficult enough.'

'Not a vast amount of messing with people's minds, then?' Now he *was* grinning.

'My work is still in development,' she defended

herself, knowing that her back had stiffened. She went through this at every annual review, defending tiny increments of progress, expecting each time to be challenged.

'Maybe you're looking at the wrong minds?'

'I think you may be right.' She had already begun to consider the question. 'I may need to widen my subject pool.'

'Starting with me.'

'You . . . I've never encountered a subject with the kind of response you have. I've never known a subject who can feel when I'm in their head.'

'I'm special, then, am I?'

'Yes.' She looked into his eyes. Felt a shiver, deep down in her abdomen. Some of it was attraction, no question, but what else? Excitement, anticipation . . . fear.

This is the most dangerous man you have ever encountered, and he doesn't even have a name.

The thought turned her cold, then hot. She should walk away. As a woman, she was ready to go. As a scientist? *Never.* She'd protected herself all these years. *You just have to handle this.*

'I think maybe I'm flattered.' His mouth twisted, half grin, half grimace. 'Whatever you need to do, I'm willing.' His voice grated, rough edged. 'Feel free to mess. If you find anything in there, let me know.' The flippancy didn't quite hide the pain.

Madison pushed herself away from the table, heart beating fast. 'We should be at the lab. There are procedures, protocols—'

He laughed. 'If I'd been awake and sensible last night you'd have tried then.'

'Well—' How could she deny it?

'Do it.' He held his hand out to her, palm upwards. After a brief hesitation she laid her hand on top and shut her eyes, concentrating.

Remembering the discomfort she'd caused him the previous night, she moved cautiously, even though this time he was expecting her. She honed a narrow, tentative probe, meeting the initial resistance as unthreateningly as she knew how. His hand tightened on hers. She poised herself to pull away if he showed any sign of distress. She wanted to get this right.

'Go on.' His voice, low and harsh, startled her. The idea that he could feel her was so alien. 'Push harder.'

She did, and felt his instant recoil. She wavered, momentarily uncertain. Then moved on, slowly.

Suddenly, like a door being opened, the resistance vanished. The change was so abrupt, she almost fell into him. There was a nauseous, vertiginous rush, whether from his mind or hers she couldn't distinguish.

Then everything stilled.

The clarity of the connection astonished her.

The analytical part of her mind held back, detached. With infinite care, she put out exploratory feelers.

Sensations and emotions came rushing towards her.

Pain from the damaged shoulder and behind it a deep, complex anguish, like a pool of darkness, that had her struggling, momentarily, for breath.

Then they were swarming past her, almost too fast to distinguish. Anger, bone-deep exhaustion, only partially relieved by one night's sleep, a thread of fear, tasting of broken glass. Desolation, kept under tight restraint. Frustration and confusion, chasing each other in an endless wheel.

He was stripping himself bare, giving her everything, without sparing himself. It was blotting out her control, blinding, just too much. Alarmed, sucked in headlong, she began to pull back.

Jay's hand clutched hers tighter, holding on as if she were a lifeline. She could feel him breathing, trying to calm the chaos. She let herself follow, inhaling air, making everything slow. Gradually the maelstrom receded.

Gathering herself together, she started back in, easing softly past the whirlpools. It was quieter here. With relief she recognised strength and resilience and a beleaguered courage that made her want to weep. Garnering power, she moved on, pushing to the centre.

It was like banging her head against sheet metal.

The core, where the history of the man lay, was wrapped tighter than a guarded fortress.

'*You can feel it.*' Jay's voice was inside her head.

Astonishment rocked through her for a second. Steadying herself and stepping up the pressure, she pushed harder. The reverberations shook them

51

both. She felt the shock through her body and the grip on her hand.

Regrouping, she tried something more subtle. Again, nothing. It was like a barrier of steel, smooth and solid. A barrier she'd never met before. She feinted, tried to sidestep, to slide in or around. Without success. She could feel the agitation building in Jay, ruthlessly controlled. But he wasn't strong enough yet. He couldn't take much more.

She had to end it.

Reluctantly she moved back, drawing on her reserves to soothe the raw edges of emotions that brushed against her as she disengaged. Her head was spinning. The table seemed to be moving.

'Are you okay?' Jay's eyes were on her, his hand still in hers. He looked dazed, as if he'd been punched. For a moment they clung together. She couldn't move, couldn't think. His eyes were the only thing stopping her from reeling into the walls. When finally she nodded, he let her go.

'Thanks.' His voice was jagged. 'I felt what you did as you were coming out. It helped.'

'Uh.' She waved her hand, then put it to her forehead. Something throbbed briefly, then stopped. 'I don't get this. Normally subjects don't feel anything. You spoke to me in there!'

'I'm not normal.' He gave a bitter bark of laughter. 'You know what I mean now. The thing like a wall.'

'It's there.' She nodded, mouth grim. 'It's like

nothing I've ever experienced. I shook you up, pushing like that. I'm sorry.'

'If you can get through, I can put up with anything.' He was studying the table, tracing a pattern with one finger. Madison sat motionless. She didn't have to be in his head to know he was struggling with what he wanted to say. 'I know we have a deal, and I have no right to ask this—' He swallowed. 'You're the first chance I've had . . . the first possibility . . . Will you . . . Can you help me?'

Something twisted inside her. He was big and powerful and lost.

'Yes.' She gave his hand, still on the table, a small shake. 'Did you really think I'd say no? You,' she pointed her finger, 'are the most interesting thing I have come across in the whole of my professional career. You will *not* get away from me. I will help. Whether I *can* is another matter. We can only try.'

He was smiling. He had the kind of smile that could get a woman into deep, serious trouble. When he'd had the beard, she'd been safe. Madison dredged up every atom in her body that was scientist, not woman.

'That's good enough,' he confirmed.

'It's going to be exhausting and uncomfortable.'

'Doesn't matter.' He brushed that aside. 'You want to renegotiate our deal?'

'Renegotiate? How?'

'I let you take me apart, do whatever experiments you want on me – you try and get my memory back.'

'Getting your memory back would be the biggest experiment I'd ever want to do.' She grabbed his hands, still fidgeting on the table. 'There are things we can try and if none of them work, we'll think up more. I'll go on the Internet this morning to see what I can find. I *want* to do this. You do not have to make bargains.'

'Does that mean I still get my hundred pounds, then?' The grin was evil, but she saw the relief and excitement under it. It lit something inside her. She chose to ignore the flicker of danger. *Professional enthusiasm, that's all.*

'Huh! Memory or not, you are a devious, scheming opportunist. You ambushed me last night. You knew I didn't have any option but to pay up if I wanted to keep you,' she accused.

'I simply worked with what was there. I think it's called negotiation. I wasn't asking to stay. You were the one who offered me money.' He paused, frowning. 'If your porter had put me back on the street—'

'—I might never have seen you again.' The desolation that swept over her made her tighten her grip on his hands. She saw his reaction of surprise. 'Sorry.' She let go. *Shouldn't be doing that. Physical contact with the subject to be kept to absolute minimum. Strictly a need-to-touch basis.* She crunched down on a peculiar feeling, low in her belly.

He was frowning. 'Actually, I'm not sure about that. It . . . it's kind of hazy, like a lot of stuff . . .' She saw exasperation flare in his eyes. 'I don't

54

know if I would have gone far. For the last couple of days I've felt as if something was drawing me here, to this part of the city. That I knew I had to find . . . something. Does that sound as weird to you as it does to me?'

'Not necessarily.' She breathed. 'Maybe you have connections here – or you might have heard the men from one of the homeless hostels talking about working for the lab.'

'Maybe.' He considered the idea. 'Probably. Why else? I don't remember it, but that's not exactly a surprise. Yeah, else why now? Why not when I first woke up?' His shoulders sagged.

Madison sat looking at him uncertainly, watching the way he went into himself, containing the misery. Unbelievable courage. Should she—

She got up abruptly and began clearing the table, not quite sure why she wasn't going to tell him that she'd only arrived back home two days ago, after three months in Washington, DC.

The tower block was huge, dwarfing most of the surrounding buildings. Faceless glass and metal, it could have been part of the skyline anywhere in the world – New York, Tokyo, Hong Kong. The lower floors housed the kind of outfits that anyone would expect to find in the City of London – brokers, insurance houses, legal firms.

The top floor was different.

The directory of the building's occupants, which covered one wall of the sleek, minimalist foyer, many floors below, contained no listing for these offices. The Organisation liked to preserve its anonymity – it owned the building, although its ownership was not acknowledged in any official documents. The Organisation, a collection of nominally autonomous local cells, without even an official name, existed for one purpose only – to make money. The people at the very top were shadows: men, and a few women, who walked the corridors of power on five continents, sustained by profit and vast influence, never acknowledging responsibility or blame, protected by violence as stealthy as it was ruthless. No one crossed the Organisation and lived. That was the legend. But if you worked for them that didn't matter. The Organisation made money. Unbelievable amounts of money. In unbelievable ways.

Alec Calver strode along the wide, silent corridor. He stopped when he reached the door at the end, straightened his tie, looked up into the overhead camera and knocked.

The intercom panel beside the door crackled. 'In.'

As the door closed behind him, Calver took a moment to adjust. After the subdued illumination of the corridor, this office was flooded with light. Only high-flying birds and the occasional plane ever overlooked it.

'Alec.' The man behind the desk gestured to a chair. 'Sit.'

Calver didn't let his impatience show. Let the

56

guy have his power trip. He placed the file he held in the centre of an otherwise empty desk.

'Madison Albi?'

'Subject B,' Calver corrected. He took the chair indicated, hitching the knees of his impeccably pressed trousers. In contrast, the man behind the desk looked like an unmade bed. The expensive suit was rumpled, tie askew. The top button of his shirt strained under the pressure of a neck the thickness of a young tree. A fuzz of coarse hair was visible over the button. The hair extended, too, at the cuffs of his shirt, down over the backs of the broad hands. The CEO resembled nothing so much as a large ape. The mind inside the ape was as sharp and unyielding as a steel trap.

'Developments?' He prodded the file.

Calver nodded, without speaking.

'Good.' The CEO moved restlessly. 'I still think we should have bugged the woman's apartment, and the laboratory.'

'It's still a possibility,' Calver conceded. 'But bugs need someone to monitor them – which means bringing in more operatives, simply to listen to her taking a shower, or feeding the cat.'

The ape behind the desk gave a strangled noise that passed for a laugh. 'The shower sounds enticing. I will pass on the cat.'

'Which is a good thing, as she doesn't have one.' Calver let a small smile through.

'A beautiful woman.' The CEO leaned back in

his chair. 'A superlative body, housing a gifted and inventive mind. Does she bring these talents to her sexual encounters, do you suppose?'

'I wouldn't care to speculate – sir.' Calver kept his eyes down to hide the glint. 'She is known to be fastidious in her choices. There's been nothing of that nature since the death of her fiancé, nearly two years ago.'

'No?' The CEO breathed out the word, considering. 'An excellent move on our part, then. She sees men socially?'

'Yes, but mostly colleagues and no one in particular. Her most frequent escort is Jonathan Ellis.'

'The faggot from the lab?'

Calver looked at the view. 'They go to the theatre together.'

'She'll be ripe, then, to put someone new in her bed. So – is subject A going to get lucky?'

'It's to be hoped so.'

'Anything we can do, to help it along?'

'No.' Calver shook his head, eyes hooded. 'But there's every chance. Propinquity is a great aphrodisiac.'

'Hmm.' The other man ran a finger over the file. 'You have a tail on them?'

'Not yet.'

'No bugs and no tail? How the fuck d'you expect to know what's going on?'

'It only needs the lightest of surveillance at present, sir. Trust me on this one. Anything more might attract attention. Remember who we're dealing with. This way we have capacity to increase, should it become necessary.'

'Plenty, as you seem to be doing fuck all at the moment.'

'Everything is going according to plan, sir.'

'You're not watching and you're not listening, but everything is going according to plan. Just dandy.'

'It's all in there.' Calver nodded to the file.

'Précis for me. How do we know the contact has been made?'

'We know.' There was satisfaction in Calver's voice. 'This morning Madison Albi began to trawl the Internet for information on amnesia.'

When Calver had gone, the CEO rifled through the file, grunting in approval, before dropping it into the drawer of the desk and locking it. The information was presented in the most guarded terms. In the unlikely event of anyone but himself or Calver reading it, almost all they would get would be that subject A was male, subject B female. There was nothing on the page about the scope of the project, or the untold billions of pounds, dollars, euros and yen that it was expected to generate.

On the other side of the building Alec Calver entered an empty room. Passing through it, he shoved open a door, kicking it shut behind him. One hand loosened his tie; the other patted over his pockets.

'Sod it!'

'Here.' The shaven-headed giant, lounging in front of a computer screen, tossed over a pack of cigarettes. Calver caught it and extracted one, pocketing the remainder with a swift glance upward to the smoke sensor above him. The complex wiring, designed to keep the building smoke-free, had been carefully dismantled and rerouted away from this room.

The man at the computer clicked his fingers. 'Packet.'

'What?'

'I want the packet back, you thieving bastard.'

'Oh.' Alec dug it out and handed it over. 'Sorry, Vic. Mind on other things.'

'Yeah,' Vic agreed sceptically. 'So – did we make King Kong happy?'

'Ecstatic, as far as I could tell.' Alec lit the cigarette and leaned on the desk, drawing deep, and blowing a perfect smoke ring in the direction of the defunct detector. 'He's still banging on about bugs and surveillance, though.'

'Plenty of time for that.'

'That's what I told him. The bitch is sharp. No point in leaving trails if we don't need to.'

Vic's eyes narrowed. 'You ever know me to leave a trail?'

'You never handled anything like Madison Albi before. This one reads minds.'

'She wouldn't need a crystal ball to read mine.' Vic made a graphic gesture. 'I'd like to handle *her*, no problem.'

'Get in line, sucker.'

Vic gave a crack of laughter. 'You, too?' His eyes widened as he sorted through the implications. 'And old hairy arse upstairs?'

'Him, too. He thinks she has a superlative body and an inventive mind.'

Vic whistled. 'Didn't think he knew words that long.' He laughed again. 'Who would have thought it, me and ape-face, brothers under the skin. Inventive. I like that. Some of the stuff I'd like to do to her might be classed as inventive.'

He gestured to the computer. A picture of Madison, taken with a long lens, had been enhanced and cropped and made into a screensaver.

'That is *crude*.'

'Like I haven't seen you looking,' Vic taunted. 'Say, how about when this is all done, we scoop up what's left of her and bring her over here? Have a little fun. Take turns like. Might be a laugh, watching ape-face fuck her.' He saw the spasm cross Alec's face. 'Pansy.'

Calver ignored the jibe. 'She still online?'

'Nah, logged off a few minutes ago.' He tapped a key, and the screensaver dissolved. 'This one is interesting. Cutting edge research on memory loss.'

'Yeah,' Alec agreed. 'Keep your eye on that one.'

'You know, I've been wondering – if the man wants bugs – it would be no big deal to add a camera or two, like in the shower and over the bed, maybe. Catch all the action.' Vic watched Calver's face out of the corner of his eye.

'It's an idea.' Calver was studying the screen.

'So – how long before they start shagging?'

'God, doesn't your mind ever get above your belt?'

'Not if I can help it.' Vic lit up a cigarette and offered the packet again. Alec hesitated, then took one, lighting it from the stub of the last. 'How long before he shags her?' Vic persisted.

'It's too soon. We factored it in, but only as one scenario.'

'The best one, though.'

'Oh yes.' Alec dragged on the cigarette.

'What's Kong think?'

'Same as you, it would appear.'

'Brothers under the fucking skin – or maybe fur.' Vic smirked. 'Good old Alec though, he's sitting on the fence. You want to watch it mate, you'll get splinters in your backside.'

A half-smile drifted over Calver's face. 'Kong wanted to know if there was anything we could do to help them along.'

'Christ! What was he expecting – we pitch up and offer them a lecture on the birds and the bees?'

'He didn't say.'

'So—' Vic looked up at Alec. 'What do you think? Really.'

'I think it's quite likely that they will end up in bed together, yes. He bears sufficient resemblance to the fiancé for us to assume that he's her physically preferred type. That was factored in, too.'

'And him? You know him better than anyone else.'

'Subject A?' Calver turned away from the computer. 'I think there's more than a distinct possibility. She is definitely *his* type.'

'You know this because—?'

Alec laughed. 'I know it because he chose her himself.'

CHAPTER 4

Madison pressed her fingers to her forehead and leaned back in her chair. She hadn't really expected the answer to Jay's amnesia to pop right out of the computer screen at her, but she had hoped there might be more. *Come on, what did you expect? A nice Wikipedia entry? Loss of memory – cure of – c.f. mind reading?*

What she *had* found had started a disturbing chain of thought.

She checked her e-mail, smiling at Jonathan's response to the one she had sent, confirming that she had made it safely through the night, before logging off. The machine seemed to hesitate for a moment, before closing down. It was slow to respond on occasions, too. Probably needed an overhaul. Which meant transporting it to the lab. Something for the to-do list. *Later.*

She sucked the end of her pen, assessing the brief notes she had made about Jay's status. She would need to make up a file. *Which might be pretty thick by the time you're finished.* She frowned. The amnesia – was it linked in some way to his ESP abilities, or just a hideously frustrating coincidence? Here she had a man who appeared to be well educated and who was interested in science, yet was living on the street. She knew, from experience, that it happened. What had put *Jay* there? Accident, misfortune, a cataclysmic life event? She doodled on the edge of the pad. *Amnesia – cause, effect – or irrelevance?* A slight shiver ran along her arm. He could feel her, inside his head. He'd *spoken* to her, while she was in his mind, yet he didn't seem to be aware of having power of his own. Was the amnesia covering something up? *Something that even Jay doesn't know?*

With a sigh she stood and stretched the kinks out of her neck, checking her watch. Breakfast TV had kept Jay quiet for over an hour. Which surprised her. She'd have bet on him tracking her down way before this.

He was asleep on the sofa, remote control in hand.

She gave him a long, considering look, then went to make tea. She tipped half a packet of biscuits on to a plate. Not one of the major nutritional groups, but hell – food was food.

Deep in thought, she licked the chocolate off a digestive as the kettle heated. Feeding a man. She opened the fridge. There *was* healthy stuff in here. Salad, fresh pasta, Sandra's home-made spaghetti sauce. She shook the container. Neil had done all the creative stuff in the kitchen. She'd been strictly slicing and chopping. Sometimes he'd let her grind herbs and stir things. She cooked a decent fry-up, and her knowledge of the controls on the micro-wave was second to none, but that was all. She puffed out her lower lip. Spaghetti sauce. *How hard can it be to boil tomatoes?*

'Garpgh.' Jay woke with the lightest touch on his arm, sitting up with a jerk and cursing under his breath as he jarred his shoulder. He scrubbed his hand over his face and accepted tea. 'Must have drifted off.'

'Not surprising.' She pushed the biscuits towards him. 'You need to eat. You'll have to put as much into this as I do. You need all the stamina you can get.'

'In that case—' He took two biscuits, raising his brows when Madison put a set of keys on the table.

'There's a studio flat on this floor. It's meant to be staff quarters.' She made a face. 'It's yours, for as long as you want. There are more clothes in the hall cupboard. We'll get whatever else you need.' She looked pointedly at his bare feet. Jay gave her a bland look and swiped another biscuit. 'First we get that shoulder looked at. I've thought of someone—' She forestalled him when he started to shake his head. 'Not a hospital.' *Not a doctor, either.* 'Hospitals ask too many questions, right? Like who you are and where you live?'

'You got it.' He shifted, not meeting her eyes. 'Did you find anything? On the Internet?'

'Nothing particularly useful.' She tilted her head.

66

'You know a lot of homeless people have been in the Forces?'

'Yeah, I met a few. Mostly ex-army . . .' His voice faded and his whole body stilled. 'You think I might be a military experiment that went wrong?'

Or maybe way too right.

She studied his face, watching for a reaction, saw him reaching and coming up blank.

'Nothing.' A frustrated sigh. 'An experiment – military, or whatever – that would mean I'd got away from somewhere.' A slight but unmistakable shudder. 'Or been turned loose. Someone may be looking for me. Or have no further use for me.' His eyes were dark, turned inward. 'If the amnesia isn't natural . . . if it was *done* to me – that's a whole new raft of who and why questions.' Abruptly he focused on her. 'I shouldn't be dragging you into this.'

'I said I'd help.' *Try keeping me out.* 'If it was done, then it can be undone.' She hesitated. 'The work I do – it's a small, tight, professionally jealous world. Not exactly public, but not secret, either. I would have expected—' She gathered the corner of her lip into her teeth. 'If something like this was going down, I'd have expected a whisper. Rumour, gossip – something. There isn't anything – which means it's very well hidden, or it doesn't exist.'

'Which makes me a *paranoid* amnesiac!'

'Not knowing who you are is grounds for paranoia.'

'Thanks for the vote of confidence.' He held her eyes. His were very deep, dark blue. She noticed the length of his lashes again, feeling a disturbing quiver in the pit of her stomach. She looked away first, reaching to pick up the empty biscuit plate. 'Shall we go and look at the studio?'

It was bigger than she remembered, with a large, light main room, a compact bathroom and a kitchen alcove that gave on to a tiny balcony. She showed Jay how the fold-down bed operated, and where the bedding and towels were kept. Everything was new, unused.

'Thanks.' He was looking round with an unreadable expression on his face.

'No problem.' She turned away, before he could say more. 'Will you be ready to go in ten minutes?'

'You brought me to a *vet*? A place that takes care of people's *pets!*' Jay stopped so suddenly, catching sight of the brass plate by the door, that Madison cannoned into him. She pulled back sharply. He was wearing Neil's cashmere overcoat. The familiar feel of the soft fabric, brushing against her cheek, made her skin tingle.

'You have a better suggestion?' It came out sharper than she intended. She exhaled. 'Animals have bones, same as people, and Joe plays rugby. He's always breaking things.'

The tension in Jay's jaw told her how much he wanted to argue. And the control as he let it go.

Doesn't take instruction well, but sucks it up when there's no alternative. Hmmm.

Joe had sandwiched them in between an anxious poodle and a hamster with a weight problem. Madison leaned against the wall while he conducted his examination. She avoided noticing the white line of pain around Jay's mouth by pretending to study a diagram of the feline digestive tract.

'Well, Doc? Is he gonna live?'

'How the hell would I know?' Joe grinned. 'As far as I can tell, your diagnosis is correct.' He nodded to Jay. 'Broken collarbone, but *don't* quote me. On the basis of personal experience, if you did it three weeks ago, then it should be on the way to healing by now. But I am *not* a doctor. I can strap it up, make it more comfortable, but you really should see a medic. One that specialises in humans.'

'Not possible.' Madison reached up to kiss his cheek. 'Thanks, Joey, you're a star.'

'Old boyfriend?' Jay settled into the passenger seat with a resigned sigh as Madison leaned over to help fasten his seatbelt.

'Joe?'

Jay narrowed his eyes as her head went back and her eyebrows soared. Either she was a bloody good actress, or she'd been genuinely surprised at the question.

'Friend, not boyfriend; we were at university together.'

She let in the clutch smoothly. Jay found himself

69

admiring the way she drove and obscurely glad that she and big, good-looking Joe had never been an item. On the other hand, there was the expensive coat he was wearing. *And everything else.* There'd been a man in the angel's recent past. He'd walked out, and left his stuff behind. Interesting. Jay studied Madison's profile. Chin a little tense. The angel had something on her mind. Was she going to spit it out? Yes?

'Joe doesn't know,' she'd pokered up, hands stiff on the wheel, 'about the mind reading. I . . . don't broadcast it. He knows I work at the laboratory – he thinks I just do drug research.'

'I can see it might be disconcerting. For friends,' Jay agreed smoothly. 'Not knowing if you were inside their heads.'

'Exactly.' The note of relief in her voice touched something inside him, but it didn't last long. 'I would never do that. Invade someone's privacy. Uh – not if I could help it.'

But you have done. If you want something badly enough. You did it last night. To me.

The back of the angel's neck was going pink.

'Not to friends.' He couldn't resist. 'But what about lovers?'

'I don't have—' She stopped abruptly.

Jay watched, fascinated, as a delicate flush rose slowly from the neck of her severe black coat. Now why the hell should that half-admission, intriguing as it was, make Dr Albi blush? And why was the sight of that fragile rose, spreading under the pale skin, making a suspicious tightness in his groin? *Shit.* His angel was embarrassed, or angry. And he wanted to taste—

He pulled himself up, staring at a sign beside the road, welcoming them to Uxbridge. Madison crunched the gears. *Still flustered.*

That made two of them.

He took a breath. He didn't much want to be in the car if she was planning to drive them into a traffic island, but an opportunity was an opportunity.

'Did he know?' He lifted his arm. 'The owner of the coat? About the mind reading?'

'Neil,' she corrected automatically. She'd recovered herself. Shot him a get-back-in-your-box-and-stay-there look. *Good girl.* 'He knew.'

She wasn't going any further than that, he could see by the way she turned the steering wheel. *So, back down now, buddy, before this gets sticky.*

'What's your doctorate?' Nice harmless change of subject. 'Psychology?'

'Chemistry.' She was parking the car beside a row of shops. He looked expectantly at her. 'Shoe shop.' She pointed. 'Then you can throw away those revolting trainers.'

Everything was fine, until it came time to pay. Madison bit her lip as Jay's hand went automatically to the pocket where his wallet should have been. She saw the recoil, then the shutters came down, leaving his face devoid of expression.

71

'I'll take care of this.' She slid her card to the cashier. 'Is there anything else you need?' She turned, deliberately neutral, towards him.

'No.' He'd mooched to the front of the shop, eyes away from her, studying the street. 'Thank you.'

When she left, he followed. She bit down an involuntary smile. His indecision over letting her carry the parcels, set against accepting the contents, was coming over her shoulder at her, almost strong enough to touch. The warmth of his fingers as he lifted the bags out of her hand sent a frisson up her arm. She flexed her fingers to dispel it, stopped and turned. 'What?'

'I want you to keep an account.' His voice was gruff and he didn't meet her eyes. 'Everything you spend.'

'I can afford to buy you a couple of pairs of shoes,' she objected quietly.

'Not the point.' His eyes came back to hers, as she'd hoped. 'Keep an account. I'll repay you. Everything. When I get straight.'

'Okay.' She wasn't going to push it. 'But you know what I'd really like, more than money.' She looked pointedly at the waste bin, standing at the kerb.

He took barely a second to catch on.

The rueful smile, as he ceremonially dumped the bag with the old trainers, had the corners of Madison's mouth twitching. She turned hurriedly towards the car.

★   ★   ★

72

'Impressive place.'

Madison pulled into her designated parking slot and turned off the engine.

'I suppose it is.'

She looked around. The lab was a long, low building, a curve of white plaster and glass, set well back from the road to Amersham, surrounded by wide lawns. She'd stopped seeing it, she realised, with a jolt. The shiny windows, close-cropped grass, tasteful flowerbeds of pale lemon daffodils, edging the approach to the double doors. She didn't look any more, not even at the flowers. It was just the place she worked.

'Good design. *Clever* design,' Jay corrected softly. 'Unthreatening,' he explained, when she raised her brows. 'All that white. Open.' He waved a hand at the immaculate green. 'Nothing to hide. Clever,' he repeated.

'Or truthful.' Madison could hear herself, a shade tart, as she opened her door. 'It's just a research foundation. Nothing bad happens here.'

'Good to know.' Jay slid out of the car and padded after her. 'Good. To. Know.'

Madison closed her ears to the mockery in the drawl.

She made her decision as she crossed the foyer to sign in, leaving Jay to negotiate the doors in his own time. Not the interview rooms at the front of the building, where she usually conducted initial assessments. Jay was coming with her, into her office. Her own domain – *private* domain.

Her mind twisted over the tangle of power and threat *that* represented.

'I'll need a visitor's pass, for Mr . . .' *Hell.* The security guard behind the desk was looking at her expectantly. Her eyes flipped frantically for a second, before settling on the monochrome canvas of lines and splatters that covered most of the wall in front of her. 'Jackson. Jay Jackson,' she repeated, louder, as Jay joined her. She saw his eyes widen, then the almost imperceptible nod, to show he understood. 'He's going to be helping me for a few days.'

'No problem, Dr Albi.' The guard thrust the book towards Jay, who slanted her a quick glance before signing.

'I suppose I should be grateful that whoever chooses the corporate art around here doesn't have a taste for Picasso.' Jay stood behind her, looking back into the foyer as she punched numbers into the security lock that accessed the main building. 'Or maybe Caravaggio?' he suggested conversationally.

Madison couldn't help the splutter of laughter. 'You got that, did you?'

'The *Jackson* Pollock, over by the desk? Difficult to miss. Is it real?'

'Probably – but too big to steal.' They were through the doors and into the narrow, glass-sided corridor that ran along the entire front face of the building.

'Wouldn't dream of it.'

74

They'd reached another coded door. Something in the way he paused made her look up.

'You can identify a piece of modern art, but you don't know who you are.' She'd already got to it. 'You know how to read, how to write. You just signed the visitor's book. You didn't have to think about it.' She swung open the door. 'You can probably drive a car and work a computer – maybe you play a sport, or a musical instrument. None of this is affected by the fact that you can't remember.' She watched the frustration roll over his face. 'Don't push it.'

Her hand was on his for only a second.

She unlocked the final door and ushered him into her office, dropping her bag and coat on to a chair. She needed some time to collect herself.

She headed for the safety of her desk, pointing to the two easy chairs that stood closest to the door and gesturing to Jay to sit, wondering if he would. She wasn't surprised when he ambled to the window to stare out. *A problem with authority, natural restlessness, used to giving, not taking orders?*

She exhaled heavily and sank into the chair behind her desk. The indicator light on the phone was blinking. She had voicemail. Routine stuff. She listened to her messages, with half her mind making notes automatically, her eyes on Jay's back. Last night all she could think of was how to hold on to him, to harvest everything she could from him. But now—

She closed her eyes, briefly. She might have

known it would be a lot more complicated than that. Even without the memory loss, this would have been a bigger, slower thing. Last night she'd been on a high of possibilities. Reckless. Now there was reality and issues piling up all around. She was probably already over her armpits in stuff that would keep the lawyers in fits for days. Kidnapping, forgery, using an alias, impersonating a member of the medical profession – but hey, the last three were only aiding and abetting. *Memo to self – stay well away from the legal department.* Thank God the Institute's director was still in Washington.

She needed to rearrange her schedule to work with Jay. She reached for her diary, then let her hand drop. Busy work was all very well. The elephant in the corner, visible only to her, wasn't going away. She could only avoid it for so long.

Face it now, or face it later.

This man has the potential to get under your skin.

She let out a shallow sigh. It wasn't the physical awareness, buzzing just under the surface. She could deal with that. Simplest thing in the world. Just ignore it.

But not if your mouth is going to run away with your mind whenever he asks you a personal question.

In the car just now, she'd started to say that she didn't have lovers – a subtle warning that she wouldn't be taking *him* as a lover – and realised, too late, how it sounded. A denial of Neil and all that they'd shared. And then she'd *blushed*, for heaven's sake! She could feel the heat again now, rising up from the collar of her dress. Confusion? Irritation? *Guilt?*

The word whispered, like an echo of pain.

She brought her hands down firmly on the arms of her chair, shaking her head to cool the flush. She couldn't and wouldn't go back there.

Briskly she pulled open the drawer of her desk, selected a new folder and wrote Jay's name on the cover. She stood, tucking it into the crook of her arm. Jay swung round from the window as she approached him. She pasted on her professional smile.

'If you're ready, I'd like to start with some simple tests.'

'Do you think this is going to get us anywhere, like this side of the next millennium?' Jay demanded as he shifted position on the sofa, scowling. 'When you said tests, I thought you were going to *do* something.' His eyes tried to nail her, accusing. 'This is just stringing words together.'

'True,' Madison agreed serenely, making a note. 'I said it was simple, but it *is* important. Look.' She fanned out the sheets she'd been using, spreading them over the table. Jay bent forward, interested, despite his protests. 'These are behavioural memory tests.' She indicated the lists. 'Each one you've completed is perfect. Even half an hour of my bargain-basement psychology skills is showing that there's nothing wrong with your semantic understanding. There's no evidence of confusion, or fugue.'

'Which means – in English?'

'Your memory is fine, except for the fact that you can't remember anything.'

His bark of reluctant laughter made her grin in response. 'I guess I walked into that one.'

Madison tried not to look smug.

Jay shifted long legs in one direction and then the other, clearly uncomfortable on a sofa which was too small for his frame. 'If you're going to psychoanalyse me, shouldn't you have a couch or something?'

Madison got to her feet. 'If you want a couch, then you have to come to my lab.'

CHAPTER 5

Madison leaned against the workbench, watching Jay. He was prowling around the sterile white room, like a wary predator inspecting new surroundings. She knew the cliché from a hundred novels. She'd never seen it in action before. As she watched, he examined the flasks and beakers set out on the side, studied her wall charts and considered the sink and the air conditioning unit. Knowing she was observing didn't seem to bother him. Finally he tested the couch, which stood under the shaded window, before sitting down on it.

'This where you want me?'

'Wherever you're comfortable.' She took a lab coat from the hook behind the door and put it on. Protective coloration, or professional barrier?

Jay eased himself carefully on to the couch, still looking around.

'Now that is *very* you,' he said softly.

'You think so?' She followed his gaze to the single personal item in the room – a framed print of a harbour scene, bright with colour. Pastel-painted houses clustered around a tiny marina. She could look at it now, without flinching. She'd been wondering when he'd get to it. 'It's Portofino. In Italy. D'you recognise it?' she added casually.

'Can't say that I do.' He turned his head from the picture. 'Think that will work? Sneaking up on me with stuff I might remember?'

'Probably not, but always worth trying.' She'd washed her hands and was preparing a syringe. 'If you don't like needles, look away now.'

'Ouch.' He was a fraction too slow in moving his arm out of her reach. 'What's in that?'

'Truth serum,' she responded, unblinking. She grinned as his eyes widened. 'In a way it is.' She pulled over a stool, to sit beside him. 'It makes a subject – oh – less anxious about the results of the experiment.'

'Loss of inhibitions?' This time his eyes narrowed. 'Am I going to wake up in an hour or so, to find you have film of me flapping my arms and crowing like a rooster?'

'Now why didn't I think of that?' She picked up his wrist, to check the pulse. Easiest thing in the world. Only the slightest flicker over skin on skin. 'I do video some sessions, but not today. Now, relax, stop talking and let me work.'

'Yes, Doc. Eyes open or eyes shut?'

She gave him her best professional glare. 'That is entirely up to you.'

She slid gently into his mind and hovered, assessing the situation. It felt surprisingly warm. As if he was welcoming her. But there was pain and tension under the surface that the drug hadn't dispelled. She refined the probe and moved in.

Madison flipped through her notes, sucking her pencil, then doodled a small diagram in the margin, a map of what she'd encountered in Jay's head. She studied it, clarifying her thoughts. The wall, barrier, whatever you wanted to call it, was clearly delineated. A regular shape, with a surface that she could only describe to herself as smooth. She'd explored the whole of the perimeter, ending back where she'd begun, only marginally wiser. She tapped the pencil against her teeth. Natural aberrations, like those caused by injury, were softer, uneven and sprawling. She caught herself up. She was doing it again. Defining this thing as unnatural. But if it wasn't natural—

She lifted her eyes as the door opened. Jonathan leaned in around it.

'This is where you're hiding.' He slid into the room. 'What have you done with—?'

'Shh.' Madison put her finger to her lips and inclined her head towards the couch. The drug and her gentle suggestion, as she slid out of his mind, had sent Jay into a light doze, while she made up her files.

'Is that him?' Jonathan came to stand beside her. He rolled his eyes. 'I take back everything I said last night about throwing him out. Darling, he's *gorgeous*. No wonder you wanted to keep him.'

'He did scrub up rather well, didn't he?' She

regarded Jay, then Jonathan, thoughtfully. For an incorrigible gossip, Jonathan could be remarkably good at keeping secrets, but she wasn't going to confide in him today. Right now she wasn't planning to share the finer points of this – or maybe that should be the murkier points of this – with *anyone*. Not until she had a better idea of what she was dealing with. She shuffled papers, trying to recall exactly how much had spilled out in last night's over-excited phone call, wincing inwardly as she remembered an uncharacteristic babble about power and connection. She really had been out of herself. Nothing to do now but keep it cool and casual.

'I've done some preliminary work.' She indicated the file. 'He seems a particularly receptive subject. Possibly the best I've ever found.' She was quite safe going that far. 'He's willing to stay around for a couple of weeks. So—' She smiled and shrugged. 'Who knows?'

Jonathan shot her a puzzled look. 'One for the journals, then?'

'Maybe.'

'Well, if he doesn't work out for you, you can certainly send him over to us. I've always been a sucker for a pretty pair of ears.' Jonathan's specialty was sound and hearing.

'You're a sucker for a pretty anything.'

Jonathan nodded, grinning. 'This is true.' He reached out to hug her. 'Hope it works out, sweet pea.' He threw another glance over at Jay. 'And if you want me and Ash, you know where we live.'

'I do. And I appreciate the way you both take care of me.' She reached up to kiss his cheek, turning him gently towards the door. 'Go now. I need to finish up here, before I wake sleeping beauty.'

Jonathan stopped in the doorway 'And you know how to do *that,* don't you, darling?'

'Go!' Madison made a rude gesture. Jonathan laughed and went.

Madison stacked a clip of papers and files and dropped them in the out tray before looking back at her notes and the diagram. The session hadn't gone badly, except for a niggling worry that had thrown her off balance. This time she hadn't been able to talk to Jay when she was inside his mind. There'd been just a blankness when she'd tried to form the words and get him to respond. He could still feel her inside his head, but all she'd got was the usual miasma of emotion and sensation. He was tired – no, make that exhausted – but neither that, nor the drug she'd administered, should have dampened his responses to that extent.

She sat with her chin buried in her hand. She had to figure out how to get that communication back. Or did she? Was that just something *she* wanted? Would it affect the wall, or was it just a blind alley? Maybe it *was* simply fatigue, dulling his reactions? She shelved the problem and moved over to the couch. Jay's hair was flopping over his face. The lines and shadows of tension had smoothed out a little in sleep, but not enough. She made a mental note to find out more about headaches and nightmares, as she studied his mouth. From this angle, no, from any angle, without question, it looked pretty damn good. Jonathan had put an idea in her head and now it was trying hard to take root. It was only healthy and natural for a girl to wonder how a mouth like that might taste. *Doesn't mean you have to do anything about it.*

With a sigh, Madison settled for patting Jay's arm. He came awake with a start that had her pressing her hand to his chest, to stop him rolling and hurting himself. Firm, hard muscles, under her fingers. She dropped her hand, fast.

'Hell.' He rubbed his eyes. 'Can't seem to stay awake.' Madison saw realisation coming into his eyes. 'That shot you gave me—'

'The after effects are mildly sedative, that's all.' She held up her arms to show there was nothing up her sleeves. 'When was the last time you had a full night's sleep? Before last night?'

He got the point. 'About . . . three months?'

'Exactly.' Madison stood aside as he swung his feet to the floor.

'I take it you didn't miraculously stumble over my whole life story, while you were in there?' His voice was carefully neutral. Its very flatness constricted Madison's chest, but there was no point in lying.

'I have a clearer picture now of the barrier.'

'That good, huh?'

'It's a start.' She looked at her watch. 'Let's go home. What we need now is a plan, and food. Pizza. I always plan better over pizza.'

Madison walked away from the ATM with a bundle of notes in her hand. Jay was propped against the car; one arm was wrapped around the other, supporting his injured shoulder. She held out the bundle.

'Your fee. One hundred pounds, as agreed.'

'Should I give you a receipt?' His mouth now was a hard flat line. *It isn't meant to look like that.* He hadn't moved.

'Please, Jay, take the money. You need it.' She curled her fingers over the notes, to protect them from the stiff breeze. 'You were willing enough last night.'

'Last night was last night.' He still didn't move. Madison looked down at the money and back at him. She didn't need to ask what he meant. Twenty hours ago he'd been a derelict, on the make. Now there was a new man evolving in front of her. Food, warmth, shelter. The line between respect and the street was frighteningly narrow. 'This isn't just money, Jay. It's independence, and a small measure of dignity. You think I don't realise how hard this is for you? Accept it, please.' He shifted his stance. She held her breath. After a couple of beats he held out his hand. She put the cash into it. 'Thank you.'

'I'm the one who should be saying that.' His voice cracked a little.

Wordlessly Madison shook her head. 'If you want to shop, I'll go and pick up some milk and then order the pizza. Meet you back here in half an hour?' Jay nodded as she turned away. 'Oh.' She turned back. 'What shall I order for you?'

'Pepperoni, jalapeño, extra cheese.' Jay swore softly. 'Great – I can remember a pizza topping, but I can't remember who I am.'

Scott was coming towards them across the lobby, with a package in his hand.

'Good evening, Miss Albi. This just came for you. Can I get a signature?'

Jay shuffled the brand new backpack up his arm, to take the pizza cartons from her while she signed.

'Scott, this is Mr Jackson.' Madison waved her hand in introduction. Scott turned to face Jay. 'He'll be working with me for a while at the lab, so I'm letting him use the studio. Could you mention it to Sandra?' she added casually, watching the concierge under her lashes.

'Certainly, miss,' Scott replied as he relinquished the parcel. 'Hope you have a pleasant stay, sir. Anything you need, just let me know.'

Scott smiled, gave a small salute and went back to his desk. Silently Madison and Jay crossed the foyer. The lift doors closed behind them.

'No recognition at all. He had no idea we'd already met.' Jay propped the cartons against the lift rail for balance as the elevator jerked. 'Looks like clothes do maketh man,' he misquoted, mouth turned down.

'The fashion industry certainly counts on it,' Madison agreed absently as she checked the package – a covert DVD of bloopers and out-takes from the official proceedings of the convention she'd attended in Washington, DC. She grinned, shaking her head. One day someone was going to get into deep trouble for circulating these. She tucked it into her bag, pulling out her door keys. Scott's reaction hadn't surprised her. She'd have been more surprised if he *had* recognised Jay as last night's tramp. With the potentially tell-tale bruises hidden by the high-collared sweater and freshly washed fall of dark hair, which also covered the cut over his brow, there was little to offer a clue. *We see what we want to see. Expect to see. This is Mr X. He looks right, speaks right, smells right, even. And so we accept him.*

She cast a sideways glance at Jay as the lift stopped. It wasn't just the clothes that had made the change. It was everything about the man.

Just who the hell are you, Jay?

CHAPTER 6

'Jalapeño.' Madison wrinkled her nose as she pushed the carton across the coffee table to Jay and unwrapped her own anchovy and black olive. 'You must have a throat lined with asbestos.'

'I still don't get it.' Jay was helping himself generously from the tub of coleslaw. 'Perfect recall – for a bloody pizza topping.'

'Don't stress while you eat, you'll get indigestion.'

That got her a spectacular scowl. She wanted to give it a round of applause, but her hands and her mouth were fully occupied with crisp dough and melted cheese. She sighed contentedly, savouring the taste. Jay's voice recalled her attention. 'We have the pizza here, so when do we get to the plan?'

'Patience.' Madison caught an olive before it fell on to the table. 'Eat first, talk after.'

Jay raised his eyebrows but didn't comment when she put a mug of coffee down in front of him and settled into her seat with a pen and a clipboard.

'This is what I have so far.' She passed over her

notes and the diagram. Jay studied it intently. She waited until he looked up.

'This is unique, in your experience?'

Madison nodded, watching closely, but keeping her body language strictly in neutral.

'And your experience is like . . . pretty wide?'

His eyes were clouded. If she went into him now, she knew she'd find fear, but he was doing a damn good job of not letting it show. Except for that tell-tale darkening of the eyes. His courage sent cat's paws over her skin.

'Pretty wide,' she agreed. 'What I've done so far is nothing more than a fishing expedition. The only way is to approach this systematically. We try one programme, in escalating steps. If that doesn't work, we try another.'

'Drugs? Like the one you used today?'

'Mmmm. There are several possibilities. I already know what I want to use. You don't have a problem with that?'

He shook his head. 'Whatever it takes.'

She shifted in her seat, gathered her knees up under her chin, and took a breath. Now for the tricky part.

'I'll work on getting your memory back,' she said levelly. 'But there are more conventional ways of finding out who you are. I think we have to try those, too.'

'You mean go to the police? I . . .' He stopped. 'I did that, after the hospital. Got as far as the front steps. I . . . I couldn't go in . . .' He put up a hand, rubbing his chest. 'I was afraid that they'd think I was raving.' He stopped again, hugging the coffee mug, chest rising and falling sharply. Madison leaned forward, with a quick flare of concern, as something dark passed over his face. Then it was gone. He gave a crooked shrug. 'Missing adults aren't really a priority for them, anyway.'

'No – although it might be worth a shot. You could be on a list somewhere.' She paused. Tried to sound casual. 'Actually, I was thinking more of a private investigator.'

She waited for the eruption. It was there, in a heartbeat. Jay's mug banged down, making the table shake.

'Which you will pay for?' he demanded.

'Yes.' She waved her hand at the room in which they were sitting, taking in the expensive furnishings, the soft sheen of an antique bureau, the muted glitter from a display cabinet of old Venetian glass, the state-of-the-art sound system. 'Look around you, Jay. I have money. I inherited it.' Her breath caught. 'I make it. I can afford to fund you on this. Don't keep fighting me over the same ground. It's getting boring.'

She flounced back, sweeping up her coffee, taking a gulp of too-hot liquid and swallowing it, feeling the burn all the way down. When her watering eyes cleared, Jay was staring at her.

'Okay.' The sheepish expression on his face evaporated her annoyance.

Even so, she gave him a long look. He squirmed a little, then grinned. Her stomach fluttered. Why did a man with that half hang-dog, half cocky smile always cut right through a woman's defences? *This woman's, anyhow.* She hauled herself back to the job in hand.

'Right, we have a private investigator.' She ticked her list. 'You know, if someone from your family is looking for you, we might get results very quickly.'

Jay's silence made her look up. His face was blank. 'You must have thought about the people who could be searching for you? Friends, family? You could have a wife – children,' she suggested gently.

The total confusion in Jay's face took her aback.

'I've never . . . I've never thought of it.' He looked stunned. 'All this time . . . I don't feel married.' He held out his hands. Madison followed his gaze. Tanned skin, broad palms, capable fingers, with calluses showing across the tips, as he turned them over and back.

'No ring. And no mark of one.'

'Not every man wears a ring. Or you could have hocked it.'

'No.' She saw him shiver. 'If I was married, I would wear a ring. I know it. The way I knew about the pizza. No ring, no wife. Unless—' His smile was lopsided. 'Unless it's her I'm running from.'

'How does that feel?' Madison leaned forward, intent. 'The idea that you're running from something?'

'I don't know. I could be. I have dreams some-times, when it feels like I'm trying to get away from something.' He pinched his fingers at the bridge of his nose. 'Nothing is ever clear.'

'You said you have headaches?'

He nodded. 'Does that tell you anything?'

'That your brain is trying hard to cope, perhaps to fight whatever has invaded it. Does the idea of a wife and children give you any kind of feeling, an emotion that you can identify?'

'Blind panic?' he suggested wryly. Madison pursed her mouth. He closed his eyes, opened them. 'Nothing. We're clutching at straws here, aren't we?'

Madison shrugged. 'I'd like you to think about it. Try to analyse whatever sensation it brings up. There's something else, too.' She tapped her fingers on the clipboard. 'This one is a bit more off the wall—' She stopped.

Jay was looking at her encouragingly. 'All contri-butions gratefully received,' he said.

Madison grimaced. 'It may not be any use at all, but I work sometimes with a voice analyst. It's part of a memory project that compares what people remember about the places they've lived, with the influences on their speech patterns and accents. I'd like to give her a recording of your voice, to see what she comes up with.'

'Born in Timbuktu, educated in Greenland, that sort of stuff?'

Madison smiled. 'Not as extreme as that, I hope.'

'I'll do it. Whatever you need, just bring it on.' He frowned, examining an idea. 'A private investigator – it would be like the reverse of what they must usually be asked to do. Won't they think it's a bit weird?' He waved his hand. 'Scrub that. I don't care if they do think it's weird.' Excitement chased quickly across his face. 'Do you really think there's a chance?'

'There has to be.' Seized by his excitement she stretched forward, to put her hands over his. 'You didn't just drop into that alley, Jay. Someone has to know about you.' She looked up into his face as his fingers twisted, gripping hers.

A hot splinter of awareness ran up her arms.

Jay's mouth was so close. She could smell lemon soap and warm skin. There was shock and heat in his eyes. Her throat went tight. She pulled her hands away and sat back, heart pumping. *Do something, say something, defuse this.*

'Ah—'

'I . . .' Their voices clashed. Jay stopped. 'Go ahead.'

'Uh – I was just going to ask if you wanted another coffee.' *That is so feeble.*

'I'll get it.' He uncoiled from the sofa.

Madison's throat went tight again as her eyes involuntarily travelled up that long, lean frame. This man was seriously built, seriously hot, and her banked-down hormones were rearing up and sniffing the breeze. *Oh hell.*

'I can do it—' She needed air. 'Your shoulder—'

93

'I'll manage.'

Unable to stop herself, she watched his rear as he headed to the kitchen. Muscles flexing under clinging denim. There was saliva pooling in her mouth now. When the door closed behind him she was on her feet and scrambling for the French windows, throwing them open and stepping out on to the balcony. Trembling, she inhaled starlit, frosty air, until her racing heart began to slow.

In the kitchen, Jay primed the coffee machine with hands that weren't quite steady. The ache in his shoulder as he swung round, too fast, to pick up the coffee, had him grinding his teeth. Grimly he focused on that, and not the heaviness low in his groin.

He leaned wearily against the counter, good hand thrust into the pocket of his jeans, waiting for the machine to start to bubble. Ten seconds more and he would have been kissing Dr Albi. At least she'd had the good sense to pull away. She'd been excited, carried away by enthusiasm and he'd been—

A goddamn idiot.

He cringed as the alarm in her eyes replayed in his head. Christ – what was he doing? That woman was the only thing standing between him and the gutter, and all he could think to do was hit on her?

It's not just you. She felt it, too.

He shook away the thought. This was down to

him to fix, not her. Just because he hadn't had a woman in – he didn't know how long – didn't mean he had to come on to the first one to show him a little kindness. More than a little.

An ache that had nothing to do with desire spasmed in his gut. She was putting herself way out there. For him. Something that had crawled, stinking, out of an alley and into her life.

This isn't just one way. She wants to play with your mind. She wants you. Yeah, in her lab, not in her bed.

The machine was letting off fragrant steam. Jay rammed his hand against the button and watched the dark brew gushing into the mugs. What the hell did he have to offer a woman like Madison Albi, except the chance to see inside his mind? She could have that and welcome. Everything else— He gritted his teeth. Everything else had to be battened down tight. Whatever the hell it took.

When he walked back with the mugs, the room felt strangely cold. He must be imagining the drop in temperature, because of the chill emanating from Madison. She was sitting very straight on the sofa, with a pile of books in front of her, leafing through the top one. The briefest glance, as he put down the coffee, told him that they were all thick tomes on psychiatry and memory. He eased himself into the chair opposite her, looking at the formidable tower of learning. If he'd known anything about body language he'd have said that Dr Albi had constructed a very efficient barrier between them – a professional barrier. But what

95

did he know? *What* do *you know? Is there something there* . . . He struggled for a second, trying to grasp a fugitive thought, but it was already gone. Chasing it gave him a crushing stab of pain behind the eyes. He closed them, waiting for the pain to fade. Easier to let it go. *Probably nothing, anyway. Your head's full of that.*

He sipped coffee he didn't want, wondering if exhaustion would overcome caffeine or whether he'd be awake later, staring at the ceiling. The silence was getting strained. He could almost feel Madison's brain skittering fruitlessly, trying to find a neutral topic; trying to get back into the casual ease of their discussion, before he'd blown it. *Help her out here.*

'The brief for the private investigator—' She jumped slightly at the sound of his voice, and something shrivelled inside him. He ploughed on. 'If someone did create this barrier in my head and I am on the run – or been discarded – asking questions could stir things up.'

Her chin came up. Was he imagining relief in her eyes?

'If it does, we need to be prepared.' She was thinking. He'd already noticed how her head tilted sideways when she was figuring something out. 'It might be a good thing.'

Or it might be bloody dangerous.

Did he feel any danger? He stared at the back of his hands, concentrating inwards. Delving as deep as he could. And coming up with nothing

96

but an unfocused sense of unease that might just be a reflection of his own panic.

What do you know? The pain shimmered behind his eyes again. He jerked back to merciful awareness of his surroundings, before he could spiral down into the dark. Madison was running through the technicalities of a series of excursions into his mind. He tried to look as if he knew what she was talking about and found, after a few minutes, that he did – or at least that he could follow a lot of what she was saying. She was good at explaining and the warmth of her voice, as she became more involved in her subject, touched something inside him. Had he ever been able to talk like this about his work?

There was only a swirling, fearful void when he tried to will himself to remember.

'Do you have any questions?' Madison was staring at him with a dent between her brows.

'Mmm.' Had he looked as if he was falling asleep? 'The stuff you're going to do at the lab? Who's going to know? Your boss, your colleagues?'

The frown had deepened. He could see her wondering why he'd asked that particular question.

'I'll need to register the programme, keep proper records,' she said carefully.

'But?'

'But at this stage I'm not going to make a big production about what we're trying to do,' she admitted. 'This is not a regular experiment. We're

97

off the map here. My official area of research is memory and communication, not amnesia.' She shifted slightly in her seat, looking narrowly at him. 'That bothers you, doesn't it? The idea of a lot of people knowing about you?'

'Yes. And before you ask, I don't know why. Another pepperoni moment.' He did though, kind of. *That nagging sense of threat again, that isn't based on anything. It's just – there.*

'I don't find it strange.' She shrugged.

'We both like secrets.' He deliberately looked off, but kept her in view from the corner of his eye. Saw the small, betraying movement of her hands, up to the gold chain at her neck. One of her tells – a dead give-away for agitation. Some sort of devil made him want to dig.

'The lab, where you work. Why does it exist?'

'Research?' she suggested dryly. 'Like it says on the tin?' She'd relaxed a little. *Not the question she was expecting?*

'Who for? Who puts up the money?'

She screwed up her mouth. 'Some funds are from the government. We get money from charities and the lottery. A number of projects have private sponsors. The current director is a brilliant fund-raiser. The lab is a very well-respected body, with a worldwide reputation – even if it is usually misinterpreted by the general public.'

'Is that really a surprise?'

'Of course not! It's far more fun to imagine a lot of scary stuff. We're just as guilty ourselves of making jokes about spooks. But the reality is often routine, even boring. We're just a research facility, trying to find ways to help people.'

When he met her stare, she stared right back.

'No connection to the military then?'

'No! Don't start on the conspiracy theories. I couldn't work for somewhere like that. And I'm not against defence – I just wouldn't want to be part of it. My talent, gift – whatever you want to call it – wouldn't lend itself to any kind of weapons use – it's too diffuse, for which I am very grateful.' From her expression, she still detected scepticism in his face. *Which may be true.* 'If you think the lab is some sort of front for weapons development, then you're wrong.'

'Sure about that, are you?'

The stiffening in her shoulders told him he'd annoyed her, but the smile she gave him was a work of art – cool poise, seasoned with just the right trace of scorn. Insider to outsider.

'I'm sure. But then, I would say that, wouldn't I?'

'Of course you would.' He held up a hand in surrender. Something inexplicable relaxed inside him when the hard-edged smile softened into a genuine grin.

'You haven't fallen amongst thieves. There's nothing sinister in what we do,' she promised. 'I admit I don't want to go public on what *we're* doing, not yet.' There was a flicker behind her eyes he couldn't read. 'When the time is right, yes – but not until then.'

'Sounds good to me,' he agreed, looking away, testing out what she'd said about the lab. Did he believe it? On the whole he thought he did – but he still had questions. *Only they aren't all about the lab.*

'How do you come to be working there?' he asked abruptly. Something shifted in his chest. *Wrong question. It should be – why are* you *working there?*

Madison looked surprised, but answered quite easily. 'I was headhunted. Friend of a friend. You know the kind of thing. Or perhaps you don't?'

'I believe I've heard of the concept.'

'But you wouldn't know if you've ever seen it in action.'

'Got it in one.' The warmth was creeping back, but her eyes were wary. Cautiously he rested his forearm against the arm of his chair, mirroring Madison's pose. 'What exactly is the setup?'

'The type of work we do, do you mean?'

She lifted her head when he nodded and the long, exposed line of her throat scattered his thoughts every which way. Scrambling, he stifled the frisson of awareness. Hard. There was too much he needed to know. He pulled his mind back to what she was saying. It came reluctantly.

'It's based on the five senses,' she said. 'My area is sight – in my case *second* sight, which translates for me into mind reading, telepathy and studies relating to memory. Other sections are dealing with actual physical sight, and things like

100

precognition. There are departments working on hearing, taste, touch and smell. We have people who are "noses", like those who work in the perfume industry, others with a particularly acute sense of taste.' On familiar ground, she'd relaxed. This was a well-rehearsed patter. 'We research cases of heightened awareness and also levels of ability in the general population – how latent talents might be stimulated and applied, in a positive way.'

'With success?'

'Some. A number of my peers are working on some interesting research papers.'

'And I'm going to be yours?' Suddenly the hesitation about sharing with her colleagues fell into place.

'Well . . .' She caught his eye. 'All right. I admit it may just have crossed my mind, for a second.' She held up her hand, laughing, then her face changed. 'Would you at least consider it?'

'I think we need to know a little more about what we're getting into first.'

His stomach contracted as the eagerness went out of her eyes. She'd instantly mistaken his caution for reluctance. *Oh blast.*

'Yes, of course.' Head down, her voice was muffled. 'I was getting ahead of myself.' She looked at her watch. 'Well, it's getting late—'

'And I should go.' He knew he'd blown it. Again. The rapport between them was at an end. Since he couldn't explain a sense of danger that he didn't understand himself, there was nothing else to do but leave. He nodded towards the pile of books. 'May I take a couple of those?'

Surprise flashed in her eyes, quickly stifled. 'Yes, of course. If you need anything else—'

'I'll let you know,' he confirmed, as he hauled himself to his feet. 'Thanks for everything.'

She shook her head, without speaking.

He turned towards the door 'Don't forget to lock up, after I've gone.'

Madison pottered about the room, returning volumes to the shelves, and retrieving the incriminating blooper DVD from her bag, to store it inconspicuously amongst her reference material, while battling a sense of disquiet. She'd made a fool of herself. Twice. Once when she'd almost kissed Jay, or let him kiss her – she wasn't sure which – and then again, over the loan of the books. She'd hidden her surprise fast, but not fast enough. Her cheeks burned. That had been – stupid – in the extreme. And hurtful. She *knew* Jay wasn't the down-and-out she'd first taken him for. But even if he had been? Why shouldn't he want to read up on something that might help him understand the position he was in? In his place, she'd want to do the same.

Involuntarily she shivered as she thought of that place. Totally alone. She knew a bit about that – but she still had her friends, her home and her work. What did Jay have? Just her – a stranger, who wanted to turn him into a guinea pig for a research paper.

The heat in her face went up another notch. Jay was an exciting opportunity, one that she'd found for herself, after years of searching. She knew, with a bedrock confidence that had nothing to do with pride, that she was the best person to help him, maybe the only person, given her experience with memory investigations. Was it so bad to want the credit for it, if and when it happened? She didn't want to risk sharing him with anyone. *But is that professional jealousy or something much more basic?*

Shying away from that disturbing thought, she moved restlessly to the window. The lights were coming on in the street below. She stared at the dark amber halo around each streetlight. The edgy feeling in the pit of her stomach wasn't all to do with embarrassment. She leaned her forehead against the cool of the glass. Jay had asked questions. The rational part of her mind had no problem with that – curiosity was natural – but there was another part that wasn't so comfortable.

Now the euphoria was evaporating – she shrugged off the hormonal haze that seemed to want to take its place – her own ability to question was kicking in. Jay didn't want people to know about him. Was that an understandable sense of uncertainty, given the vulnerability of his situation? Or was it something else entirely?

Had it been too easy, the way Jay had accepted that she could read minds? The way he already seemed to have slid into her world? Was she letting her eagerness to work with the best subject she'd ever encountered override all her protective mechanisms? For a second she felt nauseous. She wanted to work with Jay. *Needed* to. She dug her fingers into the palms of her hands. Something had created that barrier in Jay's mind. Whatever or whoever it was, it was unlikely to be good. His easy acceptance of her and the unknown source of his own power – the answers to both *had* to be lurking behind that barrier. Did she really want to go there? To an uncertain, dangerous place? *Of course you do. You just have to be very, very careful.*

She straightened up. Getting a private investigator was a start. She needed some answers, too. She'd choose carefully and pay what was asked. If Jay was a con man, or some kind of spy, if he'd been sent to test her – she was going to know about it. If he was something worse . . .

What?

You just have to be very, very careful.

Jay lay in the dark, as expected, looking at the ceiling, willing his mind to behave. For over an hour he'd been trying to nail that persistent sense of menace, checking out whether it was real. The only result was the return of the nagging pain behind the eyes. He was stuck here, in the middle of the craziest of the crazy. Mind reading, for fuck's sake! Mind reading! A long shiver ran over his skin. His whole life, his whole *being* was so screwed up, *that* felt like normal. And when he tried to sort out stuff, to make some sense of it – zap – knives behind the eyes.

With a curse he levered himself off the bed, crossing to the sink for water and one of the painkillers he'd bought at the chemist. He looked down at the small white pill. He might have bought them, but it was Madison's money. Everything he had he owed to the angel.

The thought stung.

The only repayment he had right now was blood, sweat and tears, and she could have those, any way she wanted. Have him – he shunted quickly past *that* image. Circumstances had thrown them into a weird intimacy. The last thing he wanted to do was frighten her. There was too much riding on it. She could use him for any number of research studies, if she could get his memory back – and if he could be sure that what they were doing was safe. Until he could, the fewer people who knew about him the better.

He wandered back to the bed, feeling his eyelids getting heavy as the meds kicked in.

He arranged himself on the mattress, his shoulder supported by a pillow, with the duvet drawn back over his good arm. The studio was well appointed and comfortable. He had everything he could possibly need, but the neutral décor of his surroundings had all the impersonality of a hotel room. Blank, just like he was. He tried, fruitlessly, to call up some familiar picture. Did he have a home, somewhere?

Madison's apartment was full of surprising pieces of her personality, books and CDs, candles, paintings on the walls from places she'd visited; not great art, but pictures that meant something to her. Like the Italian one at the lab. There'd been something there. Something connected to the missing lover? That was one private area he hadn't trampled into. Madison had let him into her personal space, but she still had things that were hidden.

Madison Albi was one hell of a woman. She had his life, literally, in her hands. But he had confidence in her. The thought came with a tiny shock. *Someone to trust.* Could he? His angel had secrets. And he was stuck here in the dark, inside and out, depending on her.

You are so screwed.

CHAPTER 7

Madison sat in her office, regarding the computer screen thoughtfully. She fiddled briefly with the chain at her throat, realised what she was doing and dropped her hand. She added a few lines to her proposal for her work programme with Jay, and pressed send, frowning as the machine stuttered before confirming that the e-mail had been dispatched to the Administration Office. With any luck the administrator wouldn't get round to looking at it for a few days. With more luck, he wouldn't look at it at all. He'd just file it. Madison crossed her fingers. She really didn't want to share information on Jay. *Don't want anyone telling me to put him back where I found him!*

She stood up, smiling. The new morning had calmed yesterday's doubts. She could do this. Whatever there was to find, she'd find it. If Jay was conning her, a good investigator would uncover it – and she was going to get a good one.

She looked at the clock. Time to go and stick more needles into a defenceless six-footer with a beautiful butt and a wicked smile. She'd noticed the smile. *And the butt.*

Nothing in the manual that said a woman couldn't enjoy her work.

Vic was leaning back dangerously in his chair, whistling and scratching his crotch when Alec opened the door. Alec's grunt of disgust was quickly stifled, but Vic had hearing like a cat. He straightened the chair, feet to the floor, and held up a finger.

'You too, buddy,' Alec retaliated.

Vic snickered. 'You might want to get down from that friggin' high horse if you want to see what I got for you.'

'Give.' Alec held out a peremptory hand.

Vic moved a bundle of printouts into the safety of his lap. 'Pretty please.'

Alec sized up the situation. It wasn't worth the hassle of an undignified scrap over a pile of paper. 'Pretty. Fucking. Please.'

Vic tutted and passed over the papers, spreading them with his fingers to illustrate. 'E-mail to the voice analyst woman she uses. Asking her to work on a recording of a new subject she'll be sending over.'

'Subject A?' Alec looked up.

'Who else? Private deal, not through the lab.'

'Clever girl. Kong said she was inventive.' Alec shuffled further down the bundle and laughed.

'What?'

'The research programme she just filed from the lab for Jay Jackson.' Abruptly his laughter died as he stared at the sheet. 'For Christ's sake – Jay? How the fuck did he remember that?'

Vic wasn't concerned. 'You said there might be a small amount of leakage, even with the deterrents you built in.'

'Yeah, but not something that basic.' Alec could hear the alarm in his voice and cursed mentally.

Surprisingly, Vic didn't pounce. 'Don't sweat it. The guy is bound to be thinking – trying to figure out what the hell happened to him. Your name – it's like part of you, isn't it? Embedded? It's not as if he's remembered anything else that would be of use – and you said he was good.'

'He thinks he is.' Vic's unexpected support, and the rest of the contents of the paper bundle, leached away the panic. Alec grinned

Vic caught it. 'Again – what's funny?'

'This list of drugs she's planning to pump into him. She uses half of these, he's going to feel like shit.'

'And this amuses you?' Vic rolled his eyes. 'Christ! And you used to be a buddy to this guy! Remind me to watch my back.'

'Buddy?' Alec's face hardened. 'Yeah. Buddy. I'm the closest thing Jayston Creed ever had to a best friend.'

CHAPTER 8

Madison locked her car, turning quickly as a shiver went down her back. A young woman who was unloading flat-pack furniture from the car in front, while a small, blond boy looked on, shot her a startled glance. Madison pulled herself together.

She'd had the creepy feeling that someone was watching her for a couple of days now. And it was getting stronger. She didn't know why she was feeling it. There was no one here, except the woman and the child. There never was any one. With a sigh she shouldered her bag and went to lend a hand with the boxes.

She knew where she'd find Jay. Where she always found him at this time of the afternoon. In the small, exclusive gym provided in the basement for the use of the residents. Since he'd discovered that the gym manager was a trained physio, waiting for the chance to use his skills, he'd haunted the place – when he wasn't in the lab. Madison's mouth twisted. She was poking around in his mind, filling his body with unhealthy chemicals. When she wasn't doing that he was down here, slogging to get himself in shape. Or walking. He did a lot of walking.

She reached the door and stopped. Jay was sweating in the embrace of some machine, all pulleys and leavers and shiny chrome, the purpose of which she didn't even *begin* to understand. The throb in her breasts, and further south, had her mouth twisting even further, with self-disgust. How big a cliché was that, getting a hum from watching a guy working out? It was so cheap. *Still gets you hot though, doesn't it?*

Leaving her lust at the door – some hope – she strode over to the machine, dredging up scientist, not hormone-fuelled female, to appraise what she was seeing. Jay was still favouring the injured shoulder, but in the weeks that had passed since their encounter in the alley it was visibly healing and strengthening. You could tell, just by watching the way he moved. Another thought that she didn't need to explore, with its hot trails of awareness. *Do not go there.*

Seeing her, Jay let the machine come to rest. She handed him a towel and a bottle of water, watching approvingly as he drank. The column of his throat, head back, as the liquid went down. *Grrr.* The brief vest top and sweats clung to his body, gleaming and prime in the strong lights of the gym. He rolled out of the monster's clutches. With a gigantic effort Madison hauled her mind back to the envelopes in her bag. It was just the blast of ice water in the face that she needed.

'You have something?' Jay had picked it up from her face – the way she stood – what?

'The private investigator's report, and the voice analyst's.'

'Ah.' He exhaled. 'Do we need pizza for this?'

'It's already ordered.'

Madison tipped the delivery man and closed the door. Jay had the folders spread over the table. He looked up, face bleak.

'Basically, nothing.' He flipped the investigator's report. 'No missing person matching my description. No one saw or heard anything at Paddington. Or anywhere else. And the voice stuff, it's inconclusive – maybe London, maybe the West Coast of America.' He dropped the folder to put the heels of his hands into the sockets of his eyes and emerged blinking 'This stuff is good, thorough. There's just nothing there.'

Madison pushed a pizza carton and a half-full glass of red wine towards him. He picked it up, then paused. 'Should I be having this – the drugs?'

'In the circumstances I reckon it's allowed.'

She knew how she'd felt in the investigator's office when he'd gone through the report with her. She suppressed a small pang of guilt that she hadn't included Jay in the visit. She'd had to know first what the report contained. Alone.

She'd had time to come to terms with her disappointment. For Jay this had to be a thousand times worse. They'd both been hoping – more than either

112

of them had admitted, she realised now. But for her, along with the disappointment, there had been something that had felt like relief. The investigator hadn't turned up anything positive, but he hadn't shown Jay up for a fraud or a liar. Which meant she could still continue to work with him. She didn't want to give him up. Didn't want him to walk out of her life.

This whole thing was stirring up a complex mix of emotions she didn't have time to examine. All this and lust, too? *Hell's bells.*

'I didn't call off the investigator. He'll still keep digging,' she said.

'Is it worth it?' Jay leaned forward. 'And the programme. Are we making any progress at all?'

'Of course we are.' She heard the over-cheerful, hearty note in her voice and tried not to cringe. 'I have a good picture—' she began more cautiously.

'But you can't get in,' he interrupted. She heard the urgent desperation, and the steel under it. 'In fact we're going backwards. That first day, when you went inside my head, you said I spoke to you.'

'You still don't remember that?' Madison had begun to wonder if she'd imagined it, but she'd been so sure.

'I was pretty beat up, everything is a bit blurred. But if we did it once, then we have to be able to do it again.' He bent towards her, urgency in every muscle of his body. 'I want you to step everything up. Stronger, harder, deeper.' Something flickered in his face. She could feel her own face tingling as other connotations of his words painted graphically in her head. 'The answer is in my mind. It's the only place to look. You have to use whatever it takes to dig it out.'

'Got any blood, darling?' Jonathan asked as he put his head round the lab door and gave Madison his best vampire leer.

'Since when were you the errand boy for the blood samples?' She looked up in surprise.

'Since the regular delivery man rang up about ten minutes ago to say he has a flat tyre, somewhere the other side of Amersham.' Jonathan came all the way into the room and hitched himself on to the workbench, swinging his legs.

'Mitch is taking his opportunity while he can.' Mitch was Jonathan's Head of Section. 'He isn't happy with the quality or the turn round time he's been getting back from the regular testers, so he's trying that new place. Which is why I'm here, touting for custom. Cheaper by the dozen.'

'Okay, why not?' Madison glanced at her specimen tray, knowing that all it contained were some phials of blood she'd just taken from Jay. Left too long, they could deteriorate, and she was sticking enough needles into him as it was. 'All yours.'

'I thank you.' Jonathan hopped down to take them. 'Mitch thanks you.'

'Go on. Take your blood and go.' She flipped his arm, before putting the padded envelope in his hand. Her weekly report on Jay was underneath, waiting to be filed. She picked it up. Another long line of negative results that made her stomach plummet. She still hadn't got them back to that first day when Jay had spoken to her. Had she imagined it, because she wanted to?

'Jonno,' she spoke as her friend reached the door, 'hypothetically speaking – have you ever encountered a case of a natural? Someone you can communicate with?'

'Someone *you* can communicate with, you mean? I don't do the mind stuff, remember?' Jonathan shook his head. 'Anyway, I've never heard of it. It simply doesn't exist.'

'But isn't that what we're about? What we're here for?'

'Holy Grail, sweet pea. You're looking for ways to build links into ordinary subjects. You think you're *communicating*, with someone who just walked in off the street, and you're on the way to the nice, cosy room with the soft walls.' He flapped a hand. 'Oh, yeah I know the theory – that we all have latent abilities, just waiting to be tapped or enhanced. And I agree with it, to a point, or I wouldn't be here. But a natural? A subject able to communicate, straight off? Just swimming around out there, in the gene pool? Mad, think about it. You're the slickest thing in the mind department that this place has, and how long did it take you to refine your talent until it was usable?' He nodded when he saw her face. 'You get a connection, any sort, it's going to need work. Right out

115

of the box, it's not what you'd call communication. Not straight away. Even I know that, and I'm not a mind bender.' He slanted her a searching look. 'Is this about your hot hobo?'

Madison grimaced. 'Do you spend hours thinking those up? And it's *hypothetical.*'

'It's the hobo,' Jonathan said, with certainty. 'You're stretching, Mad. The possibility of finding a natural is as likely as Mitch scoring with Nicole Kidman, next Saturday night. It'll never happen.' Concern wiped the amusement from his face. 'However much you want it. There's such a thing as getting too close to your subject, sweet pea.'

'I know.' Madison swept her hair back from her face. 'It's just that—' She trailed off, unable to put what she felt into words.

'We all have dreams. And he is a dish. I'd want to communicate with him too, but it's just a myth. Listen to Dr Jonathan now. Keep working with him to build whatever it is he's got, but keep your objectivity.' He gave her a hug and left.

Madison stared at the door. Objectivity. That was the thing. Except that every time she looked at Jay all her scientific sense had an increasing tendency to leap out of the window. Which left her just with – sense – as in sense of attraction, the man/woman kind. She'd been too long without a man and her hormones were raging. There'd been too many nights lately when she'd lain awake, thinking about Jay, in bed, on the other side of the wall. With a groan she went back to her results

116

charts. Jay's mind was her concern. Not his body. She was nest building. Recreating Neil in a man who just happened to be handy. The thought brought her up cold. She couldn't risk that all over again.

Not your fault.

'And how would you know?'

She was doing it again, talking to the voice inside her head. With that, and the prickly feeling that she'd had for weeks now, that someone was watching her, Jonathan was right about that padded cell. Jay was her subject, not her playmate. She had responsibilities. When people got too close to her, they got hurt. Jay had already been hurt plenty.

Jay walked along the pavement, deep in thought. Another week had passed, another programme of drugs, another negative result. They were running out of options. Madison was still optimistic, still willing to keep trying. She hadn't given up on him, so he wouldn't give up on her. *What the hell choice do you have, anyway? Back to the street?*

The beer cans and the DVD from the hire shop clanked together in the supermarket carrier. Paid for with Madison's money. He was a kept man. A gigolo, without the sex. *You wish.*

He squelched that one down, in a heartbeat. He wanted to be able to repay Madison, somehow, for all she was doing for him – the money, a place to live, the work in the lab, even though that seemed to have stalled. He needed to be able to do something for her, something she'd like. *Not that.*

He grinned, reluctantly. There had to be something.

He took the steps to the apartment block two at a time. A glance at the small glass-covered pigeonholes behind the front desk told him that Madison had mail, but Scott was nowhere in sight.

He found the concierge at the back of the building, at the service door, lugging bags and pots and crates of bedding plants into the service lift. Jay took a corner of what looked like a bag of small pebbles, and helped him drag it inside.

'What is all this?'

'Woman in number 503.' Scott was panting. 'For her balcony; she likes to make it like a garden up there.'

'Garden.' Jay looked consideringly at the contents of the lift. 'You think you could get some more of this stuff, for Dr Albi's place?'

'Yes.' Scott looked puzzled. 'When do you want it?'

'How about this afternoon?'

'You sure about this?' Scott gazed uneasily down at the bags of compost and nest of pots that the garden centre had just delivered. 'If I have to let you into the penthouse, I want to be sure that Miss Albi's okay about it. Maybe we should call her?'

'No.' Jay was already considering what he was

going to do with the planted strips of flowers and ivy he'd picked out, with help from the girl at the garden centre. 'I want it to be a surprise.' He looked up. 'She's letting me stay at her place, rent free. This is a way of repaying her.'

'Oh.' Scott's face cleared. 'Like kind of a present?'

'Exactly.' *Paid for with the angel's own money, but what the hell.*

'That's cool,' Scott approved. 'Who's going to get mad over a present? You want to take the stuff in now?'

Jay sat back on his heels, looking at his handiwork. The three large containers, which had already been in place on the balcony, were filled now with climbing plants. Jasmine, covered with small, white star-shaped flowers, giving off a delicate, heady scent, and something with spreading green leaves, serrated like fingers. The label said it was a passionflower. The pale yellow and purple bloom in the picture looked exotic, but the girl at the garden place had assured him it would flower in the warmer weather. He'd fastened a trellis behind the pots, so the plants had somewhere to clamber.

Two tall conical planters, in matching matt black, held variegated grasses. The green and white mounds felt like velvet when he ran his hand across them. There were more containers, two plain and one patterned, with a rich silver grey glaze, full of lily bulbs. He'd filled out the tops of all the pots with ferns and ivy and white geraniums. It looked good.

He wiped his muddy palms on his jeans and began to collect the empty bags and packets. It had been satisfying, to do something with his hands. He studied the calluses on his fingers. Was that how he'd earned his living, planting things, or making things? He reached down into the blackness in his mind, but there was nothing there. Why was he surprised? Why did he keep trying?

Because if you don't, then you're trapped in this limbo. Forever.

'Jay?' Madison closed the door of the apartment behind her, frowning. 'Are you in here?' she called, louder, crossing the hall to the open door leading to her sitting room.

'Out here.' He appeared at the entrance to the balcony.

'What's going on?' Madison took off her jacket and flung it over the back of the chair, before stepping out beside him. 'Scott was very mysterious, downstairs. Oh!' Her eyes went wide when she saw. 'Jay! It's lovely.'

'I thought maybe you would like to sit out here, in the evenings.'

'I would, I will – I've never really thought of doing something like this.' She was walking slowly from pot to pot, fingering the leaves, and inhaling the scent of the jasmine. 'I love it, I really do.'

'That's all I wanted to hear.' He shrugged awkwardly. 'I need to get rid of this mess.' He indicated the few remaining plant carriers.

'No, wait just a moment.' She put out a hand. 'I haven't said thank you. No one's done anything like this for me . . . well it's been a while.'

'It's okay, as long as you like it.' He brushed past her, head averted, carrying the boxes.

Madison stood watching him, then looked back at the balcony. The plants were nodding in the breeze. Scent washed over her. There was a tightness in her chest, and the prickle of something behind her eyes that could have been tears.

Jay had just blown a huge hole in her objectivity. Which meant she had to try even harder to give him back his life.

Sandra polished the big front window thoughtfully, watching the man from the florist unloading yet another bouquet for the lady in 401. This one was a riot of blue and purple and long stiff leaves, with a huge pink, spiky thing in the centre that didn't look like anything that grew on planet earth at all. 401's hubby was abroad, somewhere hot, and obviously missing his wife like crazy. Or else he was getting his end away over there, and the flowers were because he was a guilty bastard.

Sandra sighed and polished harder. It would be nice to get a bunch of flowers once in a while, or even a plant. Greg never thought about stuff like that, except for a poinsettia from the garage, at Xmas.

'Miss Albi was dead pleased with what Mr Jackson did with all them pots on her balcony,' she told Scott, when he came to stand beside her, ready to let in the delivery man.

Scott puffed out his chest as he swung open the door. 'You know who gave him the idea, don't you?'

'You never?' Sandra said admiringly.

'What you been doing now, Scottie?' The delivery man handed over the bouquet, winking at Sandra.

'He helped Mr Jackson plant up the balcony for Miss Albi.'

'Did he now?' The delivery man looked impressed. 'Albi? She's the hot brunette on the top floor, right? This bloke Jackson, he's her fella, is he? Lucky sod.' He gave a dirty laugh.

'Mr Jackson *works* with Miss Albi,' Scott said, stiffly. 'There isn't none of that sort of thing going on.' He hefted the flowers and stalked off.

Sandra watched him, hand over her mouth to stifle a giggle. 'You know you don't want to get him going like that.' She turned to the delivery man. 'He doesn't like people talking about the residents.'

'No one 'cept him, you mean. Go on, you can tell me.' The man nudged Sandra's arm. 'Them two having it off up there in the penthouse, are they? She finally got over that other chap you was telling me about?'

122

'Nah, nothing like that,' Sandra said regretfully. 'Pity really, 'cos Mr Jackson seems ever so nice.'

Jay lengthened his stride as he approached the apartment block. Whatever Madison had stuck him with today had worn off, leaving him clear-headed, but with a raging thirst. He shut his mind on the memory of another failure, and focused instead on the image of a long, cool glass of water, followed maybe by a beer, and a dip in the basement pool. After that he had the rest of the afternoon to fill.

He'd been turning ideas over in his mind ever since yesterday. Madison's obvious pleasure in what she'd christened her sky garden had made him wonder about other things he might do. Practical stuff – like cooking her dinner, maybe? He could do that. The kitchen in the studio was small, but adequate. He could ask Sandra for a few ideas. Nothing fancy, and not anything that would give Madison the wrong impression, or scare her. It would just be two friends, sharing a meal.

He'd almost reached the front steps, deep in plans, when the sound of a scream jerked his head up.

'Callum!' A woman was standing on a balcony a few stories up, her hand to her mouth. Even at this distance Jay could see her face was ashen. He followed her horrified gaze. Halfway along the decorative ledge that ran around the front of the building, a small figure, dressed in the distinctive red and blue of a Spiderman pyjama suit, was spreadeagled against the brickwork, alongside an even smaller bundle of black-and-white fur.

CHAPTER 9

Jay leaped past an open-mouthed Scott, heading for the lift. A quick glance showed him the lift light, stationary on the fourth floor. He swerved to the emergency stairs.

'Call the fire brigade,' he yelled back over his shoulder to Scott. 'There's a kid out on the ledge.' He slammed through the fire door without waiting to see what Scott would do.

By level four his breathing was fast, but not out of control. Blessing the hours in the gym and the pool, he powered along the corridor. The door of apartment 401 was open. A large cardboard box was flattened against the wall beside it, with more piled inside. Jay stepped over them, dodging round an enormous arrangement of exotic flowers on the hall table.

'Hello?'

'Here. Thank God!' The woman from the balcony appeared in the doorway, tears streaming down her face. 'Callum. It was only a moment. The recycling—' She made a helpless gesture with one hand. 'He's going to fall.' She crammed her fingers to her mouth, stifling a scream.

'There's help coming. You go on out there and talk to him.' Jay took her arm and turned her around. 'Keep him from looking down. Go on.' He pushed her gently towards the open balcony doors.

There was a clatter behind him. Scott had arrived in the hall, wide eyed and breathing heavily, tie askew. 'Dialled 999.' He leaned against the wall. 'Sending fire crew . . . but there's . . . big blaze . . . A40. They don't know . . . how soon. They said . . . keep him talking.'

'Mother's already doing it.' Jay shrugged off his jacket, dropping it on the floor and testing out his shoulder. He flexed his arm, grimacing. There was still some slight weakness in the muscles but it would have to do. 'We can't wait. The kid's too young. If he panics— Who's next door? Anyone home?'

'Mrs Glover. She's in Spain, but—'

'You got the pass key?'

'Yeah.' Scott was fumbling at his belt. 'But—'

'It would be easier to guide him back from this side. Plus I'm going to have to pick up the fur ball that's out there with him. I just hope whatever the damn thing is, it doesn't have claws,' Jay muttered as he strode past Scott to the door of the next apartment.

'I—' Scott was dithering, the key ring in his hand. 'The fire brigade— Mrs Glover—'

'Look!' Jay rounded on him. 'Do you really want to wait and risk having that kid splattered all over the front steps?'

Scott gave up the keys, looking green.

Jay let himself into the flat, throwing open doors until he found the room that gave on to the balcony. The place was sparsely furnished, but what there was looked expensive. Jay skirted a low table with a fragile glass vase. A second key on Scott's ring unlocked the balcony door. Jay slid it open and stepped out. The young woman was crouched inside the adjacent railing, talking softly to her son. She had her tears under control, but the knuckles gripping the bars were white. Jay gestured to her to warn the child that he was there. For a heart-stopping second both of them froze as the boy's head jerked round and the small body wobbled.

Jay let out his breath in a hiss as the grasping fingers found a hold on the brickwork.

'Callum,' he called softly. A frightened pair of dark eyes in a narrow, pinched, white face gazed up at him. Jay knelt down and leaned in, as close as he could. 'I'm Jay. I'm going to climb out to you, and then we're going to go back to your mummy. Is that okay?'

A tremulous nod. 'And Zorro?'

Jay looked down. The fluff ball quivering on the ledge beside the boy was a very small rabbit, with a band of black fur across its eyes, like a mask. 'And Zorro,' Jay confirmed.

The narrow shoulders sagged with relief. 'Zorro got through the railings. I was rescuing him. But then I got scared.' A small Adam's apple bobbed. 'I don't want to be Spiderman any more.'

'Even Spidey gets scared sometimes. But he's brave, even when he's scared.' Jay gripped the rail. 'You just hang on and pretend you're him, just for a few more minutes.'

Jay hoisted himself over the rail, testing the ledge before he put his weight on it. It was reasonably wide, an extension of the balcony floor. He edged slowly sideways, back against the wall and eyes fixed on the child, feeling his way with his hands, flat against the rough bricks.

After half an eternity of shuffling progress, checking with each step to see that the ledge would continue to bear his weight, he reached the rabbit, which was cowering in a ball by the boy's leg. Sliding down, Jay scooped it up and tucked it into the front of his shirt, hoping it would have the good sense not to wriggle.

'Zorro is fine.' The child was watching him anxiously but with complete, heart-wrenching trust. Jay shoved the hot ache in his shoulder, and the pull of tense and overstretched thigh muscles, out of his mind. He needed all his concentration for the few feet of brick and concrete that still had to be negotiated.

'Callum,' he spoke softly to the boy, as if they had all the time and space in the world. 'I want you to move one foot sideways and then the other and then stop. And I do the same. We keep doing that, until we get to your mummy.' He shot a glance at the other white face, watching their every move from the balcony. About a million miles away. 'Can you do that?'

'Think so.'

'Good. You go now. One foot and then the other. That's good. I've got you.'

Together, infinitely slowly, they inched towards safety. Jay bent to splay his hand over the boy's back, keeping him close to the wall. Zorro was warm, and mercifully still, against his chest.

They stopped finally, within reach of the balcony. Callum's mother was on her knees, hand stretched through the railing. Jay urged the boy forward, sending up a silent prayer of thanks when he scrambled over and into his mother's arms.

Jay hauled himself up, feeling his hand slip as the half-healed shoulder failed to take his weight. With a stifled curse he hung for a second with his whole body weight on his good arm, muscles screaming, before his feet found a hold and he was over, half swinging, half stumbling, on to the balcony.

A ragged cheer, followed by what sounded like applause, made him look down. He was puzzled for a moment about what he was seeing. A small crowd had gathered in the street below. People were yelling, clapping, waving. One or two women seemed to be crying. In the distance he could hear the sound of a fire siren. Callum's mother, face again streaked with tears, reached up to hug him.

'That was unbelievable. How can I ever thank you?' She was laughing and weeping, all at the same time.

'Tell you what you can do.' Jay's shirt front had

begun to undulate. He reached in, with fumbling fingers. Now that it was over, his hands and his knees were shaking, he realised in disgust. At last he got a grip on the wriggling bundle and pulled it out. 'You can find somewhere safe to put this bloody rabbit.'

'Local Hero,' Madison read aloud, voice husky. 'Jay *Johnson*, today snatched toddler Callum McBride from certain death—'

'Where the hell do they get that stuff?' Jay grunted, refusing to look at the copy of the *Evening Standard* Madison was holding.

'Mr Johnson, a research scientist at a local laboratory—' she kept reading.

'Huh!' Jay interrupted her. 'Scott must have talked.'

'Probably.' Madison brandished the paper. 'You might at least look at it. There's a picture.'

Reluctantly Jay took it from her. The shot was fuzzy, probably culled from a mobile phone, but even the indistinct lines made the little boy's plight startlingly clear. Jay could feel the sweat starting out afresh across his back. One missed step—

Something in his face must have given him away. When he looked up, Madison's brown eyes were regarding him intently. He'd never realised they had gold flecks in them, near the centre. Never let himself look. 'The worst didn't happen,' she said quietly. 'You got the child.'

'And the rabbit. Don't forget Zorro.'

'I don't forget anything.' The way she was regarding him was making him uncomfortable.

'Look – despite what it says there, I'm no hero. It was sheer bloody adrenaline that got me out there, and then I was shitting bricks in case the kid panicked. And my shoulder all but gave out. That could have been a picture of the firemen peeling me off the side of the building—' He stopped abruptly. Focusing on Madison's eyes, he hadn't properly noticed the pallor of her face, or the tension around her mouth. He back-pedalled, fast. 'Oh hell, I wasn't in any danger, except of looking a fool. That ledge was as wide as the road.'

Without thinking he put out his arms. For a wavering second Madison was still, then she came into them, head against his chest. Amazement flooded him as a sob quivered through her. She was soft and warm and *crying* down his shirt.

'Hey!' Awkwardly he patted her back, shifting so that his hip wasn't pressed to hers. The feel of her – and her scent . . . God! He was getting hard. 'It's okay. Don't—' Despite himself his arms were tightening on her. His head was tilting towards her. In a second—

She broke away, hiccupping, scrubbing her face.

'Oh damn, I'm sorry. What on earth must you think?' She retrieved the newspaper from the floor. 'Do you think anyone will recognise you, from the picture? It could be a real opportunity—' She was babbling, high pitched and breathless.

'To hell with that.' He brushed the paper out of

her hand again. 'My own mother wouldn't know me, assuming I still have one.' He grabbed Madison's shoulders, turning her to him. That was better. He could hold her like that, at arm's length. And he had to ask, even though it was as clear in his head as a voice. 'Someone you loved, they fell.' Ice dripped down his spine. Her anguish was bleeding into his mind. 'The guy you lived with? He had an accident?'

Madison was staring up at him, with a mix of horror and fascination, her mouth open and her eyes stretched, so he could see the whites. 'Neil. His name was Neil. We were engaged.' Her voice wavered, heartbreakingly. 'I was going to marry him.'

Jay's fingers were biting into her arms now, but he couldn't control his grip. The certainty of her loss and terror was driving him. 'I thought . . . the clothes. I thought he'd walked out – left you.' Madison's head jerked, in a soundless denial. 'Madison. You have to tell me, how did Neil die?'

CHAPTER 10

'He jumped off a bridge.' Madison's voice was hollow, echoing in her own ears. 'He drove down to Bristol. It was where we met – we were at the university together.' She drew in a deep, ragged breath. 'We lived in Clifton. He went back there. He parked the car and walked out on to the Suspension Bridge. And then he jumped. A week before the wedding.'

Jay swallowed. 'Could there—'

'There was no mistake. He left a note.' She winced at the memory – it had just been a jumble of random phrases, with the word sorry repeated over and over. Eight times. She'd counted. 'He'd been on medication, for depression. It came out at the Inquest. I didn't know.'

'I . . . I'm sorry.' He let go of her shoulders.

Without the bone-crunching grip she felt cold. She looked up at him, empty, but curious. There was real concern in his face, not the usual embarrassment or avid prying.

'Everyone will have told you this,' he continued, eyes focused, unflinching, on her. 'Suicide is not the survivor's fault.'

'I know.' She looked down, studying her feet, encased today in dark pink kitten heels. Close to Jay's. His were bare. A tremor ran through her. 'I've read all the pamphlets, had all the counselling. It does help.' She straightened up, pushed back her hair. 'You may as well know it all. Neil's death wasn't the first violent loss in my life.' She gulped, trying to clear a throat that was as dry as glass paper. 'When I was fifteen years old, my parents were murdered. The killer was never found. I know what it's like to be alone, Jay . . . I've lost everyone I ever loved.' She held his gaze. 'That's a fact. I'm not looking for sympathy.'

'You have it, just the same.'

She nodded abruptly.

The gesture caught Jay under the heart. Her face was stoic, her eyes dry, her back straight. The bravado and vulnerability of her upflung head turned inside him, like a spike. His hand was twitching, wanting to reach out, to touch her cheek—

The doorbell rang.

Madison stood in the centre of the room, getting her emotions under control, hearing Jay's low rumble and the lighter flow of a woman's voice. He came back after a few moments, clutching an enormous bottle of champagne. 'From Mrs McBride – I told her she didn't need to do this, but she wouldn't take no for an answer.' With an

134

embarrassed shuffle, he indicated the champagne. 'I'll go and put this in the kitchen somewhere.'

'No.' Madison shook her head, knowing her eyes were gleaming. 'I've got a better idea. Let's open it. And get expensively, irresponsibly drunk.'

'Water chestnut?' Jay fished in a narrow waxed carton and brandished his loaded chopsticks at her. Madison held out her dish and offered the champagne in exchange. Halfway down the bottle she'd decided she was hungry. They'd ordered in from the Chinese restaurant across the street. Spring rolls and noodles and sweet and sour sauce were mopping up the alcohol. She shook her head when Jay reached to top up her glass. He drained the last few drops into his own.

'I have a feeling we may regret this in the morning,' Madison said, pleased not to be slurring. She was feeling light and rather floaty and the pain of remembering Neil had bundled up into ball and receded to a safe distance. Now all she had to worry about was the man sitting opposite her. The gorgeous man sitting opposite her. Whose mouth she wanted to kiss.

She sat up, with a start. She wasn't that drunk. And neither was Jay. She could see it in his eyes as he watched her.

'What?' She swirled the dregs in her glass and put it down.

'I've never asked—' He stopped.

'Asked what?' A cool trickle of caution found its way through the warmth of the champagne.

'What's it like—' He'd finished eating and was slouched against the sofa, arms spread along the back. 'What's it like, for you, when you're inside someone's head? When you hear their thoughts?'

'Not hear. It's more like feel.' She pretended to search through the containers on the table, looking for scraps. 'I don't read people's thoughts. I told you that.'

'Did you?'

'When we first met.'

'Hmmm.' He wrinkled his nose. 'I wasn't exactly taking everything in around then. So, what is it like? What you feel?'

He was still flopped back, boneless, against the sofa. She watched him, sideways, over an empty box. If this was an interrogation, he was pretty relaxed about it. *Which doesn't mean you can be.*

She studied him, nerves alert. The open-armed position stretched the dark green T-shirt across the muscles of his chest. This man had saved a small boy's life this afternoon. She tried to process the swirl of emotion that produced, and found she couldn't.

He was waiting, patiently, for her to continue. She toyed with the contradictions in him for a moment, patience and impatience, then abandoned the conundrum. He was male, and therefore a bundle of contradictions. She chewed a finger, thinking through the alcohol in her blood. What did he want, now, at this very minute? What was he prepared to wait for? What did he expect her to give up?

'If you don't want to share, that's cool,' he said eventually, lifting one shoulder and turning away.

The shuttering in his eyes sent a spasm through her. If this was just straightforward interest . . . He was letting her wander through his mind at will, and she couldn't even answer a simple question without searching all round it for hidden traps. She wanted to tell him, to take that look away.

Now who's being contradictory? What if that's what he's counting on?

Oh, to hell with this.

She yanked a skein of hair behind her ear. 'I find it difficult to explain.' *Nothing but the truth there.* 'I don't read minds, not the way you see it portrayed on TV and film. When I go in – it's emotions, senses, all jumbled. There are colours and scents. I can taste things like fear. There are big blocks of sensation, like an abstract painting. That's in the present. As far as the past is concerned, I access memory like looking through an archive of pictures.'

'And I don't have that archive.'

You're not like the average subject, either. When I go into you, you can feel me. It's intimate. She put her hand to her mouth, to stop the thought travelling anywhere else. Like out into the air. The champagne was having more effect than she'd bargained on. She couldn't complain. It had been her idea.

'Er . . . No.' Her voice came out strangled. She did a little breathing. And with it came an idea. *Turn the tables.* 'What do you feel? When I'm inside your head?'

His chin came up and his head rested on the back of the sofa as he considered. The strength in the exposed column of his throat set something inside her purring. She wanted to nuzzle, then nip. *Do not drink champagne with this man again.* Then – *Who are you kidding? You want things like that, with or without the champagne.*

He'd sorted out his answer, and lifted his head. 'It's not painful, not unless I already have a headache. It's like a buzz. I have to concentrate, to be able to think. Sometimes it feels as if there's too much in there, with you and me, and that's uncomfortable. Sometimes it feels as if I'm on the edge of something.' A look of surprise crossed his face, at the analysis. 'Hey – I didn't know I knew so much about it. Does any of that make sense?'

'Yes.' She was intrigued, despite herself. 'You know, we ought to document this. I've never had a subject with this strong a reaction. Most can't feel anything.' *Which makes being in their minds a curiously lonely experience.* 'There are a few of my regular subjects who are learning to respond.' She clasped her hands together. 'Maybe we've been concentrating too hard on the amnesia. Maybe we should diversify. Look at other areas we might develop.' *You spoke to me once. I* know *you did.*

He wasn't moving. His eyes were opaque, then

something glinted in the shadowy blue. Reluctance. He didn't want to do what she asked, but he wasn't going to say no to her. The realisation put a sour taste in her mouth.

'We'll talk about it some more.' At random she picked up the TV guide from the table, then her interest sharpened. 'Hey, there's a double bill of the old Hammer horror movies.' She reached for the remote. 'Christopher Lee, doing his thing in Black Park.' The set crackled into life.

'Black Park?'

'It's woodland, not far from here, close to the film studios in Denham. They used it a lot for location shots. Don't you know anything about vintage British vampire flicks?'

'Apparently not.'

Madison settled herself more comfortably in her seat. 'Watch and learn, then.' She grinned as the titles rolled. 'Watch and learn.'

There was a phone ringing somewhere. Alec reached blearily for his mobile.

'*Evening Standard*. Final edition.'

Calver sat up, galvanised awake, brain spluttering expletives that never reached his lips. Kong wasn't supposed to have this number.

'What about it?' he asked cautiously.

'Page fourteen.'

Alec got out of bed. He'd dumped the paper beside his attaché case in the next room. He'd got bored at page five.

The continued heavy breathing on the line told him his boss hadn't hung up. And that he wasn't happy.

When he saw page fourteen, Alec understood.

'Low-profile operation. Utmost secrecy.' Kong spat the words so hard Alec almost instinctively moved to wipe his face. 'So why is there a picture of Jayston Creed splashed across half a page?'

'Uh – that wasn't in the plan, sir.'

'If I thought it was, I'd be eating your balls in a sandwich, Calver. Any fallout, you will deal. Understood?'

'Sir!'

Kong was rumbling on, 'That guy always has to be a fucking hero.'

'That's what we're counting on, to make this thing work.' Alec was getting back into control. 'Plus there are only about five people still alive who can identify Jayston Creed, and none of the others are in this country. No one will see it.'

'I trust not.'

The phone clicked off before Alec could make a response. He flung the paper on the table and squinted at the headline. 'Local fucking hero!'

'Hero.' Jonathan sighed and fluttered his eyelashes at Madison, grinning. 'Bulging muscles, flexing pecs. Now will you take him to bed?'

'I wish you'd shut up about that,' Madison growled, trying to get her desk in order with Jonathan perched on the end of it and the legacy of slightly too much champagne scudding around between her ears.

She and Jay had watched both horror movies. It had felt good, to have him there, but she wasn't fooling herself. Even under the influence of the champagne, there'd been a constraint between them, overriding that current of awareness. They'd been conscious of each other, but careful not to touch. One thing she had established – alcohol had no effect on Jay's loss of memory. Which was something else to put in the negative column.

She'd banged on his door, not too hard, this morning. Getting no answer, she'd left him to follow her, in his own time.

'Don't fight it. Sleep with the he-man. Broaden your experience. You know you want to.' Jonathan laughed and ducked out of the door when she threatened him with a file.

Madison put the file down and flopped into her desk chair. She dropped her head in her hands. *Wanting to* wasn't the problem.

Jay arrived, looking sheepish and a little ragged, just before lunch. He was squinting in the sunlight that bounced off the white walls. He'd shaved, but there was a tiny nick on the side of his chin. Madison had to battle the impulse to touch it. If she'd kept her hands off him last night, she could certainly do it now.

She had her implements of torture waiting for

him. He grimaced when he saw the syringes, unbuttoning his sleeve on his way to the couch.

'How's your head?' she asked, adjusting the blinds.

'So-so. Not improved by the bus ride here. You?'

'About the same.' Madison looked down at the medication she'd prepared. 'We don't have to do this.'

'Yes we do.' Jay's eyes were determined.

She pursed her lips. 'Okay, so we do. But we don't have to do it *here*.'

Jay sprawled on the sofa, with a cushion under his head. Madison, out of her work clothes and in a pink cotton sweater and jeans, had tied her hair back with a white silk scarf, winding the ends into a loose knot. She squeezed his hand to get his attention. 'Ready?'

He nodded. Madison pressed the button on the recorder, perched herself on the arm of the sofa and dropped into his mind. She approached from an angle, the way she'd learned caused the least disruption.

She knew, in two seconds, that this time things were different.

The kaleidoscope of images had shifted subtly. They were more ordered, with a sharp, bright line around them. The traces of hangover put a fellow-sufferer's smile on her lips, even as her heart accelerated in excitement.

'*Jay?*' She reached out with the probe she always

began with, automatically trying to form the form-less into Jay's name.

Something swirled. *'Yes?'*

She almost dropped the connection. *'You can hear me? Hear the actual words?'*

'I feel the words.' Puzzlement and excitement washed towards her in a silver tide. *'I can talk to you!'*

'Oh God!'

'You've done it!'

She couldn't tell if the jubilation was him or her. *'We've* done it.'

With a thrilling spurt of triumph, she pulled her resources together and surged forward. Met the wall – and bounced off with a skull-searing recoil.

'Hell, hell, hell!'

'Ouch!'

Both their brains were spinning. She fell out into safety, reeling. Only Jay's grip kept her from falling off the sofa.

'What the hell was that?'

She put up a shaky hand. 'It was like that first morning.' A measure of relief flowed through her. She hadn't imagined that communication. 'You were reading my mind as I was reading yours.'

'Telepathy.' The bitterness in his voice brought her down with a bump.

'Hey!' She thumped his shoulder, not caring whether it was the good one or not. 'We *talked!* This is progress. Something worked. We got back to where we were. We can *use* this.'

143

'How?'

'I don't know yet, but it *is* progress.' She reached for her notes, speaking fast into the recorder. Listing the drugs she'd used.

'Don't forget the champagne. What was it? Bollinger '92 or '97?' Jay enquired acidly.

She blinked, then added it to the list.

'It might have been Krug. I'll have to look at the bottle.' She was gabbling, thoughts free-wheeling. She took a hold on herself. 'If we want to repeat this, I'm never going to get *that* past the Finance section.' She prodded Jay's middle. 'Come on, be a little happy. This *is* a break-through. Sit up.'

Impatient, she reached to help him move the cushion, and only just missed brushing her breasts against his chest.

That *really* got her excitement under control.

She arranged their bodies so that they were sitting cross legged, facing each other on the wide settee.

'Now, take my hand.' She offered it. 'This time, you come to me.'

The first attempts were blunt and painful. Madison felt her thoughts being squeezed and trampled as Jay found his mental feet. Thank God she'd never made her subjects feel like this.

'*Guilt.*' Jay's inner voice reverberated softly, now she'd convinced him to scale down the volume. He was following her lead, exploring sensations.

'Green and black. Wet. Smells acrid. Why are you guilty?'

'It's more like relief, that my subjects couldn't feel me when I was a beginner.'

'Clumsy? Sorry.'

Patiently, and with more wariness, Madison went back to helping Jay refine his technique. After an hour they were both exhausted. Madison leaned against the back of the sofa, spent. *A bit like the aftermath of sex.*

She lifted her head with a jerk, afraid the thought might have spilled over. Jay's eyes were shut. He seemed to be asleep. She shook his arm gently, thankful when he didn't respond.

Her face was burning. Her breasts were tingling and tender. There was a suspicion of dampness between her legs. Oh God! It *was* like sex. Jay, sliding into her head, taking her thoughts.

Whether you want him to or not.

She shivered, rolling over a fraction to stare at Jay. Normally, when she entered someone's head, it was a mass of emotion. Like soup. Not a bloody conversation. And not someone coming right back at her. Why now? What had changed? The setting, the drugs? *Could* it be the champagne?

It didn't fit.

Nothing with Jay was normal. She had to protect herself. She had to have barriers. A girl had to learn to take care of herself.

She was still sorting through her thoughts when Jay opened his eyes.

'Again.'

Exactly like sex. She brushed the buzz away, like swatting a fly. She shook her head.

'Not the telepathy,' he insisted. 'Dose me again and try the wall.'

'You've had enough.'

The glint in his eyes was dangerous, as he rolled back his sleeve. 'Again.'

CHAPTER 11

Madison put a pint mug of water down on the table, scanning Jay anxiously. His arms were bruised with needle marks and his eyes dull with chemical hangover. She felt as if she'd run a marathon. He had to feel worse. And they had nothing to show for it. The wall was still stubbornly in place.

He was struggling to sit up. He made it at the second attempt.

'I thought you were getting coffee?'

'You need this more. Flush out the junk I've pumped into you.'

'Mmm.' He stretched a stiff neck, flexing to work out the kinks. She told herself not to watch. Then ignored her own instructions. Observation was necessary. She had to monitor the health of the subject. *Oh, really?*

Jay shook his head and picked up the mug. 'I guess I don't need caffeine. My brain is running like an engine.'

She sat down beside him on the sofa, feeling his forehead and his pulse. One damp, the other fast. 'You need to rest.'

'Would if I could.' He'd finished the water. He looked round vaguely. 'Maybe a walk. Fresh air.'

'Maybe a couple of hours' sleep.' She moved cautiously, hovering just on the edge of his consciousness, bracing herself to be pushed out again once he realised she was there. She forgot to breathe as he sensed her. His mind roiled for a moment, like a cat with its fur brushed back. Then, abruptly, he capitulated and let her gentle him, throwing a balm over racing sensations. He tipped his head back with a sigh.

'Is it so bad? To accept a little help?'

'I suppose not.' He was relaxing visibly as she worked. She pulled out when his breathing deepened and everything in his mind went blue and misty.

She folded her legs up under her, watching him. Gave in to the impulse to smooth his hair away from his face. Touch his skin. Warm. His stubble was rough to her fingertips. There was something about a man asleep. Vulnerability. Neil had looked—

Gently she pulled her thoughts back from the way they were going. This man wasn't Neil. She couldn't recreate the dead in the living, just because her heart was bruised and needy. *If you think this has anything to do with your* heart *you've got a sad grasp of anatomy.*

An unexpected gurgle of laughter rose in her throat. She was exhausted. Punch drunk. Her eyes fastened on Jay's mouth. She wanted his mouth. Wanted to run her tongue around it, inside it, feel it pressed on hers, bruising, and then she wanted to move down. His chest. Her eyes hovered over his belt.

Grimly she unravelled herself from the sofa and headed for her study.

Jay was in her trust. Whatever she *wanted*, her hands and her lips stayed *off* him.

And his off her.

It was getting dark. Jay plodded along the pavement, doggedly keeping one foot in front of the other. Cars swept by, headlights fracturing the lengthening shadows. Walking to the Common hadn't cleared his head the way he'd hoped. An hour's sleep on Madison's sofa had left him groggy, yet restless. He'd deserted Madison, with a half-mumbled excuse, to spend the evening alone in the studio, thinking he needed the space. But that hadn't been the answer. His thoughts were wearing themselves towards exhaustion, grimly, ruthlessly, moving and shifting, obscured by fog. Something in there had changed. *Who the hell knows what?*

He trudged up the steps to the apartment block, across the lobby and into the lift. On the top floor the door to Madison's place was closed. He hesitated, hand outstretched to knock, before changing his mind and swinging sharply towards his own door.

Once inside he tossed his jacket into a chair and took a beer from the fridge, pulling the single chair towards the long window and dropping into it. He sipped, staring out at the gathering night. The stars were coming out in the sliver of sky visible in the gap between the two buildings opposite. Jay shifted uneasily. Telepathy. He'd exchanged thoughts with Madison. She'd been right. He had his own power. Power like hers. Gingerly he explored the idea, waiting for the pain. Nothing came. Fog swirled, the aftermath of too many drugs, but no sudden flair of agony. Had he imagined a connection between prying too deep into his situation and crippling stabs behind his eyes?

Was he imagining all of it?

Maybe he was lying comatose in a hospital bed, surrounded by tubes and bleeping machines, while all this madness paraded, unnoticed, inside his head? It was a thought.

He swigged deeper from the beer. Fantasy, or memory? *Had* he once been that way? Everything he could see and hear now *felt* real. Deep in the back of his mind, everything felt . . . right. Progress, just as it ought to be. Which was crazy, as there was nothing in his life that could be claimed as anything near *right*.

Except Madison.

Her name was a shiver on his skin. Without her he was adrift in his own life, a walking, talking nothingness. But now, it seemed, he was a nothingness with power. Was that coming from her? Was it her *will* that was doing it, pulling things out of him that might have lain dormant? Should have lain dormant?

Carefully he set the empty beer bottle down on the floor, beside his chair. Madison was drawing stuff out of him, no question. Had it already been there? Had he known it was there? He'd had a life, and now it was gone, wrapped in steel inside his own head. Wrapped in steel. His fingers tensed on the arms of the chair. Whatever Madison had disturbed, it wasn't enough. The barrier was still there.

The wooden arms of the chair bit into the palms of his hands. He needed more. So much more. He raised his hands, pressing hard against his eyes until lights danced, trying to force them into some sort of pattern. And felt again the tantalising hovering-on-the-edge-of-certainty that he'd felt before. Something was there, if only he could make sense of it. If only he could wrench it out of the darkness—

Defeated, he dropped his hands and rose to make his way blearily towards the alcove that housed the bed. It swung down smoothly from its position in the wall, protesting gently as he threw himself down on it. He stared at the ceiling – a pure, perfect white blank, like his mind. *Your* mind? *Not pure, not white, not perfect.*

He rolled over and hid his face in the pillow, shutting it out. If only he could *think*. Gather his thoughts to a point and cut through the barrier, to what was beyond. *However terrible that might be?*

Exhaustion was pulling him into oblivion. Briefly he struggled against it. Sometimes, like now,

drifting down into sleep, he could almost sense
. . . voices. One voice. Insistent, repetitive, calling
his name. *His* name?

*Madison is not the only one who has been inside
your head.*

She'd kept busy all evening – tidying her credit
card receipts, shredding ancient bills, making
herself a simple salad and eating it standing next
to the kitchen counter, so she wouldn't be tempted
to call Jay to share it. She'd even watched some
TV. Once she thought she heard the sound of a
door slam and the whisper of the lift, but she
might have imagined it. In any case, Jay was free
to come and go as he pleased. She was not his
keeper. She wasn't anything to him. *Except a friend?*
    She was damaging him, and he was letting her.
Because he was desperate. Something had changed.
She had to figure out what it was, and use it, for
both their sakes.
    She sighed, pulling herself up off the sofa, to
close the curtains. A new moon was riding high
in a navy blue sky. The colour of Jay's eyes.
Madison grimaced.
    Abruptly, a yawn overtook her. She took one last
look at the new moon. Hope? New beginnings?
Hope?

It was dark. He couldn't breath. The air was hot
and heavy, stifling in his lungs. He had to keep
running, gasping down oxygen. Muscles in his legs

pumped, screaming. He surged on, one narrow space after another. There was light. The nameless thing was behind him. A long way behind. He'd got away.

No!

The wall reared up in front of him, out of nowhere, blocking his path. He heard a sound rising in his throat. It was here! No place left to run.

The dark stain splashed across the pale surface, just a few drops at first, splattering. Then a tide, running down the wall, black and viscous, obliterating the white painted surface, seeping over the floor, towards him, lapping at his feet, leaping towards him. He threw up his arms, to cover his face.

With a disjointed lurch it was all gone, sucked away. Relief made him dizzy. He turned, slowly, to make his way back.

He wasn't alone. She was standing only a foot away from him. She shouldn't be standing, shouldn't be looking at him. Not any more. She was watching him but he couldn't see her eyes, because she was dead. She was staring, with eyes that weren't there. He looked down and his mouth stretched wide.

The screaming woke Madison. Coming from behind her head. On the other side of the wall.

'Hold on, Jay! I'm coming.' Oh God, could he hear her? She stumbled and almost fell as she grabbed her robe. The spare key to the studio was on a hook beside the door in the kitchen. She saw the clock. Quarter to four.

She fell into the lobby, wincing at the cold tiles under her feet, fumbled the lock, finally got it open and hurtled through the tiny hall and the open door into the main room. He was sitting bolt upright on the bed, back to the wall, eyes open but unseeing.

Sweat stained the front of his T-shirt, making it cling. He was lying on top of the covers, still fully dressed.

Heart hammering, Madison stopped beside the bed. Jay seemed to sense her presence. His head swivelled. She could see the whites of his eyes. The screams had settled into a heartrending murmur of sound. With only her instinct to follow she put her hands on his shoulders, gripping hard, and shook. 'Jay.'

His head flopped, then snapped up. The way he swore convinced her he was awake. She put her hand to her mouth, fighting an abrupt wave of nausea. He was shaking. Without thinking, she pulled him towards her, cradling his head until the shivering stopped and he carefully disengaged himself.

Face going pink, she retreated to the end of the bed, belting her robe tighter. She had done more blushing around Jay than she'd done in her entire life. Well, since she was thirteen, anyhow.

'I guess I was yelling?' He had his arms wrapped around himself, shoulders hunched.

'Something like that. What were you dreaming about?'

His eyes skittered away. He shook his head. 'Don't recall. I'm okay now. Thanks for the rescue.' His lip curled.

'Jay—'

'I think I'll open the balcony doors. Get some air.' He brushed past her, still without looking at her. Madison studied his back, wondering whether to . . . The set of his shoulders told her not to even think about it. She took her dismissal and went.

Back in her own bed she sat for a long while, thinking. Something had shaken loose today. Something frightening.

Despite herself, she shivered. Jay knew exactly what the dream was, he just wasn't sharing. Its trails had hung in the room, like sticky spider threads. Dark – and violent. Why? Too many meds, too much emotion? Or were they finally getting close to a breach in the wall?

Madison sent a tentative probe out, seeing if she could connect. When she encountered nothing but dead air, she rolled on her side and curled into a ball, pulling the pillow under her neck.

On the balcony of the studio, Jay gripped the railing with whitened knuckles, hauling in cold, moonlit air. His heart had steadied, but the sick griping in his guts still lingered. The sweat on his body had cooled, turning icy.

He stood for a long time, listening to the noises from the street, until chattering teeth finally drove him in, to lie on the bed, wakeful.

He drifted into sleep around dawn. Dreamless. No more pounding down endless corridors. No more fetid, stifling violence. No more dead women; bloodstained hands.

His hands.

'I think we should take a couple of days off. Go to the sea, maybe—'

'No.' Jay shook his head, for emphasis. 'Thank you.'

Madison shifted until she could look into his eyes. 'We both need a break. You scared the living daylights out of me last night.'

'I'm sorry.' He leaned across the table, captured her hand. 'But don't you see? Something is moving. You have to press on—'

'No. And that is my considered, professional opinion. You're over medicated. We take a week off. From everything. Let your system clear.'

The horror in his face would have been funny, if it hadn't broken her heart.

'I'm fine.' His grip was nearly splintering her bones. She pulled free. His face whitened when he saw the red marks across the back of her hand. She heard him gulp. 'Two days.'

'Three. Best offer.'

He went still. The silence stretched. 'All right, three days.'

Having got what she wanted, Madison could afford to be generous. 'If we're having time out, how would you like to go to a party?'

'What sort of party?' he asked suspiciously.

'Work related, black-tie, tomorrow night. Schmoozing potential sponsors for new projects. Human face of research. Meet the scaries. Shake their hands. Eat a canapé with Mulder and Scully.'

'That is *so* out of date.'

'People who donate big money don't tend to watch much recreational TV.'

'Do you really put yourselves out there?' he asked. 'In public?'

'You bet we do. It's all in a good cause. We raise money, we continue to get paid. The research we do, it's mostly pretty straightforward, except for the occasional guy with amnesia.' She grinned. 'The thing is, everyone secretly *wants* to believe that what we do is a bit creepy. Getting a little shiver with their donation seems to make people more willing to put their hands in their pockets. It's like theatre.'

He nodded. 'That's quite smart.'

'It's all a matter of presentation. People meet us, find we only have the requisite number of heads, but there's still that little buzz.'

As they talked she could see the tension settling out of his shoulders.

'You going to wear that gold number?'

'The gold number hasn't been the same since

157

the night we met. Oil?' she reminded him. 'But I have something else you might like. In silver.'

'Sounds interesting. But you know I don't have a thing to wear.'

'That can be fixed.'

Madison dipped the tip of her tongue into the liquid in the wooden spoon, thought for a moment, then licked off the rest. It was spaghetti sauce. *Her* spaghetti sauce. It was good. This cooking thing wasn't such a big deal. Like an experiment in the lab, a little of this, a pinch of that. With better results. Prettier. And tastier. She scrunched the pepper mill over the bubbling pan, turned down the heat, and wandered to the window.

Jay was in the tiny scrap of open ground across the street with Callum, kicking a football. They were both yelling, ducking and diving. Who exactly was the five-year-old? She raised her hand to wave as Jay spotted her. Callum waggled his arm energetically too, grinning. In the absence of his father, working in Dubai, the child had attached himself to Jay with a shy but serious case of hero worship. They looked good together, scrapping over the ball.

Madison looked over her shoulder at the kitchen. Food simmering on the hob, mum watching her son and his father play. Just like family. Any minute now the syrupy voice-over would be extolling the virtues of some essential domestic product. She smiled, self-mocking. The child wasn't hers, and neither was the man. She didn't do family. She ought to have learned her lesson by now. She opened the cupboard looking for the spaghetti.

'I'd definitely forgotten how dammed uncomfortable these monkey suits are,' Jay complained, hand to his throat, as they waited in the receiving line to greet the mayor. 'This bloody collar is killing me. How can you forget being choked half to death by a few inches of starched cotton?'

Madison gave him a quizzical look. 'Stop moaning, you look great.' The suit was Neil's, unworn. Madison pushed away the idea that he'd bought it for a wedding that in the end he couldn't face. She didn't know and wouldn't grieve over it.

'You don't look too bad yourself.' Jay's eyes were scanning the silver dress. His approval warmed all the exposed skin that Madison had on show. And some that wasn't. She stiffened, then made herself chill. These events were never going to be up there in the list of everyone's top ten most unforgettable parties, but they were meant to be at least mildly enjoyable. And she intended to enjoy.

She wiggled her fingers at Jonathan, already past the line and in the room, glass in hand. He'd taken his demotion as escort with a droll look and a disturbingly dirty leer, but mercifully, no comment.

The mayor was getting closer. They shuffled forward.

'Remind me again, why am I here? Strangling?'

159

Jay spoke out of the corner of his mouth. Madison admired. How did he *do* that?

'Social integration.' The very dark brows disappeared, almost up under the fall of hair that flopped over Jay's forehead. He'd had it cut, but nothing stopped that wayward front section. 'You're going to have to get back to real life some time, whether you regain your memory or not,' she advised primly. 'May as well start here.'

He was studying the mayor and mayoress. Short, tubby and red-faced. Mr and Mrs Noah, in a child's model ark. 'This is real life?'

Madison had to control her grin. 'Yes,' she said firmly.

Despite the running commentary, Jay was relaxed. She could feel it. More at ease than he'd been since the nightmare. In the gym, playing with Callum, sampling her cooking, there'd been a black-edged undercurrent she hadn't been able to unpick.

Once past the official greeting, Madison emerged thankfully into the room to find Jonathan and his partner, Ashley, waiting for them, with drinks. She'd barely got her mouth to her glass when she spotted the director, beaming and bearing down on her.

'Madison, my dear.' He air kissed her left ear. 'There's someone you have to meet.' Short of shaking her boss's hand off her arm, Madison couldn't duck out of her duty to help charm a few sponsors. And it was, after all, why she was here. With an eye roll at Jay, she let herself be led away.

'Mad's always in demand at these affairs,' Jonathan said as they both watched her progress across the room in the director's wake. Jay looked round inquiringly. 'Female scientist,' Jonathan elaborated. 'Still a pretty rare commodity. Everyone wants to meet the lady spook, the *beautiful* lady spook, who may or may not be able to do something really creepy to you. And our director, bless his heart, has all the instincts of a top-grade matchmaker, which makes him *very* good at his job. That's all jealousy, of course. Not so many people want to meet the queer spook.'

There was a flash of pain/anger, quickly suppressed, as Ashley nudged him in the ribs, with a reproving stare, and a swift apologetic grin at Jay. 'You really want to spend the evening shaking moneybags, to see what you can make fall out?' he asked softly. He turned to Jay. 'Want to go find the food?'

Jay got himself a convenient wall to lurk beside, and a loaded plate, and watched Madison working the room, wondering why he was surprised at the skill with which she did it. Madison was good at everything she put her mind to. Despite the way she chose to live, she wasn't the archetypal nerd, with the social skills of a goldfish. Her choices, the distrust of emotion, the fear of intimacy – he could understand that, given her history.

'Madison's parents and her fiancé?' he said as Jonathan joined him. 'You know much about that?'

Jonathan shot him a startled look. 'She told you?'

Jay nodded, eyes still on Madison. The silver dress and spiky heeled shoes shimmered. So did something low in his gut. 'A little. You know what happened?'

'Madison is usually pretty clam-like on the subject – but hell, everyone can Google,' Jonathan admitted, eating a piece of stuffed celery. 'Parents – pretty nasty and a bit weird. Drive-by shooting in Tunbridge Wells, if you can believe it. Police thought it must have been a case of mistaken identity. As for Neil—' His face darkened. 'The spineless bastard didn't even leave a proper explanation for the woman he was meant to marry in ten days' time.'

'You disapprove of suicide?'

'I disapprove of anything that hurts Madison. She and Neil – it wasn't exactly Romeo and Juliet, but they'd known each other since university. That's where they met. He was a few years older, doing post-doctoral work – engineering. She was in her final year as an undergraduate. They kept in touch after she graduated. It was kind of a slow burn thing, but they were good together. He was protective, you know, but not over the top. I thought he really loved her. She was easy with him. He accepted her as she is. She had a chance of a *life* with him. Since then—'

The glance, over the wine glass, was speculative. Jay could see what Jonathan wanted to ask, but uncharacteristic discretion was holding his tongue.

'I have to say it was a surprise when Neil topped himself,' Jonathan carried on. 'He was chilled, laid-back, everything was cool. But who knows what's really in someone's mind? Except Madison, that is?'

'And she didn't?'

'No.' Jonathan looked at his empty glass. 'I need a refill.' He ambled towards the bar. Jay was wondering if skulking beside a wall and avoiding the women who were giving him assessing glances really constituted reawakening his social skills, when Madison detached herself smoothly from the group she was with. The trip that his heart gave, as she approached him, was a small, alarming surprise.

'What are you doing here?'

'Eating, and waiting for you.' He offered her his mostly demolished plate. She took a stuffed olive and put it in her mouth, then let him feed her a cracker with prawns. 'That is delicious.' She was licking her fingers, when a matron in a flowing, purple dress sailed towards them. 'Mrs Eugene. Very big corporate sponsor,' she whispered before the woman reached them.

'Dr Albi, I just had to speak to you. And your . . . friend.' Her eyes slid over to Jay. She held out her hand. Jay ditched his plate to take it. 'So unexpected,' the woman murmured. 'Madison usually comes to these things alone.' She waved a dismissive hand at the room. Jay found the curiosity in her eyes was sharp but friendly.

'Mr Jackson is . . . assisting me with my work,' Madison responded hastily.

Emboldened by Mrs Eugene's approach, several other people were drifting up. Jay found himself occupied with Mrs Eugene, while Madison was facing slightly away from him. The woman was pumping him for information, he realised, amused. Parrying her was stretching his wits, but he was managing it. Social interaction. Madison would be proud.

'And tell me, Mr Jackson, how did you and our lovely Dr Albi meet?'

Jay, distracted by the brush of Madison's arm on his back as she turned to greet a newcomer, found his thoughts a complete blank. Hubris. Mrs Eugene was waiting, expectant.

'How did we meet? Not the version with the iron bar.' He felt the stutter of shock from Madison as he slid into her mind. He telegraphed apology, and mild panic. *'Mrs Eugene!'*

'Oh . . . Washington, DC.? Conference?'

'Thanks.'

Madison stalked up to Jay as he refreshed their drinks. 'I can't believe we just did that.'

'What?' He handed her a glass. 'That's yours. The lipstick's not my shade.'

'You know what I mean. We had a conversation, in a public place, *without actually speaking to each other.*' There was a tremor in her voice.

'Yes.'

'*Oh my God.*'

'What's the problem?' He shoved his glass on the table, so that he could close his hands, lightly, over her shoulders. 'It's not such a big deal. I was floundering, you helped me out. Mrs Eugene went away happy. Why does it bother you so much?'

'I . . . I've never done anything like that before.'

He frowned. 'Can't say if I ever have.' He gave her shoulders a small shake. 'Don't panic. I won't do it again if it worries you.'

'It isn't that.'

Madison's head was swimming. Jay was watching her face and mouth. Intense. For a second she thought he might kiss her. The feeling was so strong she found her chin tilting up. His eyes were incredibly dark, and softer than she'd ever seen them.

'Madison?' The sound of him saying her name brought her back to earth. Jay let her go and she immediately felt lost. 'You've gone as white as a sheet. Take a moment. Go powder your nose or something.' He gave her a gentle push. 'Go!'

Reprieved, she fled to the cloakroom, almost cannoning into a waiter who was hovering near the door, with an empty tray. She ran cold water over hands that shook slightly. In the mirror her eyes were huge, her face pale. What did Jay see when he looked at her? A woman he could want? A desirable woman?

She shook her head. She had to put a hold on this now, before Jay detected her . . . lust . . . and

165

all the other stuff. She put a finger up to the mouth of the woman in the mirror, focusing on the smoothness of the glass under her skin. Jay couldn't know. Their conversation without words hadn't panicked her because she didn't like it. It had panicked her because it felt so *right*.

Back in the reception room, Jay had found himself an alcove. He propped himself on the edge of a table, and breathed in, deeply. His palms were damp and his throat tight. Now that Madison was gone, reaction was setting in.

He'd stepped in and out of her mind, so effortlessly that he almost hadn't noticed it. It had taken her alarm and distress to show him.

And then the impulse to give more and take more, to overwhelm her, while she was vulnerable to him, to comfort her – he genuinely didn't know what the impulse was. He'd almost kissed her, right there in the middle of the room. And she'd known; he was sure of it. She'd run when he told her to go. *Wise girl.*

He moved restlessly. A twinge of pain from his shoulder grounded him with a rush. It killed the want that was still heavy in his groin. He had to remember he was nothing. He had nothing to offer. He was worse than nobody. Even the clothes he stood up in came from another man.

Jay slumped on the studio's small balcony, legs out, back braced against the wall. The scent of jasmine, from Madison's pots, stole over the railings. The journey home, by taxi, had been a largely silent affair. He hadn't known what to say to make things right, so he'd kept his mouth shut.

He dug his hands up into his hair. He ought to go – just leave. Let Madison have her life back. He was taking her money, her time and her talent, and in exchange he was disrupting her world. She didn't need any more pain and violence in it. God knows, she'd had enough for anyone's lifetime.

He shifted restlessly. Now that Madison had put him back together again he was fit to move on. A soft shudder ran through him when he assessed how far he'd come in the weeks he'd spent with Madison, and exactly what she'd given him in terms of healing and self-respect. He didn't have his memory, but what did that matter, against Madison's happiness. He could get a job – casual work at least – and a place in a hostel. He could still work with her, if she wanted, like all her other subjects. Go to the lab, by appointment, for an hour or so every week.

He folded his arms around himself, rocking forward. Who was he kidding? It wouldn't be enough. Now that he knew—

If he left, then it had to be a total break. He had to disappear. Out of the picture, for good.

Before someone else got hurt. Before Madison got hurt.

Lurid flares of violence and blood danced, hectic, behind his eyes. He put up his hands to cover them. He'd been shutting them out, fooling himself that the nightmare was a one-off, that the visions in it weren't real, lulling himself into believing that he could be normal. He wasn't normal. He would never be normal. Maybe that was best. That he never found out what his memory had contained. He had a chance of a fresh start. Madison had given him that.

If the best he could do for Madison in return was to protect her from himself, then that was what he was going to do

God help him.

CHAPTER 12

'So – she took him to a corporate fundraiser. Big fucking deal.' Vic slung the report on to the floor. 'Christ! It's been weeks. This is so boring. She hasn't found her way into his head yet and he hasn't found his way into her knickers.'

Alec retrieved the papers, studying the photographs of Jay and Madison partying. 'Don't be so impatient. We're still well on track,' he pointed out mildly. 'You know the plan, and the projected timeline, as well as I do. They have to build a relationship. We have to give them the chance to do that. I'm sorry if you find it tedious.' He tapped one of the pictures. 'There was some sort of . . . incident . . . at the reception. Albi spent a while in the ladies and soon after that they left. Might have been an argument.'

'Might have been an alien invasion. And if they're arguing then they're not jumping in the sack together.'

'Could be a sign of . . . emotional tension.'

'Emotional tension!' Vic scoffed. 'You've got to stop reading all that romantic novel crap – they

169

fight because they really want to fuck? Give me strength! You know what I think? I think that your old buddy's too bloody noble to jump her. That, or his dick's too limp, after what happened to his wife.'

'That's an accepted medical theory is it? Being involved with violent death causes impotence?'

'*Causing* violent death might.' Vic leaned over, with a grin that left his dark eyes cold. 'Remember – I got *you* sussed, sunshine. I know what this is about.'

'You weren't there.'

'If I had been, he wouldn't have got away with it.'

'Maybe not,' Alec said stiffly. 'We'll never know, will we?'

'Nah.' Vic lost interest in the tussle and began to punch buttons on his computer. The dormant video game that had been snoozing under the screensaver sprang to life. Vic began zapping aliens at lightning speed. After a dozen deaths, he flung the control down.

'We've got to do something.' It was almost a whine. 'This is *so* boring. And Kong isn't going to be a happy ape when he gets back from LA. Sod the timeline, he's gonna expect *something* to have happened while he was away. He said, right back at the beginning, that we needed to give them some encouragement.'

'I seem to remember you thought he was out of his tree.'

Vic made a rude gesture. 'So? I've changed my mind – now I agree with the boss. He's the ideas man. That's why he is the boss, and I'm just a lowly computer jock.'

Alec snorted. 'Modesty!'

Vic gave him the finger again. 'You know that for this to work they've got to be fucking like bunnies. You're the romance expert. What do we do?'

'Sex isn't necessarily required.'

Vic groaned. 'It's the best scenario, and it'll be a lot more fun than sending fake waiters to take pictures of fat faces getting fatter.' He tapped the slew of party pictures. 'This is *crap*. C'mon, Alec, think of something. What can we do, to give them a push?'

'Sightseeing?' Jay looked up from the book he'd just taken from Madison's shelf. 'You really mean that? Like the Houses of Parliament, Tower Bridge, that sort of stuff?'

'Why not?' Madison had thought of this idea in the dark reaches of a semi-sleepless night. 'We've been focusing on what's going on inside your head. Maybe we should start looking at the outside. You had a life – you lived somewhere, worked some-where. Maybe you went to the theatre, the opera. You must have had a favourite restaurant, bar, gym.'

'You want to wander round London until I spot something I recognise?'

'Hoping you would.' She spread her hands. 'Hoping we find a pattern.'

'London is a big place. And there's no guarantee that I even lived here.'

'We'll do New York next week.' Madison let her impatience show. 'You have a better idea?'

'No,' he admitted. 'Not unless you're prepared to start on the meds again. Thought not,' he added, when she shook her head. 'Okay. Let's go see sights. Can I borrow this?' He held up the book.

'Of course. What is it?'

Jay showed her the cover, marking the place with his finger while he scrabbled for something to use as a bookmark. Madison handed over an old envelope.

'If I remember rightly there are some good papers in there.' She took the book from him. 'A lot of these were given at a symposium I attended in Switzerland. Is this the one with,' she moved the envelope, 'mapping thought patterns?'

'That's what I was reading. It seemed to make sense.' He was frowning. 'Creed and Carver. They any good?'

'The best, Creed anyway. Or at least, he used to be. There was a big scandal. I think he's dead now.' She looked at the clock. 'We'll take the Tube into town. Any suggestions on where we should start?'

'Uh, no – your idea, you choose.'

★　　★　　★

Jay shrugged his way into his jacket. Neil's jacket, he corrected himself, and stared in the mirror, trying to read his own eyes.

Madison was next door, getting ready to visit tourist attractions, and he was – bottling out of his plans to leave. Too much of a chickenshit coward to walk away and not look back. If he had any backbone in him at all, he should already be gone. He'd made up his mind to it. And had the best part of a night's sleep as a result. Dreamless. Which had made him wonder – things he shouldn't be wondering. Hopeful things.

Then, before he could haul back his wandering resolve from wherever the hell it was scrambling off to, Madison had come knocking at his door, with an offer of breakfast and her crazy plan to do the town. She'd looked at him with nothing but enthusiasm in her face, and he hadn't had the simple guts to say no.

He couldn't leave. Not yet. He needed another day, two days, perhaps a week. He needed to prepare himself, prepare her. That was the official story. The other one, the one he wasn't taking out and looking at, was telling him, in a cold whisper, that he didn't have the strength. He needed one more try at the wall, when Madison was ready. Then he would go.

He picked up his keys and walked slowly to the door, knowing what he was doing was wrong. Forget the wall. He had to haul his sorry ass out of this woman's life. But not today. Today was too complicated.

173

One more day with Madison. He felt his heart kick. He could allow himself that. What kind of a threat to her could he be in crowded places, in broad daylight? After that – then he'd see. Something might happen today. He might see something he recognised. There could be a life out there somewhere, waiting for him.

Madison twirled in front the mirror, examining her reflection with a critical eye. The skirt was a gaudy mixture of silken scraps, floating mid calf over low-slung, slouchy suede boots. She'd paired it with a soft cream cotton top and a short jacket that matched the boots. She hesitated, looking back at the plain black trousers and white blouse laid out on the bed. This was a scientific exercise, not a date. She and Jay were conducting an experiment.

She hesitated. There was no reason that she shouldn't look good while they experimented. In fact the decision she'd made last night depended on it. She'd told Jay on that first night, when she'd strong-armed him out of the car park, that she wasn't afraid of him. Now she was going to prove it – to herself. She'd decided that at about 3 a.m.

She didn't need to hide behind a professional uniform. She could take care of herself. She wasn't going to let Jay become a threat. She wanted too much from him.

Jay regarded the pale, pillared front of the Opera House with a blank expression. 'I think I can confidently say that I have *never* been here. Even though I can't remember.'

Madison laughed. The sun was shining and the streets weren't yet crowded. They'd had a second breakfast at a pavement café in one of the side streets on the edge of Covent Garden, drinking cappuccinos and sharing a muffin and watching the world go by. At her suggestion Jay had piloted them across the Piazza with perfect confidence, confirming that he had visited the area before. Maybe this was the way to unlock memory after all. The safe way.

She brushed the thought away as a man walked past her, blocking the sunlight for a second. Something hissed inside her head, making her turn to look after him as he continued down the street.

'What is it?' Jay frowned.

'Nothing.' She shrugged. 'Next trick. Can you find the river from here?'

They wandered back though the old flower market. Buskers were working the crowd. A classical quartet played Mozart and a man with a unicycle juggled with clubs. On the corner a stark white figure, looking like a statue, stood motionless on a pedestal. Not even an eye blinked. The passers by jumped, then broke into applause when the white-faced, white-clad young man suddenly moved, handing a pretty girl a red rose from out of his sleeve.

Jay saw Madison looking towards a stall selling jewellery and steered her over to it.

'Why don't you get those?' He indicated a delicate pair of silver earrings, ivy twined around a dark green stone.

'Do you think they'd suit me?' she asked, picking them up. 'I've never worn anything like this.' She held them up to her ear.

Jay looked at the way the silver strands caressed the slope of her neck and took a firm grip on his hormones. *You started this.*

Shame and honesty and a bitter-edged sense of lost chances clenched at his stomach. Might as well come out and say what was in his mind. 'I'd buy them for you, but it's your money I'd be using.'

Madison looked from him to the earrings.

'It really doesn't matter—'

'It does.' He touched the silverwork. 'If you like them, get them.'

The stall holder had come over, to make a sale. Jay wandered away, looking at an adjoining table that had all sizes and shapes of kites. Madison studied his back. What he'd said – it had implied that he wanted to buy her gifts. She handed over her money, receiving the tissue-wrapped parcel in exchange. She shook off the idea. Jay wanted to repay her for what she was trying to do for him, that was all.

'Come on.' She put all the brightness she could into her voice. 'You still have to find the river.'

He took them down to the Embankment with no missteps. Madison clapped her hands, grinning. 'This is working!'

'Is it? We already know that my, what – semantic – memory is normal. Why is this different?'

'You are *such* a wet blanket. All right.' She put up her hands. 'It might not be different, but we know that things are moving inside your head. Something we see might be a trigger.' She stopped at his sceptical expression. 'All right! I'm fishing in the dark. It's a nice day. We're having fun. You got something against fun? Tomorrow I promise it's back to the drugs and the mind stuff. Today—' She looked around. 'How would you like to go on a boat?'

Jay tuned out the cheesy commentary from the amateur comedian in charge of the microphone at the front of the tour boat and concentrated on the sights and sounds of the river; and on Madison sitting beside him, laughing and pointing as they passed the Globe and then the National Theatre and slid on towards Westminster and the Houses of Parliament. The fragility had gone from her face and he could feel kinks in his own frame, layers of tension that he hadn't been aware of, melting away.

It was just a simple day out. Two people enjoying each other's company. Not quite a date. Madison was wiser than she knew. Walking the streets, and now being on the river, had stirred something for him. Given him a new sense of connection. He had lived here. Maybe not recently, but at some time. The memory was in there, frustratingly out of reach.

He felt the tension beginning in his chest, and breathed it down. It would come when it came. Force just drove it deeper.

If this had been his home once, then it could be again. He held the idea, feeling a quiver of anticipation. The sunlight and Madison beside him were making last night's fears look like shadows. The stuff of nightmares. He'd had one bad dream. Did that really mean he had to give up on everything, in a melodramatic flourish? Warmth was spilling though him. Warmth and certainty. He and Madison could do this. He would give himself more time. It wasn't cowardice. This was real. This was hope.

They were off the gangplank and on to the dock, caught up in the press of people alighting from the boat, when Madison felt it again.

The hissing sensation, inside her head.

Alarmed, she put out her hand to Jay, just as something hit her sharply on the back of the leg.

Then she was falling.

Towards the water.

CHAPTER 13

'*Jay!*'

The silent scream had his arm snaking out, around her waist, dragging her back before she skidded off the end of the dock. Off balance, he pulled hard. They ended in a tangle of limbs on the deck.

Jay lay winded, conscious of a sore spot on the back of his head, and the much pleasanter feeling of Madison lying on top of him. She was struggling to get up. The pleasure index escalated as she wriggled against his chest. People were flapping around them. Someone else had been brought down by their fall. A child was wailing in fright.

Reluctantly, Jay sat up, then swung himself to his feet, taking Madison with him. A uniformed official was shouldering his way through the crowd. Between them they ushered Madison, and the middle-aged woman who had also fallen, to a bench out of the crowd.

'I'm all right.' Madison's voice was barely a whisper. 'What about the other lady?' Shock and guilt were coming off her in waves.

'She's okay. A bit shaken up.' Jay kept his voice

low, rubbing the back of his head. 'Oh well, that's a myth. I thought if you banged your head, your memory miraculously came back.'

'No way.' She reached up to probe with her fingertips in his hair. 'Does that hurt?'

'Only when you poke it.' He shied away. 'What about you? Did you stumble or something?'

'I was hit. Behind the knee. It just gave out.' She stretched out her leg. They both looked at the red mark that would turn to a bruise in a few hours.

'It could have been someone with a walking stick, or a child maybe, with a toy.'

The official, having soothed the woman, came over to them with a worried expression.

'The young lady—?'

'Some slight damage to her leg. If you could call a taxi?'

'Certainly sir. The company, of course, will settle the bill.'

'This is not slight damage.' Madison leaned heavily on Jay's arm as she alighted from the taxi. 'I may have broken something. I could have sued that guy. Made big money.'

'You already make big money, drama queen! That leg is not broken. *You* know that. *I* know that.'

'How?' she scoffed.

'I can see inside your head, remember?'

The flustered look she gave him had him stifling a grin.

'You have *not* been inside my head. I would have known.' Her eyes widened in disbelief. 'I *would*!'

'It's okay. Don't panic.' He should not be teasing an injured woman. Except that it was fun.

'I'm not panicking.'

She lied. He was sure of it. He could see the pulse beating in her neck. Unless that was because she was standing so close to him. Her scent, soft lemons and honey, and her nearness were playing havoc with his blood supply. His heartbeat was all over the place and everything else was going south.

'Oh!' Madison's mouth formed a soft, round circle. Her eyes were dark, pupils dilated. She had to be able to see the hunger in his own eyes. Her weight was on his arm, her breath on his cheek.

'Dr Albi!' Scott was hurrying down the steps, smoothing back his hair. 'Are you hurt?'

Madison leaned back, letting cool air between her and Jay. 'Just a *slight* accident. To my leg.' She shot Jay a barbed look.

Scott was fussing. 'Can you manage the steps? Should I—?'

'No problem.'

Before Madison had any idea what was happening, Jay had her up in his arms. Stunned, all she could do was wrap her arms around his neck. A rush of chagrin and confusion had her struggling briefly to be set down as they reached the door, before an intoxicating rush of pleasure blotted out everything else. Breathlessly she stopped struggling to cuddle against Jay's chest. She could feel his heart thumping.

'No one has *ever* picked me up like this before.'

He was striding towards the lift. 'I don't suppose anyone dared.'

'Damn right. You think that makes you special, Jackson?' She looked up, eyes narrowed.

'Hell no! Loss of memory. No sense of danger.'

The lift doors closed slowly on the picture of Scott, gawping.

'Um – I think you could put me down now.'

'Start a job, finish a job. Keys?'

Realising the futility of arguing with a man on a mission, she handed them over. Jay dealt with the door and kicked it shut behind them, before putting her down, gently, on the couch.

'Why thank you, Rhett.'

'Don't mention it, ma'am. How bad is it – really?' He was bending over her leg.

'It's sore and getting stiff, that's all.' She looked up at him, smile wavering. 'I feel so stupid. I'm not really hurt. I want to laugh, but I nearly fell in the river. You stopped me falling in the river.'

Under Jay's astonished gaze, Dr Madison Albi burst into tears.

'Better now?' Jay offered Madison a fresh tissue. She nodded damply. Her eyes and her nose were red. She looked – adorable.

'Except for feeling like six kinds of idiot.'

'Shock does strange things to the system.' He

182

got up quickly. If he stayed here— 'Hot, sweet tea.'

He bolted for the kitchen.

As the kettle heated he leaned on the counter, head in his hands. The insistent ache of the erection that was pressing hard against his zipper made him grit his teeth. He had to be able to think his way out of this. The mind controlled the body. Rationally, he was attracted to Madison because of the situation they were in. She was helping him. She was the fixed point in a sea of blackness. Like a patient falling for his nurse, or a variation on the Stockholm syndrome – captive falling for captor. What he was feeling wasn't real. It was just hormone overload.

But if it was real—

He couldn't even shape the thought. There wasn't any place for him in Madison's world. He couldn't trust himself. He'd seen how vulnerable she was, under the poised exterior. She'd had too much pain and violence in her life already. He couldn't risk the chance that he'd bring her more.

Behind him the kettle boiled.

'Tea.'

Madison looked up, puzzled, as Jay put the single mug down in front of her. 'You're not having one?'

'No.' The coolness in his voice drew her brows together. 'If you're going to be okay, I think I'll head next door. Got a few things to do. You want me to call Sandra to come over?'

'No. The leg really isn't that bad. It's just a bruise.'

'Right then. Er – knock on the wall if you want anything.'

He turned abruptly and walked out, leaving Madison staring as the door closed behind him.

'What in God's name did you think you were doing?' Alec could feel the blood pounding behind his eyes. 'You tried to have Albi pushed in the Thames!'

'I arranged an *accident*,' Vic snarled into Alec's face. 'Gave your buddy the chance to play the hero. And it worked. He carried her into the building. Real loved up, so I heard.'

'Well, you heard wrong.' Alec's voice had descended into a hiss. 'Read this morning's report.' He waved the paper under Vic's nose. 'Albi spent the night in her apartment, Creed in his. Separate, alone, *not together*.'

'All right, I get the point.' The flicker of unease behind the hostility in Vic's face gave Alec a moment of satisfaction. 'You were doing fuck all. It was worth a shot.'

'Worth a shot! If Albi had gone in the river, if she'd *drowned*,' Alec drilled his finger into Vic's shoulder, 'you think the boss man upstairs would have thought it was worth a shot?'

'Get your hands off me.' The ice in Vic's voice brought Alec up short. He dropped his arm. 'Thank you.' Vic shook himself down. 'I told my guy something simple – maybe he wasn't careful enough. I'll deal.'

The concession, coming from Vic, was a major event. Abruptly Alec's anger dissolved. 'I guess I overreacted. Hell, you scared me.'

Vic waved the explanation away. A slow grin crawled over his face. 'It was a good idea. Admit it. Romantic. It could have worked.'

'Yeah, all right,' Alec agreed. 'It could have worked. You got any more bright ideas? Ones that won't get either of them dead?'

The sun was spilling in at the kitchen window and across the litter of coffee cups and papers on the table. Madison consulted her list.

'Engineer?'

'Nope.'

'Pilot?'

'No.'

'Lawyer?'

'*Please*.' Jay made an impatient movement. 'Tinker, tailor, scuba diver, steeple jack, female impersonator – is this getting us anywhere? Other than proving I have a deep-seated distrust of lawyers?'

'That could be significant—'

'Yeah, like maybe I'm an international jewel thief.'

'You could be a spy?'

'Why would spies dislike lawyers?'

Madison shrugged.

'For all we know, I could be the head of MI5,' he suggested tersely.

'I think they would have noticed you were gone by now and started looking.' Madison dropped her clipboard on to the table. 'This is a serious attempt to see if any of these jobs resonate with you—'

'Which isn't working.'

'There is that.'

His down-bent head and the slump in his shoulders made her hand itch to reach across the barrier of the table to touch him. She twirled a strand of hair round her finger instead. Sighing, she tried again. 'You had a *life*, Jay – you had a home, worked somewhere. There are people out there who know you. You have to have left a gap *somewhere*.'

'You figure we're going to find it out, sitting here? You know how many adults go missing every year? Just walk out the door, never seen again? Maybe I lost my job, my home, was bankrupt, in jail.'

'Does any of that feel in any way familiar?'

'Maybe – some of it, all of it. I just can't *tell*.' He gestured at the clipboard. 'This is a waste of time. The only place we have to look is inside my head. You *know* that.'

He hadn't raised his voice but Madison still had to stop herself backing away from him.

'We were getting somewhere.' His eyes pinned her. 'Before you decided on the embargo.'

'That was necessary. You were over medicated—'

'I accept that,' he interrupted quietly. 'My system

is clear now. Today is the third day. Do you want me to beg?'

'Of course not, but—' She shifted uneasily.

'But what? What's the problem, Madison?'

I'm the problem. I've lost my nerve again. I'm afraid to let you in. Afraid of what you might find out. I'm attracted to you. She shielded the thought fast, just in case.

'I just think we should give it a little longer. There are other things we should try—' she began uneasily.

'No!' Jay dismissed the idea with an impatient wave of his hand. 'None of this other stuff is strong enough on its own, Madison. It's not powerful enough to break through.'

He was baffled, frustrated, angry, but holding it in tight check. Realisation stirred something in Madison's head. She frowned as he got to his feet.

'Where are you going?'

'Down to the pool, to swim off some adrenaline. If you change your mind you know where to find me.'

Madison lined up the pencils on her desk. Then the pens. That was getting her workspace tidy.

When she turned out the pot of paper clips and began to sort them into piles, by size, she recognised displacement activity.

She should be working. With Jay. This wasn't about trying other things. It certainly wasn't about him being ready.

It was about her.

She didn't want to go into Jay's mind because she didn't want to risk the connection that might let him into hers. Which was stupid and unprofessional. Science was about calculations and outcomes and risk. Being human was about fear.

She prodded the clips into a pattern, square within square. Her whole life had been about overcoming fear. For some obscure reason the sensation that had rippled over her yesterday, outside the Opera House and again, just before the fall, rippled over her again.

She leaned down to examine her leg. There was a large bruise and her knee was a little stiff. The helpless feeling of falling and then of being in Jay's arms came back to her, vividly. One frightening, the other . . . not. She'd tossed and turned for a long while last night, thinking about Jay's arms. The feel of his body.

She let out a strangled groan as her abdomen tightened. Control. This was about control. Exercising it, giving it up. She and Jay were two of a kind. She'd seen him holding in his anger. There was something there. It had given her an idea. Was it possible for Jay's control to be working against him?

If she wanted to put that theory to the test—

She gathered the paper clips and put them back in the pot. She'd let excitement and enthusiasm run away with her scientific caution from the moment she met Jay. Totally reckless. So why spoil a perfect record?

She got to her feet with a sigh. Avoidance was futile. She knew what she had to do. Face up to the fear. Destiny was down in the basement, powering back and forth across the pool.

And looking pretty good doing it.

She stood in the doorway, indulging herself and calculating her next approach. The guy had the best shoulders she'd ever seen; not that she'd seen that many. And the rear view, when he hauled himself out of the water— She lost her place in her thoughts.

He turned, scooping wet hair out of his face, and saw her. He stilled, watching her, wary. She limped over, to hand him a towel.

'You said I should find you if I changed my mind.'

CHAPTER 14

Madison fiddled with the air-conditioning unit in the corner of her lab. The room felt chilly, after the warmth outside. She thought, with a pang, of the sunshine flooding in through her balcony windows. But she'd wanted, *needed*, the formality of the laboratory, the workplace setting. It wasn't working. She and Jay simply weren't connecting.

She gave up on the AC unit and went to sit at the bench. She wasn't sure what was happening. It was as if they were both holding back. Politely skirting each other, like guests at a dull party – but that couldn't be right. She knew what she was trying to hide, and that she was going to have to fix it somehow. But what could Jay be masking? She had to be projecting her own anxiety on to him. And it had to stop.

'I think we should call it a day.' She closed her file. 'Make a fresh start in the morning.'

Jay was sitting on the edge of the couch, arms braced, head down. She went over to him. 'Are you nauseous? Do you want some water?'

'A little light-headed, that's all.' His eyes, when

190

he raised them, were bleak. 'We've lost it, whatever it was.'

'Tomorrow will be different.'

'You think that?'

She shrugged, not wanting to lie.

'This is just an experiment to you.' His eyes had gone from cold to hot. 'It's my fucking *life*.' His hand closed on her arm. Even as his grip tightened she saw the horror fly over his face. He let go of her as if her flesh burned.

'Jay!' She hitched herself up beside him on the couch, making him turn to look at her. 'What is it?' A flash of intuition gave her the answer. 'Is this about that nightmare you had?' she asked quietly. 'What did you see?'

'I don't remember. It was just the drugs, an hallucination.'

There was a film of sweat on his forehead. He put up a hand to brush it away, shielding his face. She closed her fingers on his wrist, gently pulling his arm down. He'd lowered his head, still blocking her out. She shook his arm before she let it go.

'Look – it could be important. Tell me.'

She waited in silence.

There was uncertainty in his eyes when he finally raised his head. She could almost feel the wrench as he made the decision to give it up. His face was contorted in anguish.

'I was running, endless corridors – you know the sort of thing. Then . . .' He swallowed. 'There was a woman. I couldn't see her face, but I knew her.' His voice hitched. 'There was blood – all over my hands.'

Madison pulled in a long breath. 'You think you were responsible for the blood – that you hurt this woman? Someone you loved?'

'Not loved.' The denial came out hard. He shoved his hand into his hair. 'It could explain the memory loss. Killing someone. Pretty traumatic.'

'Killing?'

'Oh yes, definitely killing. Maybe your investigator should be looking at unsolved murders.'

Madison ignored the diversion. 'You couldn't identify the woman, but you knew her. How well?'

'Intimately. And don't ask me how I know that, because I can't tell you.'

Or wouldn't? She let it pass.

'There are all sorts of symbols related to dreams,' she began cautiously.

Jay gave her what could only be described as a dirty look. 'I don't care what it says in the textbooks. This blood *was* blood – and it was on my hands.'

'I don't go much for the textbooks, either,' she admitted. 'But when you dream about something, it isn't necessarily because you experienced it. Dreams don't have to reflect things that have actually happened.' She stopped, gathering her thoughts. 'When my parents were murdered—' she paused again 'They were shot. I didn't see it. I was in school on the other side of town, but for years afterwards I dreamed about blood – in their car,

192

on the pavement. What I was seeing wasn't real, just something my imagination had conjured up. I knew that, but it didn't stop the dreams, or take away my grief and guilt because I wasn't with them when they died. I kept on seeing it, *even though I wasn't there*. I think you're a man who values control, Jay. This may have been something like that – some event that was out of your control.'

'Something I should have been able to stop.'

'Something you *felt* you should have been able to stop. However unreasonable that feeling might be.'

She watched him turn the suggestion over. The ghost of a smile came up into his eyes.

'So – me being totally anal, this could be a kind of survivor guilt, stirred up by the chemical cocktails you've been serving me?'

'It's a theory.' She hesitated, then decided to take the plunge. 'Um, you know the control thing – I had sort of an idea. About the wall.'

'Yeah?' His eyes lit up.

'I wondered if your brain could be using that trait against itself, holding on to something so tightly that nothing is getting through. It's not very clear yet, and don't ask me how we undo it, because I really don't know.'

Jay shut his mouth on the question. 'You'll figure it out.' He gave her a long look. 'Thanks for sharing with me, about your parents – and I'm sorry. No child should have to go through that.'

'What doesn't kill you makes you strong. My aunt used to say that. I'm not sure if it's true.'

He was still looking at her. 'I think you know that it is.'

Strong. Jay thought she was strong. And this, after she'd cried all over him. If only he knew.

Madison curled her feet up under her on the bed. The blinds in her bedroom were open. The fine weather had broken. There was a storm coming in, rapidly, from the west. She could hear the rumble of thunder. A sheet of bright, white lightning cracked across the sky. Ten seconds later the deluge began. Madison darted up to fasten the windows. There was a light showing next door. Jay was still awake.

She paced back and forth, watching the elements. After a while she opened the window again, just a crack, letting in the fresh smell of the rain. Jay was just the other side of the wall. She leaned her head against it. Was he sprawled on the sofa, or on the bed? On his side, or on his back? Reading or watching TV? Still in his jeans and sweatshirt or—

Her imagination failed. The image was too much to handle. It had to be the storm, making her skittish.

Oh, really? The man is sex on legs. You want him. When are you going to deal with that?

Madison threw herself down on the bed. How could she deal with it? Sexy or not, Jay was off limits, out of bounds. But if she didn't deal with it . . . she was never going to get back inside his head again.

The truth hit her with an impact like the thunder.

The three-day breathing space she'd insisted on had actually been her own undoing. Out of professional mode, her awareness of Jay as a man had escalated, without her even realising it. Now, having to shield the way she wanted him, was sapping her focus when she entered his mind.

You can't do this and still keep secrets. If she wanted to help Jay, then she couldn't conceal any more. She had to give as much of herself as she could. *Except for that very last barrier of protection that you promised never to give up?*

She pulled her knees up under her chin, rocking. Her heart was racing so fast she was afraid something was going to burst. She forced herself to inhale and exhale. She could give, but would Jay take? There were plenty of signs that he was attracted to her. She'd caught a look in his eyes that was more than attraction, once or twice. A slow smile lifted the corners of her mouth. Was *that* what he'd been trying to mask? Was Jay hiding, just like she was? Because he didn't have a name?

Madison went very still. If they were to become lovers—

Had she simply been avoiding the painful need to confront her own feelings, cowering behind a barrier of her own making, clinging to the justification that desire was unprofessional and unethical? But she was confronting those feelings now. Where did that leave her professional values, if acting on desire was the only way to help Jay?

195

Surely trying to help him had to be the most important thing? And what about the woman in Jay's past – a woman he'd known intimately, who was tied in his mind to violence? She could be his wife.

Pain crimped through Madison's chest. The private investigator had turned up nothing. If there was a woman out there with a claim on Jay, she wasn't searching very hard for him. If Jay never recovered his memory, this woman, if she existed, would never get him back. Maybe she didn't want him?

Madison curled her fingers. Jay and her? If they became lovers it would be a brief liaison, purely physical. Was it worth the risk? She held the thought in her mind – a purely physical affair, without ties? No strings, no pain?

Time out of time.

Did she really believe that they'd reached an impasse; that *this* was the only way forward?

Certainty flooded through her. She did believe it.

She jumped off the bed, needing to move, before her nerve failed her. If it didn't work, if she'd read Jay all wrong – then tomorrow she'd have to hand in her notice at work and book herself a passage to the other side of the world. But right now—

She crossed to the mirror, smoothing down her hair and undoing the top button of her blouse. Surveying the result, she undid another. With hands that shook, she reached for the perfume bottle and spritzed it into the air, walking through the cloud of vapour. The scent of lemons settled around her.

She was as ready as she was ever going to be.

The door to the studio looked more forbidding than she remembered. She could have brought the key, but that wasn't how it should go. She put her finger on the bell and pressed, then pressed again. If Jay was asleep in front of the football with the volume turned up—

Her finger was hovering over the bell for the third time when she heard sounds of movement. The door swung open silently. No ominous creaks, no warning groans. Jay stood in the frame, backlit by the lamp in the tiny hall.

He looked – gorgeous. Even better than she'd dared imagine, he was without his shirt. The soft light etched out smooth skin and sculpted muscle. Low-slung jeans clung to lean hips. His hair was flopping over his face, and his eyes were wide with surprise.

'Madison?'

She had to go up on her toes to reach him. Cupping his face with her hands, she caught him just right, with his lips parted, about to ask her what was wrong. She closed hers over them, boldly sliding in her tongue.

His mouth was hot, sweet, rich and completely beautiful. With a butterfly after-kiss to his lower lip, she stepped back.

He looked – like a man struck by lightning.

Madison picked up his hand, pressed her key into it and turned away.

Jay stood, body burning, vocal chords paralysed, and feet too heavy to lift from the floor. All he could do was watch as Dr Albi *sashayed* back to her own apartment and shut the door with a quiet click.

CHAPTER 15

It took nearly an hour.

For the first ten minutes Madison's body was vibrating too much for her to think straight. After that, she watched every minute as it crawled around the clock face, her limbs slowly turning to ice. She was composing her letter of resignation in her head and booking her passage to Borneo, Madagascar, anywhere where she wouldn't have to face Jay again, when the key finally turned in the lock.

He'd put on a shirt and his hair looked damp.

She couldn't breathe.

'Uh, did you—' He waved the key. 'Did that . . . just now . . . did that just mean what I think it meant?'

It needed two attempts. Even then her voice came out light and scratchy, not the seductive purr she'd aimed for. 'Depends what you think it meant.'

'That you . . . that you and I . . . Madison, did you just – uh – invite me to go to bed with you?'

'Er . . . yes – only if you want to.'

He closed the gap between them in two strides.

This time the kiss was fully interactive. Madison could only bring herself to disconnect when her lungs were screaming for air.

'I waited a whole hour!' She scrunched her hands up into his hair. It *was* damp. He'd showered. The stubble she'd felt when she'd ambushed him in his doorway was gone, too. He smelled of soap and clean cotton. 'What took you so long?'

'You come over in the middle of the night, turn a guy to stone, so that he can't move, and then you ask that?'

'Stone.' She rubbed against him, exploring. 'I like it.'

'Madison.' It was a low-pitched groan. Very gently he pushed her away from him. 'I want you. You've proved that – but how can we?' His voice hitched. 'You don't know who I am, what I am . . .'

He looked down at her, helplessly. When he'd recovered the powers of movement and thought, he'd stood on the balcony, in the rain, with the key in his hand, reciting the hundred reasons why he couldn't use it. He kept on reciting them in the shower, and as he shaved. He'd sat in the dark, praying to whatever god was in charge of willpower. He tried reason and he tried restraint. The taste of Madison's mouth kept wiping out his concentration.

It had been a very full hour.

He'd decided to use the key to tell her that he couldn't possibly accept her flattering offer. He had to save her from herself.

And then the sight of her had annihilated almost every speck of resolve and left his head empty and his body stiff with need. He was totally, utterly lost. But he still had to try.

'Have you thought about this? Really thought? You know nothing about me. I could have anything in my past—'

She put up a hand to cover his mouth. 'I know enough. I'll argue ethics if you want, but I'd rather make love.' He felt her chest rise and fall, sharply. 'This shouldn't be happening,' she went on. 'I have no business coming on to you when I'm already messing with your mind. The answer to your question is yes. I have thought.' She rested her hand against his throat. 'I've been . . . scared of what seemed to be happening to us. Not scared of *you*,' she qualified hurriedly as his muscles jerked under her hand. 'I don't . . . let . . . people into my life easily, but you're already there. You've given me your trust.' She looked up, her gaze steady and clear, into his eyes. 'I'm repaying that by asking for your body, as well as your mind. If you tell me that I can't have them both, then I'll live with that, and be exceptionally embarrassed in the morning. But it has to be because you don't *want* me. Not because you're afraid of what you might have been or done. That's a shadow.' She grinned. 'You know, if you're going to avoid sex until you get your memory back – you might be looking at a very long period of celibacy.'

She ran her fingers down the buttons of his shirt.

'As you've already admitted that you want me, it's rather a done deal. But I'd like to hear you say it. Again.' She smiled up at him encouragingly.

Jay moaned softly. Any ground he still held had just crumbled under his feet. 'I should never have come in here, should I?'

'It's a little late to think of that now.' Her eyes were shining.

'You know very well that you had me at hello.' The very last shard of resistance shattered. 'I want you.'

He bent his head and kissed her, long and deep, then rested his forehead against hers. 'You realise that for all we know, I may never have had sex before.'

'An interesting but unlikely hypothesis.' She grinned wickedly at him. 'And one that I'm fully prepared to test until destruction.'

'You have definitely done this before.' Madison flopped on to her back, panting. The man could kiss. They'd established that. *Oh* boy, *can he kiss.* She would willingly spend the rest of the night just kissing, but if she could have the caress of his hands as well . . . The taste of his mouth and the feel of his hands, roaming her body, exploring her skin. And hers on him. But there was more . . . So much more . . . The thought of what else they could do, of what came next . . .

Her stomach shuddered, her breasts throbbed and her toes curled. All at the same time. Her head was spinning, and they'd barely started. She stared around, blinking. Clothes seemed to be strewn in heaps on the floor, plus a pillow or two. She had only the dimmest awareness of how they'd made it to the bedroom. Every nerve in her body was pulsating in tingling life. Jay's mouth. His *hands*. 'Definitely,' she confirmed.

'I'm not sure.' Jay crawled across the bed to her, rolled her on to her side, and began kissing his way, delicately, up her spine. She squirmed as his fingers probed gently between her legs, into the sweet, pulsing heat that was driving her. Gasping, she bucked into Jay's palm as she shot to an abrupt, body-racking climax, with his mouth against her neck. *This . . . has never happened . . . like this . . . before . . . So . . . intense . . . So . . . so . . . fast!*

Then she was on her back again, his tongue doing incredible things to her breasts and travelling down.

'Jay. I can't . . .' Breathing was a waste of energy that could be expended elsewhere. She had to keep remembering to do it. Her hands convulsed over Jay's back and dug in. 'I need you, inside me. Now . . . please, now.' She was ready to beg and she didn't care.

The world stopped as Jay went still.

'What is it?' She struggled to sit up. Jay's face was anguished.

'I can't – protection – I don't have anything.'

Relief made her oxygen-starved head spin. She'd thought – never mind what she'd thought.

'The bedside drawer—' She leaned over, tipping out the contents of the box and finding them, thankfully, still within date. Jay reached for the packet, but she pushed his hand away. 'I can do this.'

Jay held his breath as her hand stroked over him, letting it out in a long shudder as she accomplished her purpose. She was kissing her way up his belly now, eyes on his face. Laughing. *Wicked angel.*

He'd spun her under him before she'd realised that he'd moved. For a second he just let his weight rest, relishing her softness. Then he eased her thighs apart. She was drenched, so ready for him that it almost hurt. He brushed her lips with his and slid into her.

She was tight, as he'd expected. Her breath hissed and he held himself still, afraid of hurting her. She put her hand up to his neck, looking into his eyes. No doubt there – only wonder and welcome. Something under his ribs kicked and his breath stuttered.

'You are so beautiful.' He brushed her hair back, cradling her face with one hand, as he thrust in deeper.

Madison closed her eyes, then opened them again. She wanted to see Jay's face as he took her. He'd filled her, stretching her in a way that had taken her to the edge of fear, just for a second. But then he'd held still. Let her accept the feel of him, the possession.

When the sweetness of surrender washed over her, he took his rhythm and began to move.

'Go on.' He'd captured her hands, urging her up, eyes on her face. Intense, dark, totally focused. On her. 'Fly. Fly now.'

With his name in her mouth she came again, shuddering, as he plunged deep inside her and spun out over the edge.

Madison lay staring at the ceiling, too sated to move. Jay was somewhere to her right. She could feel his arm, just brushing hers. All her other nerve endings were popping and fizzing and generally doing an after-sex tango. She was wiped out, but she really needed to ask . . .

'*Jay?*'

There was a slight rustling beside her, then nothing.

'*Jay?*' Sharper. '*You okay?*'

A colourful buzzing in her head. Rainbow. In pieces. Smug satisfaction oozed through her. She'd done that. The shades coalesced as he got himself together. It took a moment.

'*Er . . . depends how you define okay.*'

'*Uh, like how far did the Earth move?*' As if she didn't know.

'*A . . . considerable distance. May have rolled right over. Damned if I can tell.*'

'*Me, neither.*'

205

'*Glad about that.*'

Silence.

'*Er . . . Jay . . . Can we do it again?*'

'*Now?*' Panic was blue, shot with silver. She managed to get her fingers to close over his.

'*Not* right *now.*'

'*Thank the Lord.*' There was dark warm around the words. Desire already stirring again. So much for panic.

'*Only I think I may have missed a few of the finer points.*'

'*It all felt pretty fine to me – but yeah, some of it was . . . kind of a blur.*'

'*Again, then?*'

'*Later.*' Pause. '*You're cool with this? Talking without speaking, I mean?*'

'*No problem. Not sure how well anything is working right now – voice – whatever.*'

'*Mmm.*' He was drifting away from her. She let him go.

She woke at 3 a.m. with his hand on her throat.

He'd pushed her hair aside, nibbling at the sensitive skin behind her ear. She stretched lazily back into his embrace.

'Mmm.' A shiver of pleasure ran through her.

'You said you wanted to do it again.' His hand slid down to her breast. 'Never disappoint a lady.'

Daylight was filtering under the blinds. Madison lay in the half-light, admiring the rise and fall of

Jay's chest. He'd put back the weight he was meant to have and now that long, hard body was just about perfect. She wanted to touch. Taste. Learn. She'd already discovered a couple of places that could turn Jay's eyes smoulder hot. There had to be more. Wowee! The long legs and the curve of his hip, the line of his back. She ran the tip of her tongue over her lips.

She knew the moment he was awake, from the shift in his breathing. She looked up to find him watching her. 'Hi.'

'Hi.' He reached out a lazy arm and pulled her over to snuggle at his side. She buried her nose in his skin, snuffling, making him laugh. He hitched her up, so that she was against his shoulder. She rested her head, remembering the scar along his ribs. She nudged him, running her hand down his side until she found it. 'What was this?'

'A misunderstanding over possession of a shop doorway in the Strand and a sharpened dinner knife.'

She winced. 'Nasty.'

'Luckily the knife bounced off the bone and the guy behind it passed out at the sight of the blood. Knocked his head on a piece of masonry. I ended up taking *him* to A&E. Got him within sight of the door, and then scarpered.'

'You're making that up.'

'The truth. I swear.' He raised his hands to cross his heart. Madison twisted his arm, looking for the other scar, running her fingers over it. There was a ridge under the skin, just below the elbow. Jay squinted at what she'd found. 'I have no idea what did that. It was there when I woke up.'

'I thought it was laser work, perhaps to remove a tattoo, but it feels wrong. There's a bump under the surface.' She guided his hand. 'Feel it?'

'Yes.' He turned his palm, catching her wrist. 'But I'd rather be feeling you.'

CHAPTER 16

Madison moved about the lab, humming a tune under her breath. When Jonathan wandered in he gave her a quizzical look. 'For a woman with dark circles under her eyes, you're sounding very perky this morning.'

'Circles?' She flew to the mirror that hung beside the door, then threw the cork from the top of a test tube at Jonathan. He caught it, grinning. 'So, who was it interfered with your beauty sleep, sweet pea?' He struck his forehead with his hand. 'Silly me. I know who.' He dragged out a stool and sat on it. 'What I really mean is, how often?'

'You are disgusting, Jonathan Ellis, and I wouldn't tell you, even if I knew what you were talking about, which I don't.'

Jonathan unravelled this with delight. 'More than once then, goody.'

'Goody?' Madison gave him her best sneer. 'What sort of an expression is that?'

'I got a whole pack of them: bravo, tush, bother.' Jonathan was unperturbedly cheerful.

'Is there a purpose for this visit? Other than being annoying?'

'No.' Jonathan recognised, with regret, when the teasing had to stop. 'Although, while I think of it – Mitch wanted to know if you were satisfied with the blood analysis that was done in the other test centre. If so, he's going to make a case to he-who-should-be-obeyed-but-isn't-if-we-think-we-can-get-away-with-it to give them the contract. The other lot didn't show up again twice last week.'

'I think they were okay.' Madison tried to recall. She had a guilty feeling she'd shoved the blood test findings into her briefcase, with only a cursory glance. 'Tell him a provisional yes, and I'll let him know, soonest.'

'No rush.' Jonathan unwound long legs from the stool. 'Mitch is off until next week. E-mail him when you have a moment.'

'Jonathan guessed.' Madison was sitting on the edge of the couch, monitoring Jay's reactions to the drug she'd just injected.

'Is that good or bad?' Jay's lids were drooping. His pupils had gone wide and dark. Madison made a note. 'Bad, unless you happen to like heavy-handed jokes. You ready?'

'Mmm. All yours.'

She sidled gently into Jay's mind, and felt his welcome enfold her as intimately as his body had enfolded her for most of the night. The thought made her breasts tingle. She sensed an answering ripple of awareness in him, and stifled a smug grin. An increased pressure of her hand on his reminded them both to concentrate. Jay sighed, giving her a hot, hungry shiver of pleasure before he relaxed into the drug, compliant and passive, and let her work on unpicking the wall.

She'd been careful to limit her expectations, a long-learned skill, to avoid disappointments, and so she was pleased and encouraged by the results. Freed from the need to dissemble she was stronger and surer of what she was doing. The wall was still in place, but she knew that it was thinner and less resistant to her.

Something in Jay's head was definitely shifting.

Jay turned on his back in the water, floating, looking up at the ceiling. It was painted to look like blue sky and clouds. His conscience was telling him that he should be feeling guilty for ignoring all its arguments, and making love with Madison. His body felt too damn good to care. He'd done what he'd promised himself he wouldn't do, and the roof hadn't caved in. Though maybe it should have. He still didn't know who the hell he was, and whether what he was doing was right.

But it feels right, on so many levels. Hah! Since when did you have levels?

After a moment puzzling that one, and coming up with the usual blank, he rolled over and began to power up and down the length of the pool. All he had was gut feeling, and Madison's judgment.

Which was as good as anything he knew. It was all he had to trust.

Madison stopped, attention drawn by the window display in the small boutique. She glanced guiltily up and down the street. She was meant to be in Amersham to use the cash machine, not to shop. The display of lingerie was as enticing as it was pricey. She fixed her eyes on a dark saffron camisole that was sheer, except for the heavily embroidered band across the breast. The matching panties lay beside it.

She could go in and ask. Maybe they wouldn't have her size.

Forty minutes later she emerged from the shop with an embossed carrier and a much lighter wallet. She wandered along the pavement, swinging the bag. She was a woman, buying underwear, to please her lover. It felt . . . it felt as if something was opening up inside her, something that had been closed for far too long. She and Jay were finding pleasure together – it was a normal, human impulse to want that closeness. When Jay discovered who he was, then the world would come crashing in. They'd have to deal with reality, whatever that turned out to be, but in the meantime – they weren't hurting anyone. *Except perhaps each other?*

She shut her mind on the thought.

The minute she opened the door, she knew things weren't as they normally were. The scent of something delicious came to meet her from the kitchen, closely followed by something that looked delicious, in a blue shirt and black jeans, with a glass of wine in each of his hands. She grinned when she saw the apron she'd bought in Florence, emblazoned with the city's coat of arms, tied firmly around Jay's waist.

'Nice day at the office, dear?' He came towards her.

'Mmm.' She reached up to kiss him, running her tongue over his lower lip. 'You taste good.'

'Thank you.' He fended her off by putting one of the glasses into her hand.

She sipped, and considered him over the rim. 'Playing hard to get, Jackson?'

'I have something on the stove.'

'I'm sure the thing has an off switch.'

'No,' he objected. 'Eat first, then you can seduce me.'

'Huh!' She turned on her heel, heading for the bedroom. 'You should be so lucky!'

'I devoutly hope so.'

She was still giggling into her wine as she emptied the contents of the carrier on to the bed. She slithered out of her clothes at lightning speed, and into a wisp of dark green silk that had provocation sewed into every one of its embroidered seams. A two-minute search of the wardrobe produced a pair of spike-heel mules in almost the exact same shade. She slid them on, ran her tongue over her lips and sauntered out.

The effect, when she slinked into the kitchen, was everything she'd hoped for. Jay's spoon completely missed the saucepan he was aiming for, and clattered to the floor. His jaw wasn't far behind it.

'Dr Albi!' He didn't have any more breath to protest as she backed him against the work top and fastened her mouth on his. Her hands were under the apron, undoing his belt. His were on the sensitive skin of her back, exposed by the low-dipping silk. Then they slipped lower to cup her buttocks. The groan, deep in his throat, quivered in her mouth. His erection ground into her, hard, as he clamped her against his hips.

She reached around him with her free hand, to turn off the master switch to the cooker, squashing her breasts against his chest.

'Anything in here that's going to overheat?'

'Only me.'

Without warning he hauled her up and over his shoulder, barging open the kitchen door with one arm. She squirmed, upside down and dizzy, but loving the feel of his encircling arm and his back, powerful under her body. His palm was on her bottom, holding her firmly in place, hot and possessive through the silk. Then his fingers drifted into a tormenting caress, making her bite her lip.

'We were supposed to be having a civilised, home-cooked dinner. I got recipes from Sandra.' The aggrieved note in his voice, as he tumbled her on to the bed, didn't match the smoulder in his eyes. His mouth, on hers, was blistering. His fingers teased her nipples, wicked and demanding.

His shirt was already a heap on the floor. Everything else followed, with his mouth barely leaving hers. He pulled her over his lap, caressing her intimately through the silk. The fabric was damp and clinging, from his mouth and from her own wetness. She came, with a shuddering leap of pleasure, spread across his legs. With no respite, he pushed her upwards again.

She was gasping as he tipped her over, on to the bed, slithering her out of the wisp of silk. He rolled her on to her back, taking her in a single wild surge that flung her over the brink again. She dug her nails into his shoulders as he climaxed, pumping violently, inside her.

She was deliciously, bonelessly limp. Jay's legs were tangled with hers. She unravelled one and held it up. The green mule was still in place. She flexed her instep.

'Fuck-me shoes.' Jay had revived and rolled over far enough to watch her.

'They certainly worked,' she agreed. 'And I have a whole cupboard full of them.' Jay groaned and put his hand over his eyes. She kissed her way up his arm and along his wrist. 'We don't have to try them *all* out tonight.'

'That's a relief.' He slid his fingers apart to look at her through them. 'Can I go and finish cooking dinner now?'

'Go! I'm done with you.'

He swatted her on the bottom as he got off the bed to look for his clothes. She hooked her leg around his and overbalanced him, back on to the bed beside her. 'On second thoughts . . .'

He'd set out candles in the tiny dining room, off the kitchen. The garlicky chicken with roasted tomatoes and peppers hadn't suffered from the delay. Madison savoured the food and watched Jay in the soft light of the flames.

'What?' He reached out and caught her hand.

'Nothing.' She curled her fingers into his. 'This is good.'

He understood that she meant more than the food; she could see it in his eyes. He pressed a kiss into the palm of her hand.

'No regrets?' There was an almost imperceptible catch in his voice.

'Absolutely none.' The shadow that crossed his face had her tightening her hand over his. 'And that holds, whatever happens, whoever you turn out to be.'

'That's too big a promise.'

'I don't think so. We'll deal with who you are when we find out,' she said softly. 'And we will find out. That's a promise too.'

Madison woke in the dark, to find Jay tossing and turning in agony beside her.

'Jay!' She rolled over, to pin his shoulders and

prevent him thrashing his body against the night-stand. His hands came up to manacle her wrists, making her gasp as his fingers tightened. 'Jay!' His eyes were open, rolled back in his head. Her voice wasn't reaching him. Panic spiked adrenaline into her bloodstream. In desperation, she all but hurled a probe into his mind. There was a concussion like a firework and Jay was lying under her, limp, awake and blinking. She sat up, rubbing her arms.

'What the hell was that?' His voice was painfully hoarse. He cleared his throat and grabbed her hand, seeing the marks of his fingers. 'I held you. I hurt you.' He dropped her hand and rolled on to his elbow. He was shaking. 'I knew what was happening. I could hear you and feel you, but I couldn't get out. I was locked in my own head. I couldn't move, except to grip your arms.' He sat up with a jerk. 'Oh God! I could have broken your wrists.'

'No, you weren't squeezing that hard. Look, it's fading already.' She showed him. She stroked her hand slowly down his chest, soothing him, until she felt some of the tension dissipate.

'Can you tell me what you saw?'

'There wasn't anything. Just that I couldn't move. I was awake, but paralysed. I couldn't open my eyes and yet I knew they were open.'

Madison was checking his vital signs. 'Rapid pulse, that's all. Do you have pain anywhere?'

He shook his head and made to get off the bed, reaching for his clothes.

217

'Where are you going?' Alarm flashed through her.

'I'll sleep next door. I'm not safe to be with you. I could really hurt you.'

'I don't think so.' She put a hand on his arm, felt him flinch under her touch. 'I think you're more in danger of hurting yourself. Look at me.' She pulled him round to face her. 'I think that tonight is a sign that we're getting close. You know what I said about control? You were paralysed because of that. Your mind is desperately trying to help itself.'

'You really believe that?'

'I do.'

'And you'll still be thinking it when you wake up with my hands around your neck, not your wrists.' He stood, yanking his jeans off the chair. He had them on and zipped by the time Madison got off the bed.

'Jay.' She grabbed his hands. 'Please.' She tugged at him, relief bubbling when he let her turn him. 'Trust me. And stay with me. You're not a threat to me.' She looked up into his eyes. 'Provided you've told me the truth. There wasn't anything else in that dream?'

'Nothing.'

The torment in his eyes wasn't lifting, but somehow that gave her courage. 'I know now, if it happens again, not to touch you. You won't hurt me. Don't be alone, Jay. I know what alone is like. It's cold.' Tentatively she put her arms around

218

him. The rigidity of his back muscles resisted her for a moment. Then he lifted her hand and put it to his lips. 'You're better to me than I ever deserve.'

'You deserve more than you allow yourself.' She pushed him back to the bed, pushed him down on to it, closing her mouth over his. She kissed him until his body responded, relaxed and then tightened, and they both dropped out of space and time.

Madison tapped at the computer keys, glancing at her watch. It wasn't late, but the lab was unusually quiet. People were already winding down and taking leave, in preparation for the late May bank holiday and the long weekend ahead. Tomorrow night the lab would shut for four days. Which was why she really needed to clear her backlog of weekly returns, before someone noticed they were missing. *Plus you're not ready to go home, not yet.*

She pressed the wrong key and cursed as a line of figures disappeared. She concentrated on re-entering them with her tongue clasped between her teeth. She and Jay weren't avoiding each other. They were just . . . she didn't know what they were doing. *Going through the motions?*

Working in the lab, day-to-day, everything passed as normal. They were making a little progress, but it was slow. She thought she was beginning to see a pattern in their sessions, but she wasn't certain yet. Or what it meant.

Making love – she caught her breath. That was the only time that the pain went out of Jay's eyes. And then afterwards he'd lay immobile beside her. Willing himself not to sleep. Keeping himself out of the dreams. And she wanted so much to help him—

She cupped her chin in her hands, forcing herself back to the figures. There was an uncompleted line in the spreadsheet. She'd rifled through the papers in her tray before she realised what it was, the blood test results that were still in her briefcase. And the case was – on the backseat of the car. She glanced at the window. Rain was beating against the glass. She wasn't going out in *that* to find the case and then come back again. She filed the incomplete return and shut off the machine.

'Rain's stopped.' Madison stood at the balcony door, watching a small boy disconsolately kicking his ball about in the open space across the street. His mother was sitting on a low wall, watching. She raised her hand to wave. 'Why don't you go and give Callum a game before bedtime?'

'His or mine?'

Madison turned from the window. Jay was sitting on the floor, knees up, arms crossed around them. He'd given up all pretence of reading the book that was open and lying on the rug beside him. They hadn't spoken for at least an hour. Now, when he raised his head, the dark shadows under his eyes were plain.

'You could have an early night,' she suggested gently. '*We* could.'

Jay shrugged. She saw his shoulders tense. 'I'm not sleeping here tonight.'

Madison took a breath. 'Fine, if that's what you want.' She watched him out of the corner of her eye, saw him start.

'Are you humouring me?' His head went back, eyes glinting.

'I'm agreeing to what you want.' She walked back into the room. 'You need sleep, Jay. You're not getting any rest, here, with me. You want to sleep next door, sleep there. Just *sleep*.'

She flopped on to the floor to sit in front of him, knees up, mirroring his pose. A mocking half-smile pulled his mouth out of shape. 'Soothing the crazy man.'

'I can think of another soother.' She slanted her head. 'You up for it?'

'What do you think?' The stiffness in his neck had relaxed a fraction. He put out a hand and she clasped it, palm to palm.

Madison weighed up options. She could gloss over this, take Jay to bed, give him the respite he desperately needed. Or she could confront it, head-on. *Nobody runs forever.*

'You don't worry about whether you might hurt me when we make love – it's not even in your

221

head,' she said abruptly. 'No fear at all. So why is it different all the rest of the time?'

There was shock in his face. She saw him searching for his response.

'Making love with you . . .' The look in his eyes made something hot quiver over her. He shook his head. 'It's the only time I feel whole. Like it doesn't matter who or what I am.'

'It doesn't. You're beating yourself up, Jay – because of something that might not exist.'

'But what if it does? No, listen—' He held up his hand against her objections. 'What's going on in my brain, we're sure it didn't get there by accident.'

'So?'

'So – someone put it there. We've never really talked about why.' She could see the restlessness and the torment in every line of his body. 'What if I got away from somewhere? Somewhere *really* spooky? And the barrier, whatever it is, has been put there to block something – something grotesque.' He shuddered. 'I could be anything – a psychopath, any kind of deviant, a killer, child molester—'

'That's why you've stopped playing with Callum.' She covered his hands with hers. 'Don't torture yourself, Jay. You saved that child.' She shook him gently. 'If you had instincts to harm anyone, don't you think they'd still be there? Just like the ability to read or to recognise a tune?'

He rocked back, away from her. 'But what if

they've been deliberately excised? As a kind of cure? And we're trying to undo that process. If we open the box – God alone knows what will crawl out.'

'You want to stop?'

'No!' His whole body went rigid. She watched the battle wash over his face. Conscience, over need. This was the bedrock. What this thing was really about. She had to lean forward to hear him, he spoke so softly. 'Everything rational in me says that we should stop. That I have to learn to live like this.' He looked up, eyes anguished. 'I don't have the courage to do that. I want . . . to go on. If you will? We just have to be . . . careful.'

'So – you want me to tie you down, like Frankenstein's monster, before I go to work on you?'

'It's a thought.'

The pain in his eyes shifted slightly as she smiled into them. She put all she had of reassurance into that smile. She had to get this right.

'Jay, whatever happened to you, it is not down to you. Someone put it there. I'm surer of that every day. And I don't think it was because you're dangerous. This thing, if it's constructed the way I think it is, uses your own mind against you. I don't believe the brain would naturally work against itself in *that* way. You don't feel like a psychopath, or any of those other things, and you don't act like one. If that was true, it wouldn't just

223

be a matter of blocking something. It would mean replacing one character with another, a whole new mindset. There are people out there who are good, but not that good. Trust me on this.' She risked a look up at him, through her lashes. 'Tying you up sounds like an interesting proposition, and maybe we can explore it some time, in a recreational context . . .' She waited until she saw the corner of his mouth twitch. 'I'm not afraid of you, Jay. I don't think that you're going to turn into a werewolf when we find out what's going on in your head, but if it will make you happy, I promise to keep a gun loaded with silver bullets under my pillow. First sign of trouble and you get it – straight through the heart.'

He was smiling now, despite himself. 'You are seriously disturbed. You know that?'

'Of course I am. It goes with the job. Now get out there and let Callum beat you at football, before it gets dark.'

Madison sat on the bed. Her limbs were in the lotus position but her mind was way out still, churning information. She was sure that Jay wasn't crazy or violent. *And we'll just forget the bit in the alley when he came at you with an iron bar, shall we? Pretend it never happened?*

Giving up on the yoga – she didn't practice enough to be any good at it – she unwound her limbs. There had been violence in Jay that night, with reason, but it wasn't there now. She examined the thought. That was the truth. She knew the difference. Jay was the victim. She had to believe that.

She headed for the shower.

CHAPTER 17

The CEO was leaning against his desk when Alec entered the room. The sight of the short-sleeved sport's shirt, straining over bulging biceps, and the baggy pants in hallucinatory tartan, put a brief hitch in Alec's step, but he recovered quickly. Not quite quickly enough.

'It's a holiday weekend, Calver.' The CEO held out his hand for the report. 'Is this good?'

'I think you'll find it so, sir.' Alec handed it over with a tight smile.

'The ape plays golf!' Vic's eyes bugged for a moment, before he began to laugh. When he almost choked, Alec thumped him between the shoulder blades, slightly harder than was necessary. Recovering, Vic gave him a sharp look. Alec met it blandly.

'Networking,' he suggested. 'Lots of contacts, male bonding, all that crap.'

'Anyone who wants to bond with the ape—' Vic let the idea hang. 'He reads what's in that file, he's going to be too happy to see the little white ball. Are we geniuses or are we geniuses?'

'The critical part is still to come,' Alec cautioned.

'Yeah, I know. Don't sweat it.' Vic waved away the warning. 'Look – the thing with the river, I was in too much of a hurry. I admit it.' He grinned as Alec blinked. 'Watching them tiptoeing around each other was so bloody frustrating. And don't pretend you didn't feel the same.' He pointed a finger at Alec's chest, before curling it into a fist. 'But now we have Creed in Albi's bed – without us having to give them any more help. Plus the good doctor is what – this much?' he held up a closely aligned finger and thumb, 'away from opening the box.' He leaned back in his chair. 'We've got the sex confirmed from the gossipy cleaning woman at the apartments. Real hot sex, and I mean *hot* – lingerie, the lot. That van driver from the florist is seriously good.' He gave a crack of laughter. 'And wouldn't the guy in Dubai be surprised just how often he's sending his wife flowers!'

Alec's head jerked. 'Is he going to suspect—'

'Nah!' Vic shook his head. 'Left his credit card details, didn't he? For regular *bouquets,*' Vic drawled. 'He's just gonna be pleasantly surprised how far his money stretched. Hope the little woman is suitably grateful, when he finally gets home.' Vic leered, rubbing his hands, well pleased with himself. 'The mind stuff – Albi's lab results – they're coming in fine, too – the computer I'm monitoring and the ones your bloke in the test place is intercepting.'

Alec pursed his lips. 'I'm not sure that's going

227

to be available much longer. We may have to make other arrangements. It looks like the test place is having its contract terminated.'

'Not surprising, with half its staff on the take.'

'One technician, and a delivery driver,' Alec objected.

Vic shrugged. 'Whatever. Not really a problem, old son, Albi's *doing* it. Doesn't need us to interfere, just to keep our eye on the ball. And she's two weeks ahead of your best-case scenario. You *said* she was good.'

'*He* said she was good,' Alec corrected. 'She was on the original shortlist, but he interviewed Gina first.' A small spasm crossed Calver's eyes.

'Messy, man,' Vic sympathised. 'But now you have me on the case.'

'Yes.' Alec looked at him. Cold. 'This has to go down perfectly. We bring them in, the moment that Albi makes the breakthrough, day or night—'

'Hey, it's going to take them a little while to figure out what they've got.'

'Not long,' Alec objected. 'And when they do, they'll run. So we have to be there. We have to know, and we have to be ready. Whatever you need to put in place, you do it – now.'

'Don't get your knickers twisted. It's all in hand.' Vic looked at his watch. 'Even as we speak.'

'Dr Albi?'

'Scott?' Madison tucked the house phone under her chin, as she dumped out the contents of her handbag on the kitchen table. Pouncing on her car keys, she tumbled everything else back in, with a quick swipe off the end of the table. 'I'm just about to leave. What is it?' She picked up a toffee that had rolled away, unwrapped it, one-handed, and popped it into her mouth.

'Just checking, Dr Albi. I have the maintenance company here, for the heating systems? They need to check the block – some of the units may have a faulty component. Will it be okay to let them in later?'

'Yeah.' Madison sucked the toffee. 'Whatever you need.'

'This is ridiculous.' Madison picked her way carefully around the trestles and pots of paint. 'Who the hell authorised this, and why wasn't I told?'

'Woo – scary Dr Albi, out for blood.' Jonathan moved her out of the way of a man carrying a ladder. 'Run and hide.'

'Fool!' Madison punched his ribs. 'I just think I should have been warned that someone had decided that my office should be painted.'

'It's not just you – they're all over the place. Apparently maintenance arranged it for the long weekend, when the building was empty, but someone put the wrong start date in the order – today not tomorrow. No one's admitted to it yet – but when the director finds out who it was . . .' He made a graphic throat-slitting gesture. 'And talking of the devil.'

Madison swung round, to see the director approaching them.

'I know.' He held up his hands. 'Heads will roll, I promise you that. In the meantime,' he cast a rueful look round, 'I think that the only option is to break for the holiday,' he consulted his watch, 'six hours early. I have complete assurance from the maintenance manager that everything will be kept secure and protected.' He glared at a workman, whistling by with a bundle of dust sheets under his arm. 'But you'd better check over and lock up whatever you need. Then you can go. Have a good one.'

'Have a good one?' Madison looked at Jonathan as the director strode away.

'He has teenage children,' Jonathan reminded her. He was grinning. 'Well, you heard the boss. Let out of school, a whole day early. Cornwall, here I come. Surf's up, man!'

Madison intercepted Jay as he walked towards the lab from the bus stop, drawing into the kerb to pick him up. He looked at her questioningly as he slid into the car.

'The decorators are in – so we're out.' She peered through the windscreen. The sun was burning off early morning puddles in the road. The weather forecast was for a fine weekend. 'I think it's an omen. How long will it take you to pack a bag?'

★　★　★

'I could drive,' he suggested, half an hour later as they pulled out into the line of traffic. 'If I had a driving licence. Also if I knew where we were going.'

'Wait and see.' She was grinning.

He settled back in his seat. 'No fair. Clues?'

'Mmm. They speak another language, but you don't need a passport.'

'Good thing, as I don't have one of those, either.' He squinted at the approaching motorway sign. 'You do have an actual destination in mind? One that isn't going to be booked solid?' he queried, as she looked sideways at him. 'Bank holiday? Fine weather?'

'Don't worry. We'll have the place to ourselves. I promise.' She took her eyes off the road to look over at him. 'This is time out, Jay. No work, no mind reading. Just you and me. Deal?'

He reached to take her hand. 'Deal.'

'I think it should be down this way.' Madison turned the sketch map sideways, keeping it out of Jay's sight. She'd given up on the satnav after it triumphantly deposited them in a deserted car park.

'You *think*?' Jay asked suspiciously, tweaking the map out of her hand. 'C'mon, I've figured out from the bilingual road signs that this is Wales. You may as well tell me the rest.' He studied the map. 'Guillemot Cottage? Right. No – *turn* right – there, just past the sign that says Tenby.'

They travelled along a winding B road for a couple of miles.

'We must be getting nearer.' Madison rolled down the window. 'I can smell the sea – and there are gulls.' She turned the wheel, and they bumped into a rutted farm track. 'If I'm right . . . I've never actually been here before. Yes, there. See the sign? Oh! Wow!'

She brought the car gently to a stop and they sat in silence, taking in the view.

The cottage was small, white painted and half-covered in wild-looking clematis, just coming into flower. Beyond that there was only the sky and the gulls. Below the headland a narrow sandy bay stretched in a nearly perfect arc. A dark straggle of seaweed marked the extent of the tide, and a large rock broke the line of the outgoing surf.

'It's beautiful.' Jay exhaled. 'Who does it belong to – Jonathan?'

'It's mine.' She folded her hands over the wheel, still for a moment. 'It was part of my legacy, from Neil. He left me everything, and the deeds for this were amongst the papers. He completed the purchase the day before he died. He told the solicitor it was for a wedding present. I've never really understood . . .' She put her hand to her head. 'There are no memories here, his or mine, but he wanted me to have it. Chose it for me. I've never been able to get it together to come here before – a couple from Tenby take care of it for me – but now it's right for us to be here.'

She could feel the tension that she hadn't known was gathered in her neck and spine, beginning to unravel, like yarn. She opened the car door.

'Time to explore.'

CHAPTER 18

It was a simple two up, one down, with a long, narrow hall, a lean-to kitchen tacked on at the back of the house and a bedroom and bathroom under the eaves. The furniture was sparse but comfortable: two huge leather chairs and a wide, well-stuffed sofa, that looked far too big for the narrow cottage door. There were rugs and throws in cloudy pastels, and cushions embroidered with Celtic symbols. Local art hung on the walls, pictures of birds and old castles. The kitchen was fully equipped. Pots and pans were stacked on a shelf over the cooker. Plates and dishes displayed on a narrow dresser. There was no dust anywhere.

'Look.' Madison guided Jay to the kitchen window. Outside was a pocket-handkerchief garden, south facing and sheltered by an old apple tree and a wall that looked a lot more ancient than the building. An old wooden bench stood on a minute square of lawn. Late bluebells were flopping beneath bushes that were sharp green with new leaf. A ragged gap in the wall, where stones had collapsed inwards in a heap, gave a theatrical view of the sea.

The water mirrored the blue of the sky. It was covered in white caps where currents raced and the breeze whipped up the foam.

Madison put out her hand to find Jay's. He pulled her into his arms and kissed her, deep, damp and hot.

'You know what they say? About making a house a home?'

'What?'

He whispered into her ear, biting her lobe as she giggled. Her hands were busy already, untucking his shirt. He kissed her again, hard. When his fingers pressed between her legs, she was already moist. She squirmed as he stroked her, her hands cupping his buttocks through the rough denim of his jeans.

'Madison.' He was breathless, kissing down her neck. The other hand was skimming under her sweater. She moved, so that her breast fell into it, and purred when his fingers circled and teased. 'If you want to go upstairs—'

She shook her head, grinning, and licked his lower lip. Enjoyed the reaction. 'Here,' she murmured. 'Now.'

She grabbed his shoulders as he boosted her on to the stout cupboard beside the sink; then her fingers were on his zip and tugging. He groaned against her mouth. Her skirt had ridden up, almost to her waist. Pushing the silk of her panties aside and parting her thighs, he was inside her in one thrust. She blinked, swallowed, smiled, then wrapped her arms about his neck and her legs around his hips. For a single, intense moment she hugged him close, before easing away, her palms resting on his chest. He dipped his head, to taste her throat, as her head fell back. Squirming, laughing; shivering when his lips drifted towards her breasts, she lowered her hands to delve under his shirt, murmuring in frustration as her fingers tangled in the fabric. Buttons popped and she had what she wanted. Slick, smooth male flesh. Satisfaction hummed in her throat as she ran her hands, then her tongue, over his chest.

'You make me crazy.' He could barely get the words out. She was so wet, hot, enclosing him. He moved inside her. Clinging to him, she matched his thrusts, body bowed back against his supporting arm.

She came in a shower of sparks, feeling him spill, hot and urgent.

He was still holding her, face buried in her hair. 'The place is ours now. All ours,' she whispered, as she touched her lips against his shoulder.

Madison dropped a loaf the size and shape of a small cartwheel into the rustic basket she'd picked up at the door of the shop. One side of the shop was a bakery, the other a greengrocer and general store. She consulted her list, picking up a packet of butter and a carton of milk from the chiller cabinet. There was a display of Welsh cheese. She pointed out the piece she wanted cut to the woman behind the counter. 'What's in there?' she asked as Jay ambled over with a bulging paper bag.

'Welsh cakes.' He showed her the flat, sugar-dusted circles. 'What's Bara brith?'

'I think it's a kind of tea bread. Looks good.' She added the rich-looking, fruit-studded loaf to the rest, handing Jay the basket to go and pick apples out of a wooden crate beside the door.

In the end they bought the basket, too. They were loading it into the car, parked on the outskirts of Tenby, outside the city walls, when Jay's stomach grumbled loudly.

'What do you expect?' he defended himself. 'All I've had since eight is a plastic motorway sandwich and a couple of Welsh cakes.' He touched her arm. 'Forget cooking. What's that way?' He pointed towards a narrow, sloping street.

It was still early, but several of the eating places along the harbour were already open for business.

The restaurant they chose was small, dark and intimate, decorated with a hodgepodge of old fishing nets, glass balls, and sepia photographs of fishing boats. The tablecloths were red-and-white checked gingham and none of the chairs matched each other.

They shared a quart of mussels followed by locally caught fish, with a mountain of crisply fried chips.

'Pudding?' Jay looked hopefully at the list of home-made ice creams.

'You have one. I'll have a taste.' In the event, he fed her almost half of the bowl of strawberry and raspberry ice. 'Now I really can't move.'

'Yes, you can.' He pulled her to her feet. 'I want to walk along the harbour and then maybe up to the castle.'

The beach was emptying, as day visitors made for their cars, but many of the shops were open, catching some evening trade. As they wandered along, hand in hand, Madison felt a deep content-ment stealing over her, and a small shadow of regret.

'What is it?' Jay stopped, leaning over the harbour wall to look at the boats.

'Just thinking – of Neil.' She looked out over the darkening sea. 'Letting him go.'

Jay shifted to stand behind her, hands firm but gentle on her shoulders. She rested her back against his chest.

'It was the right thing to do, to come here,' she spoke softly, covering Jay's hands with hers. They stood for a while, watching the bustle of boats that were taking fishing parties out for an evening's sport.

Madison was the first to move. 'Do we really have to walk all the way to the castle?'

They did, and were coming back again by a different route, one that led through a tangle of narrow-fronted shops, when Madison stopped in front of a multi-paned window, displaying candles and wind chimes and painted glass. A soft, sweet scent blew out from the open door.

'I'd like to get some candles, for the bedroom.'

Jay shrugged, manlike. Madison stuck out her tongue and slipped through the beaded curtain into the shop, coming eye to eye with an enormous ginger cat, sitting on a shelf, just inside the door. She took a surprised step back. A woman with long blonde hair and an armful of bracelets got up from a small table, with a swish of skirts, smiling apologies.

'Sorry about that. He likes to sleep high. I didn't realise he'd got up there again. Go on, Humbug, move.' She prodded the cat. 'You have a perfectly good basket on the top of the fridge,' she told him.

The cat yawned, taking his time to jump down and stalk into the back quarters.

Jay had come in through the curtain. The woman looked at him, seemed to decide that they were a couple, and turned to Madison. 'What can I show you – or would you just like to look round?'

'Candles, please.'

'Scented?' The woman indicated a display. 'My sister makes them. The lavender comes from Caldy Island, where the monastery is. The other flowers and herbs are locally gathered, when she can get them.'

Madison chose half a dozen, in varying sizes and scents. The woman began packing them into a parcel, while Madison browsed the rest of the shop.

There were Celtic talismans and crystals amongst the glass and pottery. Jay, at her shoulder, picked up a squat jug, in the shape of a frog, and offered it to her. Shaking her head, laughing, she turned away, glancing down at the table where the woman had been sitting.

A Tarot pack lay spread out in a cross shape. Rich, bright colours shimmered. Madison recognised the Hanged Man and the Queen of Cups. The woman had finished the parcel.

'Would you like—' She nodded towards the cards.

'Oh . . . No . . . I don't really believe. I'm a scientist.' *Yeah, I read minds.*

The woman smiled. 'No worries. A lot of people come in and are nervous of asking.' She gave Madison a considering look, frowning slightly. For a second Madison thought she saw sympathy and understanding in the dark eyes. Then, whatever it was, it was gone.

'You don't have to believe in something for it to be true,' the woman continued softly. 'The future is the future. Even science doesn't have it all.'

Gently, she took Madison's hand, studied the palm. 'Strength. You will need it. And your man, too.' She nodded towards Jay. 'You will be strong for each other.'

The woman looked up, into Madison's eyes. 'This one's a keeper, hold him.' It was barely a whisper. Madison wasn't even sure she'd heard it. Then the woman smiled and folded Madison's fingers into a fist. 'Enjoy your stay and be lucky.'

She turned away as the cat reappeared in the doorway, dragging something behind him that looked suspiciously like a side of fresh salmon. 'Humbug! What the hell have you done now?'

'That was – a bit weird.' Madison scrubbed her palm down her skirt. The skin was still tingling.

Jay stepped sideways to let a fisherman, loaded with tackle, squeeze past them on the narrow pavement outside the shop. 'Local colour, for the holidaymakers. What she said, it didn't bother you, did it?'

'No, actually what she said was quite apt.'

'But suitably cryptic.'

'I suppose.' She wound her hand into Jay's. 'It's human nature, isn't it, to want certainties?' She shivered as cold fingers walked up her spine.

Jay hugged her to his side. 'Right now I'll settle for a future that has hot coffee and a comfortable bed in it.' He yawned. 'Does crossing the Severn Bridge give you jet lag?'

He changed his mind when he saw the fair. It was a tiny travelling set up, in a field by the side of the road, gaudy with lights and cheap music.

'You want to stop?' She was already slowing the car.

'Don't you?'

They wandered amongst the stalls and side-shows, clung together, screaming, in the waltzer and hung against the night in the miniature Ferris wheel. Madison shook her head when Jay pointed at the candy floss. Together they rolled coins at a target. Madison's eyes bugged when the stall holder handed over a large stuffed toy.

'Be grateful it wasn't a goldfish.' Jay dumped the beast in the back seat when they got back to the car. 'Is it a mouse, or a squirrel?'

'Mouse, I think. Different tail.'

Jay leaned over the seat to look. 'I think you're right.'

'Where the hell am I going to put it?' Madison was giggling as they fell into the living room of the cottage.

'How about here?' Jay arranged the mouse in the window seat. It sprawled, with its head on one side, grinning at them.

'Next you'll be wanting to give it a name.'

'What I want,' he grabbed her around the waist, dragging her down on to the sofa, 'is you.'

He was pulling off her shoes, easing his fingers over her heels, making circles on the instep. Hot desire was spiralling up her legs and finding its target, in a way that made her gasp. Jay's clever, caressing hands were travelling now, up her calf, around her knees. She couldn't breath. When he looked up, his eyes had a devilish light in them. When he reached the inside of her thigh, she thought she might melt. She was drowning, incapable of saving herself. He was laughing as he abandoned the torment and moved to pull her into his arms. She felt the vibration of his chest. *Sexy as hell.*

Jay inhaled Madison's scent, and felt his mind go flat. He wanted to throw his thoughts into her, as well as his body, but the shred of sanity that remained knew that it was wrong. He held on to his control, feeling her tremble under him. Then he let her take him, drawing him down until he couldn't tell where he ended and she began.

In bed, they made love again, lazily, by the light and scent of the candles, and then lay in the dark, listening to the sound of the sea drifting in softly through the open window.

'Glad we came here?' Madison propped herself on her elbow, fiddling with Jay's hair. His body was relaxed, his eyes half-closed.

'Uh-huh.' She had to bend to hear the mumble.

'Go to sleep.' She kissed his cheek.

'G'night.'

Madison settled a pillow behind her head. She'd extinguished the candles. The curtains were open, but it was too early for the moon. Jay was a dark shape in the bed beside her. His breathing was deep and regular. The faint, lingering scent of lavender and thyme drifted over the room. A bitter-sweet ache was radiating out from somewhere, deep under her heart. This evening had been . . .

Her mind hesitated, unable to put it into words, but knowing that special wasn't enough.

She breathed deeply, staring into the darkness, clear eyed.

A keeper. To hold. The fortune teller's words whispered in her head, crystallising what had been there for – minutes, hours, days?

She was perilously close to falling in love with Jay.

CHAPTER 19

'What do you mean, they've gone?' Alec forced himself not to grip the phone hard enough to shatter it. 'Where?'

Vic's voice was close to a whine, justifying himself. Alec cut in, brutally. 'I don't give a shit about painters and maintenance men. Where the fuck are they?'

He began to pace, kicking a coffee table aside when it got in his way. Panic was swelling inside him like an inflating balloon, shoving air out of his lungs. He had to struggle not to fling the phone after the table. 'What did the guy at the apartment block say? Word for word. Just for the weekend – you're sure of that? Definitely coming back? On Tuesday. And there was nothing in the apartment or the office to indicate that she'd broken through? They weren't running?'

The negative from the end of the phone had him breathing a little easier. 'Do what you can to find them. Call me if you do. Call me anyway. Two hours. Pump the concierge at the apartment block again. And the woman, Albi's cleaner. Does she work in the building on Saturday? Then send the flower delivery guy, she gossips to him. If she knows anything, he'll get it. I don't care,' he yelled into the phone. 'I don't *care* if it's a holiday. I don't *care* if we sent flowers yesterday. Order more. I'll pay for the sodding bouquet. I'll pay for the whole bloody flower shop! And go back to the lab. Trash Albi's office if you have to. Whatever it takes, just do it! If you don't find them? We sweat it, until Tuesday. And you might want to pray.'

'This is . . .' Madison stopped, chest heaving, to look out from the cliff walk. The long expanse of sand below had the colour of spilt champagne. The sea was coming in lazily, making patterns like lace, before running back down the gentle slope of the beach. 'Can we get down?'

'I think so.' Jay put his arm up to shield his eyes from the bright sunlight. 'That way.' He pointed to the steep path to the shore.

They walked along the edge of the sea. Madison caught her breath at the contrast between the cold of the water, washing over her toes, and the hot sun on her back. They watched the gulls and ate a picnic of fresh rolls and ham and local cheese, sitting on a sun-warmed rock. There were seaweed-crusted rock pools, with limpets and small crabs. Far out, the sea raced and boiled. The red flag, alerting bathers to the currents, flapped in the sudden breeze.

The way back to the car, once they had climbed

up again from the beach, was mostly downhill and easier.

They were on the last descent when the distant sound of gunfire split the stillness.

Madison jumped, her heart racing in panic as she turned to Jay, wide-eyed.

'It's okay. There's an army range.' He gestured to a notice, half-hidden in long grass. 'It's not close. The wind must be blowing this way.' He grinned. 'Don't worry, I'll throw myself in front of the bullets.' Jay grabbed her hand, pulled her to him and kissed her. His hands cupped her buttocks, provocatively.

'Jay!' She was laughing and trying to put a warning note in her voice, all at the same time. 'Not now, and not here!'

'Why not?' He nuzzled into the V of her blouse. 'Alfresco sex—'

The sound of a polite throat clearing, behind them, had them breaking apart, giggling. A group of serious walkers, booted and weighted down with equipment, filed decorously past them.

'That's why not.' She softened the words with a kiss. 'Look out, more coming.' They stepped off the path again to let the next party through. Madison rested against Jay, looking up into his face His eyes were clear, the colour of the sky, and the wind had ravelled his hair into a tangled halo.

It would be so easy to love this man.

She held the thought for a heartbeat, then let it go.

They had this time, and the sun, and the air, and the sea birds calling above.

Keep it simple. Don't let him know, not when you don't really know yourself.

Jay lay on his back, on a tiny square of grass, watching the patterns made by the dappled sun through the branches of the apple tree. Behind him, in the cottage, he could hear Madison pottering in the kitchen. They were meant to be exploring another castle this afternoon, but somehow his bones seemed to have melted. He didn't want to move. Maybe he'd just lie here, relaxed, for the rest of the day. At peace.

You can have this, if you want. He went totally still at the thought. *You just have to begin again. If you have Madison, why do you need your memory?*

His throat had gone dry. For a moment, even in the sunshine, darkness threatened to close over him, and then he was through it, blinking.

He could call it all off, now. Live with what he had. Stop looking for whatever was in his past. Find a job, start a new life.

With Madison

The prospect glittered in front of his eyes, like the sun on the sea. *Do you really need to know? When you could have all this?*

He sat up slowly. Could he ask Madison to give up on all the work she'd done? To wait for him, while he put some sort of life together? Some sort of future for both of them? Was he that bloody arrogant?

He rolled over, thinking that maybe he was. *Maybe?*

She was coming towards him, long and slim and beautiful, with light catching her hair and a smile to break hearts.

Especially his.

'You're very quiet.' Madison nudged him with her foot. She was sitting on the bench, watching him sleep on the grass, except that he could tell that she knew he wasn't really asleep. A small frown creased between her brows.

'Just too lazy to talk.' He heaved himself up, to look directly at her. She'd agreed to pass on the castle, with some relief, he suspected. She was looking at him now with a puzzled expression. He could feel words clogging on his tongue. Should he tell her what he'd been thinking? Ask her? *Can we stop looking for who I am? Would you give it all up, for me?* He opened his mouth, and lost his nerve. She was waiting for him to speak. 'You want to walk down to the bay?' was what came out.

The way down was steep but the perfectly empty sweep was worth the effort. They walked beside the water. Jay looked back at their footprints in the wet sand. So close. Meant to be together? 'Madison . . . if I was to—'

She turned towards him, face alight. 'Did you see that? I think there's something out there.' She pointed out to sea. 'Some sort of big fish – or maybe a seal? If we climb up there, on that rock, we can see better.'

They decided, in the end, that it might be a seal.

Going back, the ascent to the cottage demanded enough breath to keep conversation to a minimum. By the time they reached the top, Jay had made a decision of sorts. He'd keep his mouth shut, at least until they were back in London.

Don't wreck something this good.

'How about dinner and a movie tonight? I think there's a cinema in Tenby.' Madison handed him a beer and clinked ice into a glass of mineral water for herself.

'You mean a proper date? Scary movie, popcorn, necking in the back row?' He grinned. 'You're on. How do we find out what and where?'

'There might be something on the tourist information website. I'll get the laptop from the car.'

'I can go.'

'No, it's okay. I want to look for my other sunglasses. Go sit in the garden and drink your beer.' She shooed him out, laughing.

Madison opened the boot and pulled out the computer. Her briefcase shifted, banging her hand as she lifted the laptop. A brown envelope was poking out of the pocket on the side of the case. She was stuffing it back in when she realised what it was. The missing test results.

She vacillated for a moment. She'd said no work this weekend. Wednesday would be soon enough to enter them. On the other hand, it wouldn't take more than a second and the job would be done. And as she could never seem to remember to do it when she was actually at the lab—

She pulled the results sheet out of the envelope.

'Madison?' Jay came around the side of the cottage and found her, sitting on the back seat of the car, with the door open. 'What is it?'

'This.' She put a piece of paper into his hand.

'Hey, I thought we had a deal? No work?' Her expression stopped him. Something cold nudged his heart. 'Okay. What am I looking at?' He could see it was lab results, lists and graphs of chemicals and percentages.

'Here.' She pointed to a name at the bottom of the list. 'These are your test results from a few weeks back. I've been monitoring the residual levels of chemicals in your blood.'

'And?' The concern on her face sent a spike of alarm into his guts, though the percentage against the compound was reassuringly tiny. 'What is it? Arsenic? Radioactivity?'

'It's something very experimental. They're testing it, in Switzerland.' She looked up. He saw fear in her eyes. 'It shouldn't be there, Jay. I never gave it to you.'

CHAPTER 20

'Simplest explanation is that it's a mistake.' They were sitting in the garden. The paper lay on the bench between them. Jay tapped it. 'You said you'd never used these test people before. They're not reliable, that's all. You've had other results, before and since, from your regular test place, that show nothing. These guys have transposed a symbol, mixed up results, something.'

'No.' Madison's hand spasmed into a fist. 'This isn't just something you pick up at the pharmacy, Jay. It's a specialist compound. As far as I know it's only available from one source. It isn't like anything I've used. From what I've read, it wouldn't have the same effect at all. Quite the opposite, in fact. The pharmaceutical company is trialling it as a way of blocking negative emotions, for people in extreme mental distress.' She picked up the paper. 'The amount here is negligible, but the residue of this stuff stays in the body for up to twelve months. That's one of the problems they're finding with it.' She stared at him, eyes troubled. 'I think this is what was used to make the barrier,

Jay. And someone has been tampering with the results at the lab, to stop us finding out.'

'Staring at it all evening isn't going to change anything.' Jay prised the paper out of Madison's grip and steered her firmly indoors towards her jacket and the car keys. 'We had a date, remember? Dinner? Nightlife in the fleshpots of Tenby?'

He held his breath. His immediate impulse, to leap in to the car and head back to London, to hammer on doors, demanding answers, had lasted only a second. The sight of Madison's pale, worried face, as she studied the results, had brought him up short. Sanity rushed back in an instant. They had a breakthrough, a small fragmentary clue, that was all. A clue that might lead to greater things, if it was followed up with care and discretion. And that wasn't going to be achieved by kicking down doors on a holiday weekend.

At the moment, all he could do was reassure Madison and try to wipe away that frown. 'Dinner?' he prompted again. 'We can give the fleshpots a miss, if you don't fancy them.' He was rewarded by a weak grin. He put his hand under Madison's chin and gently raised her head, brushing a kiss across her mouth. 'Forget it.'

Her hand quivered in his for a moment when he reached to take it. Then she let him lead her out to the car.

Dinner, of an enormous platter of seafood, accompanied by a well-chilled rosé wine, leached some of the tension out of her nerves. Jay's refusal to endlessly analyse what she'd discovered was both frustrating and curiously soothing. In the end she gave in and did her best to put the whole thing out of her mind.

The night was warm. They wandered the narrow streets of the small town, hand in hand. Many of the shops were still open. Soft light, the occasional burst of music and racks and rails of stock spilled into the street. The pubs and bars were doing good trade. Jay piloted Madison around a clutch of tables set out on the pavement, looking enquiringly at her and miming raising a glass. She smiled but shook her head.

Their meandering progress took them towards the harbour. It was getting dark. Lights from boats anchored out in the bay glittered over the water as the craft bobbed in a soft swell. Madison leaned into Jay as they stood near the harbour wall. They eventually turned inland again, walking along a familiar street.

The shop where she'd bought the candles was at the end. It was closed. Madison peered through the thick glass of the windows. There was no sign of life, no lights or movement. Not even the cat stirred behind the panes. For some reason the silent shop sent a shiver running through her, until Jay wrapped his arm around her shoulder and pulled her close to the heat of his body.

'Tired?' Jay backed her gently against the kitchen door, corralling her with an arm on each side of her body. His kiss was deep and questioning. Madison shook her head, clinging to him, her hands twined around his neck. Without speaking he lifted her into his arms and carried her upstairs. They made love slowly and silently, to the background noise of the sea.

The next day it was raining. The sky was a solid, dense grey and water ran in sheets down the windows.

Weather to match his mood.

Jay stared out of the kitchen window, watching the deluge against the glass, hoping that Madison would sleep for a while longer. He pushed his hand through his hair. He'd done a pretty good job last night, diverting her thoughts, and his own, from those blasted test results, but today . . .

Why the hell did she have to find them here?

And where the hell do they take us?

Unease, like a queasy mist, floated through his blood, blood tainted by a drug that wasn't supposed to be there. He clenched his teeth on the sudden urge to scrub at his arms.

You can't scrub this away – this is what you are. What you're meant to be.

A faint, distorted image, that might be the reflection of his face, floated against the backdrop of rain. He put out a hand to trap it, knowing that all he would encounter would be cold glass. That was him – trapped behind a wall of glass, watching himself, noting his emotions – horror frosted over with a strange detachment.

Where you're meant to be.

He pulled his hand away, as if the glass burned. 'You're just bloody confused and not thinking straight.'

Abruptly he turned from the window to open the fridge. Breakfast. Keep busy, keep the questions at bay. Keep it light; don't let Madison worry over it.

Above all, don't let Madison worry over it.

Focusing on the plash of the rain on the windows he set coffee to brew. When it was done, he carried it upstairs. Madison was still sleeping. Her hair made a sprawled halo on the pillow. Spiky lashes flickered against sun-kissed skin, delicately dusted with freckles. Jay's heart turned over in his chest, with an emotion he couldn't name, as he set down the steaming mug and crept back downstairs.

'Forecast says clearing later.' Jay looked up from frying bacon.

Madison stood in the doorway, in her robe, clutching the empty mug. A perky dragon grinned at him, coyly, from under the handle. Jay didn't need to read her mind; her face told him everything she was thinking.

'Hey.' He put out a hand. 'You have to stop brooding about it. You said yourself the results were tiny. Your testers probably thought they were too small to bother with. These guys were just more efficient. Yeah, I know.' He answered the objection in her eyes. 'Yesterday they were unreliable.'

257

He brought the pan to the table and dished bacon on to a plate, slid an egg beside it, guided Madison to a chair and pushed her gently into it, putting a fork into a hand. 'Eat.'

Relief lifted his heart when she smiled wanly and began cutting bacon. He reached out and touched her hand. 'Don't worry any more about it. It's a holiday, nothing we can do until the lab reopens.' He fixed his eyes on her face, intent, his hand moving up to stroke her hair. 'We always knew something put the wall in place. Now we know what. That's a gain. You'll figure out a way to use it. The rest—' He shrugged. 'It still could be some sort of mistake. If it's not, then now we have somewhere to look. We can find out who could have got access to this stuff, and who in the lab might be working with them.' He saw the pain in her face, at the thought of someone in her own lab betraying her. 'There might not be anyone involved from your place. It only has to be one person,' he reassured quickly. 'Delivery man, messenger, someone like that. This could be a real, practical lead. Something we can use – but *not* today.'

She put down her fork with a sigh. He could see her turning over what he'd said, and accepting it. He let out a pent up breath.

'How did you get to be so – rational?' She picked up the fork again.

'In the circumstances, it's the only way to be.'

He sat down opposite, to tackle his own breakfast.

This thing is ongoing.

With an effort he shut his mind to the implications that were swirling there – someone watching him, watching Madison. Someone who knew what they were doing. Someone who wanted to stop him finding out what had been done to his memory? *Someone who knows who you are.*

Madison's eyes were on him, huge in a strained face. Bitter regret, and a thread of fear, were suddenly overwhelmed by a quick, savage burst of anger. It caught him like a blow, under the ribs. All she'd done was try to help a stranger – now she was in the middle of God knew what.

He had to blot all that out of his mind, in order to blot it out of hers, until they could do something about it. Until he could make a plan.

He poured coffee, thinking of a diversion. 'There's applewood in a bunker outside the back door. We could light a fire. Assuming you've had the chimney swept recently, that is.'

'Yes and yes.' She smiled, making an effort. His heart lifted a fraction. 'Sounds good. And I promise not to brood.' She answered the question he hadn't asked. 'There's a Scrabble board in the cupboard next to the fireplace.'

'Oleaginous? That's really a word?'

'Means greasy.' Jay flipped a tile into place. 'What am I going to do with a Z and two Ys?'

'Nothing.' Madison pushed the board aside and crawled across the sofa to him. He welcomed her into his arms as she nestled back against him, watching the fire. The scent of apple smoke hazed across the room. Madison lay back against Jay's protective warmth, watching the pictures in the flames. Fairy castles and hills and fugitive faces, forming and shifting and crumbling to ash. The only sound was the ticking of the grandmother clock and the drip of rain on the windowsill – and Jay's soft, snuffling snores.

She turned in his arms, half amused, half indignant. He didn't stir. He was sound asleep. Mouth open. She looked around for something to drop into it, then decided it was too cruel. She shifted the book of research papers that Jay was still reading, to stop it digging into her leg, and rolled sideways to look at him.

'Anyone home?' She put a gentle finger on his chin, tracing the faint stubble, letting the roughness trickle desire into her. If she was to wake him now, fuzzy with sleep . . .

She dropped her head, close to his face. His eyelids were flickering. For an instant concern flashed through her, then it subsided. This wasn't a nightmare.

He was dreaming. She edged in closer, fascinated.

Dreams. The subconscious. *No one can control the subconscious.* What if—

She turned away, staring into the fire. She had no right to probe Jay's mind when he was asleep, and unaware of what she was doing. It went against every code she tried to maintain for herself. But this wasn't about knowledge any more. It was about need, and they'd almost run out of places to go on that.

She edged back, putting her arm across his chest, wondering if he was going to wake, not sure whether she wanted him to or not.

She felt, rather than heard, the sigh as he relaxed into her embrace. Her teeth snagged over her bottom lip. She didn't have to do this. She could just hold him. Comfort him with the warmth of her body, the subliminal awareness of her presence. Nice, touchy-feely, unthreatening. Keeping the nightmares at bay.

And when he wakes you'll still be running out of places to go. Except that you know – now – how it was done.

But not why.

With a last tiny quiver of conscience, swiftly muffled, she slid gently into Jay's mind, and began to nudge his dreams towards that smooth, shining wall.

CHAPTER 21

'Christ!' His head was splitting, as if someone had rammed a pile driver into it. In amongst the pulsing pain he knew . . . He remembered . . . 'Jayston Creed.'

'The *renowned* Jayston Creed. Mind-reading genius.' Madison's voice was low and hoarse, acid in his ears. His eyes finally focused. She was standing next to the couch. Emotion was flaring off her, compounding his confusion. 'Known to his friends as Jay. And still alive, and practising, I presume. *He* did this.' He could hear the wobble in her voice, under the acid. He reached out blindly, but she was too far away to touch.

Madison swallowed down the lump in her throat, ignoring the outstretched hand. She'd been such a *fool*, not to see. 'He must have made quite an impression, the remarkable Dr Creed, to make you assume his name, when you couldn't remember your own.' Jay – *Jay?* had been strong enough, *God how strong*, to carry that precious scrap of memory through the mayhem that had been done inside his head. The imprint of the

262

man who had done this to him. *I will not cry, damn it.*

'That's my name.' The voice was muffled. She had to lean forward to hear him.

'No.' She shook her head so vehemently her vision swam. 'I know you're not Creed.' She raked her eyes over him. 'Try again – who are you?'

'I . . .' *He* – she was back to that again – had his hand to his head. 'That is me.' His voice was still muffled. 'I'm Creed.'

Anger and bitter disappointment fizzed in her chest. 'I don't think so.' With a vicious lunge she scooped the Creed/Calver research papers that he'd been reading up off the floor, brandishing the author photographs under his nose: Calver – a slight, dark man, with a thin face and a widow's peak, and another – taller, darker, with a pleasant, forgettable face. 'That's Creed.' She stabbed at the picture. 'And it's certainly not you!' *Not those eyes, those cheekbones, that mouth.* 'So, who the hell *are* you?' she demanded again. 'And what is this? A test, to see how good I am? An audition, to put me through my paces before your boss graciously invites me to join his team? I assume Creed is your boss?' Her voice hitched. 'I can't *believe* I was so stupid.'

Cruelly, monumentally stupid.

She flung away from the couch, wanting to hit something, afraid it might be him. Oh God, she should have known! She thumped her fist into her palm. *Jay – Jayston – the connection was staring you*

263

in the face, but you were so taken up with your own importance, your own clever *investigations. So taken up with* him.

She should have realised – but how could she have known? *No one* knew what had happened to Creed. After the trial, he'd simply disappeared. The strongest rumours, from people in a position to know, were that he was dead. He'd been at the cutting edge of medical mind control, but when it all went hideously wrong, his reputation had plummeted. Before that – well, he'd been the man who *wrote* the bloody book. A legend, for his talent.

And now she knew. He was still alive, somewhere. Still working. Still recruiting. And he'd sent *her* a sample of his skill.

She forced some semblance of command over her limbs, reaching down to the table. 'Here.' She held out her hand.

The man with no name – sexy body, but no name – had dragged himself up into a sitting position. The heel of his hand was pressed to the bridge of his nose. She could almost feel his pain. She pushed the glass of water and the capsules at him.

'Madison, I have to— Let me explain—'

'Just take these,' she interrupted. She wanted him clear headed when she bawled him out – right before she threw him out.

Fury clogged her chest. He was reaching for her, with his mind. She got a brief flash of confusion and chaos, gaping holes where memories were leaching through, before she blocked him, shoving him back viciously, like a fist in the face, enjoying the sight of him wincing away from her.

Wordlessly, he held out his hand for the glass and the tablets. As she dropped the pills into his palm she bit down on her reaction to the warmth of skin on skin.

All that was *so* over.

'Wait for those to work. Stay out of my way until they do. Then we'll talk.' She didn't wait to hear his response. She had to get out, before the tears overwhelmed her. She headed for the garden.

The clouds had parted, briefly, and the rain had stopped. Water dripped off bushes and the limbs of the apple tree. The bluebells had been battered by the rain but one or two were lifting their heads again, towards the light. She stood for a long time, looking out at the grey sea.

Betrayal. That was a new one. Her parents had left her, Neil had left her, but it hadn't been like this. This man – whoever he was. He'd *played* her. Wound up her emotions, like a ball of string. For what? She would find out, before he went.

When the tears had finally petered out, she went back to the house.

She opened the kitchen door. She could hear the shower running in the bathroom upstairs. She scooped up her car keys and drove down to the village, a straggle of small shops beside the road. Although it was a holiday Sunday, the doors of the small general store were open. An optimistic array of ice cream and barbecue essentials was advertised in the window. Madison bought a pint of milk, and a paper, and then sat for a while in the car, reading the headlines, without seeing them.

When she finally returned to the cottage he was standing in the window, watching the track, sipping from the coffee mug in his hand. She sensed, without being told, that he'd wondered if she would be coming back. *Good.*

The way his hair clung to his head she knew it was still wet from the shower. He was wearing a black cotton sweater and chinos they'd bought, together, a month ago. She wanted to slap him, punch him, kiss him mindless. But she wasn't going to do any of those things.

He was going to answer her questions. And then she'd drive him wherever he wanted to go. And that would be that. She closed her mind to the cold, ragged-edged hole in her heart, and slid out of the car.

He'd got to the kitchen by the time she opened the back door.

'You want coffee?' He nudged the pot across the table towards her, then stepped away. Giving her space.

His voice was subtly different, she noticed. The mid-Atlantic intonation of someone who had been educated or trained in the States. They'd even altered that in the programming. Attention to detail. The work of a genius – and Creed was a genius.

He was hovering in the doorway, looking pale and – apprehensive? Would he tell her now who he really was? Not that it mattered. She filled a mug. He'd put out two. It wasn't going to get him any brownie points. She opened the milk and poured, then gulped greedily. The coffee was what she needed, to put some heat into a body that felt as if it were turning to ice. She didn't need to be grateful to him for it, though. She could have made it for herself.

'Headache?' she asked eventually, to break the silence. She didn't really care, except that she wanted him functioning well enough to get the hell out of her life.

He was watching her, not speaking. She shifted uneasily. His eyes were riveted on her face, as if he was trying to decode every nuance of her expression. There were lines of tension around his mouth that hadn't been there yesterday. Nothing was as it was yesterday.

'Gone,' he responded finally.

'Good.'

His mouth spasmed at the flatness of her voice. 'I guess you'd like an explanation.'

She shrugged. She was going to get it, and then decide whether she believed it. But he'd sweat first.

'What I want is, you, out of my house.'

That rocked him, she saw with satisfaction. Got him where he lived, wherever that was. He hadn't expected it. Would the slick bastard think he could sweet talk her into letting him stay? Temper flared,

267

brisk and hot, melting some of the ice. She banked it down. She needed to be in control here.

'I have a few questions,' she said casually.

Technical stuff. Nothing personal. Like why? Or – did any of this mean anything? The things she wanted to know were for the good of science and the furtherance of learning, stuff like that. So the next time some genius decided to hook her, for whatever experiment he was conducting, by dangling a piece of beefcake with a hard-luck story in front of her, she wouldn't be caught again for an idiot. He was watching her warily. Letting her make the running. Clever guy.

'After I have my answers, you can pack. You can keep the clothes.' She sure as hell didn't want them. 'I'll take you to the station. There's a train from Tenby to Cardiff. You can get a connection there to London. I presume you have friends, someone to pick you up?'

Damn, why had she asked that? She didn't want to know. Didn't care. Didn't want to imagine him with his mates, laughing about how easy she'd been. Her nails bit into her palms. Easy – in every way. And much too stupid to recognise the product of a leading mind in her field, even when she had him on her investigating couch.

Her heart jerked when he finally spoke. 'I'll answer what you want and then I'll leave.' His eyes were sharp. She watched him inhale, then swallow. God, she was still so attuned to his body. 'I think I can guess how you feel.'

Mister, you have no idea.

'Once I'm gone,' he continued, 'I think you should stay here for a while. Don't go back to work too soon. Take some time.' He jerked a hand through his hair, raking it hard back from his forehead. She watched the line of his arm, the movement of muscle under the sweater. 'Will you at least promise me that?'

'Why should I promise you anything?'

He grimaced. 'Last request of the condemned man?'

She frowned, unable to see where this was going. Why did he want her out of the way? Something to do with the lab?

'It's no concern of yours what I do.'

He shook his head. 'I don't know what you're thinking.' His smile was grim. 'And you won't let me in to find out.'

Jay closed his eyes, to block out Madison's accusing stare, while he pulled together whatever of himself he could get a hold on. Fuck. He was so bloody tired. His body felt as if it had been beaten all over with sticks. As for his mind . . .

He'd dared to hope that breaking through the wall might be a victory, not a defeat. That they'd laugh, cry, make love. That they'd *know*. Instead, all he had was a head full of shards. Bits and pieces of memory that still didn't come together, and the seeping knowledge that what was behind them wasn't anything like he'd imagined.

It was worse.

Life-and-death worse.

And somehow, in breaking through, he'd lost Madison. *And if you don't have her, then you don't have anything. It's over.*

He couldn't do what had to be done alone, or he'd never have started this mess. Now he could see it for what it was. A mess. He'd been so bloody blind. *You should never have dragged her into this.*

But then she'd only been a woman in a photograph, a résumé, a handful of brilliant lecture notes. She hadn't been real.

Now she was real in a way that was searing his heart.

He'd put her in danger.

It was up to him to get her out.

He put his empty mug down on the table. She was angry at the deceit. Humiliated. He could work with that. She wanted him gone. He'd go. Draw the fire away from her. If they had him, then maybe they'd let her alone.

His tired mind took a moment to see the flaw in the reasoning. The whole thing needed her, or none of this would have happened. So they'd be hunting for her. *But if they couldn't find her?*

If he refused to co-operate, she would be no use to them. Back in London he wouldn't last long. If he went to the press? The authorities? If he played it right, there'd be a bullet in his head before nightfall tomorrow. If he could just work out the best way, the fastest way . . .

Obliterate this damn freak of a mind of yours, once and for all.

Madison stood, waiting for him to speak, her emotions too near the surface as she watched him. She ought to be going after him, getting the answers she'd demanded, but somehow she couldn't get the words in order. The expression on his face tugged at her. He was struggling with something. He looked so . . . confused. Lost, and still in pain. Why did she have to be so aware of his feelings?

'You have questions,' he said at last. 'I have one.' His eyes were dark and clouded. She couldn't read them. *Didn't want to.* 'The thing is . . . I don't have all of it.' Was he stalling? 'Whatever you did to break through . . . What did you do?' Curiosity flashed in the dark eyes. She hesitated.

'You were dreaming. I directed your dreams. Got your subconscious to dismantle the wall, from the inside.'

'Brilliant.' His face lit with something that disturbed her, down deep. 'So simple. So perfect.'

'I shouldn't have. Not while you were sleeping. It wasn't ethical.' Did she wish now that she hadn't?

He brushed the objection away. 'It worked.'

'Did it?' She couldn't help herself. 'You said it wasn't complete.'

'Not entirely. Maybe it needs more work.' There was something like hope in his eyes. She baulked.

271

She'd have to take him into her bed, her arms; hold him while he slept. *No way.*

'I'm sure one of your colleagues, or Dr Creed himself, will be able to complete the process, now it's begun,' she said primly.

Unexpectedly he dropped into a chair; put his arms down on the table. 'We may as well get that one straight. I *am* Creed.'

Anger flashed over her. White hot. 'Don't tell me that. I've met Creed. Listened to him lecture. Shaken his hand. He even signed that bloody *book* for me. You are *not* him.'

CHAPTER 22

'I am Jayston Creed. The man who signed your book is called Eddie Jones.' Jay's head was down. He seemed to be finding something fascinating on the scarred surface of the old pine table. 'He was one of my first associates. There was a mix-up when we presented research papers together at a conference in Berlin. A news service used his picture instead of mine.' Jay's voice had no intonation, the flatness of exhaustion. Madison flopped into a chair. This sounded like the truth.

'Big conferences – they were never my thing. I preferred to press on with the work. Eddie was good at putting stuff over to large audiences. The next big event . . .' He shrugged. 'We just kept up the deception. At first it was kind of a joke – seeing if anyone would notice. It worked, and it seemed like a good idea, so . . . from then on, Eddie became the face of Jayston Creed.'

'But there were other pictures, from the trial,' she objected.

She saw him flinch. Had he really expected that she wouldn't know?

'Archive shots, or snatch stuff, taken with a long

lens. Eddie and I, we look enough alike to pass. It was a closed court. The security services saw to that.'

'That's who you work for now? The security services? They shut down the trial and got you out? Everyone says you're dead,' she accused.

He shrugged.

She sat back, not wanting to believe him. Unfortunately it made sense. To someone employed in the world she inhabited. No way would she want to work for the people he represented. She *never* wanted to be that kind of spook, living in a shadow world. Her life was complex enough already. 'How was it done? The barrier?'

'As you thought, an enhancement of the control function. You were right on the money, Madison.'

She didn't want to hear the praise. 'And that's what this was about, was it? Testing me?'

'There's always a place on my team for a fresh mind.'

'Not this one.' She felt dizzy. She realised it was relief. This was about what this bastard wanted, about *him*, not about her and her work. It had crossed her mind, sitting in the car in the rain, outside the general store, with its sad little holiday display, that Creed might have another reason for this charade – that he was testing the extent of her powers for her employers. It didn't look like it. No one was checking up on her. Her life could go on as normal. Once she got this man out of it. 'I appreciate your flattering interest,

274

Dr Creed, but I don't have any plans to change my job in the near future. Of course, I may well be wanting to write this up, for the professional journals.'

She got a nasty spark of pleasure from putting the knife in.

'You may not get the chance to publish it.'

'Threats, Dr Creed?' She pushed back her chair. 'I know I'm naive, but I've always believed that the truth will out. Somehow.'

She got to her feet. It was time to finish this. She had all the information she needed. This whole charade had been a perverse, demented job interview. The man had to be more than three-parts crazy. *Hold that thought.*

She shut her mind to the clamouring curiosity that wanted to ask for the real story. *Did you kill your wife, Dr Creed? Did you get away with murder?*

And the anguish behind the curiosity. *We made love.When you were inside me, did that mean anything?* She blanked the thought, forcing all the power she had into it. No memories about lying in the arms of a murderer. No wondering if she could, even now, learn to trust this man.

'I think we're finished here. Do you want a lift?'

'Thanks, but I'll walk.'

Madison opened her mouth to argue, then shut it. Why did she care? He'd go as far as the nearest phone and call up whatever backup team he had in place. There'd probably be a fast car to collect him within the hour, maybe even a helicopter.

Backup team – the ones intercepting her results at the lab? It fitted.

And never mind if it messes me up with my current employer – having someone else sniffing around. Thanks a bunch, you arrogant bastard.

The fresh pulse of anger was hot, but it didn't do much to warm the cold place inside her.

She stood beside the sink, well away from him. No excuse for him to brush close to her when he left. That cold place in her heart yearned for one last touch, but it wasn't going to happen. If he touched her she might still unravel in his arms. She couldn't even trust herself.

After a pause, when he seemed to be gathering himself together, Jay got up. He reached for the waterproof coat that was hanging on the back of the door.

'I'll go now. I don't need to take anything with me.' He stopped, eyes searching her face. She kept it averted, watching him covertly from under her lashes, keeping her mind veiled, blocking out any probe he might send in. He took a step towards her. Instinctively she leaned back, ready to move. He raised his hand, then dropped it again, in a curiously forlorn gesture that added another unwelcome layer of ice to the ache in her heart. She felt sick. *Just leave, why don't you?*

'You should stay on here, Madison.' His voice was low, but unexpectedly urgent. 'The forecast is for more fine weather. Take a longer holiday. You deserve it.'

She caught her breath at the barefaced cheek, but even outrage wasn't going to make her look at him. 'You're not my boss, Dr Creed, nor likely to be. Goodbye.'

He hesitated for a moment longer, eyes still fixed on her profile. Then, at last, he turned to open the door. 'Goodbye, Madison. Take care.'

The door closed. She heard the crunch of his step on the gravel path for a few paces and then – nothing.

With a swift pounce towards the table, she snatched up the mug that he'd used, hurled it at the wall, and burst into tears.

Jay turned his collar up and began walking along the empty road. Rain had soaked his hair in seconds, running down his face. His head was still fuzzy. Regret was pulling, like a sickening mill-stone, on his neck. He wiped his hand across his eyes, not sure whether all the wetness was rain.

If only . . . Saddest two words in any language. He straightened up. No point in going there. He'd known the price of failure before he got into this.

If he could save Madison, then it wouldn't be a failure.

CHAPTER 23

She'd run out of tissues. Which meant it was time to stop crying.

There was a long stain of coffee on the kitchen wall, with the debris of the mug below. She got a cloth and dustpan. A small cut on her finger from the broken pottery almost made her cry again. She sniffed, wiping her nose on her sleeve.

She'd had what . . . a lucky escape? A close encounter of the worst kind?

She sat down heavily on the floor. So many things were slotting into place. She had never met the real Creed. *Not until you picked him up one night in a dark alley*. No wonder she'd always found their official meetings curiously flat, and disappointing. She'd shaken the hand of Eddie Jones, the substitute, not Creed, the real deal. Jonathan was going to love this story. As soon as she got back.

She looked around the room. She could pack the car and be in London in four or five hours. Lock this place and throw away the key. Erase all traces of Jay from the studio and the apartment.

Get her work back on track – pick up all the projects she'd let slide in the last two months. Be ready for a fresh start on Wednesday, when the lab reopened.

It sounded like a plan.

She got to her feet. The rain was coming down in sheets. Anyone foolish enough to be out walking in it was going to get really, really wet.

The book Jay had been reading was still face down on the floor in the other room. She picked it up, smoothing down the spine. Should she take it with her, or leave it here? Would it be a useful reminder never to trust a glib stranger? Or would it turn her stomach every time she looked at it? She put it on the table, until she could decide.

The cushions on the sofa were still dented from where he'd been lying. She straightened them and plumped them up, smoothing the fabric with hands that were not quite steady. The mouse from the fairground was squinting at her from his place on the window seat. She picked him up to hug him to her chest, resting her face in soft fur.

Tears were rising in her throat again. She sucked them back.

She put the mouse down on the table. She'd take him back to London. Donated to a charity shop, he had a chance of making a child happy.

Uncomfortable shivers of recollection were replaying in her mind, like scenes from an old film.

She saw herself sitting across the table from Jay, eating food that he'd cooked for her. She'd promised him that night that she'd have no regrets, whoever he turned out to be. She bit her lip. Implicit in that declaration there'd been a second promise – that she'd stand by him, whoever he turned out to be. *But that was then, before you knew that the whole thing was a scam.*

With an effort she put the image out of her head, along with the picture of Jay standing by the door, before he'd walked out into the rain. Of the outstretched hand that she'd pointedly ignored. What purpose would have been served to take it?

You know, for a con man, he didn't have much to say in his own defence.

'Whose side are you on?' She was talking to herself again! With a grunt of irritation she gathered up a pile of magazines and slung them into the basket by the hearth that held kindling.

Maybe she wouldn't let this place go. She could rent it out. There were so many young people who needed a home, priced out by second homers, like her.

She sat down on the sofa. Jay had wanted her to stay here. She frowned. He'd been insistent on it. Almost as if he wanted her promise not to return to London.

What's in London that he doesn't want you to find?

Was there some other part of his elaborate scheme that she hadn't discovered yet?

Elaborate scheme. She picked up a cushion and hugged it to her middle. The whole thing had been completely over the top. All that, just to test her and maybe recruit her? *Come on – would they really want you that badly?*

There was more to this.

The conviction went through her with sickening realisation. For a moment she felt faint, then her sight and her thoughts cleared. She'd been too wrapped up in her own emotions to see it. Jay had given in, and got out, far too easily. Almost as if he wanted to avoid any more questions. And fogged with betrayal, she'd let him go. *Oh no.*

She threw the cushion on the floor and surged to her feet. The keys to the car were in her pocket. She tossed her coat over her shoulders, to protect her from the rain, and made a run for it.

She stopped the car at the junction of the track and the road, peering through the deluge. Which way?

On a gamble she turned right. Nothing but high hedges and sheets of rain. He had a head start on her, of at least half an hour. Would he have already reached a phone? Hitched a ride?

When she spotted the phone box, beside the road, her hands clenched on the wheel. Heart in her mouth, she half-rammed the car into the hedge and scrambled out, not quite sure why.

The broken glass and the shattered handset,

dangling lifeless from the wall, made her heart lurch. The rain had already plastered her hair to her skull and seeped in at the neck of her jacket, but she barely noticed. She flung herself into the driving seat. What would Jay have done when he found the vandalised phone?

Should she go on? Or go back?

She chose on.

The road was narrow, barely wide enough for two cars to pass, the hedges on either side towering and impenetrable. She couldn't even see into the fields beyond. She ploughed forward, uncertain of her choice, head shifting from side to side as she hunted for a place to turn.

She drove past him.

He was standing on a narrow strip of verge that bordered the lane, almost one with the rain, sheltering in the inadequate lee of an elder bush. Barely thinking, she threw the car into reverse, blocking him, so he couldn't get away from her. She reached across the seat to open the passenger door.

'Get in!'

'I don't—'

She leaned out of the car and yanked at the first thing she got a hold on. His feet slipped on the wet grass and she felt the impact as he collided with the side of the car. She kept on yanking, with a death grip on the sleeve of his coat.

'All right. I'll come quietly.' She didn't let him go until he'd squelched into the seat beside her and she'd leaned across him to shut and lock the door. 'Madison, I don't know what this is about—'

'You lied to me.'

'We've been through all that – if you followed me to—'

'No.' She waved the words away. 'All that, back at the cottage. That was the lie.' *Don't cry now.*

She put up a hand to the nape of his neck, and pulled him towards her. As she slammed her mouth against his, she opened her mind. Power erupted between them, like a fountain of emerald sparks. She let him go. He was shaking. Or maybe it was her.

'You lied.' She was surprised how even her voice sounded.

'I let you assume—'

'It's the same thing, Jay.' She twisted to look at him. He really was soaked. Dark, drenched patches stained the waterproof jacket and his hair was a mat of soggy rat's tails. She started the car, backing halfway into the hedge to turn it. 'Put your belt on.'

'Um – this is kidnapping.'

'In the country, in a downpour, no one can hear you scream,' she informed him tartly. 'You're coming back to the cottage. And when I've dried you out, you're going to tell me everything.'

'Or?'

'Or I turn this car around again and we head straight to London, to the lab, and whoever has been helping you to set me up. Maybe they'll tell me what this is all about.'

She didn't have to look at him to know he'd given in.

She waited downstairs while he changed, drying her own hair with a towel. And keeping her ears open for sounds of escape, wondering what to do if he tried to run.

She didn't have to decide, but she had begun to glance uneasily at the clock. The fresh logs she'd tossed on the fire were burning steadily by the time he came in and sat down beside it. He was watching her warily.

'Right, this time I want the truth.' She planted herself in the chair opposite to him. 'Did you stage this charade to test me for yourself, or for my employers?'

His eyes widened at the second part of the question. Madison felt a warm trickle of relief to her bones. That spectre had still been lingering in her mind. *At least the lab isn't involved. Your job is safe. It may be the only thing that is.*

'It wasn't a test – at least – look, Madison. I know you have no reason to trust me, but could you do it anyway? Let me leave. Stay here. Don't tell anyone where you are.' His face was haggard. She couldn't read his eyes. 'By the end of the week it will all be over.'

'What will?' She stiffened in alarm. 'This isn't a terrorist thing, is it? Oh God!'

She was fumbling in her pocket for her phone. Jay was out of the chair and on his knees in front of her, hand over her wrist, before she depressed the first nine.

Her skin burned where he touched.

Then her mind shuddered as his thoughts leapt into hers. She tried to recoil, until she realised that he wasn't invading her. He was pulling her into him.

'Not terrorism.'

All her senses told her it was true.

'What then?'

He was reaching still, trying to surround her with soothing waves of reassurance. The distraction wasn't strong enough. *He* wasn't strong enough. With a mental push, she parried the connection, but his fingers were still tingling on her wrist. He'd touched her, which gave her the right to touch him. She skewered his chest with her finger. 'You set me up. Made me look a fool. This whole thing was a great big experiment. So what the hell was it for?'

Suddenly she was mad, good and mad. Spits of power spilled out of her and into him. She could feel them landing, searing. Feel the sudden exhaustion in him that stopped him blocking them. He was just taking the hurt, letting it burn where it touched.

The fight went out of her.

'Jay.' She put her hand to his face, ran her fingers along his cheekbone. 'Please tell me. Whatever it is, it has to be better if I know.'

He was still kneeling in front of her. He let her go and flopped backwards, on to the floor. 'You're not going to let this rest, are you?'

'Damn right, I'm not.'

'Not even if knowing can put you in danger?'

'I'm already in danger.' She didn't know where that certainty had come from. 'That's why you want me to stay here, out of sight.' She felt curiously calm. Somewhere inside her a little bubble of hope was forming. *How crazy is that?* She nudged him gently, with her foot. 'If I know what it is I have to be afraid of, maybe I'll understand the need to hide. So tell me.'

'I don't think I can.' He got wearily to his feet, took her hands and guided her towards the sofa, pulling her down with him. 'My head is still falling apart. You've seen it.' He gave her a dog-eared smile. 'I feel like shit, and I don't have the energy left to talk. You'll have to come in and take it.' He closed his eyes. 'Please.' The plea was low and quiet. It did something to the pit of her stomach.

'I . . . okay.' She put her hand to his forehead, easing his head back against the sofa, stroking his hair, until she felt him relax. It took a few moments. He was wired and so was she. She pushed into his thoughts, and met residual resistance. 'Let go.'

'Madison.' She had to lean close to hear him. 'What's in there . . . is bad. I'm sorry, so, so sorry. I didn't know I was going to love you.'

Her mouth had just enough time to form a gasp of astonishment, her heart to give an incredible bound. Then the last barrier of his defences went down, and she fell, like silk, into his mind.

CHAPTER 24

Madison was sitting on the toilet, with the top down. She wrapped her arms around herself, to stop herself from shaking. It didn't work. Her teeth were chattering. She gritted them as hard as she could.

She knew it all now. And it had to be real. She'd been right inside Jay to get it. No one could hide that well, not even the real Jayston Creed. There was no way that what she'd seen was anything but the truth. Nothing hidden.

He *was* Jayston Creed.

He was sleeping now, downstairs. She'd pushed the right buttons to close him down for a few hours, before she pulled out. He could use the rest, and she needed time alone, to sort out what she'd seen. Felt.

She'd already known some of it. It had been headline news all over the world. For the press, all their Christmases had come at once. They'd torn the heart out of the story, like scavenging coyotes. It had everything. Sinister, reclusive scientist; innocent, suffering victim; beautiful, tragic heroine. Add in the scary mind games, experts running out of control, the whiff of spooks in the background. It was made to run and run.

Madison got up, slipping the bath robe that was hanging on the back of the door around her shoulders, in an effort to get warm. Jay's scent enveloped her. She screwed up her face, snuffling back tears. She had to focus.

The story wasn't complex. Three years ago Jayston Creed and his wife, Gina, had set up the ultimate experiment. Two minds, working in tandem, to control a third. A daring, last-ditch intervention to reclaim a friend, victim of a massively debilitating head injury. It had been a phenomenal risk, and a catastrophic failure. The patient had died. Gina had survived two weeks, to die in hospital, her mind, it was whispered, shattered beyond repair. She'd been three months pregnant. The baby wasn't Creed's. Jay's trial for murder opened and closed on the same day. The prosecution offered no evidence. While the press screamed about deals, and cover-ups, Jayston Creed had walked away, presumably into the arms of the security services.

And disappeared.

That was the public story. Now she knew the real one.

Jay lay back, with his hands behind his head, letting his thoughts organise themselves. All the moves were coming back to him. He'd faked sleep, let Madison believe she'd put him out. He reckoned she needed the space. He was feeling a whole lot better. Just having her crisp, clear thought patterns, sorting through the lumber in his head, had grounded him. *No longer alone.*

He bit his lip. She had it all now, every last miserable detail. And if she was the rational woman he took her for, she'd run like hell. He hadn't concealed anything. He hadn't been in a position to, and anyway he owed her. He'd given her all the what's and the why's. All the things he'd never told any of his other interrogators.

There'd been plenty of people asking questions – first the hospital authorities, then the police, and finally the suits from MI take-a-number-from-one-to-ten had arrived, to prod through the debris of three lives. His own colleagues had been the most difficult to handle. They'd all been desperate to find out how he'd managed to screw things up so royally. Initially sympathetic, and willing to close ranks around him, they'd grown increasingly hostile as the press backlash began to wash up at their doors. He'd alienated them all with his refusal to speak, until he had very few supporters left.

He'd told no one what had really gone wrong in that London hospital room. Until today. Someone else already knew though, which was why all this had begun.

He pulled himself off the couch, and padded to the kitchen to fire up the coffee machine.

★　　★　　★

Madison jumped a foot in the air when the bathroom door swung open.

'You ready to talk now?'

She gaped at him. 'You're not asleep.'

'Uh . . . no.'

Why did you think he would be? You're looking at a master. At the master.

'I made coffee,' he offered.

'Is that meant as a bribe or an apology?'

'Whatever fits.'

'I could have been naked in here.' She got up, shedding the robe, and stalked past him.

'I've seen you naked.'

Her glare, back over her shoulder, told him that now was a good time to shut up.

He took the hint.

He'd made coffee and toast, she discovered, when she got to the kitchen. A whole pile of it, neatly buttered and keeping warm under the grill. Her throat felt stiff and the back of her eyes stung.

She swung round. 'Before we go any further, I want to ask something.' She saw him brace. 'What you said, before you went under—'

'Yes?' he asked cautiously.

'What did you mean?'

'What do you think I meant?' he hedged.

'You said you loved me.'

'Er . . . Is that a problem?'

'No, you bloody fool!' She stepped towards him. His arms closed around her.

'Could you . . .?'

'I don't know . . . I feel . . .' The flash of disappointment in his eyes, quickly masked, made an ache in her heart. But she couldn't give him anything but honesty. 'I care about you, Jay. If we make it through this, ask me again.'

His head jerked up. 'No. You're not getting—'

She warded off his words with her hand. 'What happens if we run away from this? We keep running, always looking over our shoulders.' She shook her head. 'The only way out is to go through with the plan you made. I'm going to help you, Jay, whether you want me to or not.'

CHAPTER 25

Emotional trauma had the odd effect of making her hungry, Madison discovered. She munched her way through most of the toast. Jay pushed a piece around his plate, trying to persuade her to change her mind. Tension vibrated off him.

'I saw Gina die.' His face was set, pale. 'I realise now that all I felt for her was infatuation. She set out to seduce me and I fell for it. But even with what she did to me, it hurt to watch her at the end.'

'Then it's up to you to keep *me* alive.' Madison licked butter off her fingers. *And me, you.* 'Gina was working for this mysterious company, right from the beginning?'

'The Organisation. It's a collection of hundreds, maybe thousands, of companies, some real, some shell – a multi-global. A hydra, with heads all over the world. Into anything and everything that will turn a dollar – preferably a million or two of them. Or a pound, or a euro, or a yen – they're not fussy. No morals, scruples or conscience. They wanted the mind experiment. Gina must have been recruited a long time before she met me. They collect talent, and she had it. I was looking for a female assistant – a match of Yin and Yang – you were on the shortlist. I saw Gina first. She made a play for me. I was flattered, just plain stupid – mesmerised. I gave her the job, and a wedding ring. We worked together for two years before she chose her moment.'

'In the middle of the three-way experiment.' The devastation she'd glimpsed in Jay's mind came back to Madison, like an echo. 'Gina tried to take over the experiment – take *you* over.'

'She came damn close to succeeding. I didn't see it coming. Our marriage—' He raised his shoulders, let them fall. 'We were arguing a little. Going through a rough patch, I thought. But we were still working together. There was no problem with that. You know how it is. That morning everything was fine. Gina was excited, a little scared, energised.'

He breathed, deep. 'I had no warning. Things were going well. We could have done it. Dan was responding. We were making new pathways, teaching him to function again, using other parts of the brain. And then there was a surge of power. Gina let me see about the affair and the baby, but not who the man was. I still don't know. Some of the tabloids suggested it was Dan – that what I did to them both was revenge. The fact that they were sketchy on the details of exactly what it was I *had* done, didn't stop them speculating, or wheeling out so-called experts with their ideas. A lot of former colleagues made the front page on that. You find out who your real friends are.' His mouth twisted. 'Dan might have been the father of the baby – he and Gina were quite close, but it could have been any of the men in our circle, or a stranger. I really don't know.' He shrugged. 'It's not important. The man, the affair, even the child – from what I saw, in those few seconds, I don't think any of it mattered to Gina – it was just a weapon in her hands. She used it to distract me, long enough to get a hold. She was trying to overwhelm me, to control *my* mind, permanently. Then she could set up whatever experiment she wanted – whatever her masters wanted. She'd been working for them, feeding back information on everything we did, for the entire time I knew her.' His voice was bleak. 'I had to fight her – in my old friend's brain. I thought she was going to kill us both, or drive us mad.'

His voice was low and anguished. 'I lost it. Threw everything I could at her. Dan died. I blacked out. You saw. When I came round Gina was curled up in a foetal ball in the corner of the room. She couldn't even speak. And her eyes . . .' He shivered. 'She looked . . . as if she was already dead . . . I did that. To my own wife.' He bowed his head. 'She came close to killing me, for money, but I'll always be the person responsible for her death. When the police arrested me, it felt like justice. I wouldn't give them answers. They had the right man, the one who killed

Dan and Gina. They didn't need to know how. Probably wouldn't have believed it. I thought I was saving some of my dignity and her reputation . . . I was a fool. It turned the press against me. Plus there was a subtle campaign of smear and misinformation. People wanted me isolated. I've never been sure if that was the bad guys or the good ones. Maybe it was both.'

He spread his hands. 'The papers did get it right on several counts. The security people persuaded the prosecution that putting me on trial would bring out issues that shouldn't be made public.'

'But they weren't the ones who made you disappear?'

His mouth curved, but without amusement in his eyes. 'They were expecting to, but I had money, enough to buy a new life. A lot of professional acquaintances dropped me like the proverbial hot potato. Can't say I blame them. Our world is hard enough to manage at the best of times. Eddie Jones, my alter ego, made it clear that our association was over as soon as I was arrested. He'd signed on for a few lecture tours and a bit of glad-handing, not a murder trial. I believe he's since had plastic surgery – I'm sorry about that.' He paused, looking into the distance. 'Now my parents are gone, I've no close family, but there were still a few friends left who were willing to help me. They got me started on my journey off the map. After that, I made my own way. To all intents and purposes, Jayston Creed died.'

'Until you decided to resurrect him.'

'Until the Organisation did.'

'This man Alec Calver – you trust him.'

'He was my chief assistant, and a friend. We collaborated on a number of projects. I've never had any cause to doubt him.'

'He found you.'

Jay nodded. 'He let it be known, discreetly, that he was looking. I was still in contact with one friend I've had since school. He's nothing to do with the mind-reading community, but he was my link back, through tortuous routes, just in case something came up that I needed to know. I was curious about what Alec wanted, so I agreed to meet him – on neutral territory. He knew more than anyone about what happened in that hospital room. He was first on the scene – he helped me try to revive Dan and Gina, but it was hopeless – they were beyond help. He was determined that he was going to give evidence to support me at the trial, but it didn't come to that.'

'He wasn't one of the ones who got you away?'

'No, I didn't want him involved; his association with me had damaged his career enough. But he didn't give up. When I disappeared, he set about infiltrating the Organisation. They hadn't given up on the mind-control project. He came to me with the outline of a plan, one that could finish this thing once and for all.'

'An outrageous plan.'

'It had to be outrageous to work. Complex. The

Organisation is a sophisticated piece of machinery. They like complex. It's what they do. They have to think they're in charge.'

Madison gave him a narrow look. 'The control thing again. Do I have this right? The Organisation now has a one-off, whizz-bang computer that can capture the mind-control pattern. They want to force you to repeat the experiment – getting it right this time. Their plan is to freeze-dry the results, and sell them on to whoever will pay, for whatever purpose they want – terrorism, industrial espionage, whatever. Your plan is that you and Alec will destroy the machine.'

'Exactly.'

'And to do this, they had to find you and abduct you. And you let them.'

'Yes.' Jay shifted in his chair.

'And this is where I came in. Because you had to repeat the preparation and conditions of the original experiment, as exactly as possible.'

'Yes – except that Alec will be the receiver – an adept who can participate if needed.' Jay grimaced 'And, as far as the Organisation is concerned, keep me in check.' He shook his head. 'It's recording the *process* that is important, not the detail of the outcome, provided the process works. If we build new pathways in Alec's brain, they will have the pattern – which can be used anywhere, on anyone.'

Madison waved aside the explanation of what would happen afterwards. She understood the implications. That wasn't what she needed to know. She pulled in a choppy breath. 'You had to have a female mind reader. Yin and Yang.' Now she was getting to the difficult bit. The part that hurt.

'Madison—' He'd seen it in her face.

'I was the one you picked,' she overrode his interruption. 'You let them take you. You let them take your memory. I understand that they had to think they were coercing you, but why that?'

His mouth twitched. 'It was because of you. You're an authority on memory and connection, known to work with down-and-outs. They sent you a subject you couldn't resist.'

'You mean you and Alec sent me a subject I couldn't resist,' she corrected. 'You wanted my curiosity. You engineered my involvement. You were trying to test me—'

'That was the Organisation's agenda, not mine. I knew what you were capable of. But it was only part of it. We had to be . . . We needed time . . .' He tailed off, shifting uneasily in his seat.

Madison took a deep breath. 'Yin and Yang. We had to be co-operating, willingly, to reproduce the experiment. More than co-operating. We had to know each other, to have worked together. Very closely together. We were *meant* to have an affair.'

'I . . .' He met her eyes. 'I'm not going to lie. The optimum scenario was a female with whom I had an emotional and physical bond.'

'Is that what we have? An optimum scenario?'

'Madison, don't.' He leaned across the table to

take her hand. 'You know it's not like that. And if you don't, you should. When I started this—' He paused. Madison could feel him weighing his words. 'You were an unknown woman, a means to an end. I was at absolute rock bottom when Alec came to me. I'd turned my back on my whole life – faced the fact that I would probably never use any of my powers again. It was a chance. Something I *could* do. A kind of restitution. It looked— It was simply moves to be made – counters on a board. In a few weeks you've turned that around. You know it's true. You've seen inside my head. I had no idea, Madison, that it was possible to change so much. I don't know what else to say, except that I'm sorry.'

'You took an appalling risk.' Her voice wavered. 'What the hell were you thinking of? You gambled your memory on my skill.' The enormity of it made her whole body shudder. 'Your identity. What if I hadn't been able to get you back? If I'd done damage, blundering around in the dark? I could have harmed you beyond repair.'

'Ten months ago, it didn't matter. My life wasn't worth anything to me, except as a weapon for bringing down the Organisation. Jayston Creed was less than nothing. I never expected to love you.'

Madison put her hands over her eyes. Fear swirled around her. To do this she had to trust Jay. With her life. And if she didn't— 'If I'm not a part of this, if they find out you tricked them – they'll kill you, won't they?'

Horror grasped her heart, and squeezed. 'That's what you were thinking when you left here. You were going to draw them away from me.' His silence told her it was true. 'They've been watching us.' She remembered the cat's paws down her spine, the feeling of being observed. 'They've been monitoring my work at the lab, changing my results there, or at the test centre. They have someone on the inside.'

'Not at the lab itself, as far as I know. Contractors – maintenance or cleaners maybe. And . . . at the apartments – probably Scott.'

Madison shivered. 'He might be willing to provide information, for money. Scott likes money. But they don't know we're here?' Prickles of apprehension were running down her spine again, the illogical temptation to keep checking over her shoulder.

He shook his head. 'I don't think so. There's no record of this place. No one knew we were coming here. We're off the radar. At least—'

Her chin came up as he hesitated. He was rubbing the scar at his elbow. 'Alec and I . . . I didn't tell Alec everything. I . . . I wasn't confident about what would happen. How he might react . . .' He hesitated. 'I organised some private backup.'

'Security services backup?' She let out a long sigh when he nodded. 'Do they know you intend to destroy the machine?'

'Not exactly.'

'Jay – how many ends are you playing against the middle?'

'As many as it takes. The thing is . . . This is a tracking implant.' He indicated the scar. '*They* know where we are.'

'Oh.' She digested the information. 'I see. Theoretically, they're the good guys. But of course, they want the machine as well.'

'I have that impression.'

Madison felt slightly sick. 'Once the Organisation knows that the wall is broken, they will be coming for us?'

Jay nodded. 'I imagine that's why the decorators arrived early at the lab – increased surveillance. They probably have someone else at your apartment, too.'

'The heating contractors,' she confirmed absently. 'So,' she went on shakily, 'we have to complete an experiment that has never been done successfully, double-cross the bad guys *and* the good guys, wreck a computer, and get out with a whole skin. I can't believe I just said all that.'

'You can still back out—'

'And if I do, how long will you last? The Organisation will just move on to the next woman on your list. Or they'll kill you. They'll kill you whatever happens.' She could see the certainty, with appalling clarity. 'There was never going to be a way out for you, was there? Once they got what they wanted, captured on the computer, they'd kill you, to make sure that you never repeated it for anyone else. And probably me, too.' Her voice cracked.

'There was a plan B. After we'd wrecked the thing, or if we couldn't take the machine down, Alec was to get you out. That was why I needed backup from the security services. I didn't tell Alec, but that was the point when they were to step in. I don't know how it would have worked. *If* it would have worked . . . I gambled with all our lives. I think I was a little mad. Can you forgive me?'

Madison swallowed hard, willing the fear away. It retreated. Not far, but enough. But she wasn't quite ready to answer his question.

'You gambled most on me. That you could make me part of your scheme. That you could use me, the way Gina used you.'

She saw the shock of the words go through him.

'I . . .' He steepled his fingers against his mouth. 'I don't have anything to say in my defence, except that I bitterly regret it now. And I'd undo it if I could. But then we wouldn't have met. Quite simply, you're the best thing that's ever happened in my life. I realised that, the moment I got my memory back. I hope you can believe it. It's not much recompense for the disaster I've brought with me, but it is the truth.' He put his hands down flat on the table. 'I still hope you'll change your mind and let me try and sort out this mess alone, but it's your call, Madison. Whatever you want, I'll accept.'

'We have to make this work,' she said quietly. 'I'm going with you, Jay, but as a partner and an equal, not as a helper. I'm doing it with both eyes open.' No matter how much she wanted to run and hide. 'The only way either of us has a future now is to go through with your plan.'

The rain had stopped. Madison paced down the path, wet vegetation brushing her ankles. She needed to walk, to burn off adrenaline and order her thoughts. She wasn't going anywhere near what she'd just agreed to do. That would only paralyse her with terror. Which left Jay . . . and her. The man she'd come to . . . care about, didn't exist. What she had in its place was more complex, more dangerous. The physical attraction hadn't gone away. Jay Jackson or Jayston Creed, the man's body was the same.

A reluctant smile forced its way through. The man was hot and she wanted him. No change there. But the rest of the package?

She skirted the last boulder in the path, and slapped down on to the rain-drenched sand of the beach. There was a dog racing in and out of the waves, barking at the gulls. She stopped to watch as his owner threw a stick, hunching into her jacket.

It wasn't just a matter of forgiveness. Jay had involved her in his experiment with a calculation that she couldn't ignore. His remorse was genuine; she had no doubt of that. But whether she accepted it? That was one issue. The other was bigger. *Do you want a relationship with Jayston Creed? Do you want this man to love you?*

She found a rock that had dried out in the stiff breeze and perched on it, sorting through her emotions with as much honesty as she could find.

Had part of Jay Jackson's appeal been his desperate need for her help? Jayston Creed didn't need her in the same way. He was brilliant, and flawed. A man who could threaten her, professionally and personally. A man who had the power to unlock all her secrets. Mentally her guard had to stay up, even though she hadn't sensed him trying to read her. She could feel him though, on the edge of her mind, hoping she would let him in.

She looked back at the cottage, high on the cliff. *How far can I trust you, Jay?*

Can I trust you at all?

CHAPTER 26

His breath was misting the glass. Jay braced his arm on the window ledge, watching the small figure trudging along the beach below. He hadn't offered to go with her. He'd known, without being told, that Madison needed to walk alone. The temptation, when she was near, to focus his power, to reach out to touch her, mind to mind, was almost overwhelming. But that wasn't the way to go. It wasn't just a matter of ethics and an unwilling subject. He knew, bone deep, that he couldn't reach her that way. Not on a level that mattered. His mouth twisted. It didn't stop him throwing out the occasional lure, when temptation got too strong. No, not lure – invitation. A thought, hovering in the air, for her to pick up, if she would. So far she hadn't, but he wasn't giving up hope. Except – what could he say to her, inside her mind, that he couldn't say face to face?

He took a deep breath. What exactly did Madison have to gain from letting him inside her head? *Are you simply looking for connection to meet your own needs? Seeking the warmth of her mind to comfort the chill in yours?* Not that it mattered. Madison's

306

impeccable defences remained in place. And he didn't blame her. But it was achingly lonely, here on the outside. *And no more than you deserve.*

His thoughts were turning the pit of his stomach to ice. He rested his forehead on the pane. It was cold and clammy to the skin. *Cold within and cold without.* He was bleeding out inside. As he deserved to be. He'd thought his life was over when he'd walked away from the wreckage, after the trial. He hadn't even come close. If Madison turned away from him—

She'd agreed to help him, but if she couldn't forgive him—

You chose to do this. What were you? Crazy? Oh sure – Alec convinced you this crock of shit could work, but man, you were more than halfway there.

Madison was sitting on a rock now, watching a dog splashing in the water.

You can't blame this one on Alec. You were already on that path.

If you'd never begun this, you'd never have met her. If you hadn't begun it, you'd never have put the most precious thing in your life in danger.

It had all worked like a charm – better than a charm. The amnesia programme that he and Alec had sweated over had miraculously held up, almost completely intact. And they *had* sweated. His stomach churned at the memory. The Organisation had never doubted that he had been their prisoner, apparently in fear for his life, forced to do as they demanded. They were convinced that everything had been achieved through Alec's expertise and massive medication. In reality it had taken his and Alec's pooled skills, a few carefully selected drugs, sheer bloody-mindedness – and luck. And it had worked, except for that one lapse, the tiny slip that had let him remember part of his name. All the rest of the list had stayed in place. And what a list! He could barely believe that it *had* worked. The powerful connection when he and Madison met, to entice her in; his initial resistance, so that she wouldn't suspect she was being set up; his compulsion to avoid any kind of authority; the test of Madison's powers offered by the apparently impenetrable wall; the gradual breakdown of its defences, in stages, as her cleverness undermined it, and their emotional bond grew stronger. *Emotional bond? Don't you mean love?* Success that ebbed and flowed, to keep her involved and interested.

So much fell into place, now – the headaches when he'd tried to probe his own mind too deeply, the way he'd been quite comfortable around Madison's extraordinary talent, his illogical certainty that everything was as it should be, when it was quite patently not so, his awareness of a strange core of detachment, even in the middle of a personal nightmare. They'd planned and planted it all. It was a textbook performance. One for the journals. And Madison had been . . . amazing.

And now he was in love with her. He shifted his arm, leaning against the window frame, staring out without seeing. His mind turned relentlessly in on itself – returning in an endless circle to that sickening moment when he awoke and realised who he was, and what he'd done. He'd known immediately, with stunning certainty, that he'd never been in love before, but that he was now. The leap of joy his heart gave lasted barely a second, before the horrific implications of what he remembered wiped it away.

Jay came painfully back to awareness of his surroundings. Madison was retracing her steps along the beach. He turned away from the window. For a moment he stood, undecided. One last attempt to convince her to run, and not look back? *Oh, yeah, like that's going to work.*

The sigh came up all the way from his boots. Madison was right. The only way now was forward. Which meant he had to protect her, in every way he knew.

He headed for the phone.

The way up to the cottage was steep. In parts steps had been cut into the rock, to ease the ascent. The bushes on either side were still heavy with water drops. Madison took her time, avoiding a soaking and husbanding her breath. The view, as she stopped at one of the tiny natural terraces in the cliff, was a meld of grey on grey. Sea and sky meeting and stretching on forever. Until they fell off the end of the world.

She hadn't reached any new decisions. She

hadn't really expected to. All she could do was feel her way. Guard up, as always. Ever since her parents had died in a hail of bullets. Since before that. She pushed the idea out of her head. Not a thought to harbour around Jayston Creed.

The man who said he loved her.

There was a jeep parked beside her car. She walked around it and let herself in quietly, through the kitchen, hanging up her jacket and shaking out her hair. In the mirror, on the wall beside the sink, she discovered a surprisingly normal reflection. The redness of her eyes had faded and her cheeks were rosy from the sting of the wind. She stepped into the hall. There was a low murmur of male voices behind the door of the living room. She couldn't distinguish the words. She put her hand on the door and pushed.

Jay was standing beside the fireplace, every line of his body tense. His head came up when he saw her. Had he hoped that she'd change her mind, that she wouldn't come back?

The second man was sitting on the sofa, with his back to her. All she could make out was the top of a sleek, blond head. Not Alec Carver. He was dark. Unless he, too, had a body double.

As she walked into the room the man rose from his seat, and turned.

If she'd tumbled into the rabbit hole, she hadn't stopped falling yet.

Jay stepped forward.

'Madison, this is—'

'I know who it is,' she forestalled him. Part of her mind was impressed how cool her voice was. 'Hello, Craig.'

Jay's face, she decided, was well worth seeing. Total incomprehension. Not that she was much better, but she wasn't going to let it show.

'You've already met?' Jay's voice sounded rusty.

'You could say that,' Madison nodded. 'Craig was meant to be the best man at my wedding. He was Neil's closest friend.'

CHAPTER 27

'Hello, Maddie.' Craig spoke for the first time. He offered his hand. After a second's delay Madison took it, then leaned in to peck his cheek for good measure. Her nerves were tightening like wires, but she was damned if she was going to reveal it. Jay looked as if he'd swallowed a bag of nails. Craig was the only one, of the three of them, who appeared in any way relaxed. *But then, he'd known what was coming.*

He was watching her, eyelids slightly narrowed. Probably realised what she was thinking, even without mind-reading skills. 'You're looking well,' he said blandly when she dropped his hand and stepped back.

'And you,' Madison responded automatically. Polite chitchat, when her mind was screaming *what the hell are you doing here?*

Which was nothing to what was going on in Jay's head, if his eyes were any indicator.

'Shall we sit down?' Craig indicated the sofa. Madison, finding her knees were suddenly not up to the job, collapsed into it. Craig took the chair.

312

Jay, after a brief hesitation, propped himself against the arm of the sofa. Madison took a moment to admire the territorial manoeuvring.

'I called Craig—' Jay began, and then stopped.

Madison's knees might be unreliable, but her brain had gone into overdrive. 'The Security Service, the ones you're working with. Craig's your what? . . . Handler?' *And he'd been close, close enough to get here in an hour.*

'That's quite a jump,' Craig said evenly.

'Assuming that someone I thought was a corporate accountant is really some sort of high-class government agent?'

Craig bowed ironically at the compliment of high-class. Memories clouded Madison for an instant. His sense of humour had always been one of the things she'd liked about him.

'Believe me,' she continued, 'around here it's no jump at all. Unicorns, dragons, flying pigs. Bring them on.'

Craig shrugged, aiming a mildly sheepish grin at Madison. She averted her eyes, unwilling to be drawn back into old alliances. *If things go to plan, you will double cross this old friend.* She shifted uneasily, before her resolve stiffened. Craig's masters would take everything they wanted from Jay and from her, if they could, without scruple. In the name of national security. She sat up straighter.

Jay's hand drifted in, to settle on her shoulder. Analysing the warmth and the grip, she decided it could stay there. 'How far have you got?' She flashed a glance between the men.

'Not much further than hello. I've only just arrived,' Craig offered.

'Not enough time to explain that he already knew you.' Jay shot the other man a pointed look. 'Which has *never previously been mentioned*, if my recollection is accurate.'

Craig shrugged again, unconcerned. 'Need-to-know basis.'

Madison felt the tension in Jay ratcheting up a few notches.

Time to get back on-message. 'You want to tell us what should happen next? I assume you've worked something out?' She looked up, directing her question at Jay.

'Only an outline, of the more obvious parts.' He looked from Madison to Craig. Craig nodded that he should go on. Jay cleared his throat, speaking slowly. 'This isn't exactly a full-scale plan. Just as far as I've got. The way I see it, we return to London tomorrow, as if everything is normal. Once there, we restage the breakthrough, for the Organisation's benefit. I'm assuming your office and lab will have been bugged over the weekend.' He looked over at Craig. Craig nodded again. Jay took a visible breath, before continuing, 'Alec will be in charge of picking us up. Craig's people will be in place to make sure nothing goes wrong.'

Madison suppressed an inappropriate impulse to laugh, that might have its roots in hysteria. The capacity for something to go wrong – well, it was a lot higher than for it to go right.

'Fine,' she said, channelling calm.

Craig was frowning. 'You're comfortable, going along with this?'

'Perfectly.' *Liar.* She gave her best impersonation of relaxing against the sofa. 'There are a couple of things I would like to know from you, though, before I finally commit.' Jay's hand jumped on her shoulder. She ignored it. She fixed her eyes on Craig. He was looking uneasy now.

'Anything I can do.'

'You can tell me the truth.' She breathed deep. Part of her didn't want to do this. A larger part understood that she had to. The question that had been growing in her mind was too big. She tilted her head, to look directly into Craig's face. There was no easy way. She just had to say it. 'Was Neil working with you? Did he love me, or was I just a job? Was I about to marry a *real* spook?'

CHAPTER 28

Craig's expression said it all. Madison's vision misted, then refocused. In the back of her mind a hundred loose ends began to knit together.

'He loved you. Don't doubt that.' Craig's voice rasped. There were lines of tension around his mouth. Jay's hand dropped from her shoulder. She couldn't look at him. Her focus was totally on the other man. She thought about sending in a probe. *Only if it's necessary.*

Craig's head jerked, as if he'd heard her. She knew he hadn't, but the awareness of what she was had to have crossed his mind. *One to you.*

Craig cleared his throat. He raised his hand, but let it fall again in an unfinished gesture. 'At the start, you were an assignment. Get close and observe. Then Neil fell for you.'

'But why?' Madison put her hand to her head. Apprehension squirmed in her stomach. 'Why were you interested in *me*?'

'Come on, Maddie, you're not that naive.' Craig moved impatiently. 'The unit I'm attached to—' He jerked his head at Jay. 'Ask him. Officially we don't exist, in practice we keep track of those with unusual . . . gifts. Why do you think you were headhunted from that pharmaceutical job? It was to put you somewhere where we knew you'd be safe. Neil was part of that.'

Madison processed that, heart floundering. Everything she thought she'd achieved in her life, everything she'd prided herself on – her independence, her professional competence, her ability to take care of herself. Craig had just handed her a plate full of ashes. People she didn't know existed had been manipulating reality to keep her cocooned – out of harm's way – and she'd never even suspected it. Even the man she'd agreed to marry.

'I was just a job.' Her voice was barely a whisper. 'Neil . . . in the end he couldn't face the wedding.' Ice crawled over her chest. 'He jumped off that bridge because he couldn't bring himself to marry me.'

'No!' Craig came up, almost out of his seat. Madison saw the indecision in his eyes. Confusion swarmed through her. What wasn't he telling her? She was poised to leap into him, to get the real truth, when she saw him make up his mind. Instinctively she braced her shoulders.

'Neil didn't jump off that bridge, Maddie.' Craig's voice was rough and urgent. 'He *loved* you. He wanted to protect you. He would *never* have left you like that. Neil didn't commit suicide because of you, or the wedding. Neil was murdered.'

CHAPTER 29

Madison rocked back with shock. Automatically she jerked her knees up under her chin, wrapping her arms around them, folding in to protect herself. Jay slid down on to the sofa and gathered her close, holding her against his chest.

'Are you sure of that?' he barked out the question.

Craig nodded grimly. 'The whole thing was carefully staged. Neil wasn't suffering from depression, or on medication. The way it was put together was clever enough to satisfy the police but there was evidence, if you knew what to look for. Not least the fact that he'd never have done that to you.'

Craig looked straight at Madison. She could see him weighing up how much more he could share with her. She pulled herself up, out of Jay's protective embrace.

'You've started now. You may as well tell me the rest.' She curled away from Jay, so that she was sitting upright. He let her go. She trailed her fingertips over his, in acknowledgement, but her attention was all on Craig. 'Who would want to murder Neil, and *why*?'

'The Organisation.' It was Jay who answered. Madison heard the hollow edge of horror in his voice. She put her hand over her mouth.

Craig nodded again. He'd given up any attempt at dissembling. Madison found herself wondering, with a small detached part of her mind, how deep in trouble he was getting by talking to her like this. Or had that been calculated, too? Did he have permission to divulge if necessary? How would she ever know? She'd never seen his face look so bleak.

'We—' Craig began, then stopped, clearly unsure how to go on. Madison waited, not offering him any help. In the end he sighed. 'We think Neil was killed in order to expose you. There were two other women on the original shortlist for Creed's experiment, one in Finland, the other in Japan. The woman in Japan lost her husband in a hit and run, the other's partner died of unexpected complications after routine surgery. We didn't put it together until it was too late. The Organisation was paving the way.'

Jay swore, soft but vehement.

Madison's eyes were swimming. Emotional overload. She forced her nails into her palm. She didn't want to let the tears fall. 'It's nearly two years since Neil died.' She turned to Jay. 'When did you start planning this?'

'Ten months ago.'

She shut her eyes. 'That is . . . horrible . . . grotesque.'

'The Organisation's roots are long, and they dig deep. They have no boundaries.' Craig's voice was hard. 'They've been planning this a lot longer than anyone else. They always wanted that experiment.'

Fury came out of nowhere, clean and bright, scouring out the pain. Madison felt the vestiges of her tears dry, burned away in a red glare. She clutched the rage and held tight. 'Well, they're not bloody well going to get it!'

After they'd thrashed out a plan, in as much detail as was possible, Madison walked with Craig to the jeep.

'Maddie.' He put his hand on her arm. 'Are you really okay with this? When I found out you were the one the Organisation had chosen—' His craggy face crumpled. 'You don't have to go through with it. I can get you away. The whole purpose of my unit is to stop people like you falling into the wrong hands. Creed and I can cobble something together—'

'And get yourselves killed in the process?' She saw the knowledge in his eyes, though he was never going to admit it. Somehow it made her stronger. 'I've said I'll do it. So I will. There's something else now – I have to . . . for Neil. If I don't . . . then he died for nothing.'

They stood in silence for a moment. Craig spoke

first. 'Uh – are you and Creed?' He jerked his head towards the cottage.

Madison nodded. 'He says he loves me.'

She looked down at her feet. There were traces of sand on her trainers, from her walk on the beach. That seemed like a century ago. In half an hour, in half a second, the whole foundation of a world could change.

'He kind of reminds me of Neil. You trust him?'

Madison shrugged. Not water she wanted to swim in with Craig.

He slid his hand under her chin, lifting her face up. 'You don't have to be guilty about Neil, Maddie. He was where he was because he was doing his job and because he loved you. He was a professional, one of the best, but he must have slipped up. They should never have got to him. He intended to resign, once you were married, and hand the surveillance over to someone else. I guess he let his guard down too soon.'

Another thing that only took a second.

'But if it hadn't been for me—'

'Done is done,' Craig cut her off. 'You attract strong men, Maddie. They can take care of themselves, Creed included. He put himself through a lot to get here. He wants to take the Organisation down.'

'He spent three months on the streets.' The question had been haunting her. 'You were monitoring him all that time? Why did it take so long? A week or two would have been enough.'

321

'Ah.' Craig looked away. 'That was plan A, but then your return from Washington was delayed. He was already out there. Everything was on hold until you came back.'

'Freak!' Madison let the outside door slam behind her. The noise reverberated through the cottage. Crockery danced on the old-fashioned dresser.

'Madison?' Alarmed, Jay came into the kitchen at a run.

'I'm a freak. A jinx. Everyone who touches me . . .' She raised her hands, warding him off. 'Three people around me have been *murdered*. You were on the streets for three months, *just to get my attention*. Anything could have happened. Those kids could have kicked your head in. You could have contracted TB, died of pneumonia—'

'Madison.' Jay caught her hands and reeled her in. 'None of that happened. And none of the other stuff is your fault.'

'Neil *died* because of me – because I have something *corrupt* inside my brain, something evil. I've tried so hard to stay away from hurting people – but everyone who's ever been close to me has been hurt. If that doesn't make me a freak, *what does*?'

'If you're a freak, I'm one, too.' He had her close to his chest now, hands on her back, desperate to calm her. She was shaking in his arms, in a way that frightened him. 'I'm sorry, Madison, I had no idea about Craig and Neil.'

'Why would you?' The tension eased abruptly

from her limbs. She sagged against him, as if she was suddenly too exhausted to stand. He lifted her off her feet and carried her through to the next room, putting her down on the thick rug in front of the fire. She sat shivering. He took her left hand, rubbing it between his own. The right hand was at her throat.

'Hearing about Neil like that,' he said urgently. 'It had to be a shock. But you are *not* to blame. He was a professional. He was trained. The risks were part of his job. And your parents – how can that have anything to do with you?'

For a second, her eyes were pools of pure anguish. Then he saw the blankness close over them, like a curtain. Her hand was tangled in the chain at her neck. 'Careful. You'll break it.'

'What?' She looked down. 'Oh.' She uncoiled her fingers.

'You always do that, when you're upset.'

'I suppose I do.' She squinted down at the necklace. 'It was the last birthday present my parents gave me.'

He could feel her body relaxing into the warmth of the dwindling fire. The panic seemed to have left her, but her face was pinched and exhausted. He stood, pulling her to her feet. 'I think you should go to bed. Get some rest.'

Madison woke in the dark. Automatically she reached out for Jay. Her hand hit cold sheets. She dragged herself on to one elbow. Jay's side of the bed was empty. She pushed her hair out of her face and fumbled for the clock. 2.30 a.m.

He was asleep on the sofa in front of the ruin of the fire. The pillow and the blanket, which was tangled around his legs, told their own tale. Madison stood for a while, taking in the lean length of his body, feeling something stir. He'd kicked his shoes into a heap on the rug, but otherwise he was fully dressed. One arm was flung above his head. His shirt had parted from his jeans. A smooth stretch of abdomen was on display, with an arrow of hair delving under the waistband.

She reached down and kissed his cheek. Stubble – and tension in her belly and across her breasts. His eyelids opened reluctantly, then he was up and on his feet in one movement.

'What is it? What's the matter?'

'Nothing.' She put her hand on his belt. 'Why are you sleeping down here?'

'I . . . I didn't know whether you'd want—' He stopped. His eyes went dark as he studied her face.

'I want.' She put up her arms and pulled his mouth down to hers. 'Come to bed.'

They clung together, two shapes in the darkness. No sight, just sensation. Skin against skin, breath, urgency. Madison prowled Jay's body, mouth avid, gasping as he flipped her on to her back and pinned her wrists. She writhed under him as he drove into her with one single, deep thrust. His mouth was on hers, swallowing speech, swallowing everything.

She shattered in the dark, dragging him down with her.

Jay put his hand against the bathroom wall. The plaster was rough under his fingers. Madison was sleeping. He'd come in here to think. She'd trusted him with her body, with a fervent hunger that had robbed him of breath, for which he was monumentally thankful, but she still hadn't let him anywhere near her mind.

In twenty-four hours they'd be back in London, and the machinery would be in motion.

He looked across the hall, at the closed door of the bedroom. Would Madison surrender her defences to him, when the time came?

CHAPTER 30

When he got back to the bedroom there was a hint of light seeping around the edge of the curtains. Madison was awake, and sitting up. She pulled back the duvet, welcoming him. He held out his arms, but when she shook her head he settled down with his hands folded behind his neck. She'd found a nightdress to put on. Long and white, with lace at the neck. Demure, but sheer enough that a man wouldn't give up all hope. He studied her profile. It didn't look like they were going back to sleep.

'Something on your mind?' he asked at last.

'Curiosity.' She looked at him, over her shoulder. 'I was wondering. How did you get to be *the* Jayston Creed?'

'My past, you mean?' He laughed, thankfulness flowing through him at the easiness in her voice. 'You might not believe it, but it was all an accident.'

That had her attention. She turned round, face alight now with interest. 'Go on then, tell me,' she ordered.

'Yes, ma'am.' Accepting that they were going to

talk, rather than make love, he made himself comfortable, punching the pillow. 'Jayston Creed, the authorised biography. The first bit is boringly, and I *mean* boringly, ordinary. Born 36 years ago, in Nottingham, although we later moved to London, father a GP, mother a teacher. It was always assumed that I'd follow my father in being a doctor.' He shrugged. 'I wasn't really sure about it, but there wasn't anything else I wanted to do more, so I started in medical school. Mum had died six months before, from cancer. Dad – he just lost it, after she was gone. I don't know . . . maybe because he'd felt powerless to help her? He was drinking and he had a fall in the garden. Fractured his skull. A neighbour found him. That was just before Christmas, in my second year. I don't have any other family. A couple of distant cousins, in Australia, but I've never met them. After my second year, there was an exchange programme with a place in the States. It was a chance for a complete break, so I applied. And that's where it all started. Pause here for ominous music.'

Madison's brows rose in surprise. 'Not before? Nothing when you were a child?'

'No.' He passed on the interesting avenue her remark opened up. They could explore that later. At the moment this was about satisfying Madison's curiosity, not his.

He rolled over, smothering a grin when he saw the flick of impatience cross Madison's face. Better get on, before she decided he needed some encouragement. *Uh-oh, too late.*

He caught her hand and squeezed it when she reached out to prod him. She gave him an indignant stare. If he knew what was good for him, he'd get on with the story.

'Like I said, it was an accident. Literally. I was trying to teach a couple of basketball players the finer points of cricket, the ball went where it shouldn't and I was knocked out. When I woke up three days later, in hospital, there it all was.'

He shifted position, to prop himself up on his elbow. 'It was the most terrifying moment of my life. I was twenty-one years old, in hospital, with a killer headache, and I could hear what everyone else was thinking.' He stopped; the desolate chill of memory rode over his skin, and then was gone. The warmth of Madison's presence could make anything right. *God, you can't lose this woman.*

'Thinking?' She jerked him back to the present. She'd leaned forward to study him. He had to resist the impulse to pull her closer. There was real confusion in her voice.

'More or less. It wasn't organised, just coming at me in waves. I was petrified, afraid I was going mad. I could have ended up in a psychiatric unit, but there was this doctor—' Another chill at a might-have-been. If he'd woken in another hospital—

Jay shook off the memory of horror. It hadn't happened. 'He realised what was going on. It turned out he had a little power himself. He was part of this loose arrangement, a kind of informal academy of other like-minded medicos. He pointed me at one of them, the one best able to help me make sense of what I'd become. Once I was discharged from hospital, the academy took over. They taught me to control things, how to use the power and how to scale down the volume and tune out, except when I needed it. You know what it's like – totally exhausting, if you don't control it. You only really make sense of stuff when you learn to focus, and once you do – well, you know how much concentration that takes. One-to-one, and close up. It's a darn sight easier with you, of course, because the patterns are there and we both know what we're doing. When you're not actively keeping me out, that is.' He slanted her a look, getting a small nod in return 'Yes, well – I had some great teachers. I learned fast. And that was that. I was one of them.' This time he smiled at the recollection. 'I have to tell you that they were a pretty eccentric bunch. Some of them were downright geeky. Most of them were conspiracy theorists, anti-establishment, rabidly anti-military – you can imagine. None of them treated me as if I'd landed from Mars, which was the main thing as far as I was concerned. I finished my training in the States. I'd found out the kind of doctor I wanted to be.'

'And that was the start of *the* Jayston Creed.'

'Yes. Those people, they were doing some amazing things. A lot of them were working with the diseases of old age, dementia, stroke, a couple of the less geeky ones worked with the cops, doing something with trace energy at crime scenes. I never got a handle on that one. The medical side, it was all about amelioration and palliative work, helping people make the best of what they had left, after trauma – anger management, dealing with the effects of personality change, the sort of thing that goes with a disturbance in the brain. I was working with head-injury patients. I began to think that there could be more, that we might be able to get in there and do something more radical.'

'I read some of the early papers, the ones where you started to develop the technique,' Madison said.

'Then you know that I found that I couldn't do it alone. There wasn't enough power, that's the only way I can put it. So I started working with other adepts. Eddie Jones was one of them. When the mix-up in pictures happened we went along with it. Eddie liked the travelling and the glamour. All I was interested in was the work, plus I am absolutely crap at public speaking.' He spread his hands. 'What the hell – it worked. Alec Calver was my main assistant. He is *seriously* good, but even with him, there was something missing.'

'That's when you decided you needed a female collaborator?'

Jay nodded. 'You were one of the ones that I considered. I'd heard a little about you. But when

I met Gina, I filed the rest of the list. It took us a couple of years to get the co-operative technique right between us. We were having some success, but it was much too soon to put it into action. Then Dan's car ran into a tree . . .' He covered his eyes. 'The rest you know.'

Madison turned towards him, drawing down his hand, and planting a kiss on the palm. He smiled.

'Your turn,' he suggested softly, watching her face.

'The life and times of Madison Albi?' Madison closed her eyes. Could she do this? Trust? Share? The answer came back to her, strong and clear. If there was ever going to be anything between her and Jay, then she had to.

'With me – I've always had it. When I was a child, I didn't really understand. I can remember things. When I was about six, being at a birthday party, knowing which gifts the other child really liked and which ones she absolutely hated, which of my fellow guests was getting overexcited and would be in a tantrum before the end of the day.' She smiled, ruefully. 'My parents played it down. Just a funny childhood quirk, like having an imaginary friend. By the time I was a teenager I could always tell what my friends were feeling. Not thinking, but emotions. Everyone said how I *really* understood them. They used to come to me with problems, like I was some sort of agony aunt. I didn't have a clue about what they should do.

Heaven knows what sort of advice I dished out. And then my parents were killed.'

She sat still, remembering the urgent conversation with her father, the frightening things she'd learned. *Another place where your world changed.* She'd made promises that day. Promises she'd kept. It had been her fifteenth birthday. Two weeks later her parents were dead.

Jay put his hand on her back, stroking up and down, comforting. Madison relaxed into his hold. 'I went to live with my aunt. She worked for a place very similar to the facility I work at, but this was on the outskirts of Bristol. My parents never really wanted to acknowledge what I was. I think they hoped that it might just fade away. Perhaps things would have been different, if they'd lived . . . My father . . .' She shrugged. 'My aunt was the one who helped me make sense of it all.' *Helped a grief-stricken teen, with a freakish talent.* 'I decided I wanted to be normal, ordinary. I went to university, studied chemistry, and met Neil. We dated, off and on. When I graduated, I got myself a job with a pharmaceutical company. I tried to bury what I was, but it was still there. I wasn't always good at resisting. I worked on a few projects with my aunt's colleagues, contributed to a research paper or two. My aunt was like your geeks; she wouldn't have any truck with the military or anything to do with weapons. With her it was the pure science.'

Madison twisted around to face Jay. 'When my

aunt got cancer, I gave up work to nurse her. When she died, I wanted a fresh start. The offer of the job at the lab came out of the blue, through one of my aunt's friends.' She stopped, with a grimace. 'That obviously wasn't what I thought it was.'

Secretly she'd been so proud to be asked. It had felt right, using her power to try and do some good – but it had all been part of someone else's plan. To keep an eye on her. She shook off the melancholy reflection. She had accomplished things in her work. *No one can take that away from you.*

'Neil had kept in touch,' she went on, slowly. She wasn't going to think about the reason for that, either. 'He was living in London, but he came back most weekends. Things were getting serious between us. There was nothing to keep me in Bristol, so I accepted the job and moved to London. I turned my life around.' She sighed. 'Now I know it was all engineered: Neil, the job, everything.'

'It doesn't change your achievements,' Jay said gently. 'And Neil loved you. Craig was quite clear on that.' He tucked a lock of hair behind her ear, letting his fingers rest against her cheek. 'You're a very special woman, Madison Albi, and don't let anyone tell you different.'

She sank back, and rolled into his arms. There was comfort and strength there. She let herself savour it, turning her face into his shoulder. The words of the clairvoyant in the shop in Tenby murmured through her head – *you will be strong for each other.* 'Do you really think we can do this?'

He didn't pretend to misunderstand her. 'I don't know, but I think together we have the best chance. I should never have got you into this, Madison. But now I have, I can't think of anyone else I'd rather be with.'

They lay together, just holding, for a while.

Jay glanced towards the window. 'It's getting light. Our last day.' The words hung between them. With an effort Madison shook off the whisper of fear. She smiled into his eyes.

'What do you want to do today?'

'Well if the sun shines, we could explore a castle. If it doesn't—' He looked down at her, speculatively. 'We could stay here for the rest of the day.'

'That is a decadent suggestion.'

'I get very decadent around beautiful women. One beautiful woman,' he amended hastily, catching the glint in her eye. He pulled her closer.

The touch of his mouth heated her skin. Her lips trembled over a moan. She turned into him, letting go of it all – fear, promises, everything. There was only them, a man, a woman, in the sanctuary of a bed. No talk, only feeling.

CHAPTER 31

Madison stood and watched as Jay reached into the car to pack the last of the luggage. The long, lean length of his back and legs, taut now as he stretched over the driver's seat to toss something into the glove compartment, sent a frisson along her spine. She knew that body now, as intimately as she knew her own. In dark and daylight, by candle light, by starlight, she'd held, touched, tasted. Every inch of that tanned skin. And still she wanted him.

Unaccountably, tears welled in her eyes. She turned away as he straightened up. The cottage was locked and secure. Already it had a closed-off, deserted look. She sucked in her cheeks, looking up at the blank windows and the tendrils of clematis spreading over the roof, the delicate pink blossom moving slowly in the fresh morning breeze.

She might never come here again. Unless—

The key to the front door bit into her palm as she curled her fingers around it. She had a brief, reckless impulse to throw it into the sea. Instead she put it carefully into her handbag. Just in case.

When she turned around, Jay was leaning on the roof of the car, watching her

'Last walk on the beach?' he suggested, head tilted.

'Why not?'

He held out his hand. She took it and gripped tight.

There were clouds scudding over the sky, some high and white and fluffy, others dark, low-flying ribbons, threatening rain. The sand went from warm gold to dank brown as a denser ribbon blocked out the sun. Madison held her breath until the cold shadow passed. They were making for the rock in the centre of the beach. They'd crept down here last night, to the flat surface that ran around the edge, and made love, hard and fast, before the incoming tide swept in. The sea hadn't got them, but she'd nearly broken her neck afterwards, climbing the path in the dark.

When they reached the rock Jay sat, drawing her down beside him. 'You want to go over it, one last time?'

'No.' They'd looked at it from every angle, planned for everything they could. Faced all the consequences. 'Not unless there's a way to change what happens after.' She knew the answer, but she still had to say it.

'Not that I can see.' He buried his hand in his hair. 'I've tried.' He shrugged, an uncharacteristically helpless gesture that went into her like a blade. 'There isn't any other way. We agreed—'

'I know,' she broke in. 'It's just that we do all that and then—' Her voice trailed away. He understood. Why say it?

He'd dropped his hand from his head and was looking out to sea.

'Life doesn't guarantee happy endings.' He grinned at her, lopsided. 'Hell, what are the odds that we even make it through the experiment?'

'Pessimist.' She gave him a shove. He shoved in return, then pulled, and she ended up in his lap.

Madison looked up, into his face. Her heart was balanced on the edge of something that couldn't quite make it to her tongue. She buried her forehead against his shoulder instead.

'Hey!' He smoothed her hair, then her back.

'I'm okay.' She slid off his knees and on to the rock, wincing as the hard stone hit the back of her thighs. 'I can't believe we came down here last night.' She looked round. 'If someone had seen us they'd probably have called the coastguard. Was it—' Abruptly she swallowed what she was about to say.

'Like that with Gina?' Jay understood what she had been about to say. 'Sometimes, at the beginning. I remember a few wild moments in the lab, but that was before we were married.' She could see he was thinking about that. 'Neil?'

'No.' She traced the scar of a fossil in the surface of the rock. 'Neil made me feel safe. I guess that that was part of his job.' She curled her legs up under her. She'd begun to come to terms with what Craig had revealed, but there was still a way to go.

'So – it's official – we make each other crazy.' Jay reached out and took her hand. 'Some of what I felt for Gina was love, but it doesn't come anywhere near what I feel for you. I'd die for you, Madison, simple as that.'

'Don't say it!' She put her free hand over his mouth. He kissed it and twisted away.

'I'm hoping not to have to put it to the test.'

He sprawled easily against the rock, watching a couple of seagulls flying low over the waves.

The fact that he wasn't asking her for a response made part of her ache to give him one. She just couldn't get past that final internal defence that stubbornly refused to fall. She'd loved Neil, but Jay challenged her on levels she barely comprehended. If she gave her whole self to him, there wouldn't be anywhere left to hide, not even in her own mind. Despite everything, she still wasn't ready. And yet, if ever there was a moment for a declaration, it was now.

She gazed up at the cliff. Once they started back, they'd be setting something in motion that neither of them could stop. There was still time for them both to run. She looked at the cliff and the cottage, standing alone at the top, and then at Jay. Some of the best moments of her life would be left behind her here. Moments spent with this man, and she still couldn't tell him that she loved him.

Their plans were made. Now Jay was staring out to sea.

'Penny for them?'

He turned towards her, shaking his head slowly . . .

Madison didn't look back as they climbed away from the sea and the rock and the bay. She had to focus forward now. On the things they'd agreed must be done.

Jay watched Madison as she climbed the path ahead of him, spine straight and chin defiantly high. A sticky thread of apprehension was trying to crawl through his guts. Halfway up, he turned to look back. The breeze had sharpened while they were on the beach. A cold shaft lanced into his chest. He looked down at the sea and the gulls. Once they left here, nothing that happened would be within his control.

He watched a lone gull soar off into the sky, with a piercing, unearthly cry, and felt something turn in the pit of his stomach. Madison had given him everything and nothing. They made love, but when he held her in his arms she still wouldn't let him into her thoughts. The fierce hunger inside him was like a bereavement. He wanted to lie in her mind when he took her body. *And if wishes were horses . . .*

He turned again to the climb. It was Madison's call. As long as she let him inside her head for what they had to do, it would be enough.

And she had given him hope. Something precious. And dangerous.

He didn't have any right to ask for more.

'There is one other thing—' Madison indicated as she pulled out into the line of motorway traffic. 'Alec Calver. He's working for the Organisation. And with you. Are you sure about that?'

'No.'

The bald answer had her glancing sharply across the car.

'We have to watch out for him, too?'

'I think we watch out for everyone who isn't us. And keep the mental guards up. We don't take any extra risks.'

CHAPTER 32

'They're back. Drove in two minutes ago,' Vic announced tersely and hung up.

Alec staggered away from the phone, as if he'd been punched, overbalancing a small chair and sending a shower of ash and sour-smelling liquid on to the floor. A litter of overflowing ashtrays, half-drunk cups of coffee and empty whisky bottles covered most of the surfaces of the room. Those that were still upright. In the last twenty-four hours he'd overturned and trashed a lot of the furniture. With a grimace of disgust he crossed to the window to throw it open, letting out the fug of dead air and smoke. He, and the room, stank of sweat, and stale booze, and fear.

Relief and fury swam up through his chest.

'You bastard, Creed. You *bastard*.'

Vic put down the headphones as Alec entered. He hadn't shaved and his fingers were stained yellow with nicotine. He eyed Alec's cautious movements. 'Rough weekend?'

'What do you think?' Alec picked up the headset. 'Am I listening to the apartment or the lab?'

'The apartment. They'll be in the lab tomorrow morning. Apparently they made progress over the weekend. Now Albi seems excited about something she's found in a book. Dream therapy?'

Alec's face split in a grin. He exhaled, still shaky with reaction, after hours of tension. 'Didn't I tell you that this woman could do it!'

'You did,' Vic confirmed. 'She's planning to research some stuff tonight. Creed's cleared off to the studio, to let her get on with it.' He shrugged when Alec stared at him. 'I'd do the same – there's footie on the box at half nine.'

Alec grimaced, then settled in a chair with the cans over his ears. 'Get the collection unit in place. Twenty-four hour standby. They don't drop off the bloody map again.' He shot Vic a warning glance. 'We monitor every breath – neither of them goes for a pee without us knowing about it.'

Vic raised his hand in acknowledgement. 'All fixed, no sweat.'

'It better be. If she breaks through and we cock up, then we'll need a deep hole to hide in. Ape-face will start with our balls in a sandwich and go on from there.'

The coffee shop was crowded, loud with the buzz of conversation. People swapped stories of their holiday weekend, while waiting for breakfast orders to take with them to work. Craig was already paying for his coffee when Madison approached the counter. He stood next to the bar that held spoons and other accessories, sipping, as she stirred sugar into two lattes.

'When?' he asked softly.

'Half an hour?'

'That works.' He swung towards her. 'Don't worry, Maddie, we'll be right behind you. We have the implant on Creed. We'll always know where he is.' He hesitated, and then put down a small object next to her coffee containers.

'A computer flash drive?' She cast a hunted look round, alarm spiking through her over-stretched system. 'Craig, if you're changing the plan now—'

'No – it's for you. It's not a drive, at least it is, but it's a tracker, too. I got it for you, for backup. Just in case.'

She hesitated, then pocketed the gadget. 'Thank you.'

'I've got an obligation to Neil, Maddie. He'd expect me to look after you. Take care.' Craig headed for the door. 'And good luck.'

'I think we should try this.' Madison wriggled her jaw, which was stiffening up with the effort of acting natural. Somewhere in her lab was a bug. Craig's team had confirmed it, with an early morning sweep.

She tried to ignore the itch between her shoulder blades at the thought of someone listening. The urge to search for the thing was almost over-whelming, but she had to resist it. She'd managed to hang on to her control last night, alone in the apartment.

She dragged her concentration back to what she was doing. Jay was looking at her, waiting for her to feed him his lines. 'I know it sounds strange, but I think it might work. It's worth trying.'

Jay smiled but she could see the brittleness in his movements. 'Do I have this right? I go to sleep, and then you take over my dreams?' The scepticism in his voice sounded almost too realistic. She shot him a sharp look. 'You feed me coffee, then you want me to sleep?' he asked, blandly.

'So, don't drink the coffee.' She took it out of his hand. Their faces were close. She turned slightly. Jay's lips brushed hers. She rested her forehead against his cheek. She wanted to cling. She wanted to run. For an instant her resolution quailed. Jay must have felt the tension in her.

'We can do this.' His voice was a breath of encouragement, close to her ear.

'I know,' she whispered back. She hung on to him for a moment longer, gathering strength from the comfort of his hold. Then she raised her voice. 'You lie on the couch and see if you can sleep. I'll get on with some work. If you do fall asleep, we'll see what happens.'

Madison waited fifteen minutes, then five more, just in case. She shuffled paper, turned the computer on, printed out three pages of a report at random and muttered facts and figures under her breath.

Jay was doing a fairly good impersonation of being asleep, with snuffles and snores. Was a bug that sensitive? If it was, then it would be picking up her heartbeat any second. It sounded like Big Ben ticking in her ears.

She walked slowly over to the couch, putting her feet down firmly, to register movement. When she got there, she made a noise that she hoped sounded like someone finding her subject was out for the count.

For a horrific second she thought that Jay really had dozed off, until he squeezed her hand. She pulled out a stool and drew it up beside him. She felt slightly faint. Now was the worst part. They had to recreate what she'd done at the cottage, for an audience.

Moving jerkily, she clicked on her recorder and began speaking, identifying herself, Jay as the subject, the time and the procedure she intended to undertake. She paused, waited, and spoke again.

'A small change in the interior climate.' She waited ten beats. 'I'm redirecting energy towards the barrier.'

God, this was rubbish. Was anyone likely to be convinced? Panic hammered through her. Jay's eyes were open. He nodded reassuringly and began to moan. When he squeezed her hand again, her stomach kicked.

'Signs of massive deterioration in the barrier.

Oh, my God, it's happening!' She dropped the microphone. It clattered under the couch. 'Jay? Are you all right? Can you hear me?' She had her hands on his shoulders. How had they got there? She swung away as he sat up, cursing.

'Jay, can you hear me?' she repeated. 'It's all right. Take your time.' Madison waited, counting off a minute, then another, as they'd agreed, to give the listeners time to assimilate what was happening, but still braced for the lab door to come crashing in. Her breath was catching in her throat. What if they'd miscalculated? If the people monitoring them didn't understand? Jay was muttering loudly, in disjointed fragments. He grasped her hand and squeezed it. She folded her fingers into his. 'What's going on? Can you tell me? Talk to me, Jay,' she pleaded.

'Jayston Creed!'

'What?' She dropped his hand and backed away, then turned for the door, as they'd rehearsed. 'What have you remembered?' It wasn't hard to make her voice scratchy with alarm.

'Oh God. *Creed*, I'm Creed.' He was on his feet, beside her at the door. 'Do you have your car keys? We have to run, Madison. We must get out of here, now, before they come.'

Madison was afraid her heart was going to explode out of her chest. She channelled all the panic and confusion she could find into her voice. 'Who are *they*? What have you remembered? What's going on? Jay?'

He pulled at her arm. She scuffed her feet on the floor to sound like resistance.

'We don't have time, Madison, we have to get out now!'

He banged open the door one-handed, dragging her with him. They erupted into the corridor.

Instantly Madison felt the brush of fresh air on her face. The fire door at the end of the passage was open. A man in dark clothes, his face hooded, was standing beside it. There was a gun balanced across his elbow.

The scream Madison gave wasn't faked. Jay's fingers tightened on her wrist as he made to pull her the other way.

There was a second man, covering the door to the main corridor.

And behind him it was opening.

Jay steamed towards it. Madison had a glimpse of Jonathan's shocked face in the doorway. She saw his arm move sharply sideways and heard the crack of glass. The wail of the panic alarm split the air.

The man at the door swung something upwards. Jonathan went down in a heap, with barely a groan. The man swung back, ramming what was in his hand towards Jay.

Jay collapsed to his knees, and then fell forward, sprawling across the corridor.

Her screams covered by the sound of the siren, Madison shrank against the wall, edging backwards. She saw the eyes of the man who had brought down her lover and her best friend through the mask that covered his face. They were hard, glittering black.

Then something dropped over her head and she was lifted off her feet.

CHAPTER 33

It was a blanket and it was stifling her in its musty smelling folds. Sweating, and struggling to breathe, she fought her way out, fear shrieking adrenaline around her body.

Jay was beside her. The dread that they might have been separated receded.

Grimly, she ran her hands over his body, checking for injuries. It was hard to see in the dimness, but she couldn't find anything. No sign of broken bones or blood on her hands. What they'd used must have been some sort of tranquilliser. Jay was unconscious, but he wasn't hurt.

She sat back, forcing her mind to calm. Of course they wouldn't hurt him. They wanted him fully functioning for what they intended to do. She looked round, swallowing a wave of nausea, trying to take stock of their surroundings.

They were lying on the floor of a van and it was moving at speed. She got to her knees and grabbed for something to hold on to as they bucketed over a bump in the road. Everything lurched.

When she was stable enough to glance over her shoulder again, Jay was attempting to sit up. His face looked green in the half-light, but his eyes were focused. She put her arms around him to hold him steady as the van bucked again.

'What was it they hit you with?' She spoke close to his ear, to combat the noise of the engine

'Stun gun, I think. It's okay. I'll be better in a minute.' He shook his head and shifted, to brace himself against the side of the vehicle. 'I'm sorry, Madison. I've got you into this.' His voice broke.

For a moment she stared at him, confused. Then she realised, with a sudden snap, that Jay was staying in character, in case they were being observed. She shuddered. She could so easily have given them away.

He seemed to sense her alarm. His grip tightened.

'What is this?' The quaver in her voice was frighteningly real. 'What's going on, Jay?'

Alec let himself into the room and locked the door behind him. Madison Albi was sitting stiffly in a chair. Her hands were free but her ankle was padlocked to a chain fastened to the wall.

They stared at each other. She really was quite beautiful, Alec admitted silently. The paleness of her face and the fear in her expression couldn't change the wealth of chocolate-brown hair and the large dark eyes. It was the eyebrows that made her face so distinctive, he decided – naturally shaped, with a fine slanting arch. The chin had a dimple in it, but it still looked stubborn. Alec smothered a grin. Creed hadn't had an easy time with this one. He would do better.

'Dr Albi.' He inclined his head politely as hers jerked up. 'I am Alec Carver. I believe Dr Creed may have mentioned me.' He watched her carefully, gauging her reaction.

She was shaking her head. 'I don't know you. I don't know where I am. I don't know what you want with me.' She had that chin up, brave despite the quiver in her voice. Alec strolled across the room and sat on the edge of the table that stood in the centre. He waited for her to speak again. He knew she would. He didn't have to wait long. 'I work at a specialist research centre, from which you or your associates snatched me, and the subject with whom I was working. I have no idea what you want with us. But I have to tell you, the alarm was raised. The police will be looking for us by now.'

Alec allowed himself a small smile. 'I doubt if they'll find you. At least not in time.' He saw the flash of panic in her eyes, quickly controlled. 'I apologise for the rather violent nature of your arrival here,' he said smoothly, hitching up a trouser leg. 'We require your participation in an experiment, Dr Albi. After that you will be free to go.'

'Free? Experiment?' Her voice rose. With temper, not alarm, Alec noted with interest. 'Just what is going on here?' she demanded. 'If you'd wanted to do some sort of experiment, you could have approached my employers—'

'This is something rather unusual.' Alec watched her face intently, his respect for her growing. The woman was still frightened, but she wasn't letting it overwhelm her. 'You and Dr Creed—'

'The man you brought here with me is an amnesiac, whose name is Jay,' she interrupted. 'Just before you kidnapped us he made a partial, maybe a full, recovery of his memory. I didn't have time to make a proper assessment.' Her glance now was almost waspish. 'He started yelling about being Creed, and that we had to get out. He seemed to know that you were coming. On the way here he also talked of an experiment. Not very coherently.'

Alec bent over to study Madison's face. There was nothing there but confusion, some fear, and that interesting spark of anger. Her expressions really were quite transparent. No need to chance a mind probe – he could *see* what he needed, without taking the risk of opening a dangerous channel between them. No point in gambling his defences with a woman as talented as this one. He sat back, satisfied. 'In that case, Dr Albi, it falls to me to explain the situation.'

The ridges in the surface of the bench were digging into Jay's hip. His head was clear; the effect of the stunner had worn off. Not a weapon he'd encountered before – extremely fast and effective – and probably new and experimental. The Organisation demanded the latest and the best. Sometimes they were even prepared to pay to acquire it. He tried to turn, to ease some of the pressure, but the bindings around his legs and arms brought him up short. He settled down again, willing himself to ignore the ache in his limbs and the sweat of apprehension pooling at the base of his spine. He'd anticipated that he and Madison might be separated. He'd hoped to be wrong.

Anxiety for her had just begun to knot hard in his stomach when the door of the room opened with a bang. Jay ducked his head against the bright lights blaring in from the corridor. The man standing in the entrance was tall, with a shaved head and very dark eyes. Vic, the computer expert, the one who had made the machine.

He was also the man who had been waiting for them by the door of the lab, the one with the stun gun. Jay could sense his caution. He was staying in the passageway. Jay almost smiled. Clearly Vic had checked with Alec about his approach. He wasn't taking any chances with mind games.

'Your memory back?' Vic barked.

Delay wasn't going to achieve anything. 'Yes,' Jay said.

'Then you know what you're here for. Alec is talking to your girlfriend, he's persuading her to co-operate. Everything goes well, she walks away. You want her to do that, you co-operate, too. Think about it.'

The door banged shut again.

★   ★   ★

353

Madison licked her upper lip nervously, channelling all her distress and confusion. Alec Carver was still sitting on the end of the table, swinging one leg. Tentatively she tried a veiled mind probe. It went in without difficulty, only to hit a well-constructed defensive barrier. She flattened the probe immediately, automatically checking that her own shield was in place. Jay hadn't underestimated the man's power. She put her hand to her head.

'Jay really is Jayston Creed? And you want us to repeat the experiment that killed his wife?' she asked, shakily.

'Don't panic,' Alec warned. 'The first experiment failed because Gina Creed wrecked it. You won't be doing that. Plus, Jay and I will be taking care of you. You have nothing to worry about, Dr Albi, if you're prepared to co-operate.'

'If I do what you want, you promise I'll be free to leave? And Jay?' She let the hope spill into her face, watched Carver smile.

'I think that you and I are going to be able to business, Dr Albi.'

Madison felt as if all the blood had drained from her body when the shaven-headed man shoved Jay into the room. She was at his side in an instant, steadying him, blessing the fact that Carver had taken the padlock from her ankle and left them alone. Jay leaned against her for a second. She touched his face, the briefest spark of contact. Her eyes went hard when she saw that Jay's hands were cuffed. Silently he shook his head.

Clearing her throat, she went back to the script. 'You're really Jayston Creed?' She looked him in the eyes, and focused. *'Alec told me everything. That you and he were working together. He even apologised.'*

Jay's eyes widened. He nodded. *'I got Vic – if I co-operate, you can walk away.'*

'Can you do what they want?' She turned up the uncertainty in her voice as high as she could. *'Alec promised all of us will get out.'*

Jay's brows rose. 'I can do what has to be done. With your help.'

'What do I have to do?' she asked aloud. *'I tried a probe on Alec. It didn't work. He was too well defended.'*

'Vic didn't stay around long enough for me to try.'

'You're sure that you want to do this?'

'Do we have a choice?'

'I don't think so,' he said.

'Then I have to do it.'

Jay leaned against the table. 'This is what I need from you.'

CHAPTER 34

'This is too bloody easy.' Vic hauled a piece of equipment, that Alec couldn't identify, into place. 'Both of them agreeing? This fast?'

'You're just mad because you didn't get to beat anyone up,' Alec suggested, grinning.

Vic glowered. He dragged the stun gun out of his belt and pointed it. 'Don't push me.'

Alec held up his hands in mock surrender. 'What are you going to do? Zap me? I don't think so. Not with *him* watching us.'

Alec cast his eyes upwards. Vic followed his glance and cursed, softly but graphically. The CEO was standing on a wide metal gantry above them, looking down.

Vic groaned under his breath. 'Does he have to be here?'

Alec's grin widened. 'He thinks so.'

'Tosser.'

'Him or me?'

Vic just gave him a death-head stare.

Alec prowled around the space. The manufacturing unit had been stripped and was now awaiting refitting. The Organisation had acquired the whole of the small industrial estate which surrounded it six weeks before. It would be sold on again, before the end of the month. The unit was close to the river, spacious, quiet and private.

Jay and Madison were tucked away in the warren of workshops and offices that ran along the front of the building. The empty factory floor had the open area for the equipment Vic needed. They'd waited until evening, and less congested roads, to move in the largest and most sensitive pieces. Bleak, industrial walls stretched up, bare and unforgiving, into the gloom of the pitch roof. A skylight showed a darkening sky and scudding clouds. 'Did you check the perimeter?' Alec asked, as he wandered back to where Vic was positioning chairs. He'd recovered from the terror of the weekend, but the fear that Jay had run, leaving him hanging in the wind, was still a bitter memory in his mouth.

'Do I have to do every fucking thing around here?' Vic snarled. 'Parker and Kelly have been all round, twice. There's nothing out there. Only a lot more empty buildings. Do you really think the cavalry is going to come rushing over the hill?'

Alec shrugged and looked away.

'Cavalry or not, I still think it's too fast. *They* could be up to something,' Vic grumbled. 'We should have sweated them a little longer.'

'That might have been possible if the alarm hadn't gone off at the lab. The plan was to get them away quietly.' Alec ignored Vic's deep scowl. 'People will be looking for them, which is why we need to be sure there's no one out there,' he explained, with exaggerated patience. 'Don't worry about the experiment. We can do it. Albi doesn't know what's hit her. She was ready to grab the first way out that offered. Creed killed his wife.' Alec's hands tightened into fists. He unfolded them, with a deliberate gesture. 'This time he's going to do the noble thing and try to save the lady. Why wait?'

Vic turned his back on him, pointedly, and started to plug in leads and power cables. A portable generator hummed.

Alec looked critically at the three chairs that faced each other in the middle of the jumble of computer gear that the men had unloaded. 'Are you nearly done here?'

'Yeah.' Vic was booting up the machines. Lights blinked. A low-level buzz was audible as he punched buttons. 'You sit there,' he said, indicating the chair. 'I'll be behind Albi, she will be facing Creed. Then if either of them gives us any grief, well—' He patted the stunner.

'Dr Albi doesn't understand enough to be a problem. And Creed won't give you any trouble,' Alec asserted. *He's going to be trusting me, right to the end.*

'You reckon?' Vic gave Alec an enigmatic look. 'You nervous?' he asked curiously. Alec avoided his eyes.

'Of course I'm nervous. Last time this was done, two people died. But this time it's going to work. Do you need me to do anything?'

'No. These babies are up and running. Three machines, networked. Each of you will be hooked up to one. I feed you what power you need. You just stay open, and give me everything you can. Any glitches I can clean up later when I lay down the programme. I just need to get the moves that Albi and Creed make when they start to change things in your head.' He shot Alec a baffled look. 'I still don't get that you're up for this. They're going to be inside your *brain* man! Messing with your *mind*!'

'Not for that long,' Alec said confidently. 'There are vast areas of the brain we don't use. Creed will be working in one small part. It will only take a few seconds for you to get what you want.'

'And then you get what *you* want.'

Alec smiled slowly. 'I do. Better be ready.'

'Don't worry about that.' Vic patted the nearest machine. 'What about Albi?'

'Not a problem. She's the powerhouse. She keeps things running while Creed does the fine tuning.'

'And that's what Gina did?'

'Yes.' Alec leaned over to straighten a chair by a centimetre. 'That's what Gina did.'

Madison's hands were trembling. Her stomach had given up trying to climb out of her throat and was see-sawing rhythmically, like a fairground ride. She still had enough presence of mind to glare at Vic and to knock his hand away when it strayed down to her breast as he fixed sticky pads, with wires attached, to her forehead and the back of her neck. He grinned and made an exaggerated kissing motion with his lips. She turned her head away, studying the other two men.

There'd been a small disturbance when Jay and Alec had come face to face. They'd eyed each other, like scrapping dogs. Which was exactly what Alec had told her would happen. Behind Vic's back he gave her a reassuring smile.

'I want these things taken off.' Jay held up his cuffed hands.

'You don't need—' Vic began to argue.

'Remove them.'

Madison's head shot up. There was a man standing on a metal landing above them. It must be a man, even though it looked like an ape. Vic slouched over and unlocked the cuffs. Madison studied the gantry. It ran the length of the building. There were steps up from the main floor, at regular intervals. A ladder stretched up from the gantry into the depths of the roof.

'If you're ready, Dr Albi?' Alec put a gentle hand on her shoulder. 'I'll be taking my place in just a second. Then we can begin.'

Madison inhaled. The see-saw in her stomach, the betraying hands and the sweat on her hairline, all faded from her thoughts. She looked over at Jay. His face was set. His hands were on his knees. Unmoving.

Alec was fastening electrodes and settling in his chair.

Madison sensed a movement above. Automatically she looked up. The man on the gantry had stepped forward. He was leaning over, intent on the scene below him. As he stooped over the rail she caught his eye. With a small gasp of surprise and shock, she jerked away from the contact.

'Dr Albi?' Alec had caught her sudden movement. 'Is anything wrong?'

'No. I'm fine.' She waved away his concern. Mercifully he didn't pursue it. She bent her head, looking at the floor. The man above didn't seem to have noticed anything. With another deep breath she sealed away the horror she'd learned in that second of connection, to retrieve later.

When she raised her eyes, Jay was looking at her. He nodded, one small dip of his head. His mouth was a tense line. He had to be thinking of the last time he attempted this. With a relinquishing sigh she thrust aside her doubts, cleared her mind, and let go.

Immediately she could feel Jay reaching for her. She opened her defences a little wider, and pushed forward, entranced. Jay was spinning a connection between them, like a bridge. She could pass along it to him and he to her. With her eyes closed she could almost see it, a narrow golden arc, glimmering between them. Power flickered off it, like butterfly wings.

Behind her she was conscious of a change in the

note of the machines. Vic's presence was a darkening cloud behind her. The bridge wobbled. With a shimmer of guilt she concentrated forward again.

Jay was strengthening the structure. Power was spiralling off it now, like droplets of hot rain. He was edging back, letting her take the weight, encouraging her onward; to assume responsibility for the bridge.

She eased forward, surprised at the smoothness. Jay was urging her towards him. She felt warmth roll over her. She exhaled, and the bridge glittered and sang.

She felt the tiny flutter of surprise that flowed down the span from Jay, and knew she was smiling. The note of the computers had changed again. This time she used the sound, weaving it into the shining arch.

She was all the way across now, using her concentration to hold the continuation in place, feeling the reserves of life force lurking in the back of her head, paradoxically boosted by the connection and the outlet of skill – golden particles, streaming through her. She fed on the energy.

She reached Jay's mind and felt dark blue silk brush around her. She tasted lilies. Approval and welcome surrounded her. She basked like a cat. She could stay like this forever, suspended here. *This* was who she was. Her essence.

She moved her thoughts and knitted something complex, just for the pleasure of it, a grandiose bulwark, at the end of the bridge. She wanted to clap her hands at the joy of it.

She read Jay's amusement and acknowledgement, but also his caution. Sobering, she settled again, holding the structure.

She felt the pattern inside Jay shift.

The bridgehead was moving on. Energy darted outwards. Now there were two bridges. Her to Jay, and Jay to Alec.

It was happening.

She urged the power forward.

CHAPTER 35

'Brilliant. Fucking brilliant.' Vic was almost hopping out of his skin, watching the patterns forming on the three screens. 'It's working!' Carried away, he called up to the CEO, who raised a hand like a shovel in response.

Vic turned back to the computers, crouching over the machines, eyes darting from screen to screen, tweaking the settings, watching the lines pulse and shift in unison.

She had his back. Jay could feel her presence, like a silent warrior guarding the pass. He spun more strands forward, building the structure and testing if it would hold. He could feel the edges of Alec's consciousness now – total concentration and some fear. He reached out to reassure. Madison was following him, one step behind, keeping them both stable, giving him the platform on which to work.

As if we've done this all our lives.

The new structure was solid now. He moved across it, balancing both spans. Sparks flew as Madison drew on more power, to let him step over and into Alec's mind.

He had the connection. His internal sight split. He was poised, looking back and looking forward. Janus, linking the three of them together.

He pushed on, heading for the part of the brain they had identified.

The space was dark, red and enfolding. He conjured light. The brightness flared. Too strong, too soon. He controlled it, damping it down as the bridges blinked. An overload of power. The feed Madison was giving him was incredible. Behind him, she had steadied them.

Secure, Jay began to weave again, connecting the small pathways in Alec's brain that would make the link. Alec was quiescent, holding down his power, letting it rest like fog on the sea. Jay felt the other man's reaction as he skated over a synapse. He banked down the flush of triumph as the links began to form. When they were finished, Alec, who couldn't currently hold a pencil, would be able to draw.

Amazingly, Jay found himself able to think and reason outside the delicate work he was doing. The energy coming from Madison was unstoppable. He could feel the cool clarity of her mind in every move he made. He reached for another connection.

Alec kept his energy as flat and diffuse as he could, husbanding his resources. He could feel what Jay was doing, like a buzz in the corner of his brain; feel the unions snapping into place. Any time soon Vic would have all that he wanted.

It would be done.

Alec tested the last link, as it clicked into place. That was his cue, to let his power go, feeding it back to blow the machine, supported by Jay, and Madison. He and Jay had rehearsed it. But not like this.

With a leap like a smile and a surge of control, Alec reached out, pulling in the energy from Vic's computer, as he and Vic had practised, feeling it swell and hammer in his brain. He turned and sank hooks, like claws, into the golden bridge, making its surface ripple. He felt the bridge scream.

Then he began to flow along it, a dark torrent, into Jay's mind.

It was like a claxon going off. Madison coughed as the sound of sudden anguish vibrated in her mouth. Darting along the bridge, she saw at once what was happening. The darkness was visible to her, eating the connection between Alec and Jay.

'*Alec's turned,*' she telegraphed the words to Jay. She got back only a stutter of affirmation.

She could feel him, fighting for his life, inside his own head.

Vic hunched over the computers, a manic gleam in his eyes, but his hand rigidly controlling the pinwheel. Edging the current up. *This baby was rocking.* He risked a glance upwards. Creed's face was contorted; eyes rolled back, body rigid. Alec's features were smooth, like a mask of triumph.

Jay was losing ground, but only an inch at a time. The first irresistible tide had washed across half the bridge, in a sweep of destruction, turning it black and dead before Jay could muster his defence. Now the advance had slowed to a trickle as Jay battled. Madison could feel him, pushing Alec hard, trying to break the band that was holding them. She pulsed kinetic force towards him, in slow measured beats. Now Alec was waning. He'd begun to fall back.

Jay flared out along the bridge, storming forward with his last reserves of energy.

In a half-second, Madison, with an oblique view, saw the trap. In horror, she felt Alec draw strength as he might draw breath. And surge.

Jay was going down, floundering against the black tide. If Alec poured in and through Jay's mind and on to the second bridge, Jay would be gone.

For an instant of pure panic, she froze.

She felt both the bridges waver and the echo of Alec's hunger bouncing off Jay, like a cry in the dark.

Her nails bit her palm as her fingers curled into a fist.

She had no direct connection to Alec, and no time to forge one against the kind of defences he would undoubtedly have in place. A direct attack would be a distraction, forcing him to fight her, but it still might not be enough. And could she do it? She'd never used a mind connection in a hostile way. *Too much risk. Too much risk.*

Her nails were biting deep enough to draw blood.

Her only sure way to Alec was through Jay, along the connection already in place. If the tide on the bridge wasn't forced back, if the link was ripped away from Jay without being closed, if he was left isolated, exhausted and without power, with the bridge between him and Alec still burning and the surge of black fire making its way inexorably towards him . . . She didn't have time to analyse all the hideous implications and what they might mean. The only way she knew, the way she was certain of, lay ahead. She had to use what had already been built. Positive against negative, light against dark. Through Jay's mind, to block Alec, then pour his power back and reclaim the bridge.

'*You're done. Move.*' The message to Jay was barely a thought, more like an instinct.

Exhausted determination came back at her. He was panting, all but spent, but still resisting with everything he had left. '*Break . . . save.*'

She didn't answer, just pushed out to him, feeling for his trust. After a tortured second of incomprehension she sensed him understand. Relief screamed over her as he opened to her. The agonised lurch rocked them both as he fell aside to let her through. To engage with Alec. She steadied herself in an instant.

For a split second, she thought of her father. 'Sorry, Dad. I have to do this.' With a prayer for forgiveness, she lowered her last, most intimate defence.

Everything went still.

Then, rising like light, she hurled everything she had, everything she was, through Jay's mind, to the bridge beyond.

CHAPTER 36

The explosion was still vibrating off the walls. All the metal in the building was rattling. Shards of rust pattered down from somewhere in the rafters, like brown rain. Madison opened her eyes to the smell of burning.

She could hardly see. The flash of blue light that had accompanied the blast had dazzled her. She waited for her sight to clear. Vision came back slowly.

In front of her Jay was doubled over, head in his hands. Alec was on the floor, tumbled beside his fallen chair. Madison turned behind her, to the source of the smell.

All three computer monitors were shattered, black and smoking. Vic lay sprawled across the furthest one. His eyes were wide and staring. A faint blue haze seemed to be dancing over his body. As Madison watched, the blue glow crackled into nothing.

She got up shakily, testing her legs. They would just about hold her. Her ears were still ringing. What the hell had she done? Nausea rose in her throat.

She crossed uncertainly to Jay. He straightened up as she approached. Relief flooded through her when she saw that his eyes were normal. She leaned against him, resting numbed hands on his shoulders.

'Madison—'

'You will all remain perfectly still.'

Madison almost broke her neck from the speed with which her head jerked up. She'd forgotten the ape-man in the gallery. The gun he was holding was large and looked very serviceable. The snout swung towards her.

'Dr Albi, you will ascertain if Mr Carver is alive. Dr Creed, you will stay where you are, with your hands where I can see them.'

Mind racing, Madison picked her way over to where Alec was slumped. His face looked grey, but he did seem to be breathing. With distaste she put her hand on his chest. She felt a heartbeat. As she straightened up a blinking light caught her eye. Alongside the ravaged monitors, the massive black box of the power drive was humming busily.

She tilted her head to look up. Ape-man was leaning over, the gun resting on the rail. 'He's alive.'

The massive head nodded. 'Please return to Dr Creed.'

Madison did as she was told. The man with the gun was looking both ways along the gantry. At first she thought he was looking for the best way down. Then it hit her, with a start. Where were the rest of the hired help? Why hadn't anyone come running at the sound of the explosion?

She was spinning round, to scan the doorways, when there was another enormous crash, followed by the clattering of metal on metal.

Then all the lights went out.

CHAPTER 37

'Jay.' She felt for his hand. It was warm and firm in the blackness. 'This has to be . . .'

'. . . the backup.'

'Do we want to be here when they arrive?'

'Not if we can avoid it.'

There were voices and torches. Dark shadows flitted cautiously over the staved in door at the furthest end of the building.

'Up, I think.' Jay pointed towards the faint silver outline of the stairs.

'What about him?' She didn't need to explain who she meant, the man with the gun.

'He'll be doing the same thing we are, looking for a way out.' Jay pushed her gently forward. She was going, when she remembered the power unit.

'Jay – the computer, part of it is still working.' She pointed to the blinking green light.

With a soft curse Jay swept up one of the chairs and slammed it against the power drive. There was a hiss, and a shower of sparks, and flames spurted.

'Not any more.' He hustled her towards the staircase. There were distinct shapes at either end of the factory floor now, men in combat gear, moving steadily forward. The light from the blazing computer bounced over the gantry.

'Look.' Madison pointed. Alec was pelting down the metal landing. As they watched, he reached the ladder to the roof and started to climb.

'How did he get there?'

'When the lights failed. He must have been waiting his chance. That's the best way out. There'll be a fire escape, over the roof.'

Madison's legs were still wobbly. She needed a moment before she tackled a ladder. 'You go after him.' She urged Jay on. 'I'll follow you.'

He moved, then turned back, pulling her against him for a swift, hard kiss.

'I love you.'

'I love you,' she whispered.

He was smiling as he raced to the stairs. 'I know you do – now.'

Madison had made her way, shakily, to the top of the stairs, when the power came back on.

One of the security force was standing at the bottom of the staircase, staring up at her. The others were crowded around the fire and Vic's body. She shuddered, fighting down nausea again. When she looked back to the gantry, her heart nearly stuttered to a stop. Directly in her path was the ape-man. He no longer had the gun.

Madison didn't have time for thought, or hesitation. Pure adrenaline took over. She kicked out smoothly, aiming for the man's crotch. He doubled over with a scream as her foot connected. Madison dodged to one side as he overbalanced. The heavy body rolled down the steps, right into the arms of the advancing security man.

'Ask him what happened to his wife,' she yelled down as the ape-man was pulled roughly to his feet. 'Tell them to look in the concrete under the pool.'

The bellow of rage the ape-man gave told her that the brief flash she'd had into his mind, the clear, cold picture, straight from his memory – a smile of satisfaction, a shrouded bundle and pouring concrete – had been right on the money. She sprang for the ladder.

It was cold on the roof. Jay stopped just outside the door of the fire escape, waiting for Madison and getting his bearings, uneasily aware that Alec was out here somewhere. The dormer that housed the escape entrance was at the end of a row of skylights. It gave on to a tiny platform and a narrow railed walkway that stood out from the roof, bisecting its slope and running its whole length. Above, the glass of the skylights, protected by wire mesh, stretched towards the roof ridge. Below the tiles were steeply pitched. The end of the walk was in shadow. Jay hoped, fervently, that there was a ladder there connecting to the adjoining flat roof. He was wondering what sort of repair the whole thing was in when Madison hurtled through the door. He caught her. She was panting.

'Hey! Is anyone behind you?'

'Don't think so . . . for a while . . . busy with the ape-man and the wreckage.' Her voice broke. 'Jay, I killed that man.'

'Don't think about it.' He pulled her roughly into his arms. 'You had no way of knowing what would happen, and he was willing to kill us. Remember what we agreed? Right now, we have to get out of here.'

'Yes', she said, visibly pulling herself together. 'Which way?' She turned in his hold, to peer around.

'Left. It looks like it leads to the next building. The other way is a dead end. It's just the end of the roof.' Jay pointed and froze as a figure staggered up from a sitting position in the darkness further down the walkway, and began to lurch towards them. Alec.

The moon drifted out from a veil of cloud, glinting on metal. The gun in Alec's hand was wavering alarmingly.

'Oh, hell!' Madison sat down abruptly in the doorway. Then she raised her voice, 'Alec, if you're going to fire that thing, then do it and get it over with. You might like to take the safety catch off first.'

Jay shot her a startled glance. He got a how-should-I-know shrug in response. 'Worth a try,' she whispered.

'He only has to press the trigger.'

Madison shook her head. 'He's afraid of the

thing. Look at the way he's holding it. If he does any damage, it will be by accident. But it's still damage. If he thinks it's just an encumbrance . . . See.' Alec was turning the weapon uncertainly in his hands then, with a sudden gesture of impotent fury, he tossed it away from him. The gun clattered off over the tiles. Jay let out the breath he'd been holding. He moved forward until he could see Alec more clearly. There were tears on the other man's face. Alec lifted his arm to wipe them away on his sleeve.

'I thought we were friends,' Jay said softly. 'Why did you do it, Alec? Was it for the money?'

'No.' Alec's head swivelled violently. 'It was for Gina. I loved her. We were lovers.' He thumped his chest. 'It was *my* baby. She died . . . I wanted you to feel what she must have felt. It was *working*.' He turned towards Madison. 'You . . . it should have worked. Then you . . . You have more power than *he* has—' Disbelief quavered in his voice.

'Yes, she does.' Jay turned thoughtfully to Madison. 'But she kept it very quiet.'

Madison flapped a hand. 'Look, we can stay here, having a conversation about this, until that lot down there finish what they're currently doing and come looking, which will not be long. Or we can find out how to get down. I vote for getting down.' She stood up and advanced towards Alec. 'You go first.'

Jay caught her shoulders and put her behind him as Alec turned and began to stumble off. 'I think the fight's gone out of him. But I'm not taking any chances.'

'You believe him? About Gina and the baby?' Madison asked quietly.

'Yes. I don't know why I didn't think of it. He was the obvious person.'

'You trusted them both.'

He looked back at her. 'And talking of trust – what you did in there. Thank you, my love, for trusting me.'

'You trusted me first,' she said awkwardly. 'But now, I think you should be keeping your eyes on where you're walking. I don't like the feel of this stuff we're treading on.' She pointed as a piece of metal broke off and clanged away into the night. 'It hasn't been maintained in years.'

Another piece broke off and clattered after the first.

The moon was gliding in and out of the shifting clouds.

Jay slowed his pace, peering from side to side, trying to trace Alec's lurching progress ahead of them. He raised his voice 'Alec, slow down. It's not safe.'

The only response he got was a startled cry, as Alec disappeared.

CHAPTER 38

Instinctively, Jay leaped forward. The walkway vibrated violently. Madison shrieked a warning as splinters of metal flew off into space. He halted, took a moment to balance himself, and then began edging along the rotten slats.

Alec was sprawled over the sloping roof, one hand grasping a broken strut. Jay leaned down.

'Alec,' he called softly. 'Can you hear me?'

Alec's head came round, painfully slowly. His eyes were black pits, bottomless with fear.

'Madison,' Jay spoke over his shoulder. 'Can you move down to the next part of the walk? It looks more stable. Get to the other roof, if you can. It'll be less weight on this stuff.'

Madison wanted to argue that she should stay, but she kept her mouth shut. He needed to concentrate. She eased past him and scrambled across the gap that Alec's fall had made, as carefully as she could. She cleared the remainder of the walk, found the ladder and reached the flat roof of the next building, with a muttered prayer of thankfulness. From here there was a wide fire escape down to the ground.

She turned back, dreading what she would see.

Jay was inching his way closer to Alec, hand outstretched. Horror lurched in her throat as Alec's hand clamped around Jay's wrist. She couldn't hear their voices any more, but she guessed that Jay was trying to persuade the other man to shift his body sideways, so that he could get a better grip. Alec moved awkwardly towards Jay. Under his foot a tile detached itself, and went rattling down the roof. Both men stopped moving.

From the ground below, Madison could hear the sound of sirens. There would be fire trucks for the blaze. They would have ladders. If Jay and Alec could just hang on, help was a few feet away. *A short drop.*

Madison shuddered. If she could get down, she could get help. She turned towards the fire escape, and then turned back. She didn't know if Jay could see her. Would he think she was deserting them? She was too afraid to send a message into his mind, in case it was enough to distract him.

He was half kneeling, half lying, over the roof, one arm wound around the solid part of the walkway. He was very still. She could see the breeze ruffling his hair. Alec's jacket flapped out, like a flag.

She had made up her mind to go for the fire escape when the men began to move. She watched, mesmerised, as Jay drew Alec, with infinite slowness, towards safety. His head was bent. She sensed that he was talking to Alec, keeping up a flow of encouragement that was making the other man's progress more smooth and sure. As she kept her eyes fixed on them she could see Alec growing steadier. He was in a rhythm, easing more confidently towards safe ground.

She put her hand to mouth, biting her knuckles. If Alec could get his feet on to something solid they would make it. Madison bit down harder on her hand, imagining the stress on Jay's arm and shoulder. He had to be taking most, if not all, of Alec's weight. But the other man was closer now. There would be a second, when Alec would have to let go of the strut that supported his other side.

He let go.

Jay hauled back, and up, pulling him on to solid metal.

Madison let her hands drop as Alec reached the safety of the walk, sprawling across it like landed fish. All the breath hissed out of her lungs. There were tears on her face. She couldn't stop shaking. She could see Jay was panting with effort, his chest rising and falling in shuddering gasps. He was still on his knees. Alec was up now, on his feet.

Madison screamed the instant before Alec bent to yank Jay past him, down the roof. Jay dodged away, braced against the rail of the walk. Alec's arm went wide. Momentum carried him forward. His feet slipped as his body slid sideways. He tottered, limbs flailing. Jay was struggling to his feet, reaching out.

Madison watched the two figures like a tableau,

serenely lit by the moon. For a moment she thought Alec was going to get his balance. He seemed to be suspended, hovering against the sky.

Then he dropped, shrieking, into the empty air.

CHAPTER 39

'He tried to kill you. You helped him and he still tried.' Madison was sitting on the steps of an ambulance, parked amongst a cluster of vehicles at the rear of the building. The Thames gleamed, impassive, alongside. The wind had dropped. It was a perfect night, still and clear. She could hear noises floating up from the water, a snatch of music as a pleasure boat, full of partygoers, churned slowly past. There were a few people on the highest deck, craning to watch the fire trucks, turning away in disappointment when there were no flames to be seen.

Madison couldn't stop shivering. Someone had wrapped a blanket around her shoulders and put a mug of tea in her hand. The tea was disgusting, but she was drinking it anyway. It gave her trembling hands something to do. Jay was hunched against the side of the vehicle. He'd thrown his tea away. A splash of blood stained the sleeve of his shirt where he'd scratched the skin and removed the tracker. The pieces were ground into the concrete surface of the car park.

'Alec paid for it.' Jay's voice grated.

There was a small huddle of people beside the building, dealing with the broken body. A shadowy figure came to the edge of the group, looking in their direction. Jay raised a hand in acknowledgement. The figure turned away again. Muffled orders were shouted. A dark-painted van crawled on to the site and stopped. The ambulance driver and his mate moved out of the huddle to greet it.

Jay stroked Madison's hair. 'Don't think about it,' he implored softly.

Madison reached up, found his hand and squeezed. 'So many deaths.'

'But this is where it stops.' Jay pressed her hand in return. 'We can end it here.'

'Can we?'

'If we do what we agreed.'

'I . . .' She felt so tired. She knew reaction was setting in. She tried to fight it. Tried not to feel again the raw fear as the black tide washed towards Jay's mind, not to see Vic's burned face and staring eyes. 'What . . . what did we do in there? How did the energy feed back like that?'

'Alec was calling on some sort of electrical power. Vic was feeding it to him, through the computer. It had to be. The guy's work was incredible. Those machines were almost organic. But he met something stronger.'

Madison looked up, too drained to understand. 'You,' Jay prompted gently.

'Oh.' She let the word out long, like a sigh.

'You never let me see what was really inside you. You never let anyone, did you?'

Madison shook her head. 'Two weeks before he died, my dad finally talked to me, about the mind reading.' Her mouth twisted at the memory. 'He told me to be careful who I trusted. He made me promise never to show everything. Not to a colleague, employer, lover – no one. Then afterwards he refused to speak about it again. The mind power, it came from him. But he never acknowledged it. I think maybe that's why my parents were killed. That it was something he had done, or that he knew. I think my dad guessed what might be coming, but he couldn't stop it.' She made a weary gesture that bent Jay's heart. 'I can see now that my father was afraid of what was in him. Perhaps he had reason to be, I don't know, but he loved me and he wanted me to be safe. When I went to live with my aunt, she was different. She didn't hide what she was. She helped me come to terms with what I could do. I resisted it, for a long time, but it was too strong in the end. But she agreed with her brother, that I shouldn't let people know everything, to keep myself safe. In there just now . . . I couldn't do that any more. You needed me. I had to let go.'

'You trusted me.' Jay's voice was very soft. He touched her cheek.

'You did the same for me. You stepped aside and let me through.' She gulped some of the tea. 'I don't think that I want to do it again. I know now

385

what I'm capable of. It's too difficult to control,' she said bleakly. Then she looked up. 'I love you, you know. I couldn't keep that a secret, either.'

'Yes—' He didn't get to finish the sentence. Madison saw him tense as a figure loomed through the darkness towards them. 'Now we have to get ourselves out of this. Game face,' he whispered as he swivelled round to meet the newcomer.

Craig's body armour bulked out his silhouette, but he'd taken off his hood. He looked them both over, and then nodded, as if satisfied.

'Which of you is going to run?' he asked conversationally.

'I am.'

'How did you know?' Madison's heart jolted as her voice collided with Jay's.

Craig gave her a slow smile. 'I reckon if I can figure it out, you sure as hell could. The two of you together? Even without what happened in there?' He jerked his head back to the factory building. 'My people are going to want to harness that – whatever it was.' He raked an enquiring look from Jay to Madison. When neither spoke, he shrugged and looked off, studying the river. 'At the very least, they'll want to stop it falling into anyone else's hands. They're not so happy right now about the way that machine got busted. Going to want to hold on to the source material. Plus, there's going to be a shitload of questions.'

He shifted his stance, watching the Thames flow by. Jay was silent, clearly waiting. Madison could barely breathe. When Craig moved, her lungs were screaming. He was holding out a set of keys to Jay. 'My jeep is parked down there in the road. Dump it as soon as you can. I guess you two have made some sort of arrangement?'

Jay looked down at Madison. 'We have.'

She got unsteadily to her feet, shrugging off the blanket. 'Arrangements can change.'

'No.' Jay took the keys. 'We agreed.' He closed his hand over them. 'Thanks, Craig. We owe you.'

'Just get yourself out of here, safe.'

'Helping us will get you into trouble,' Madison objected.

Craig gave a characteristic shrug. 'I can hack it. This is the last thing that I can do for Neil. That's why he bought the cottage,' he said unexpectedly. 'It was meant to be a starting point, for dropping off the map. After the honeymoon, when you came back from Portofino, he was going to try to persuade you to disappear. He wanted to make a new start, somewhere he wouldn't always have to be looking over your shoulder for the bad guys. And the not-so-bad guys.' A twisted grin curled his mouth as he scanned the activity around the warehouse. 'It didn't work out for Neil. You've done this before, Creed.' He looked back to address Jay. 'You can make this work.'

'I hope so.'

Jay pulled Madison into his arms, resting his head against her hair. 'I love you. Don't forget that. Be strong.' He could feel the wetness of tears on her face. He held her away from him, brushing the moisture off her cheeks with his thumbs. She sniffed, shaking her head. Unable to speak.

'I love you,' he repeated as he bent to claim her mouth.

The kiss told him everything. It was sweet and soft and rippled with pain.

And over far too soon.

'There's going to be a lot of fallout from this.' He glanced up at Craig. 'You'll be looking out for her?'

'Yeah.' Craig was still studying the activity around the building. More cars had drawn up. Raised voices and slamming doors. 'I don't want to hurry you, but the cops have just arrived, to take over. My people will be pulling out of here pretty soon. Someone is going to be coming this way before that happens, to scoop the two of you up. If you're leaving, it ought to be now.'

Jay hugged Madison, hard, then disengaged himself from her arms 'Take care.' Madison's throat was too choked to reply. She pulled him to her for one last, tight embrace.

A man had detached himself from the group around the building and was moving towards them. Craig strode forward to intercept him. Behind the two dark figures, Jay let Madison go.

She watched as he stepped silently away from

the ambulance and walked between two parked cars. And out of her sight.

She couldn't stop the tears running down her face. She didn't try. They just kept coming. Beyond her control.

CHAPTER 40

'You okay, sweet pea?' Jonathan put his hand on Madison's shoulder.

'Oh – yes.' She jerked her eyes away from the calendar, hanging over her desk. 'What time is the staff meeting?'

'Half an hour. You want to get a coffee first?'

'You go on. I'll follow you. I promise,' she said.

Jonathan looked her over critically. 'How *are* you doing, really?'

'Not too badly.'

Not now that the intense questioning was over and she had been allowed back to the lab, to resume normal life – although all her movements were undoubtedly being monitored. She'd even looked at Jonathan sometimes and wondered; which was mean and disloyal. She'd told him most of the story and his support had been as generous as his astonishment. She was just feeling over-stretched and tearful. Not herself.

She smiled to reassure Jonathan, pleased when the concern faded a little from his eyes. 'I have something to finish up in here. I'll see you in five minutes.'

When the door closed behind her colleague, Madison went back to the calendar and the tiny red dot in the centre of the 0 of the tenth of June. Now it was the twenty seventh of July, which might mean nothing. Stress could play havoc with a woman's hormones. She and Jay had always been careful, except—

The memory of the kitchen on the first day at the cottage came flooding back. Jay boosting her on to the unit beside the sink, his laughter against her throat, his skin, smooth under her fingers, her breasts crushed against him. The scent and the taste and the feel of him. It had been fast, spontaneous, loving. Her stomach contracted with longing.

She crossed to the window, to look out. Jay had stood here, when she'd brought him to the lab on that first day. The ache, that was a permanent feature in her chest, intensified from dull throb to white heat. She dragged in a breath that was halfway to a sob, then shook it off, lifting her chin. She'd known how it would be, when they'd made their decision to part. There was no going back now. Especially not now.

She turned back to the desk, leaning over to punch out a number on her phone.

'Hello? Yes. I'd like to make an appointment with Dr Griffiths, please.'

'You want an extended period of leave?' The director was frowning. 'Madison, in the circumstances—'

He stopped. 'I'll do what I can, of course, but your return here—' He paused, clearly uncomfortable. 'You know the security people remain unhappy about your part in . . . the incident with Dr Creed. I gave certain undertakings, because I felt that it was important that you should be somewhere you felt secure—'

'And I appreciate that, very much,' Madison interrupted the director quietly. 'I know what you've arranged and I'm grateful. I do understand the position you're in. It was made quite clear to me that I was on probation here.'

Craig had done all he could to shield her when Jay's absence was discovered. His rank and standing in the service, very much higher than she had ever imagined, had protected him from suspicion, but as predicted, his superiors had not been happy. Jay's disappearance, apparently into thin air, and her reluctance to speculate on that, or to provide precise details of what had happened at the warehouse, to cause the death of two men and the destruction of an important piece of equipment, had not gone down well. Withdrawing into herself, she'd weathered the repeated interrogations, even the suggestions that Jay had run out on her, leaving her behind to face the music. She knew differently. They'd talked about it. Harder to hide together than alone, when the authorities would throw all they had into finding them. This way the focus was divided. Jay had wanted her to be the one to go. But she hadn't been sure she could do it.

It had been like tearing her heart out, but she'd made him promise. To stay, under the eye of the authorities, they would never be free. This way – she had to hope there was a chance.

In the end, Jay had given in.

That secret hope had helped her withstand the barrage of questions, about Jay, about the events at the warehouse, about her own skills. Disappointment at the loss of the machine and its creator had refocused her questioners on Madison's own expertise. Finally, once they'd established that her individual talent was unchanged by collaboration with the notorious Dr Creed, and that she still identified only memory pictures, or feelings and emotions when in contact with regular subjects, Craig's shadowy bosses had reluctantly agreed to draw a veil over the whole incident. The director had been a tower of strength in the complex tests they'd ordered. If he'd detected any increase in Madison's power, he hadn't drawn attention to it. There had been one arrest, after the police had dug up a swimming pool in a garden in Surrey and found the body of a young woman. Craig had hinted that the papers and computer records found in the ape-man's safe had provided a welcome distraction to the investigators. There had been reports of several spectacular crashes on the stock market of companies connected to the Organisation.

No charges had been made over the two deaths at the warehouse. But Madison knew she would have to live with the consequences of that night for the rest of her days – the sight of Vic, lying dead at his machine, and Alec plummeting into darkness. Those ghosts would always be with her.

She bit her lip. The director was waiting, puzzlement and concern in his face.

'Madison?'

'Sorry,' she said. 'I was distracted. I understand the difficulty, but I'll still have to have the leave.' She smiled wryly. 'I won't be going away, or leaving the country,' she reassured him.

Her smile softened at the confusion and irritation in her boss's face. 'I think you'll find that you can't refuse me,' she said gently. 'This will be maternity leave.'

CHAPTER 41

One year later

Madison kissed the downy head resting against her chest, and smiled. Amanda Jayne gave a contented gurgle, reaching for Madison's hand, curving tiny pink fingers over her mother's thumb. Madison made approving noises and tickled a small stomach.

'Uh-oh.' Both their heads went up as they heard a noise in the hall. 'Sounds like that's the post. Letters for Mummy.'

Tucking her daughter more securely on to her hip, Madison wandered out to pick them up. It was a fine day, so they would be going to the park later. Madison would tell Amanda Jayne all about the ducks on the pond and the boys playing football and the baby would keep dark blue eyes fixed on her, exactly as if she understood. Or she might just go to sleep.

Madison scooped up the letters. A bill, a holiday brochure, a postcard from Los Angeles. She turned it over and read the message from Jonathan. Ashley was settling into his new job. Jonathan was perfecting his surfing technique and enjoying being a kept man during Ashley's period of secondment and his sabbatical from the lab. The sun shone every day. When was she going to visit them and bring their goddaughter?

'You want to go, poppet?' She jiggled the baby on her hip. 'In a big airplane? To see Uncle Jonathan and Uncle Ash?'

Amanda Jane blew a bubble.

Madison turned the last envelope over. Her heartbeat had kicked up a little at the sight of the padded bag. She unsealed the flap and tipped the contents out. It was there. After so long, the signal lay in the palm of her hand. It looked like an expensive piece of marketing, an extravagantly embossed invitation to visit the local car showroom to try out the latest models in stock. The key, attached to the card – *unlock your future driving pleasure* – was impressively realistic.

Madison stared down at it, her heartbeat sounding in her ears. She could barely breathe. Elation, joy, heart-wrenching longing – and sudden panic. She grasped the corner of the hall table, fighting her emotions. *Normal, everything has to be* normal. *In case someone is still listening.* She'd spent a year living quietly, working methodically, dressing plainly – subdued and passive. Flying under the radar. Waiting for this moment.

Madison leant against the table, eyes closed. The baby, gripped a little too tightly in her arm, began to whimper.

'I'm sorry, poppet, was Mummy holding on too tight? Silly Mummy.' She lifted the child to her shoulder and nuzzled her cheek, hand folded over the key. 'It's a lovely day – how would you like to go for a ride on a train?'

She packed the bag with care, putting in the essentials, then stood back to examine it. Only the sort of thing a nervous new mother might put together for a day out with her baby. Her heart was still pounding. She forced herself to move slowly and carefully as she emptied the bag again, tucking in the large stuffed mouse, and below it, the tissue-wrapped wisps of scarlet silk. Smiling, she discarded a few of the larger items from the original pile, loaded the rest of the contents back in, and closed the zip. Then she fitted Amanda Jayne into her carrying sling and picked up the bag.

Madison hesitated on the edge of the platform, stopping at the last minute to let the doors of the Tube train close, without getting on. Alone on the platform she looked up at the signs, whispered a soft reassurance to her daughter, and headed for the southbound line.

She'd rehearsed it in small, unconnected bursts – the rapid succession of buses, taxis and tubes that would obscure her trail, the small but significant changes to their appearance in the mother-and-baby room of a large department store, the last stop at the coffee shop where the envelope containing their new identities, that had been waiting safely under the counter for weeks, was passed over, so casually, with a cup of espresso. Madison grimaced as she sat down to drink it. She hardly needed the caffeine. Her nerves were at jumping point, her chest tight with tension. It was a miracle that Amanda Jayne was dozing peacefully in her brand new baby sling. Her new *blue* baby sling.

Madison looked down at her watch. Two hours and forty minutes since she left the flat. She was almost sure she hadn't been followed, but there was one way to find out. Closing her eyes she sent a probe out into the crowded café, smiling when it turned up empty. Craig was an excellent planner and teacher and she couldn't have done it without his help, especially in the matter of obtaining their new identities. He was a good man, with an enduring sense of responsibility to a dead friend and colleague. She was deeply grateful, and glad to be finally ending that responsibility. Very soon she would be off Craig's hands. Then, in a few days, but from a different starting point, she would follow the route overseas that Jay had taken when he'd first disappeared, and had travelled again a year ago. A route to the other side of the world.

It had worked then. She sent up a silent prayer that it would work now. Just one more time. Then they would be free.

Her hand closed on the strap of her bag as the stab of longing went through her, iced with fear. Nothing could go wrong. Not now. She'd moved like a ghost in her own life for a year – fading into the background, colourless, causing no ripples. No suspicion.

Shaking off the cold breath of trepidation down her spine she stood, gathering her things. It was time.

The express train from Paddington wasn't crowded. Madison sat in the quiet carriage trying to read, wondering if she was being observed by a CCTV camera. There was nothing to see. She didn't *feel* as if she was being watched. She crossed her fingers, and hoped. Craig had told her how to minimise the risk, if there were any cameras, but it was impossible to completely avoid all chance of surveillance. Amanda Jayne snoozed in her lap, unconcerned. They spent the night at a hotel near Cardiff station. The second train was smaller and slower, pottering through the countryside, stopping at small villages and halts, with unfamiliar names. Madison fed and changed her daughter and watched the scenery.

The SUV was parked a short distance from the cottage, nose towards the track. Madison breathed a sigh of relief. There had been a moment of panic when she alighted at the station and a tide of fear had inexplicably washed over her. She'd come to a dead stop on the platform, limbs turning to ice, before realisation dawned. Not her, but a woman walking just ahead of her, journeying back from hospital and a terminal prognosis. Madison sent out what comfort she could, and saw the woman's step lighten a fraction.

Hugging Amanda Jayne, she'd hurried to the bus stop.

Madison took a deep gulp of sea air. Gulls were circling overhead. From below she could hear the sound of the waves. She took the key from the envelope out of her pocket and aimed it at the lock, face lighting up as the vehicle responded. There were tickets and maps in the glove compartment. Madison leafed through them, before tackling the baby carrier that she'd bought in Cardiff. Amanda Jayne, safe on the back seat, in a nest made from a rug, looked on, with what might have been a puzzled expression, as her mother dealt efficiently with the fastenings and fittings for the car seat.

'It's a good thing I thought of a seat for you,' Madison told her. 'You know your daddy is going to flip when he sees you.'

She'd made Craig swear that he wouldn't tell. She'd been too afraid that Jay would try to come back. She grinned at her daughter. 'I'm quite good at keeping secrets. And you're the biggest secret of all. The most wonderful secret,' she assured her daughter, as she lifted her off the back seat.

The ferry from Fishguard sailed on dark water, into a moonless night. By morning they were docking in Ireland. Madison drove the vehicle carefully down the ramp and threaded her way through the dock buildings, heading west. They stopped for lunch in a small town, then meandered on, always moving westwards, along unfrequented roads.

She missed the turning twice, and had to double back. When she finally made it, she understood. She'd been expecting a disused aerodrome. It was actually just a flat field, with a tumble of derelict barns at one end. The small plane waiting in the lee of the largest one was sturdy and freshly painted. The pilot showed no surprise at having a baby unexpectedly added to his unofficial passenger list, simply directing them to the best place to sit in the small hold, amongst towering piles of cardboard boxes.

'Is his dad going to get a shock when he sees him?' he asked, grinning, as he showed her how to fasten the seat belts.

'Um . . . yes. You could say that.' Madison tilted her head, frowning. 'Do you know . . . er . . . Dad?'

The pilot put his finger to his lips. 'No names, no pack drill.' His eyes glittered with amusement. 'Make yourselves comfortable and hang on tight. Take off might be a bit bumpy.'

Madison stood in the stern, watching the silver line of the ship's wake, trailing out behind them. Around her the darkness of the ocean melded into the darkness of the sky – black-on-black. On the port side distant lights showed the presence of another vessel, but otherwise they were alone on the inky sea. She leaned on the rail, savouring the warm breeze in her face. When she tipped her head back, the stars were huge and bright above her. Engines beat rhythmically under her feet as the small cargo vessel ploughed onwards, into the night. Everything she'd ever known was thousands of miles behind her. In front of her . . . a new life. She shivered at the leap her heart gave. It was time.

Closing her hands on the smooth wood of the rail, staring down into the water, she turned her thoughts inwards.

Waves. Gulls. A beach. A picture forming – colours etched on glass. The beach below the cottage, that last day. The hardness of rock at her back. The softness of sand under her fingers . . .

Their plans were made. Now Jay was staring out to sea.

'Penny for them?'

He turned towards her, shaking his head slowly. 'It's just . . . here, today . . . knowing that this will be the end,' he said quietly. 'Once we've done what we have to do.'

Madison nodded. 'And you're taking your farewell,' she confirmed softly. 'Prospero, promising to drown his books?'

Jay tilted his head, to slant a glance up at her. 'I hadn't thought . . . but I suppose it's apt – the magician renouncing his power, once he's used it for the last time.' He reached out to take her hand. The smile was as sad as the fingers were warm. 'When this is over, if we make it that far,' he gave a small, wry grimace, 'we can never attempt anything like that again. It has to be buried, and stay buried.'

Madison let out a measured sigh. 'Was it hard, last time – giving up your work?'

'Yes. No – I was so full of self-disgust, hate – guilt. Especially guilt. It felt like a suitable penance. I got by – but I was only living half a life.'

'You know there is more to you than just the ability to read minds.'

'I hope so. If we survive we'll find out.' He raised her hand to his lips. 'If we do, will you marry me?'

Madison swallowed over her stuttering heart. 'Well, I didn't see that one coming.' Suddenly she laughed, leaning closer to rest her forehead against his cheek. 'If we survive – and what are the odds – that would be a whole different world.' She twined their fingers together, interlocking. 'If we get through this, ask me again. Two halves together might just make a whole.'

Madison came back to the present slowly, as the images in her mind faded. She was standing on deck again, looking out to sea and preparing, as far as possible, to consign her own powers to the deep. Idly she followed the star-lit wake of the ship. Left unattended, would the power dwindle to a shadow of itself? To small, personal manifestations, like this ability to make living, breathing mental pictures of the past, that she had been refining for the last twelve months? Would her power be used in the future only to record small hopes and joys – milestones of the baby now asleep in the cabin behind her, lulled by the throb of the engines?

There are worst things that can happen. Much worse.

Involuntarily she shuddered – dragging her mind away from a derelict warehouse and the smell of burning. Pictures of the past had consoled her over the long, empty months of waiting. If she never read another mind – what then?

Emotions swirled around her in the sultry night – poignancy, regret and – a measure of relief. She smiled. It wouldn't be simple to turn her back, but it would grow easier, with time.

There were other ways to use the power of the mind. Standing straight, she leaned against the rail. Summoning her concentration, she flung her energy out into the darkness, letting it travel and build. Create. Eyes closed, she focused on the empty air beside her. Slowly, painstakingly, the sensation of a form grew beside her. Joy bubbled in her chest. They were so much closer now, as the ship sped on into the night. *Now* it was possible. *Now* she could *feel* him, like a warm breath on her skin.

When at last she opened her eyes golden trails of light popped and fizzed in a form that was almost real. Laughing, she turned fully to face him, putting out her hand as his came up in response 'The answer is yes, and I love you,' she whispered.

'. . . love you.' It might have been the echo of her own voice as the trails glowed bright, then faded into the dark. The whole thing might just have been a trick of the light.

'Not long now, my love. Not long,' she promised the night and the stars, before turning back to her sleeping child.

The sun was coming up over the valley. The early morning air was cool. Madison shivered slightly as she studied the vivid green of the vegetation in the field at the base of the mountain. They'd spent last night at a small B and B in the nearest town. Amanda Jayne had been fractious and grisly and Madison had been glad to stop and rest before the final stage of the journey. She hadn't wanted to arrive late at night, tired and travel stained, with a wailing baby. *We girls have to have some pride.*

And she'd needed that time. To . . . gather herself. New world, new life.

Now the morning was getting into its stride, glittering with promise. She stopped the hire car at the viewpoint, just before the descent, shading her eyes. Her heart was jittering under her ribs.

The track was visible, snaking down in a gentle incline. The farm was nestled at the bottom – the sprawling main house, and a jumble of outbuildings and barns.

There was a man standing in the field closest to the road. He looked as if he'd been standing there for some time. He seemed to be waiting for something.

Madison got back into the hire car and pointed

it down. She was almost at the bottom when the light of the sun caught the windshield. She saw the man in the field react to the flash. Even at this distance she could see dark hair flopping over a tanned face. Madison's heart gave a gigantic leap. Her hand went out, to find her daughter's.

'Nearly there, poppet.'

She put both hands back on the wheel to steer the car for the last few hundred yards, to the farm gate.

In the field, Jay began to run.